it CHICKS

by

Tia Williams

JUMP AT THE SUN
HYPERION PAPERBACKS FOR CHILDREN
NEW YORK

Also by Tia Williams
The Accidental Diva

Coauthored by Tia Williams
The Beauty of Color:
The Ultimate Beauty Guide for Skin of Color by Iman

Text copyright © 2007 by Tia Williams

Ing. 12/17/07 8.99L

If you purchased this book without a cover, you should be aware that this book is stolen property. It was reported as "unsold and destroyed" to the publisher, and neither the author nor the publisher has received any payment for this "stripped" book.

First Jump at the Sun paperback edition, 2007
3 5 7 9 10 8 6 4 2

Printed in the United States of America
Text design: Elizabeth Clark

Library of Congress Cataloging-in-Data on file
ISBN-13: 978-1-4231-0406-3
ISBN-10: 1-4231-0406-4
Visit www.jumpatthesun.com

To Chocolate Drop and Backseat Fearless, the eternal teenagers

ACKNOWLEDGMENTS

I'm so grateful for the advice of the sassy-fabulous teenagers—and you know who you are—I met while writing at the Seventh Avenue Starbucks in Park Slope, Brooklyn. Miss Conceited, Lalipopz, and Exclusivbitch—thanks for the window into your MySpace-and-Chris-Brown-obsessed world! And a huge thanks to all the performing arts school kids, current and former, who helped me with details: Lilli Cooper, Max Moran, Jason Moran, Nzingha Isis, Andrea Fairweather, Chanel Neal, Marie Ransom, Nina Edmonds, and Hollis (no last name necessary).

A big fat kiss to everyone who helped made my cover so fantastic: Candice, Meli, India—you girls are the very definition of "It Chicks"! Sam, Kibwe, and Tippi—I'm the luckiest girl in the world for bagging such an outrageously A-list styling team. And a huge thanks to Beth, Jill, Arlene and Rodger at Disney, for pulling it all together.

Mountains of gratitude to Kelli Martin, my big fancy editor, who thinks folks still say "heavy petting." We made it, girl! And, as always, I owe everything to my agent extraordinaire, the chic and smart Mary Ann Naples—every day I'm thankful to the Publishing Gods for sending you my way. Somebody give this woman a medal for talking me off so many ledges.

I couldn't have written a word without the support and understanding of my wonderful family—Andi, Aldred, Devon, and Lauren—who love me even though I'm a lunatic. And were it not for the saintlike patience and encouragement of my husband, Adam (who, after two years of marriage, is now qualified to pen a self-help book called The Fire and the Fury: Life with a Writer), I'd be lost, just lost. It may sound silly, but I also have to thank my *miniature pinscher, too—whenever I was blocked, Chappie would rest his paw on my keyboard and give me a little nudge. This one's for you, Puddin'.*

And a big shout-out to my "Shake Your Beauty" ladies for keeping me on my toes and wildly inspired, every single day. Love ya, mean it.

1.
TANGIE ADAMS, SUPERSTAR

"I SEE YOU, *beee-yatch!*"

Surprised out of a semitrance, Tangie spun around to see Skye, her best friend since kindergarten, hop out of a Lincoln Town Car and come running over. A relieved grin crept across Tangie's face. Finally, somebody familiar! For what felt like 200 years, Tangie had been waiting for Skye by the front doors of the Louis Armstrong Academy of Performing and Creative Arts. Standing alone as streams of first-day-of-school-giddy students breezed past, Tangie felt certain she was radiating a deeply uncool "new kid" vibe.

It wasn't helping that her hand was covering her mouth, as if she were suffering from a lethal case of bad breath. Of course, she'd happily have claimed halitosis rather than admit the truth—that she'd waited till the very first day of school to attempt Nairing her upper lip. The sad thing was, the only person Tangie truly minded seeing her 'stache-shaped burn was C.J.—and he was so over her he probably wouldn't have noticed. It was so tragic. And this should've been the happiest day of her life!

After all, she'd *finally* gotten into the school of her dreams after suffering the most hellish year and a half.

It had all started when, days before her eighth-grade graduation, she'd found out that C.J. and Skye—her two best friends from one of Manhattan's most competitive private lower and middle schools, Carrington Arms Prep—had been accepted into Armstrong's illustrious freshman class, while she'd been rejected. Actually, this shouldn't have come as such a shock, since Tangie's audition had been a disaster.

Stressed by her dad's elopement with a twenty-year-old, barely-English-speaking foot model, she totally fell apart during her tryout routine, the "I Can't Do it Alone" number from *Chicago*. She could dance that piece in her sleep, but performing before judges in a studio crammed with hundreds of bitchy-faced dancers, her *competition*, all of them picking apart her every move—well, that was totally different.

Tangie had breezed through the first two eight counts, and then abruptly frozen, the steps vanishing from her mind. For five seconds she had stood in front of the judges, paralyzed in her *All That Jazz* stance (i.e., right knee popped, "jazz hands" jutting out from her sides)—until the reality of her situation washed over her. Then had come the nervous breakdown.

Tangie had burst into messy tears, wailed "I suuuuck!" and fled from the studio, not stopping until she reached the girls' locker room. Trembling with humiliation, she had locked herself in a stall and plopped down on the toilet for a good cry. She knew Armstrong would never take her now.

And she was right.

Tangie had then been forced to spend ninth grade at her neighborhood high school in Fort Greene, Brooklyn, friendless and depressed. Not only had she not known a soul, but on the second day of school she had been jumped by a hulking homothug-ette named Tisha, for allegedly "thinking she was cute," (Um, what was cute about Tangie's "whatever, my life's over anyway" uniform of ancient Seven jeans, a faded American Eagle T, and a frizzy ponytail?) Everything sucked.

While Skye and C.J. were part of an elite group of the most

talented kids in the city, busy experiencing glamorous Armstrong rites of passage, Tangie was hiding out in the nurse's office during lunch and watching her *Fame* DVD on repeat all night long.

Thank God that Armstrong also held auditions for incoming sophomores (that was the last time students could—if you failed, it was a wrap). By the time tryouts rolled around again in the spring of her freshman year, Tangie had spent months psyching herself up. Even though she'd sort of OD'd on Red Bull, she still managed to pull out her A-game.

During her audition routine, she had pretended she was starring on her favorite TV show, *So You Think You Can Dance*, and she had been the front-runner, the plucky audience favorite. The four hundred or so wannabe Armstrong students staring at her from the barre-lined studio walls weren't intimidating— *please*, they were simply her worshipful fans, cheering her on and holding up signs saying things like "DROP IT LIKE IT'S HOT, T!"

And instead of getting freaked out by the bored-looking dance department dean watching from the judges' table, Tangie imagined her raving to *Access Hollywood*'s Billy Bush, "Thank God this year's *So You Think You Can Dance* winner is shaped like a *real* girl—Tangela Adams and her juicy booty are going to set the dance world on fye-ah!!" All Tangie's positive visualization worked, because she got her acceptance letter in the mail two months later!

All Tangie had ever wanted to do was dance at Armstrong, and now it was really happening. But was it worth it if C.J. hated her? She didn't know whether to laugh or cry.

"Wassup, Miss Tangela Adams!" Skye almost knocked Tangie over with the force of her enormous hug. Which was shocking, since at five feet eight inches and 105 pounds the girl was supermodel-skinny. Actually, she and her almost identical-looking big sister, Eden, with their sexily slanted greenish-gray eyes, golden bronze skin à la Tyra, and butt-grazing, honey-streaked hair, could've been supermodels (okay, the hair was a bit much—too-long extensions, a few split ends if you looked closely—but they'd both have sooner inhaled a box of Dunkin' Donuts Munchkins than get a trim). Instead, they were gorgeous, aspiring movie stars.

Eden had already had a taste of stardom as a child actress; from age eight to age twelve she had played Kendra, the youngest sister, with all the bratty one-liners, on the hit TGIF sitcom *Family Chatter*. Even though Skye didn't have a major TV show on her résumé, she'd been a supersuccessful child model (if one calls a stint as the girl with the curls on the cover of Just For Me's hair-relaxer box supersuccessful).

Despite Skye's secretly feeling like the Ashlee Simpson of the family, the Carmichael girls were socially unstoppable. With their money, talent, and showbiz pedigree—their dad was a Broadway producer; their mom starred in a famous eighties nighttime soap—they were bona fide It chicks: the ones every girl wanted to be and every guy wanted to be next to.

"Hey, girl!" Tangie squeezed Skye back just as hard, thrilled to be relieved of her position standing guard by the doors; she'd looked like a hostess at Outback or something.

"Congrats, Tangie," slurred Eden, kissing her on both cheeks. Hyperaware that everyone was gawking at her, the vacuous, Valium-addicted queen of the senior class had practically sauntered up to them in slow-mo—it was a very Halle-Berry-emerging-from-the-sea-in-*Die Another Day* moment. "I always *knew* you'd make it."

"In the end, the judges couldn't resist my classic ballerina bod." Tangie was joking, obviously.

At five feet five inches, tall with size 32D breasts, a tiny waist, and a Beyoncé-caliber booty, she did not look like the typical Armstrong dancer. She had the kind of body that always got annoying attention from boys (on the street, in the grocery store—everywhere), but in the professional dance world, she was considered chubby. It had never been an issue before, though, since she'd never trained on that super-intense, every-day-after-school-and-weekends level.

Tangie was only allowed to take dance during summer vacation, and Debbie Allen's Dance Academy camp—or DADA, as all the dancers called it—was filled with girls who were amazingly talented, but generally normal-shaped, like her. But at the Armstrong tryouts, Tangie realized that the stakes were higher, when she found herself drowning in a sea of Skinny Bitches—superintense, hypercaffeinated ballerinas who'd been groomed to be professional dancers since they were in diapers. At DADA, she'd been the hottest hip-hop dancer in her grade level, but now she was just a face in the crowd.

Whatever. Even though she didn't have their training, Tangie *knew* she could dance. It was in her bones.

"Hell, yeah," said Eden, not getting Tangie's joke. "So, how come we didn't see you at the Hamptons house all summer?"

Skye hit her sister in the arm. "Duh? You know she goes to DADA every year."

"Oh, *truuuue.*" Eden swayed slightly. She'd popped her daily Valium pills in their dad's Town Car, and they were just starting to kick in. "Yeah, I spent a couple summers at Stagedoor Manor upstate. Remember that, Skye?"

"I remember," said Skye, with a sour expression. What she remembered was that their mom, Alexa, hadn't let Skye go to the star-making performing arts camp (alumni included big names like Robert Downey, Jr., and Natalie Portman) because she had had embarrassing chicken pox scars. Alexa had remarked that Skye's skin resembled an ostrich skin handbag she had had in the seventies.

"Listen, Tangie," continued Eden, "lemme give you one piece of Armstrong advice."

"I'm all ears."

"Oh, Tange, that reminds me!" interrupted Skye. "Mommy said for my sixteenth birthday I can get my ears stapled back!"

"You'll still look like Curious George," snapped Eden, glaring at her attention-whore sister. "Listen closely, babe. This school is good times, but remember: *in the jungle, never forget to wear insect repellent.*"

With that bizarre statement, she floated away like some

Prada-outfitted apparition, her oversize Dior sunglasses taking up half her face.

Skye rolled her purple-lined eyes at her sister. "Depression. Not one of the great looks."

Not one of the great looks. It was Skye's favorite thing to say. She thought it sounded sophisticated.

"What's *up* with your sister? I mean, besides the Valium."

"Trey."

"No new developments, huh?" Tangie shook her head sadly. Until the previous spring, the gorgeous actress and sexy hip-hop dancer had been Armstrong's golden couple, at least on the surface. They were like Ciara and Bow Wow (though Trey was much taller). Tangie was devastated—she'd always looked up to them as the perfect couple, ever since she and Skye were twelve, when they used to spy on the for-ever-horny duo making out in the Carmichaels' living room. Back then, Tangie's daydreams about being a teenager had always involved having a boyfriend as sexy and popular as Trey Stevens.

"It's like the end of an era," Tangie continued, wistfully. "I was so used to them being together, you know?"

"Sweetie, everyone was used to Ja Rule and Ashanti collabos, too, but that doesn't mean they were any good."

"True."

"She's still tripping. I'm her closest confidant, so I had to listen to her all summer." Skye rolled her eyes and changed the subject. "So, have you seen him yet?"

"Who?" Tangie's stomach dropped.

"The Dalai Lama. What do you mean, who?"

"Oh, you mean *C.J.*?" Tangie said his name as if she'd never heard it before. "Nope. Why, what's up?"

Skye just looked at her, one hand on her hip.

"Okay, whatever." Tangie sighed, giving up the act. "I've been actively pretending not to look for him all morning. I wonder if he knows I even *go* to Armstrong now."

"Oh, *honey.*" Skye gave her another one of those fiercely strong hugs. "If it makes you feel any better, he barely talked to me all summer, either—and I had nothing to do with it. You know how my cousin gets when he's in one of his moods."

Tangie nodded. She knew all about his tortured moodiness. It was one of the things about him that made her knees weak.

"Alexa"—Skye called her mom by her first name—"invited him to dinner with the family a couple weeks ago, at Pastis." Pastis was one of the hottest, most celebrity-packed restaurants in Manhattan. Tangie knew that C.J., a guy for whom the phrase "keep it gutter" was a personal mantra, must have loathed it. "I tried bringing up the situation, but he was all shady and . . ."

"Yeah, things aren't that great," said Tangie, not wanting to hear the rest. "We haven't really talked much since your party."

"Ya'll haven't talked in *three months?*" Skye was not helping matters. "I thought you'd write while you were at camp. At least!"

Tangie shrugged but didn't say anything. She could feel the tears coming, and she didn't want to streak her bronzer.

As far back as she could remember, she and C.J. had been inseparable: the kind of friends that finished each other's sentences and knew each other's deepest secrets. She adored Skye, of course, but so did Skye—she was almost pathologically self-involved. But C.J was different.

He knew the most intimate things about Tangie, secrets she'd never told anyone else. Even though they'd never really hooked up, it was somehow understood that they had a kind of soul-mate thing. Which was bananas, since when they had first met, as sixth-graders, the only thing they had had in common was their scholarship to Carrington Arms Prep.

While Tangie had grown up on the leafy, Victorian brownstone-lined blocks of Fort Greene, Brooklyn, C.J. had grown up in the infamous Marcy projects (yeah, yeah, yeah, *those* Marcy projects, and no, he didn't know Jigga). He was raised by his father's mother, an eighty-year-old, severely asthmatic woman. C.J. never knew his dad, and his mom, Vickie had died of an overdose when he was still in grade school. That was when he started getting into trouble, becoming the mascot for a group of notoriously thuggy teenage boys, going on drug runs, and learning how to hustle. C.J.'s sick grandma couldn't handle the smart-ass wannabe Pablo Escobar, and after he sold a gram of cocaine to an undercover cop, she sent him to live with his mom's ridiculously rich sister, Alexa. Of course, it took a serious amount of begging to make Alexa take her ghetto nephew in—she was terrified he'd be a bad influence on her princess daughters, Skye and Eden.

Sometimes, Alexa would send the kids out to play and then search C.J.'s room for his hidden stash of weed, quickly smoking out in her walk-in closet. It was while she was snooping in his room one day that Alexa found his sketchbooks. Blown away by the funky portraits and complicated, mural-like graffiti, she forced C.J. to apply to Skye's and Tangie's arts-driven private school, *and* he won a scholarship.

To make a long story short, he started sixth grade at Carrington Arms (where he and Tangie became inseparable), and, being his naturally charming, irresistible self, eventually convinced Alexa that he'd cleaned up his act; so she let him move back home with his grandmother. Which was just what he wanted.

C.J. had been miserable living with the Carmichaels. What with Skye's parents' loud, drunken fights and their drill-sergeant approach to managing their daughters' careers, the Carmichaels' swanky West Village duplex apartment felt way more dysfunctional than his roughneck Brooklyn block.

Now, Tangie was the one feeling dysfunctional. When they auditioned in eighth grade, she and C.J. had made a stupid pact that if either failed to get into Armstrong, the other wouldn't go. They'd left Skye out, because a) Junior Carmichael, her legendary Broadway producer dad, had donated tons of cash to the school, and so she was definitely going, and b) she'd never have agreed to something so self-defeating. Tangie knew it was ridiculous to expect C.J. to turn down his acceptance—even for her sake. But it still hurt like hell.

Tangie thought she had handled things gracefully until Skye's first of Spring party School's a Wrap party in June. It was exactly three months ago, though it felt like years.

Skye's penthouse apartment was overflowing with all of her fabulous new friends from Armstrong's freshman class, people that Tangie didn't know. They were doing routines from dance class, gossiping about psychotic teachers, giggling hysterically at inside jokes about end-of-year recitals; everyone was having the time of their lives—except for Tangie. Her cheeks were sore from fake-smiling, but she was determined not to look like a pathetic, left-out loser: The Girl Who Bombed at Armstrong Auditions.

All night long she'd been trying to make her way over to C.J., but he was constantly surrounded by a crowd—mostly girls, of course. And now she was trapped in a ridiculous conversation with one of Skye's new BFFs, Kamillah, who was going on and on about how her bra size had increased since she lost her virginity.

Tangie was dying to escape, so she squeezed past the crowd and snuck into Skye's parents' bedroom, which she knew was blissfully off limits to the party. There was a small terrace off the master bedroom (one of the huge perks of living in a penthouse apartment in Manhattan's superfancy Greenwich Village), which had a postcard-perfect view of lower Manhattan. Tangie flopped down on one of the chairs and inhaled the unseasonably warm night air, trying to relax. It was peaceful out there—the thumping bass of Skye's iPod playlist and the incessant, animated chatter sounded a million miles away, and slowly, Tangie drifted off to sleep.

Minutes—or maybe hours—later, she heard the door slam behind her. C.J. was leaning against the door with an amused grin, a half-lit blunt hanging out of his mouth.

"Who we hidin' from?"

"Jesus, C.J., you scared me to death! What are you doing here?"

"You tell me," he said, sitting down next to Tangie.

She wanted to be irritated with him for not paying attention to her all night, but she couldn't help smiling. This was how it had used to be, before Armstrong. Just C.J. and Tangie, chilling. He playfully knocked his shoulder against hers, and she rolled her eyes.

"What?" he said.

"Nothing," she replied, tucking her wild curls behind one ear. "I'm just surprised to see you away from your fan club."

He chuckled and took a deep drag. "You're nuts."

"How'd you even know where I was?"

He looked at her. "You seriously telling me you ain't know I've been staring at you for the past three hours?"

"Omigod! Whatever, C.J." She acted nonchalant, but inside, her stomach was flip-flopping.

"I really couldn't help it if I wanted to. I mean, the Olsen Twins been hollerin' at your boy all night long."

"You're so stupid!" She exclaimed, bursting out laughing and punching him in the arm. The Olsen Twins was Skye's and C.J.'s pet name for Tangie's seriously voluptuous breasts. "I can't help it; this shirt has a built-in bra!"

"Seriously, I had to find you, 'cause my head's about to explode. All these Armstrong chicks talk about is rehearsals and industry BS. So shallow."

"You don't have to say that to make me feel better. Listen, I'm over not getting in. I'm happy you have new friends." She looked at the Mexican-tiled floor of the terrace. Tangie hoped her "really, it's all good" attitude was convincing.

"You're happy I have new friends, huh?"

"Yeah. And I heard you're messing with that girl, Christie. I think Skye told me she competed on *America's Most Talented Kids* a couple years ago with JoJo and Cheyenne—or is she the one that came in fourth in the Miss Teen New York pageant? That was her, wasn't it, with the frizzy Vivica Fox weave? She seems cool."

C.J. gazed at her intently, his brow furrowed over his sexy, honey-brown eyes. Tangie knew that look—weed always put him in a super-open, confessional mood, and he was clearly about to get deep with her.

"Why you always do that? Okay, yeah, I been messin' with Christie. And what? You know it don't mean anything."

"You don't have to explain, C.J. Really, I don't care."

"Jesus, T., let's be real, for *once*. I mean, let's go there." He took a deep drag off the blunt and exhaled, hard. He'd been going back and forth in his mind for months about this conversation, "You know how I feel about you. I've always . . . well, you know it's always been you."

Tangie felt as if she'd been hit with a paintball pellet. What exactly was he saying? Could this finally be happening?

"But Skye's right, you ain't the kind of girl I can half-step with. I gotta come correct." He was doing a lot of gesturing, trying to get the words out. "I've just been killing time with these hoochies, trying to get my shit together enough to step to you."

Tangie flinched. How romantic. "So, basically, you were just putting me on hold until you got all the other girls out of your system."

"Putting you on hold?" C.J. started to panic. He'd expected her to melt in his arms at the declaration that she was his one and only, but instead she was twisting it all around! "No, I'm saying the *hos are a wrap*! You understand? I'm ready to do this, ma, just me and you."

"Yeah, now that you've had every jump-off in Manhattan, you're ready to do this! Why wasn't I worth it two months ago, or a year ago?" Tangie's stomach was churning. "What makes things different now? How am I supposed to believe I'm any different from your other girls?"

"Because you are, T.! The other chicks were *whatever* to me. It wasn't real." He looked at Tangie, trying to see if she was feeling him, but her face was blank. So he decided to try to be funny. "I'm sayin,' there's only so many ménages a brutha can have before he gets bored."

Tangie's jaw dropped practically to the floor. "Ménages? *You've had a ménage à trois?* Omigod, C.J., you're a bigger slut than I even knew!"

"Come on, ma, you know I'm playin'! When you ever known me to rock a threesome? I mean, I go hard, but not *that* hard." Clearly Tangie didn't believe him. He had to think quick—he was sinking, fast. "All I was saying was that the old me is done. I wanna be with you, T. For real."

"So, now that you're bored, you're finally noticing your faithful standby, your reliable good girl, Tangie. Thank you very much, but I'll pass." She stood up, furious, ready to storm away. But C.J. was too quick for her.

Flicking his blunt over the terrace railing, he pulled her to him by the front of her terribly delicate BeBe peasant top and kissed her.

After four years of "let's be just friends," he kissed her.

It was her first kiss, but he didn't know that (thank God he didn't know that). He totally took her breath away. With the full moon and the sultry night air and her beautiful C.J., it was the most romantic moment of her life.

For a couple of minutes, Tangie forgot how mad she was. She forgot everything—that the entire Armstrong freshman class that she so desperately wanted to be a part of was inside, that she was past her curfew, that her father had married a child bride. This was the moment she'd waited forever for, and she wanted C.J. never to let her go.

But then he did, and reality came rushing back. Tangie burst into tears.

"Okay, I'm confused." He looked like a kid who lost his toy.

"I can't do this. I don't wanna be the girl you're with 'cause there's no one else left."

"But that ain't it, ma. I . . ."

"I just can't."

C.J. couldn't say anything. He stood there in a dejected stupor for a couple moments, baffled. He'd just told Tangie that he held her above every other girl he'd ever been with, that she was the one for him, and that he wanted to be with her exclusively—and she was *playing* him! Stunned, he walked back inside in a daze.

Tangie walked through the party a few moments later. She was surrounded by loud, happy strangers, and she felt lower than low. Suddenly overcome with the urge to get extremely, wildly, uncontrollably drunk, she went into the kitchen and surveyed the counters, which were littered with trays of lime Jell-O shots, bottles of Corona, and red plastic cups filled with vodka. She wasn't exactly sure how to start, so she quickly downed a little bit of everything.

The details of what happened next were fuzzy. All Tangie remembered was staggering back out into the living room and knocking into C.J. and a pretty Indian girl in a micro-mini jean skirt. After calling him a "skanky playa," she loudly announced, totally out of nowhere, that C.J. was part of Armstrong's "hood outreach" program. As soon as she said it, she was instantly both sorry and sober. She didn't even know where that horrible comment had come from. It was completely unlike her, and it couldn't have been farther from the truth.

She apologized a thousand times, but C.J. walked right past her. (In the distance, she heard some chick say, "Don't trip, C.J., I'll be next.") As long as she lived, Tangie would never forget how hurt and betrayed he looked. The worst part was, she couldn't blame him.

"Wait, you never even wrote him from camp?" Skye was still in shock that their feud had lasted all summer.

"No, I wrote him. I just never heard back," Tangie finally managed to say.

"Okay, y'all really need to get over this nonsense." Skye rolled her eyes. "I mean, the boy asked you to go with him. Yeah, it was in a stupid way, but clearly C.J.'s not the most sensitive guy in the world."

"I mean, whatever," said Tangie, dying to drop the subject. "We're really better as friends."

"*Please!* Why don't you two just rise up and do the damned thing already? Seriously, all that sexual tension can't be good for the circulation."

Speechless and embarrassed, Tangie's cheeks burned fuschia.

"Whatever. You wear me out," she said, dismissing the issue. Skye had a low threshold for depressing topics, especially when the story wasn't about her. "Just work it out before my back-to-school party on Friday night. It's gonna be off the hook!"

"I know, right? I have to figure out what to wear."

"I'm really feeling your bohemian-chic vibe."

Tangie beamed, thrilled at the change of subject. Ever since she had received her acceptance letter, she'd been dreaming up the perfect first-day-of-school ensemble—something cute and trendy, but not too hungry. She'd settled on a sexy tank, a sparkly, Indian-ish peasant skirt from Urban Outfitters, and cork wedges. She had even gone to her hairstylist the day before; he was the only one who could coax smooth ringlets out of her frizzy, shoulder-length curls. She had a tan from dance camp in L.A., and her rich, walnut-brown skin looked all sparkly and sun-kissed. For the first time in forever (save for her flaming red upper lip), Tangie actually felt as if she looked good.

"Yeah? Do I look like an accomplished Armstrong dance major with a brilliant career ahead of me?" Giggling, Tangie turned out her toes to form second position and swooped into a deep plié.

Skye slowly looked her up and down, bit her lip, and paused.

"What?"

"No, it's nothing," she said, shaking her head and beaming. "You're looking very 'hot tamale'!"

"You, too," said Tangie, admiring Skye's Earl Jeans micro-mini and her lace-trimmed cami. "Where'd you get that top?"

Skye twirled around and posed, one hand on her hip and the other behind her head. "Scoop. Don't you love it?

"Okay, now that our ensembles have been approved, let's go inside. You don't wanna be late for new student orientation, especially since I'm in the video!" She paused abruptly. "What the hell happened to your upper lip? Did you, like, contract E. coli at camp?"

"Oh, no, you noticed? No, no, no!" Tangie's hand flew over her mouth again. Just as she had been getting comfortable. "I, uh, had a violent run-in with a bottle of Nair."

"*Nair*? Honey, *no*, always get a professional wax, at least a week before showing your face to the public!" She noticed Tangie's dejected expression, and quickly switched her tone. "You know what? Whatever. We'll tell everybody you were making out all night and it's just beard burn."

Tangie grinned. "I love it, let's go."

"Cool! Hey, you don't think I look like Curious George, do you?"

2.
IZZY DUZ IT

". . . ALONG WITH EXCELLING AT YOUR CORE academic require-
ments, you're expected to hold down a demanding four-hour schedule
of departmental classes in your major." The portly, incredibly smug
dean of admissions, Mr. Jaworsky, pronounced it *shedge*-ool, the British
way, though he hailed from Queens. His Orientation speech had
lasted thirty-five minutes. "You'll also be responsible for technique
seminars and after-school rehearsals for showcases, concerts, and the
winter and spring festivals. If you put as much into your experience as
you take out of it, you will have fun. *But it will not be easy.*

"Our goal at Armstrong is to prepare you for an incredibly
rewarding professional life as a creative person, but we also want you
to be realistic. Some of you will make it big, a bunch of you will
barely earn a decent living, and *the rest of you will struggle.* But being
an artist is a *way of life*—you do it for the love of the craft, and it's a
calling, *not a choice.* Most of you were the best dancers, actors, artists,
singers, actors, playwrights, and musicians in your schools, after-
school classes or companies. Here, you are *one of many.* Remember
that if you don't take your time at Armstrong seriously, there's
always a thousand kids who'd *murder* to take your place. That said,
welcome to the new school year!"

The new freshmen and sophomores at the Orientation seminar rustled uncomfortably in their chairs. This speech was truly over the top, even for a group of naturally dramatic people. Who *was* this guy?

"I see why folks call him Professor Hard Knocks," the girl sitting next to Tangie whispered.

Tangie giggled. "I know, right?

"My name's Aziza, but everybody calls me Izzy."

"I'm Tangie. Hi." Tangie looked at the girl for a moment, frowning. Even though she was sitting down, Tangie could tell the girl was supershort, maybe five feet, if that. She had sharp cheekbones, a spiky, burgundy-streaked faux-hawk, and deep-set black eyes accentuated with gold liquid liner; and she was absolutely striking, in an edgy, exotic way. Her style was funky: beat-up cowboy boots; slouchy camouflage shorts; a chunky, metallic leather belt; and a tank top reading: I'MA BE LATE, THO. "Wait a minute," said Tangie. "We know each other, don't we? Did we meet at auditions?"

Izzy grinned, nodding. "I was waiting for you to notice."

Tangie couldn't believe it. What were the chances that she'd sit down next to the girl that had saved her ass during the audition that had gotten her in.

The May day had been overwhelming—a sweltering ninety degrees outside, with no air-conditioning in the hallway outside the studio where the hundreds of dancers waited to try out, and the air thick with nervous energy (and hair spray—those buns had to be *tight*).

Tangie had been drinking Red Bull all morning, and all of a sudden, her heart started to beat way too fast. Feeling faint, she slipped out of the line and bolted for the girls' locker room. There, Tangie saw an itty-bitty girl in black-and-white striped leggings and a cropped T sitting on the floor stretching, a cigarette hanging from her lip. Too hopped up and queasy to speak, Tangie rushed over to the sink and began splashing cold water on her face.

"You okay?" asked the girl.

"Uh, yeah, I'm fine." She was not fine. Looking in the mirror, Tangie realized she looked as though she hadn't slept in years.

"Blow, huh?"

"Excuse me?"

The girl lowered her voice. "You on somethin'?"

"*No!* No, I just had too much Red Bull." Tangie was slightly insulted. "And I'm nervous. I'm trying out for dance today, and I'm going in with the next group."

"Yeah, I'm trying out for dance, too. Actually, I'm trying out for everything." The girl stubbed her cigarette out on the tiled floor, got up and walked over to the sink next to Tangie's. She came up only to Tangie's earlobe. "Listen, my number is nine hundred seventy-two. I'm in the last group. If you want, you can trade with me. I always heard that it's good luck to go last."

Tangie looked at her. Who was this girl, offering to compromise her luck for a total stranger? Either she was crazy, or the most generous person Tangie'd ever met.

"I'm serious." The girl unpinned her number, handing it to Tangie. "When I go in, I'll make sure the little guy with the clipboard switches your name with mine. I'll just say it was a mistake."

"Really?"

"Yeah. You look like you need to marinate for a minute."

Marinate for a minute. That was something C.J. would have said. Tangie took the girl up on her offer. She had to. She felt as if she were going to vomit all over the bathroom (and two minutes later, she did). And the extra time worked. Tangie *killed* the audition.

And here they were again. It was fate. "This is crazy! How are you? Congratulations on getting in!"

"Yeah, you, too," Izzy said nodding.

"I *really* have to thank you," Tangie said, still amazed that they had run into each other again like that. She looked at the girl in awe—this girl was her guardian angel! "I don't think I would've gotten in if it weren't for you. Seriously, I was freaking out!"

"I guess it was just meant to be, right?" Izzy smiled at her.

"So, *Aziza*, huh? Wow, I love your name." Tangie hoped she didn't sound idiotic. "Does it mean something?"

"It means my parents are Ethiopian, and even though they raised me here, they thought if they gave me a nice Muslim name I wouldn't talk back or screw before I'm married, like my wayward American peers." She grinned. "Hi, I have no first-generation issues."

Tangie had no idea how to respond to that, so she burst out laughing. Professor Hard Knocks jerked his head in her direction, paused, and then continued his diatribe.

"Whoa." Izzy raised a gold-hoop-pierced eyebrow.

"Anyway, I hear you on the whole parents thing," said Tangie, now feeling as though she could say anything to this girl.

"Word? Have you also been grounded since 1999?"

"Well, no. But my dad, last year he married this foot model from—oh, God, I don't even know how to pronounce where she's from. . . . Anyway, she speaks, like, almost no English and is obsessed with black history."

"Obsessed with black history," Aziza repeated, one eyebrow raised. "I don't get it."

"I mean, for example, we have this blackboard in the kitchen. Like, for leaving notes or writing down where you're going or something. And every morning, *every single morning*, she copies down some little factoid from this ancient encyclopedia she carries around. Stuff like 'Madame C.J. Walker invented the hair relaxer in 1917 and eventually became the first female Afro-American millionaire.'"

"Stop playin'!" Aziza threw her hand over her mouth to muffle her giggles. "She did not say 'Afro-American'!"

"I'm so serious," said Tangie with a smile. It was the first time she had been able to see the humor in the situation. "I guess that's the way she tries to relate. It's like she thinks black people walk around trading trivia about Frederick Douglass and Nat Turner."

"So, your mom's normal, right?"

"I wouldn't know. I . . . well, I don't know that much about her." Tangie couldn't believe she was divulging this much information. "My mom moved to Europe when I was nine to dance with some fancy modern jazz company in Stuttgart, Germany."

"Oh, word?" Izzy nodded, impressed. "So you get it from her, then. The dancing."

Tangie shrugged, pretending to study a hangnail. "I wish. I'm not nearly as good as she was—*is*. I mean, I saw her dance professionally a few times. She was a Rockette."

"A Rockette? That's hot. And she lives in Europe? At least you get to visit and get away from it all, right?"

"No, not really. She sort of, like, left for good. She wanted to find herself, or something. I don't think she was feeling the whole 'wife and mother' moment." Tangie paused. "I don't know that much about her, actually," she repeated, shrugging.

"Hey, I'm sorry. . . . I ask too many questions."

"No, no, it's cool," Tangie said with a reassuring smile. "Whatever, I don't really think about it."

Izzy nodded sympathetically. "You know, my mom isn't the greatest, either. She basically stood by while my dad . . . well, let's just say Claire Huxtable is not in danger of losing her job."

"You and your mom don't get along?"

"Oh, I don't live with my parents. I haven't seen them in a while. I'm on my own."

Tangie waited for her to elaborate, but Izzy was silent. *O-kaay, so what does "on my own" mean?* She remembered reading somewhere that when Drew Barrymore was a teenager, she legally emancipated herself from her crazy, drug-addicted mom and moved out on her own.

"I never talk this much," said Izzy, with a smile.

"It's funny, neither do I."

"I think we're bonded forever now."

Tangie grinned. "Yeah, we're the too-much-information twins."

"The TMI twins!" Izzy's eyes sparkled. "I'm so loving that!"

Professor Hard Knocks cleared his throat again and glared at the two girls. Izzy waved sweetly, then he resumed talking.

Izzy lowered her voice to a movie-theater whisper and continued, "So, did you end up picking dance as your major?"

"Yeah, I only tried out for dance. I'm a sophomore dance major," Tangie said proudly. "Hip-hop's my specialty."

"I got in for dance, but I didn't pick it."

What? Tangie couldn't imagine being invited to join Armstrong's illustrious dance department and turning *them* down!

". . . And I sing and all, but I ended up going with art. I love to draw and sculpt and design." Izzy grinned. "I'm a Renaissance chick, for real. Because I write rhymes, too. I'm an aspiring rapper."

"For real? I love that!" Tangie wished she didn't sound so squealy and girlie.

"Yeah, just call me Izzy Duz It." She grinned, expectantly. "I just made that up, like, two days ago."

"Cute!" Ugh, why did she sound so vanilla? "I bet guys think the whole rapper thing is so sexy."

"Not if my flow is iller than theirs. But luckily, the guy I'm kinda feeling isn't an aspiring rapper, like every other guy you meet."

"I know, right? It gets *so* played out. And if they're not rappers, they're beatheads." Tangie rolled her eyes. She was glad C.J. wasn't that predictable. She sighed. He was such a brilliant artist.

The art teacher at Carrington Prep had used to plaster his office door with C.J.'s stuff. She thought of the portrait he had drawn of her, that was hanging over her bed. It always shocked her, how beautiful it was. She *wished* she looked like that—was that really the way he saw her?

Izzy read her mind. "So, you got a man? I'm assuming so, from that beard burn!"

"Beard burn? Oh, you mean . . ." Her hand flew to her upper lip. Thinking quickly, she giggled and put on a whole coy act. "No, I sort of accidentally hooked up with a friend—not a good look, right? But yeah, there's somebody I really like—well, *used to* like—but now we're not really talking. It sucks."

"Look, don't trip. It's a new year. Take it from me: *from the ashes the phoenix will rise again.*"

What was with everyone giving Tangie crazy advice today? "So, the guy you were talking about: is he your boyfriend?"

"Nah, we just kick it and stuff. I just met him, over the summer. He's older, which I love—a sophomore."

"Wait, what grade are you in?" Tangie assumed they were the same age.

"Freshman. I know, I know, I don't look it. I've lived mad lives for a fourteen-year-old," Izzy said quietly.

"Really?" Tangie was intrigued. "I can barely handle the one I have."

Izzy was staring at Tangie. "Please tell me those are false lashes, because if they're real I might have to kill you."

"What?"

"You have cocker spaniel eyelashes! You're not even wearing mascara, are you?" Izzy leaned in, studying Tangie's face. "I'm just itching to slap some liquid liner and mascara on you. You'd look exactly like Halle in those Revlon ads. You can trust me, I used to be a makeup artist at the Saks M·A·C counter."

"Wait, don't you have to be eighteen to work there?"

"I'll tell you everything if you let me make you over," Aziza grinned, naughtily. "Meet me in the freshman bathroom during morning break?"

Tangie nodded, beaming with excitement.

It sounded as if Professor Hard Knocks was finally wrapping up his monologue. "One more thing before I close. I'm sure most of you have already heard about Armstrong's mandatory Self-Awareness Sessions?"

"Oh, God, my friend Skye told me about this," whispered Tangie, with a grimace. "I thought I was being Punk'd."

". . . Here at Armstrong, we believe it's very important for artists to be in touch with their *deepest emotions*—it always makes for the most *honest* art, no matter if you're a dancer, an actor, a painter, or what have you. So, at least once a week you'll report to your assigned counselor for a one-on-one, fifteen-minute Self-Awareness Session. Here, you can talk about whatever's on your mind without being judged, graded, or recorded in any way. The sessions are *strictly confidential.* Their only purpose is to *enhance* your *performance.* Understood?"

Izzy looked at Tangie, pointed her finger to her temple miming holding a gun, and pretended to fire away. Tangie nodded and rolled her eyes.

"In closing, people, don't be intimidated by the size of this school. We have a *million* types of people here, and a *million* ways to make friends. A good way to start is by introducing yourself to your neighbor, *right now.*"

The TMI twins looked at each other and grinned as a rush of awkward, first-date-ish chatter filled the auditorium. They were already friends.

3.
THE BADDEST BITCH

"GOD, MARISOL, I'M SO *NOT* trying to do the whole 'Eden Carmichael' thing today." Eden and her best friend, Marisol Hernandez, the self-proclaimed "next Mariah of the millennium" were in the senior girls' locker room sneaking a cigarette. "I'm still in mourning."

Eden was a wreck, though it was impossible to tell from her flawless face.

"Look, don't trip," said Marisol, exhaling grandly. "Let people gossip about shit they know nothing about."

"The thing is, *everyone* knows what happened, Mare. Thanks to my exploiting-the-details-of-Eden's-life-gets-me-attention sister."

Eden still couldn't believe the indignity of it all. What guy in his right mind would cheat on her? Truth be told, Trey had never been the world's most faithful boyfriend, but Eden had not been able to break it off for good. First of all, being one half of a golden couple was fun. Second, Trey was almost unbearably sexy. With his rich, cognac-brown complexion, *sick* body, and lush dreadlocks tied in a thick, almost phallic knot, the boy could've stepped out of a Sean John ad. The yummiest part was that, even in his unfortunate Advanced Ballet Classics uniform of thong, leotard, and tights, Trey still had serious bad-boy swagger. Of course, the spoiled son of a wildly successful attorney was about as hood as Will Smith—but as one of the only straight guys in his department, no one could blame him for fronting.

Even though she'd turned a blind eye in the past, Eden would've looked like a total fool had she stayed with Trey after Le Prom Scandal (and Eden was not one to mess with her image). What started out as the glitziest, most romantic night ever—the dance was held on junior ballerina Courtney Van der Maal's yacht on Long Island Sound—quickly degenerated when Eden wandered into a bedroom to find Trey with his entire head buried under Courtney's dress.

". . . Never really liked him anyway, and besides, I read in *Cosmo* that it's better to talk to guys less sexy than you, because they'll want you more. Eden, are you listening to me?"

"Yes, dammit, yes." Eden snatched Marisol's Marlboro Light out of her French-manicured hand and took a deep drag, wishing it were weed. She was in no mood to hear one of Marisol's long-winded, touchy-feely speeches about finding inner strength (Marisol was always going on and on about female empowerment and loving yourself, blah-blah-blah).

Eden knew what was coming. She stopped Marisol before she could even get started. "Okay, you know what? Kill the 'I am somebody' drama. I am not J. Lo in *Enough*. I know I'm better off without Trey. It's just that the reason we broke up is so humiliating. How could he make me look so, so . . . wack?"

"Um, hello? *You're* the wack one in this scenario?" Marisol was incredulous. "May I remind you that, starting today, Dance Fever will be taking a beginner's hip-hop class with tenth graders?"

Right after Prom, Marisol and a bunch of her girls were over at her house keeping Eden from diving off her fourteenth-story penthouse balcony when somebody turned to *106 & Park* and started screaming. In plain view of the entire BET-watching world, there was Trey, dancing backup on the premiere of Missy's new video,

"Lose Control." Two days later, Eden anonymously slipped a tape of Missy's new video into dance dean Ms. Carmen's school mailbox.

At Armstrong, professional gigs were strictly banned—no agents, managers, commercials, or any nonschool shows or performances. The punishment for getting caught was taking departmental classes with a lower grade for an entire semester. Getting pushed back was embarrassing enough for Armstrong kids, most of whom had egos the size of Rhode Island—but for seniors, it was career suicide.

During their first semester, the seniors were at their show-offy peak; they were all unofficially trying to outdo each other in order to land a standout spot in the senior festival, the lavish interdepartmental senior production performed at the end of the year in front of New York City's hottest talent scouts. For Trey, one false move would mean the difference between a hot solo choreographed by Crazy Legs himself—or passing out programs while contemplating a career in taxidermy.

"It's true, revenge is sort of sweet," Eden grinned. "In a way, I hope he finds out it was me. Can you *believe* how stupid and careless he was to do that video?"

"Yeah, 'stupid and careless' pretty much sums him up." Marisol made a face. "Okay, yes, Trey's fine, and yes, he's talented—but he's also an obnoxious smart-ass with a huge chip on his shoulder. I don't know how you put up with his ego."

"Me, either." Eden would never admit it, but that was part of the reason she liked him. His cocky, you-know-I'm-the-bomb attitude was so sexy. Well, sometimes.

"You were the best thing he ever had, Edie."

"I feel sorry for him, actually. To not only lose me, but all hope of getting a good part at the showcase?" Eden was on a roll. "He's so over at this school. He can only go down from here, but I'm going *waaayyy* up!"

"Besides, Trey is just a trifling high school boy. Don't you want something more?" Since she was fifteen, Marisol had been dating much older guys—always with careers in show business. She thought Trey was cute and all, but she never understood why her gorgeous, talented friend would waste her time with some kid who couldn't help her career.

"Please, Mare, I . . ."

"We're eighteen now; we should be dealing with some real high rollers. Do you realize Mariah started dating with Tommy Mottola when she was, like, nineteen, and he was, like, a hundred and three? Look at what he did for her career. I don't mean to sound shallow or whatever, but in our industry, we have to think of dating as a business proposal." She took a deep drag of the cigarette and exhaled in a quick, hard puff of smoke. "You had your cute high school relationship, but playtime's over."

"But there's no one else," Eden mumbled sheepishly, feeling sorry for herself.

"I don't mean to sound like, conceited, or whatever, but we're . . . um, *major*. Don't let Dance Fever forget who you are."

Eden cocked her head, eyeing herself in the mirror. She flipped her hair over her shoulder and pursed her lips. She was hot, and she knew it. In a flash, she shook off her sad face. "You're right! We're *Eden and Marisol.* Who wouldn't want to holler at us, right?"

"I mean, *hello?*"

"Yeah, but why am I still miserable?"

"Because, honey, you spent the summer so depressed and isolated that you've lost touch with your *Eden-ness*. Remember the weekends Trey used to 'allow' you to come out with me? Within seconds of walking into Bungalow 8, you were beating back Wilmer freakin' Valderrama with a damned stick." Marisol felt that most of life's problems could be solved at a club. Of course, it helped that her cousin Manny was a doorman at Marquee. "Okay? Reclaim your power!"

Eden immediately perked up. "Hell, yeah, girl! This is my

senior year. I'm gonna have fun! And frankly, I get tingles just knowing Trey'll be pop-and-locking in Advanced Beginners Street Funk—not just with tenth graders, but with the totally unco-ordinated ones who were rejected in their freshman year."

"See?" Marisol grinned conspiratorially and stubbed out her cigarette. "Now who's the baddest bitch?"

4.
LADIES LOVE COOL C.J.

Hippa to the hoppa and you just don't stoppa
Diddy's on my nuts like my name's Big Poppa
Sucka MC's you know I leave 'em unconscious
Rock the Polo like Kanye but ain't that obnoxious
When I roll up on the set best expect a tongue-lashin'
Your style's a disaster, son, you might wanna cash in
Bustin' up your marriage now you look like Shar Jackson. . . .

"SHAR JACKSON? You're sick, money," said C.J., shaking his head. From the second that study hall had started, he'd been locked in a cipher with Blackadocious, the poet and rapper formerly known as Raj Jamison; Vineet Naveen, a *crazy* drummer and the hardest Indian boy anybody knew; and Kyle Clark, a Japanime addict and Armstrong style icon.

"Yo, Black, I thought you were on the conscious tip," said Vineet. "You ain't said nothing about black is beautiful or your Wiz, or whatever."

"Aw, man, that shit don't sell," said Blackadocious. "Nobody wants to hear me spit about love and consciousness, nahmean? Look, has Common *ever* gone platinum? Did anybody truly 'welcome back' Mase after he caught religion?"

"True, true," said Kyle, whom everybody called Deuce, for his habit of saying everything twice.

"I'm really feelin' your commitment to the revolution, Raj," said C.J., sarcastically.

"Look, stop playin'. You know I ain't answering to that slave name."

"But why *Blackadocious*, though?" C.J. finally said what they were all thinking. "It's like, the word won't come out of my mouth, like I got a mental block. It's just so, so . . . *extra*. It sounds like some shit out of *Superfly*. I mean, why not call yourself Soulbrotha or Jive Turkey?"

"Jive Turkey," muttered Kyle to himself, with a chuckle. "He said Jive Turkey."

"Aw, man, go 'head," said Blackadocious. "You just mad 'cause I found a higher calling."

"Why y'all hatin' on my man?" said Vineet, always on Black's side. "And the name Blackadocious ain't no crazier than *?uestlove*, right? Yo, and he's ill as hell." The Roots' percussionist was Vineet's personal hero. He tried to find a way to bring him up in almost every conversation they had.

C.J. stared at him, pityingly. "It's *imperative* that we find you a girl this year."

"Listen to this, man," said Kyle. "*Ladies Love Cool C.J.*, ya heard? *Ladies Love Cool C.J.*"

Just then, a very preppy white actor who'd been nervously staring at them for fifteen minutes finally got the courage to approach them. He was almost walking on tiptoe.

"Uh, uh, hi, um, my name is Steven? Is your name C.J.?" He was staring at Blackadocious.

"You don't wanna know his name, believe me," said C.J., rolling his eyes at Raj's new pseudonym. "What's up? Do I know you?"

Steven's voice lowered to a shaky whisper. "I, uh, wanted to buy a dime bag? I mean, if you're still selling pot. If not, that's cool, I just . . ."

"Wow," said Vineet, turning red with secondhand embarrassment.

"My man," began C.J., laughing a little. "How you gonna roll up to me and *assume* shit? You don't know me like that, money."

"Oh, yeah, I uh, I know. . . . It's my friend, he told me . . ."

"I don't know what he said, but maybe you should walk that way," said C.J., appalled. Of course he was still selling, but this idiot had broken all the rules of buying weed. You never say anything in front of a group (what if one of them hadn't been tight with C.J. and reported him?), you make eye contact with the seller, and he goes off somewhere by himself.

"Oh, cool, man, I'm sorry. Forget what I said. You guys, just forget I said anything, okay?" With that enormous fumble, Steven disappeared, and C.J., Vineet, and Kyle tried not to burst out laughing.

Meanwhile, Blackadocious's lips had been moving a mile a minute. "Okay, y'all wanna hear some conscious rhymes? Lemme find out I gotta prove to my own mans and dem that a brutha's flexible. Yo, Vin, drop a beat."

Bobbing his head, Vineet began drumming out a midtempo rhythm on his Western Civilizations textbook, and Blackadocious launched into another slightly wack freestyle. While he rambled on, C.J. thought about Kyle's remark that he was a ladies' man.

Okay, yeah, C.J. had a lot of girls, but the only girl he'd really liked—and liked since he was a kid—had disrespected C.J. like he'd never been disrespected.

Making things even more complicated, he'd met another chick over the summer at the Virgin Megastore in Union Square, where he worked on weekends (he also worked part-time at Foot Locker in Times Square—his friends' "you must be Jamaican" jokes were endless). He would never forget how they had met.

She was standing in the back of the store, staring up in awe at the graffiti mural that the store manager had commissioned C.J. to paint along the back wall. Not only did C.J. think it was his best work, the mural had actually won Virgin Mega's major design award.

The girl walked over to C.J., who was stocking CD's, and asked him a single, heart-stopping question. "Is that Lee Quinones's work?"

He was so shocked he almost dropped a stack of Three 6 Mafia CD's on her feet. *Lee Quinones?* He was basically the founding father of New York City graffiti—he'd pioneered the art form on subway cars in the early eighties. Not only did this girl know who he was, she'd actually compared C.J. to him! He fell for her, then and there. The polar opposite of Tangie, this girl was superchill and uncomplicated, almost like a guy—but kind of mysterious in an edgy way and sexy as hell. And they never butted heads.

But was what he had with her better just because it was easier?

Hell if I know, C.J. thought, rubbing his forehead. Ever since he had lost his virginity at twelve to the hot thirty-year-old CVS pharmacist who'd hooked him up with his OxyContin (to *sell*, not to use), he'd always had a steady stream of girls. It was easy for C.J. Pulling girls was something he didn't really have to think about; they came to him. But had he ever slept with a girl he really cared about? No. In fact, there was only one girl he'd ever cared about, and he'd never even come close to sleeping with her.

Tangie. Tangie was an angel, *his* angel. She was too good to pull into the madness of his life. And as much as C.J. wanted to lock her in a room and have his way with her for, like, days and days, he almost felt safer being just friends. Maybe what had happened at Skye's party was for the best. Because if he ever had gone further with Tangie, he was scared of what would happen next. It would be intense, it would be *real*, and C.J. didn't know if he could handle all that. His focus right now was on making money.

He was the man of the house, with adult responsibilities. With so much drama in his life, it was easier to mess with chicks who didn't really matter. He did know one thing: if he had learned anything growing up with a junkie who let random alcoholic "uncles" knock him around on the daily, it was that what people said or did when they were drunk was how they *truly* felt—so somewhere deep down, Tangie must've meant that "hood outreach" remark.

He also knew that, despite his kicking it with another chick, not a second went by in which he didn't fantasize about finding Tangie and kissing her until they both forgot what they were fighting about.

It was morning break, the twenty-minute recess between second and third period, and, as promised, Tangie met Izzy in the freshman wing girls' locker room. Neither one of them had anticipated how packed the locker room would be. There were giddy girls *everywhere*—stretching their long, ballerina-skinny legs against the tile walls, practicing vocal exercises in front of the mirror, shrieking with laughter over crazy Armstrong audition stories. The atmosphere was crackling with a sense of almost hysterical relief—after working their asses off for years, their dreams were finally realized. They were now Armstrong kids, members of a very exclusive club.

Meanwhile, Tangie and Izzy were members of their very *own* exclusive club. The new friends had managed to carve out a very small space on a wooden bench in front of the showers. Beaming at her work, Izzy grabbed a vintage hand mirror out of her camouflage messenger bag and held it in front of Tangie's face.

"Oh. My. God. Who *is* that?" Mesmerized, Tangie slowly moved her face to the right, then to the left, never taking her eyes off the mirror. Izzy had worked some kind of magic. The only makeup she ever wore was a bit of M·A·C Lipglass in Ornamental, and a touch of Cover Girl bronzer on her cheeks; sometimes, for performances at dance camp, she would put some glittery stuff on her eyes. Generally, Tangie thought eye makeup made her look slutty. But Izzy had made her look like a movie star.

"What did you *do*?"

"I curled your lashes, put on two coats of mascara and some black pencil just on top. It's called BAD Gal, by Benefit. See, I just winged it out a little on the sides." Izzy pointed this out to Tangie in the mirror, and Tangie nodded. "Oh, and I used this bronzy Urban Decay shadow, Midnight Cowgirl. It really pops on deep, sienna-brown skin, like yours."

"I would never, ever, say something like this—but I look good!"

"Good? Girl, you look like you should be onstage with Michelle and Kelly!"

They burst out laughing. Tangie felt incredible, invincible. Any worry she had had over seeing C.J. that day was completely oblit-erated—the second he saw how sexy she looked, he'd have no choice but to forgive her.

"Seriously, you have no idea how pretty you are. It's kind of endearing, but you should *own* it. You're so sexy!" Izzy grinned hap-pily, pleased at her little experiment.

"I can't wait for Skye to see me. She's gonna die!"

"Who's Skye?"

"She's my best friend. You'll really like her. She loves makeup, too." Tangie couldn't wait for them to meet. It was kind of nice to have met her own friend, not to have to depend solely on Skye's crew. And Izzy was fabulous.

"Hold up. This girl loves makeup, but she never told you that your lashes are a *mile long*? That you not wearing mascara is *criminal*? Tangie, celebrities pay mad change to look like you."

Izzy had a point, but she didn't know Skye. She really wasn't one to pile on the compliments—though, of course, she'd big you up if you complimented her first.

"She's a little, well, she's supportive in other ways." Tangie gave her back the mirror and changed the subject. She wanted to know more about Izzy. "So, do any of your girls go here?"

"Nope. I don't . . . well, most of my friends are guys, anyway."

"Where do they go to school?"

"Um . . . lots of places. Some are older. I traveled a lot as a kid. I moved around, so I lost touch with folks. Sometimes it's better that way." Her eyes darkened. "I'm kinda starting over, you feel me?"

"I think I know what you mean about starting over," Tangie said, trying to relate. "When my mom left, all I wanted to do was go to a new place where no one knew me. Just start over, fresh."

"So then you know where I'm at."

Tangie nodded, and without saying anything, she slid her hand across the bench and took Izzy's hand.

Surprised, Izzy's caught Tangie's gaze, and for one split second, she looked very young. Tangie didn't know what Izzy had gone through, but if it was anything like what she'd experienced four years ago, then Tangie felt for her.

Skipping a beat, Izzy gave Tangie's hand a quick squeeze, grinned, and let go. "We just had such a WB moment."

Tangie giggled. "A very special episode of *Everwood,* starring the TMI twins."

And then they went back to talking about makeup. As Izzy gave Tangie an in-depth explanation about the merits of eyeliner, Tangie thought about the fact that, for the second time that day, she'd discussed her mom with this girl. Even though they'd just met, this much was obvious: they were kindred spirits.

5.
SOCIAL CLIFFS NOTES

TANGIE WAS EXPERIENCING MAJOR SENSORY OVERLOAD. It was lunchtime, and the packed courtyard off the underclassmen cafeteria was abuzz with Oh-My-God-How-Have-You-*Been* chatter, the sounds of Hot 97, musical theater majors singing show tunes, and a small group of nebbishy boys and awkward-looking girls practicing musical instruments larger than themselves.

It was crazy—everywhere she looked there were dancers twirling, singers warming up their vocal chords, artists sketching, and actors clutching their hearts and pretending to suffer strokes. Watching the boisterous, uber-confident Armstrong kids, Tangie couldn't help wondering if she really and truly fit in at this school.

She knew she was a capable dancer, but Armstrong was a whole new level of competition. These kids looked as if they'd been performing in front of sold-out audiences since birth. *Whatever, give it a chance*, she told herself. *By next year, you'll be break-dancing on tables with the best of them.*

Tangie and Skye were sitting at the bench where, every day, Skye and her friends Kamillah Decker and Regina Leon hung out at lunch gossiping, flirting, and avoiding carbs of any kind.

As they waited for Kamillah and Regina to be let out of boring geometry class (freshmen and sophomores had their academic classes in the morning and their studio classes in the afternoon), Tangie sat nervously picking at her tuna fish sandwich, while Skye administered a crash course in sociology.

"You look like a deer in the headlights," announced Skye. "Erase your face, mama. What will the neighbors think?"

"Sorry, how's this?" giggled Tangie, flipping her head back and working the seductive pout she'd learned on *America's Next Top Model*. "I'm sorry, I'm just nervous. This is the second year in a row where I'm surrounded by thousands of people I don't know. And let's face it, last year was not a good look."

"But you have me, now! And you won't have to worry about anything because I'm giving you the Armstrong Social Cliffs Notes," said Skye, reassuringly. "I was so lucky to have Edie to help me before I started. A lot of kids aren't so lucky, and they never find their, well, their social footing. It's really a shame."

"I feel so privileged," deadpanned Tangie. "Sure would've loved to get those Cliffs Notes *before I got dressed this morning*." Two seconds after walking into the building for the first time, she realized she was the only dancer in the school rocking an actual "outfit." Everyone else was following the dancer's unwritten dress code: denim miniskirts and plain H&M T-shirts over practice outfits of leotards, tights, and ballet slippers. And no loose hair—it was all about a high bun. So, seconds before Orientation, Tangie flew into a bathroom to change into her leotard and tights and trade her sparkly peasant skirt for Skye's Earl Jeans mini. Then she piled her hair on top of her head in a messy knot (and, in the process, smushed to death her for-once-perfect curls). Voilà . . . *très danseur*!

"It all worked out, didn't it?" said Skye, absentmindedly. She put on her prettiest smile and waved at some guy across the courtyard. Tangie couldn't help wondering, though—why hadn't Skye said anything about the dancer's dress code that morning, when she had complimented Tangie's look? "Anyway, back to the Cliffs Notes. Where was I?"

"Theater majors." Tangie was dying to take another bite of her delicious tuna fish sandwich, but she'd been looking around: though it was lunchtime, no one was eating. Slowly, she wrapped the sandwich up and stuffed it back inside the brown paper bag.

"Good girl," said Skye, watching her. She handed her friend a piece of fat-free diet banana bread from her specially packaged Zone lunch. Starving, Tangie tore off a small piece.

"Thanks," muttered Tangie.

"Listen, it's okay. You're new. You didn't know that nobody really eats at lunchtime." Skye was talking to Tangie, but looking right past her, as if she were constantly checking to see who was walking by. "The Armstrong lunch crowd is like a microcosm of the entertainment industry—we're all too worried about our careers to eat!"

"Good to know," said Tangie, drily.

Skye tossed her hair and waved at some guy. "That's Michael Craig. He's the junior actor that took me to the prom last year. Such a nice ass."

"Skye! Hello? Are you talking to me or posing for the paparazzi?" Tangie was officially annoyed now. And it didn't help that Skye hadn't noticed her new makeup look. In the hallways, boys were breaking their necks to stare at her, but she couldn't get one compliment out of her best friend.

"Omigod, I'm sorry." Skye kissed Tangie on the cheek. "What were we talking about? Oh, yeah, it's *drama* majors, not theater majors." she said. "First off, actresses are the most popular girls—and I'm not saying this because I'm in drama, it's just true. I think it's because we're pretty and sexy—you have to be to work these days. And we're natural hams, so there's the whole outgoing thing. Basically, we're cool with everybody. Actor *guys*, on the other hand, are conceited, shallow, and dumb as shit."

Tangie smirked. "If anyone heard you right now . . ."

"I know I sound like the shadiest bitch, but trust me, Tange, this stuff is common knowledge." Skye raised her eyebrows and shrugged, as if to say, *Sometimes the truth ain't pretty*. "Now, on to the female dancers, who everyone refers to as Bunheads."

"*Bunheads?* You've got to be kidding, Skye." Tangie was slightly offended.

"What? It's a very affectionate term! Mad girls think Bunheads are stuck-up, but they're just haters. You know how it is . . . it's that regal posture you guys have, and the gracefulness. And, oh, those long, lean bodies." She stopped her speech abruptly, realizing she was talking to a dancer whose body looked nothing like this. "You know, I'd *much* rather have your boobs and booty than be a stick figure. You're lucky, because you've got the *sexiness* of an actress and the regal *posture* of a dancer—the best of both worlds!"

"You saw how well Jay Z and R. Kelly's Best of Both Worlds tour went," Tangie reminded her, sourly. "R. ended up with a face full of mace."

"You're so funny," Skye said, giggling. Some cornrowed guy walked past them, muttering something unintelligible but clearly obscene to Skye. She laughed hysterically and threw a carrot at him. Sighing, she turned her attention back to Tangie.

"So, what was I saying? Oh, okay, most male dancers are gay. And the ones that aren't, usually the hip-hop dancers, make the hugest deal out of being straight—they're major playas who bone everything that moves."

"Basically, you mean Trey, right?" Tangie sighed. "Poor Eden. I hate to believe that about him."

"Believe it. It's like, he tries to be overly street, to compensate. Like, you'll catch him playing dice in McDonald's and you'll be, like, wait, didn't I just see him in *tights?* Anyway, they get all the girls. The coolest guys, though, are the creative arts majors—you know, the writers, the painters, etcetera. There's a bunch over there, under the tree. I think they're juniors."

Tangie nodded. They were huddled in a cypher, freestyling. Definitely the type of guys C.J. would chill with. "Wait a second, they're not smoking weed at school, are they?"

"Please, those guys *stay* puffin'. They're all about old-school and underground hip-hop, independent films, sneakers, and drawing cartoons. Oh, and graffiti. You always know when you're sitting at the desk of an art kid, because the desk is all tagged up. But they have the most flavor, you know, in that Pharrell-slash-Kanye-slash-Seth-Cohen-from-*The O.C.* way." Skye sighed, dreamily. "And Seth Cohen is one white boy who could get it," she said under her breath.

To Tangie, graffiti and C.J. were practically synonymous. Trying to change the subject, she said, "What about music majors? You haven't said anything about them."

"'Cause they're sort of boring. Once in a while you'll get a sexy bass player or something, but on the regular, instrumentalists are nerdy and quiet. But the most annoying? Vocal majors. They're forever singing. They don't even *talk* to each other; they'll sing entire conversations. Like, 'Caa-aan *YOOUU* pass me the *PENN-ciiiiiiil?*' Not one of the great looks. Oh, and those operatic chicks are the worst, in the bathroom singing at the top of their lungs in freakin' *Italian.* They sound bananas."

"Who sounds bananas, your mom?" Standing behind Skye was a gorgeous girl in Afro-puffs and a vintage dashiki she'd converted into a minidress. It was Kamillah. Next to Kamillah stood Regina, an aspiring filmmaker and Skye-worshipper (she was half black and half Filipino, and her exotic looks had immediately earned her a place in Skye's crew on the first day of school, freshman year).

"My bee-yatches!" Skye hopped off the table and practically squeezed everyone to death, as if they hadn't spent almost every weekend of the summer at her parents' Hamptons mansion.

"Yo, yo, yo, T-Neesy! I'm so psyched to see you again! Remember, we met at Skye's School's a Wrap party?" Kamillah, a fast-talking fashionista from Harlem, was a drama major, like Skye. "Miss Pie in the Skye says you're a triple-threat superstar!"

Triple-threat superstar? Um, no—to be a triple threat, you had to dance, sing, and act. What exactly had Skye told them about her?

Tangie wished she could be flattered, but she knew the girl far too well for that. Hyping up her friends was just another way for Skye to make herself look good. Everything associated with her had to be the greatest, the hottest, the best—she didn't *know* low-budget.

"Tangie? I'm Regina. It's a total pleasure to finally meet you," said the cutie-pie wearing cornrows gathered up into a bouncy, jet-black ponytail. "When Skye told us you were a principal Alvin Ailey dancer at only eleven—well, I wasn't surprised. I guess child prodigies stick together, right?"

Tangie glared at Skye. *A principal Alvin Ailey dancer at eleven?* She'd never taken an Alvin Ailey class in her life. She was about to correct Regina, but then she noticed that Regina was gazing into her eyes. "Omigod, you have the prettiest lashes I've ever seen," Regina exclaimed. "Are they real?"

Kamillah leaned in and studied her face, then shrieked. "Goddamn, girl, I'm so-o-o jealous! Your eyelashes look like fucking *spiders!*"

Tangie grinned. Finally! "Thanks! My friend . . ."

"Wow, T., your eyes *do* look incredible," commented Skye. "Really pretty. Anyway, what was I saying? Oh, yeah, Regina . . ."

What the hell? Skye had always been a little self-obsessed, but this was *beyond.*

". . . She's a *sick* screenwriter and director. Aren't you?" Skye said smugly.

Shrugging, Regina made some hardly audible, self-deprecating comment.

Skye shoved her. "Why do you always put yourself down? It's so unsexy. Anyway, last year she cast me in her freshman film project, and we've been friends ever since. *Finger Food* was the most gorgeous lesbian love story. Remember, I told you about it?"

"Oh, that's right, it sounds fabulous." Tangie had zero recollection of a lesbian student film, but played along.

"It wasn't anything special," murmured Regina. "But Skye was beautiful in it. Her performance gave me the chills."

"I bet that's not all it gave you," murmured Kamillah, naught-ily. Regina glared at her.

Tangie noticed that Regina had pulled a worn spiral notebook out of her bag and was opening up to a page in the back. "Do you have homework already, Regina?"

"No, actually, it's . . ."

"She's taking notes for a documentary on showbiz kids, so watch what you say," interrupted Skye. "Seriously, it's gonna be her senior project. I personally love that she's constantly taking notes on every-thing, because it'll come in handy when I'm famous and want to remember my high school years for my memoirs. Or my *Driven* episode on VH1." Skye was only half joking. The girls just stared at Skye. She was so extra.

"Ah, shit," said Skye. She'd been digging around in her lipstick-red Prada messenger bag and had just slammed it down. Fixing her striking, greenish gray eyes on Regina, she stuck out her bottom lip in a mock pout. "I forgot my sugar-free Red Bull. How the hell am I supposed to stay alert in mime class?"

"I think they sell Red Bull at that bodega on University and Thirteenth," said Kamillah, popping a tuna roll from Monster Sushi into her mouth.

"Oh, do you want me to run over there?" Regina perked up, as if on cue.

"Would you? I'd love you forever, Reggie-Reg."

"I'm all over it! Don't talk about anything juicy while I'm gone." With that, Regina trotted away, risking detention for leaving the school grounds.

"Aren't you even going to give her cash?" asked Tangie. Skye looked at Kamillah and giggled, as if to say, "Poor Tangie, she's so out of it."

Meanwhile, Kamillah was grimacing at Skye as she took a bite out of something that looked straight out of *Resident Evil*. "What are you eating, babe?"

"Oh, this?" Skye flashed her most convincing, it's-all-good smile. "It's apple-flavored tofu in wheat broth. Alexa has me on this new diet. I gained a little pudge over the summer, and she straight-up went ballistic."

"You're insane, you don't look any different," said Tangie.

"Are you kidding? I ate all summer."

"Why can't you just eat a real apple? Fruit's good for you."

"You're so cute, Tange. No, real apples are loaded with sugar. These tofu thingies have zero caloric content." She shrugged, making a big deal out of looking as though it were no big deal. Taking another bite, she moaned in ecstasy. "Mmm, I actually love the way it tastes."

Kamillah shrugged, "All I got to say is, you can act your ass off."

"Um, sweetie, can we discuss your ensemble?" Being the object of ridicule, no matter how harmless, was Skye's biggest nightmare. She was a master at quickly deflecting it by calling attention to someone else.

"What's up with the Afro-puffs and the dashiki? Admittedly, I'm feeling how you bloused it out with the slouchy belt, but still, isn't 'Africana' sort of 1988?" Skye looked Kamillah up and down.

"Oh, girl, it's Blackadocious. Over the past couple weeks, he's gotten mad conscious, and a girl's gotta respect her man's aesthetic."

Skye rolled her eyes and changed the subject. "Anyway, I was just giving T-Nizzle the social tour of Armstrong. Any gossip I'm missing?"

"Oooh! I have very interesting news, but it's really Regina's moment. Let's put it on ice until she gets back."

"Oh, whatever," said Skye, her eyes bright at the prospect of titillating gossip. "She'll live—what is it? Don't *even* tell me she's coming out. I don't care what everyone says; that girl's way too cute to be a lesbian."

"Huh? No, you ass. It's about her Little Sister." Kamillah was referring to a prestigious mentoring program where a sophomore, junior, or senior acted as a "big sister" or "big brother" to a new student in a different department. The whole thing was supposed to help new kids get accustomed to Armstrong while developing an appreciation for majors different from their own. "She sounds a little too . . . *vivid* for Regina, poor thing. Supposedly, she's this total wild child with a scandalous past—she's, like, the talk of the morning."

"Sophomore?"

"Freshman."

"Oh, then, who cares?" sniffed Skye.

"No, this is good," said Regina. "Apparently, she was one of those poor, starving babies on the infomercials with the flies all over them and everything?"

"*Damn.*" Skye shuddered in horror. Tangie just looked at them both, wondering where this could possibly be going.

"I know, right?" Kamillah continued, leaning closer. "But somehow her family got lucky and moved here when she was five. And she had this totally fucked-up upbringing, and she kept running away, and in junior high, supposedly, she was Beanie Siegel's jumpoff, and he put her up in a room at the Tribeca Grand. Anyway, allegedly there was a baby or something, because she has a mysterious one-year-old sister she's, like, *mad* attached to, and she had to take eighth grade twice! And then there was some rehab situation, and somehow she got in here through her connections to the Ethiopian embassy." Kamillah paused to catch her breath and continued. "But here's the thing: she's drop-dead gorgeous, right? Like, every guy wants her. And she's so dope she's having none of it."

"Okay, wait, I need you to classify the dopeness."

Tangie could see Skye's wheels turning—she was trying to decide if she should befriend this chick. Skye collected pretty things, people included. And to rule out competition, it was always smarter to have the hot girl on your side—no matter how scandalous she was. "Is she sexy dope, pretty-but-stiff dope, she-can-dress-her-ass-off-which-covers-up-the-fact-that-she's-not-that-cute dope, or what?"

What she's really asking, thought Tangie, is, *Is she cuter-than*-me *dope?*

"Yo, this girl is, like, on the next level, apparently. She's rockin' a faux hawk, she's got this mad, edgy Gwen Stefani–ish style. And she's Ethiopian, or Somalian, or something like that, so she's got exotic, Cleopatra-ish features."

Tangie's jaw hit the floor. "Wait a minute, I—"

"Hold on, I haven't gotten to the best part." Kamillah paused for dramatic effect. "Are you ready? Supposedly, she rolls *hard* in hip-hop circles, and, I'm not positive, but I heard she let the entire G-Unit hit it."

"No." Skye was appalled. They weren't even cute.

"Would I lie?"

"Hold on," said Tangie, not buying any of it. "I think I know who you're talking about. Is her name Izzy?"

Kamillah thought a minute. "No, it was something like Eliza or Asme. Wait, it was Aziza—oh, you're right, and folks call her Izzy. Why?"

"I sat next to her at Orientation, and she's really cool. Honestly, I don't think all that stuff is true."

Skye shot her a look as if to say, *You're the New Girl; don't start acting like you know what's going on.* "How do you know?"

"She seems really, I don't know, *nice*. And different, definitely, but not a crazy whore," said Tangie. "Oh, she's the one who did my makeup!"

"Okay, the slut does have skills," admitted Kamillah.

"She did your makeup?" Skye's eyes narrowed in suspicion. Her bestest friend had already gotten close enough with some random freshman to trade makeup tips? She didn't like this one bit.

"Yo, you guys," said Regina, squinting. "Is that C.J. over there?"

All the color drained from Tangie's face, and she spun around so fast she almost got whiplash. He was standing in the doorway to the courtyard with his back to them, talking to some guy. Nodding,

C.J. gave him a pound, and then turned around. Alone, he walked out into the courtyard, his slow-moving swagger more familiar to Tangie than her own face. As he scanned the crowd for his boys, he glanced up and caught her gaze. He looked at her with his deep, soul-crushing eyes for what felt like an eternity. Then, he looked away, turned around and went back inside.

He was gone. He hated her. Tangie wanted to die.

6.
YOU KNOW HOW GOOD I AM

". . . FIVE-*SIX*-SEVEN-*EIGHT*-AND-*ONE*," bellowed Ms. Carmen, facing her Advanced Beginners Street Funk students, her back to the huge wall mirror. As she pounded the floor to the beat with a gnarled wooden cane, she bellowed each count of the short but seriously complicated routine she'd just taught. The students whipped their mostly skinny-as-a-rail bodies around while a bored-looking senior, a blond music major experimenting with white-boy dreadlocks, beat an African drum to death. The studio smelled like old sweat, hair spray, and desperation. The thirty or so kids were terrified, and it showed.

The class was for sophomore dance majors who either were new to Armstrong or had been less than stellar in their freshman core curricula—so everyone was dancing her heart out, eager to prove that she belonged in a more advanced class. But no matter how graceful the pirouettes or how masterful the jetés, Ms. Carmen was not about to show that she was pleased. With her lush, loose, jet-black, wavy hair (done in a style that, on a student, would easily have gotten the girl thrown out of her class for the day—one of her favorite mantras was "No bun? You're done."), a low-cut leotard, and signature bloodred lipstick, Ms. Carmen was the sexiest teacher at Armstrong—there wasn't a single boy in the dance department who didn't secretly lust after her. She also happened to be one of the most important music-video choreographers of the late eighties and nineties, and a notorious hard-ass.

Which was why it was a thousand shades of wrong for Tangie to be seven minutes late on the very first day of Ms. Carmen's class.

Lunch ended up being from hell. Watching C.J. publicly ignore her like that—it was way too much to deal with before noon. After that, she was totally distracted. So she said something about having to change her tampon, and crouched in a bathroom stall until hearing the fourth-period bell. Then Tangie realized she had no clue as to where the dance floor was located (the senior aides had given a tour of the hella-normous school during Orientation the previous week, but who plays close attention when one is that excited?). She sprinted out into the supercrowded hallway. Why did it seem that everyone knew where they were going and what they were supposed to do but her?

And then the panic thing started happening. Tangie's cheeks burned furiously, and her palms started sweating. Did she belong at Armstrong if she was *already* lost? Everyone else seemed so sure of herself, so busy and purposeful and confident, racing off to Symphonic Application or Watercolor Basics or theater movement class. She spotted a group of obvious Bunheads (they were wearing cropped wrap cardigans over their leotards and sported the signature toes-turned-out duckwalk that was the mark of a trained dancer) and made the quick-thinking decision to follow them, since they were obviously going her way.

Wrong. Tangie realized they were not headed for the dance wing when she found herself outside, behind the Armstrong auditorium, watching the dancers spark up the fattest joint she'd ever seen.

So, after practically catching a contact high (and suffering through a decidedly NC-17-rated elevator trip starring two desperately-in-lust boys rocking matching booty-shorts and tongue rings), she finally did what she should have done to begin with and asked a hall monitor for directions. And there she stood, ten full minutes after the final bell, panting and sweating in front of a group of strangers.

Ms. Carmen signaled the drummer to cease his assault on the African drums. Turning to face Tangie, she hollered, "Oh, no, you didn't!"

"I, um, I'm so sorry, Ms. Carmen," she muttered, dropping her tote in the corner and scurrying to the back of the group. Everyone turned to stare at her. She wanted to die. "I'm so, so sorry—I'm *never* late! I'm new, and I got turned around and . . ."

"Okay, the first thing you need to learn to make it in my class, Pumpkin, is that you're on *my* time." Ms. Carmen leaned against her wooden cane, looking Tangie up and down. "The second thing is, I'm not going to interrupt my class to hold your hand when all these other dancers have managed to get here on time. See, it's like that song: 'I don't care how you get here, just get here if you can.'" A natural born performer and ham, Ms. Carmen actually belted out the lyrics. "So, *can* you?"

Tangie nodded vigorously and nervously fingered her bun, praying for the moment to hurry up and pass. From somewhere to her right, she heard a snicker.

"Well, since you feel that the rules don't apply to you, Tutti-Frutti, and you don't know the counts I just taught, I'd love to see what you've got."

"What I've got?" Tangie had no idea what that meant.

"You heard me. Come up to the front," she said, gesturing for Tangie to come forward from where she stood cowering in the back of the group. Horrified, Tangie wove through the cluster of dancers—all clearly suffering major secondhand embarrassment—and stood before Ms. Carmen, her eyes on her ballet shoes. "Now, I want to see what you can do. Freestyle for three eight-counts. Casey, play something midtempo." Casey, the blond, dreadlocked senior, grunted a reply and tossed his butt-length mane behind a shoulder. "Are you ready, Sugar, or should we wait another ten minutes?"

"No, no, I'm ready," Tangie whispered, her entire body trembling. Her classmates all moved to the back of the room to give her space, some leaning up against the barre running along the back wall, others sitting cross-legged on the floor. She could feel thirty sets of eyes boring holes into her back. Instantly, she became acutely aware of her boobs. Standing there in front of a class chock-full of classic ballerina bodies—with wiry arms; nonexistent T&A; and sinewy, mile-long legs—all of her insecurities about her short, curvy body came rushing to the surface. *The Black-Eyed Peas were clearly thinking of me when they wrote "My Humps,"* she thought with a grimace. She felt as though everyone were staring at her 32Ds and wondering how a chick with cleavage deep enough to smother an infant would ever be able to dance backup for Ciara.

But whatever. She was a dancer, and Ms. Carmen was asking her to dance. It was what she did best; it was the only thing that made her feel truly beautiful, interesting, sexy, *Alive*. She squeezed her eyes shut and transported herself to her "good luck" place.

One of Tangie's most vivid memories of her mom came from when she was about five, and her mom was playing Dorothy in an off-Broadway production of *The Wiz*. At the end of the performance, her mom pulled her onstage, took her hand, and twirled her around, over and over, so her flouncy, polka-dot skirt flew out around her. Cameras were snapping everywhere, people were tossing roses at them, and from that moment on, Tangie knew she wanted to dance. It was her favorite memory of her mother.

So now, for good luck before she performed, she clicked her heels together three times like Dorothy in *The Wiz*. It had worked during Armstrong auditions, and Tangie prayed it would work this time.

Before she knew it, the surly senior began pounding on the drums again. All eyes were on her. And something in Tangie clicked. She took a deep breath, closed her eyes, and then threw herself into the dance, feeling the beat of the drum in her blood, doing exactly what her body told her. She was categorized as a hip-hop dancer, but her special "Tangie flavor" had so much more than what the usual video-style dancer did—it was a mix of jazz, ballet, and African dance, with some gymnastics thrown in there, too.

Tangie danced and danced—hurling her body into a flying somersault, bending backward into a shoulder fall, launching into a sky-scraping pirouette fouette. She let it all out, the heartbreak of C.J., the humiliation of showing up late to her first Armstrong dance class, the worry that things with C.J. and Skye would never be the way they used to be. Tangie danced past the three eight-counts, going and going until Ms. Carmen finally said, "Okay, okay, enough. Enough!"

Hearing that, Tangie spun around in a final pencil turn and landed in a jazz split (her front leg straight in front of her, with the back leg bent upward). She held the pose, sweating and out of breath, feeling truly alive for the first time in months. When she stood up, Ms. Carmen gave her a nod and a very small smile.

Tangie held her breath in triumph. Then Ms. Carmen yelled at her to join the rest of the class, and it was only at that point, when Tangie turned around and faced her classmates, that she even remembered that they were there. Blushing furiously, Tangie speed-walked through the cluster of dancers to take her place in the back. Did they think she was a show-off? Was she going to get jumped again for thinking she was cute?

"Not bad," whispered the frighteningly skinny, aristocratic-looking Asian chick to her left. Like the world's most flexible stork, she stood on one leg and nonchalantly held the other one up by her ear, stretching her hamstrings. "You have amazing energy. And really nice lines."

"Thanks," Tangie whispered excitedly, thrilled to be complimented by a real, live, Armstrong dancer. "Omigod, how humiliating to have to freestyle in front of the whole class on your first day."

"Please, are you kidding me?" With an all-knowing air, the Asian stork waved away Tangie's embarrassment. "You got singled out by the most powerful instructor in the dance department."

"Yeah, but it wasn't for a good reason. It was punishment."

"It doesn't matter," the stork said, gracefully falling forward and touching her nose to her knobby knees. Instantly, Tangie copied her. "Attention is attention. Every Bunhead in here's *praying* that Ms. Carmen'll notice them, even for a second. Come Fall, Winter, and Spring Fling time, it'll mean the difference between getting a Spotlight solo and landing in the back row of the chorus. See, no one cares *how* you get noticed, babe, the point is that you were noticed."

Tangie nodded slowly, totally getting it. She had a lot to learn.

"It's just Armstrong Politics 101," shrugged The Stork, lifting her other leg to her ear. "I'm Gigi, by the way. Gigi Cho." With her itsy-bitsy leg still in the air, she thrust a dangerously emaciated hand in Tangie's direction.

"What's up? I'm Tangie."

"Just in case you're wondering, I don't have an eating disorder."

"What? I . . . I didn't think you did," Tangie quickly lied. Not only did this girl make Tangie look like a pre-gastric-bypass Star Jones, she was a mind reader.

"So, are you new?"

"Yeah. I'm a sophomore, but it's my first year."

"Are you a ballet major?"

"Actually, no. I'm hoping to do hip-hop."

"*Reeaally?*" Gigi frowned, looking her up and down.

"How about you?"

"Ballet, of course," Gigi said, stretching out her other leg. "I started pointe when I was only five years old. Believe me, I'm only taking street funk to fulfill a requirement."

O-kaay, thought Tangie. How bitchy! Gigi was acting as if hip-hop were not as legitimate as ballet.

"So," continued Gigi, "where have you trained?"

Tangie couldn't belive it. That was another thing—every dancer she'd talked to had asked about her training within seconds of saying hi. "Well, I've gone to Debbie Allen's Dance Academy camp every summer for five years."

"Yeah, but that's summer camp. What about during the school year? Any classes at Joffrey Ballet School? Or School of American Ballet?"

Tangie shook her head timidly.

"Well, what about National Dance Theater? Or even Broadway Dance Center? You must've studied *somewhere* in elementary or middle school, or how else would you have gotten into Armstrong?"

Tangie shrugged, feeling like a total idiot. "I don't know, I've never taken any of those classes. But I'm not a ballerina, so . . ."

"It doesn't matter. Even hip-hop dancers need training."

"Well, I guess Debbie Allen was good enough for . . ."

Gigi abruptly turned away to speak to the willowy brunette on her right.

Ms. Carmen announced that they had one more minute to warm up before learning another eight-count of the routine. Tangie sat down on the floor and spread her legs as far as they'd go, bending at the waist to stretch out over one knee. When she raised her head, her heart skipped a beat. Breezing into the studio was the most beautiful boy she'd ever seen (well, next to C.J., of course): chocolate-brown skin; cheekbones that would make Mekhi Pfifer growl with envy; sexy dreads tied in a messy knot; and perfectly muscular, but not gross arms.

What the hell was Trey Stevens doing in a sophomore class?

He leaned against the wall at the front of the room, folding his strong arms across his broad, muscular chest. His eyes lazily scanned the class, giving "Wassup, ma?" nods to a couple of girls. When his eyes landed on Tangie's, he stopped. A slow, lazy grin spread across his face and, in front of everybody, *he winked at her.*

She would have sworn she'd imagined it, had the first two rows of dancers not turned around to see who the hell Dance Fever was silently hollering at. Her heart stopped—did he recognize her from when she had been a kid hanging out at Skye's house, sneaking glances at him and Eden making out? Had he just seen her dance? All aflutter with a mixture of embarrassment and excitement, Tangie gave him a dumb little wave and then, realizing she was still sitting spread-eagled in her thigh stretch, slammed her legs shut.

Sensing that her class was preoccupied with something behind her, Ms. Carmen finally turned around. When she saw Trey leaning against the wall, her mouth twisted into a tight, angry knot. "Well, you have some nerve, Mr. Stevens," she spat furiously, her cheeks turning a deep maroon color. "Your video appearance all but proved that you think you're too hot for Armstrong rules, but, if you're interested in graduating, you'd better take my class seriously. Why'd you even bother showing up this late?"

Trey shrugged, making no move to join the rest of the dancers in the cooldown. "Considering I took this class three years ago, I'm asking myself the same question, Carm."

Collectively, the class gasped in shock. Carm? He actually called her by her first name! And why was she blushing?

"Mr. Stevens, I refuse to let you waste everyone's time. I want you gone, now."

"Cool. I'm out, yo," Trey growled, snatching his jacket up off the floor. "Peace."

"I don't care how many times you've taken this class," Ms. Carmen yelled, stamping her cane on the ground for emphasis, "as long as you're in my studio, you'll respect my rules. You're not above this class, Trey; I don't care how good you *think* you are."

"Don't front, Carm," Trey said, looking her dead in the eye. "You know how good I am." Throwing up the peace sign at the class, Trey stormed out of the studio, slamming the door so hard that a framed poster of Isadora Duncan went crashing to the floor. Steam almost visibly rising from the top of her head, Ms. Carmen stomped into her office just off the studio and slammed the door. The class was thunderstruck. The bell sounded, and everyone rushed for the locker rooms, buzzing about what a *bad ass* Trey was.

But Tangie lagged behind, surprised by what she'd just seen. All those years he had been dating Eden, Tangie had always imagined that Trey was a golden-boy gentleman. Clearly, Trey Stevens's ego was totally out of control.

That's not to say he wasn't sexy as hell.

Ms. Carmen felt as if she were having déjà vu. Had she met Tangie before? Maybe, but she definitely would've remembered this girl. It had been a while since she'd seen a dancer with this much talent in such a raw place—some dancers learned so much technique that their natural abilities were watered down over time. Tangie was the opposite. She needed tons of work, but she was good. *Really* good.

After class, as her students were filing out of the studio, Ms. Carmen stood in her office doorway and called to the last girl left.

"Excuse me, Pumpkin?"

Tangie picked her bag up from the floor by the wall and turned around. "Yes?"

"What's your name?"

"Tangela Adams. Well, Tangie. Everyone calls me Tangie."

Ms. Carmen froze. "What? Say your name again?"

"Taaangie." She said it very slowly, as if she were explaining something to a very small child.

It was weird—Ms. Carmen seemed to go a little pale hearing her name.

"Tangie." She repeated the name, then nodded silently to herself. "Okay, Tangie, the sophomores have a free period now, yes?"

"Uhhh, yeah, but I . . ."

"Good. I need you to meet me in my office in ten minutes. Okay?"

Tangie nodded, smiled uneasily, and hustled out of the door.

For a long time after everyone had left, Ms. Carmen still hadn't moved. She hadn't been so shocked since Paula Abdul, her biggest competition in music-video choreography in the late eighties, had decided she was an accomplished enough singer to judge *American Idol*. So this was Tangie. Ms. Carmen had been wondering when she would run into her.

7.
A FIGHTING BITCH

FOR C.J., THE FIRST DAY OF SCHOOL had been wrong from the moment he woke up. He'd been up all night with his grandma, who was suffering a terrible asthma attack, and with her wheezing and hacking was even more verbally abusive than usual ("Cedric James, you better get your skinny black ass in here and pick up your motherfuckin' dishes—my name ain't Flo, and I ain't no waitress!"). He usually found her downright raunchy language hilarious, but not at four in the morning. Since he woke up late, he almost missed his appointment outside of Not Ray's Pizza with Kevvy-Kev, Bed Stuy's premier weed guy. Kevvy-Kev's stuff was the best in Brooklyn, and it kept Armstrong's ultraprivileged stoners happily "baked, dude" for days at a time.

Luckily, even though C.J. was twenty minutes late for their meeting, Kevvy-Kev was still hanging out at their meeting place, kicking it with some customers. Quickly, he picked up enough stash to last the entire month and broke out, only to discover that the C train to Manhattan was stalled, because a severely cranky homeless guy refused to budge from some old lady's lap (it seems she was sitting on his house—welcome to New York, right?). He ended up hailing a gypsy cab to school and, in true C.J. "Don't Knock the Hustle" Parker style, he got out of paying the full twenty-five bucks by charming the hell out of the female driver. He pretended to think she was Mary J. Blige, asking her for her autograph and acting all starstruck (as if MJB would have been caught dead pushing a hubcapless Caddy for extra cash). And in a ridiculous end to a ridiculous morning, when he finally got to Armstrong he ran away like a scared little bitch when he saw Tangie.

But C.J. didn't want to think about that right now. He had more pressing matters to deal with.

He was in intermediate charcoal sketching class, sitting all the way in the back row next to the only other black kid in a room full of Chuck Taylor–clad, floppy-haired hipster white boys with a hard-on for Japanime and hemp-wearing hippie chicks that sat under trees during lunch listening to Phish and sketching pictures of horses. It was a seriously intense class for the first day of school.

They'd just been given their first project, which would count toward one-fourth of their final grades. The teacher, a bushy-eyebrowed former downtown muralist who, in a very "The Artist Formerly Known as Prince" way, made his students refer to him as The Illustrator, was explaining the rules.

"Okay, so for the first quarter we'll be studying the human form," he said, pacing up and down the paint-spattered, gray cement floor of the studio. Sunlight was beaming in through two floor-to-ceiling windows (The Illustrator preferred his students to work under natural light), catching every speck of dust on the floor. Years of former students' paintings, photographs, and sketches lined the walls, the edges curling up. The studio smelled like oil paint, glue, and charcoal-smudged fingers.

"In two weeks, you'll turn in an 8.5 x 11 charcoal portrait of a person. A real-life *human being*."

C.J. smirked and shook his head. This man was a fool.

". . . Must be male or female and in any pose as long as it's full-length. And it must be a nude. Any questions?"

A white boy wearing baggy Rockawear jeans, a do-rag, and dog tags (they were engraved with the name "Body Count") raised his hand. "Are we allowed to sketch off a photograph? Meaning, if I draw Buffie the Body, does it count?" The class giggled at the mention of the famous video vixen, but The Illustrator looked as though he were losing his patience.

"No, you can't use a photograph. Are we going to be mature here?"

Izzy, sitting right next to C.J., leaned over and whispered in her low, raspy voice, "Are we gonna be mature, here?"

He raised his eyebrows. "I don't know, you tell me."

"I know what you're thinking."

"What I'm thinking?"

"You're thinking, 'Damn, I really wanna ask Izzy to pose for me, but she's just so-o-o sexy, yo. What if I can't control myself . . .'"

C.J. snorted, and The Illustrator slammed his hand down on his desk. "Maturity, folks. If you can't handle a simple nude, you don't belong at Armstrong."

"Listen to the man," whispered Izzy with a smirk.

C.J. leaned over to her. "How'd you get so damn cocky?

"What, you already forgot Jones Beach, Fourth of July weekend?"

He shook his head, smirking. Izzy was nuts. "Whatever, ma. You wouldn't do it."

"Why wouldn't I? It's for art, right?" Izzy bit her bottom lip mock-seductively. "I got the time if you got the place, baby."

C.J. didn't remember a damn thing The Illustrator said after that. He was completely thrown by Izzy, always. Never in his life had he met a chick so raw, so in-your-face wild. But no matter how tough she acted, the fact was that Izzy was a very young girl. And C.J. had dealt with enough young girls to know that they might say one thing, but mean something totally different.

Izzy acted as if posing nude didn't mean anything. But for a girl, sitting naked in front of a guy for hours on end—all vulnerable and exposed and shit—that was *deep*, maybe even deeper than sex. You only went there with someone you were really serious about, someone you could trust (after all, the wrong guy could exploit the hell out of a girl, putting her naked ass all over his MySpace page or something). Of course, Izzy could trust him: he was a good guy, but he absolutely did *not* want to be serious. Before C.J. drew her portrait, he wanted to get a few things straight.

After class ended, C.J. walked Izzy back to the freshman wing. As they talked about random, first-day-of-school stuff, each wondered if the other would bring up the fact that Izzy's offer was hanging in the air between them.

C.J. went first.

"Hold up, were you just messin' around in there?" C.J. was leaning against the wall, coolly watching the crowd while Izzy loaded her oversize art portfolio into her locker. An expert businessman, he was brilliant at looking out for potential customers while simultaneously making a girl feel as though she were the only female in the room. It was so obvious when a kid wanted to buy from him—he could always tell from their darting, should-I-or-shouldn't-I eyes.

Izzy shrugged almost impatiently. "Of course I'm serious."

"Then I must have some bomb-ass karma," he said, shooting Izzy one of his most devastating grins. She just nonchalantly rolled her Cleopatra-lined eyes and curled up one side of her mouth in the way she knew was irresistible to all guys. Izzy was all about preserving her unimpressed cool.

No matter how unbearably cute C.J. was in his crisp white T, Sean John track jacket, and sideways Yankees cap, she was not about to give him the upper hand, especially since it was obvious that that was the kind of chick he was used to. She'd had enough experience with boys to know not to get all girlie and vulnerable before she knew she *owned* them.

"I'm saying, ma, you sure you're trying to, like, go there?" C.J. held his breath. He liked her, but he didn't want to be roped into a huge boyfriend-girlfriend thing. It was just his general rule: he only dealt with girls he *knew* were down with no-strings-attached sex. He wasn't trying to lead anyone on or hurt anyone's feelings—he just wanted to chill.

"Yeah," said Izzy, boldly staring him in the eye. "Why not? It's about art. That's why we're at this school, right?"

He just looked at her, one eyebrow raised. "I mean, it really would be about art—you know, nothing more. I'm saying, I like you, but I'm not trying to do a serious thing, and . . ."

"Listen, C.J., don't get it twisted." She took a step back away from him and planted her hands on her hips, all don't-even-go-there-with-me attitude. "We had a cute summer and all, right?"

"Yeah."

"But it was a summertime moment. The reason I wanted to talk to you after class was because I think we should chill, now that school's started."

You could've knocked C.J. over with a feather. This was not how he'd expected the conversation to go. *She* was breaking things off with *him*? "What . . . uh, what do you mean?"

"I know what you're thinking. You're scared I'm gonna get all pressed and giddy 'cause you kiss *a-iight* and draw pretty pictures. Let's be clear. I don't do girlfriend, and I don't do possessive. Got it?"

C.J.'s eyes widened, but he said nothing. This was definitely a new thing for him.

"I'm offering to pose nude for you because *I want to*," she repeated slowly. "Naked don't mean a thing to me; I've posed for artists before, many times, and I just want to add to my collection. That's all. Something to show my grandkids when my boobs are in my shoes."

"I seriously doubt they'll *ever* be in your shoes," C.J. said, eyeing her chest with a playful grin, trying to lighten the mood. He'd never been so caught off guard in his life.

"I mean, I like kickin' it with you and everything, but I'm new at this school, and I'm not trying to be tied down to one boy. So, before we go any further, I just want you to know that it's not going to be a boyfriend-girlfriend thing. We can still chill, but we should keep things open." She cocked her head, waiting for his response. "We clear?"

C.J. didn't know what to say. Was this a joke? It was like he'd met the female version of himself. He knew a lot of girls, like his cousin Skye, who pretended to be straight-up players. Izzy, though? Izzy was a different story. She really and truly thought like a *dude*. She went *hard*. And she wasn't pretending not to need him—she really, really didn't.

And suddenly, that made C.J. want her all the more.

"C.J.?" Jokily, she knocked on his forehead with her hand. "You there?"

"No, I'm here. Yeah, yeah, I hear you, completely. And I agree. Let's just be cool."

Smiling, Izzy got on her tiptoes and wrapped her arms around his shoulders, looking up at him. "Look, The Illustrator's one of the teachers deciding who gets to try out for Spotlight Artist on Visual Arts night. You know, during Fall Fling."

"Yeah, I know."

"I believe in you, that's all. I just want you to draw a kick-ass picture so you get Spotlight Artist. Seriously, you deserve that shine."

"Thanks, ma. I appreciate that." C.J. looked down at her, the corners of his mouth turning up. He had an uncontrollable urge to kiss her. *Hold up, this was not how this was supposed to go!* "You really wanna pose for me, huh?"

"It'll be fun. Are you scared?"

"Scared would not be the word. Hyped, yes."

Izzy smiled, tilted her chin down and looked up at him through her long, mascaraed lashes. "Cool. Let's do this, then. But remember, this doesn't mean I'm trying to hit it. It's about the art," she repeated firmly, while slowly licking her lips.

C.J. nodded slowly, staring at her mouth. *Art, my ass*, he thought. *We both know better than that.* Backing Izzy against her locker, he slipped his arms around her waist and gave her a deep, slow, unbearably sexy kiss. It was so good he almost forgot about the fact that she'd just flipped the script on him so hard his head was spinning. *Almost.*

As C.J. and Izzy were locked in their kiss, they couldn't help overhearing a couple of girls gossiping as they walked by.

". . . I know, right? Well, I heard she used to roll hard with the Roc-A-Fella crew," whispered a cute dark-skinned chick with shaggy, blond-streaked extensions.

"Oh, word?" Her friend, a tiny, around-the-way Asian girl, was rocking a Lacoste tennis dress and door-knocker earrings that read "Janine" in cursive. And she was appalled.

"Yeah, Kenya said something about Izzy letting Common *and* Jay Z hit it. And supposedly the entire G-Unit!"

"*What?* That's madness, yo. Jay Z? I mean, he has the hottest chick in the game wearin' his chain."

"Oh, please, you don't think he still has hos in every area code? I mean, this is Jay Z, okay? No matter how fly Beyoncé is, she knows what's up. I mean, you know how those hip-hop playas are."

As they walked past Izzy and C.J., the Asian girl shook her head. "Shady."

By this point, Izzy had broken the kiss and was glaring at the girls, in total disbelief. These bitches had the nerve to be talking shit right in front of her! And who the hell was Kenya? Her tiny hands formed fists, and C.J. started chuckling, laughing it off.

"Just be easy," he said, putting his arm around her, protectively. "If I paid attention to everything every motherfucker said about me, where I come from and all that, I'd be in jail."

She looked at him as if he were crazy. "Oh, but they're messing with the wrong bitch. You think I'm trying to sit back and let Dumb and Dumber spread lies about me?"

"But you know it's bullshit, so why are you tripping?" he said, trying to calm her down. She was still huffing and puffing, so he tried to lighten the situation. "Plus, you're five feet tall and eighty pounds soakin' wet. You ain't hard."

Jokes didn't work, either. Izzy was so furious she could hardly see straight. Those girls didn't know anything about her—her past, who she was, nothing.

She slipped out from under C.J.'s arm and stormed over to the two girls. Izzy tapped the black girl on the shoulder, and the girl whipped her head around in surprise, dropping her sheet music.

"We got a problem?" Izzy was a full head shorter than the girl, but her 'tude made her seem six feet tall. The freshman hallway was thick with nosy kids, most of them beginning to crowd around the two girls in hopes of witnessing the first fight of the year.

The girl and her friend were visibly nervous. "I mean, I think *you're* the one with the problem," the dark-skinned cutie said.

"Bitch, you don't even know me," said Izzy, poking the girl in the shoulder with her index finger so hard the girl jerked backward. "I'm a fightin' bitch, okay? I'll snatch that triflin' weave out your head so fast you won't know . . ." And then she actually *did* snatch some of the weave out of her head.

"Chill, chill, chill," said C.J., stepping up and pulling Izzy away from the girl kicking and clawing.

The girl blurted out, *"Bitchy ho!"* and scurried away. Meanwhile, the Asian girl that had talked so much smack had long since disappeared into the crowd, nowhere to be found.

"Ain't nothing to see here folks, keep it moving," said C.J. to the crowd of drama-seekers who'd circled around the girls. He dragged Izzy back over to her locker and tried to calm her down, but her chest was heaving and her cheeks were flushed and she was going on and on about "punk-ass tricks." So he stood back and let her get it out of her system until, finally, she took a deep, cleansing breath and quipped, "Yeah, I'm tiny, but I'll tear out some Hawaiian Silky in a heartbeat." She laughed it off, and it was over.

But C.J. didn't think her little episode was funny. He thought it was hot. *Izzy would've thrown down, right then and there*, he told himself, in total awe. *This girl is gangsta.*

And he loved it.

Name: Trey Allen Stevens
Class: Senior
Major: Dance
Self-Awareness Session #: TS 1

Eden hated sex. She was frigid like what?! I mean, it wasn't nothin' I done wrong. I'm a pimp, son, you better act like you know. Anyway, yeah, so a playa used to have to beg for some. She'd be like, "Unh-unh, my hair!" Whatever. I did love her. I miss her. But she's really a wrap, yo. I ain't got time to worry about what she's tryin' to do. It's my senior year, shit is crucial, ya heard? I'm coming for these pansy-ass dance mothafuckas. Ain't nobody at this school can see me. You got a nigga can bring it harder? Send him to me. You got a nigga who can beat out two hundred professionals for a front-and-center spot in a Missy video? Send him to me. Hip-hop dance is my God. It's my carbon monoxide.

Trey, humans die from carbon monoxide inhalation. Do you mean carbon dioxide?

Yeah, yeah, yeah. Carbon dioxide. Whatever, man. T.I. said the shit best: I'm fast as lightnin', bruh; you better bring your Nikes, bruh. What you know about that, playa?

8.
SYMPATHY FOR SOLANGE KNOWLES

"AH FEEL ALL THE TIME LAHK A CAT, BRICK," moaned Skye in her best desperate Southern belle accent. "Just lahk a cat on a hot tin roof!" She grabbed the back of the chair with one hand, her script with the other. Her bottom lip was quivering, and her furrowed brow was bathed in a thin layer of sweat. Even from the audience, the class could see her entire body trembling like a Chihuahua.

"I'm embarrassed for you, Maggie. You're makin' a fool out of yourself," growled Nick, the new guy in Skye's Southern Playwrights theater class. He was leaning on a crutch, his face a map of agony and frustration. Nick was totally believable as an injured former pro football player who was too caught up in his own depression to sleep with his sexy wife.

"I don't mind makin' a fool of myself ovah you," whispered Skye, her voice shaky with pent-up emotion. "Oh, Brick. Why d'you have to be so damned good-lookin'? No matter how hateful you become, I'll always remember the way you used to make love to me. You were so sweet . . ." Skye took a step forward toward Nick, reaching out to touch his cheek. Recoiling, he slapped her hand away.

"Why don't you just die, Maggie? It'd make things a lot easier for you."

"Die? *Die?*" Skye pronounced it "daah." "But I'm alive, Brick! Maggie the Cat is *alaahve!*" She stormed back up to her pretend husband and stood kissing-length away from his face. They held it for a couple of seconds, Skye's birdlike chest heaving and Nick's hypnotic, ocean-blue eyes flashing at her. The air was fraught with tension.

"Um, thank you very much, Skye and Nick," hollered Mr. Tracy from his seat in the front row, finally breaking the highly dramatic moment. The much-beloved, out-and-proud drama teacher rose and walked up onstage. "That was very nice, very nice. Taut. What'd you think, class?"

With the exception of Kamillah and Regina, clapping enthusiastically from the front row, the class was not impressed. Weak applause rang out from the sophomore-filled second and third rows. Skye's classmates were used to her soaking up all the praise in their drama classes, and were deeply over her.

Last year, they had been given Tennessee Williams's famous play *Cat on a Hot Tin Roof* as a summer reading assignment, and they had been expected to come to Mr. Tracy's first class prepared to give a line reading. No one was surprised that Skye was picked to go first, because she got superstar treatment in all their drama classes. Her "I-can-do no-wrong" status in the drama department was annoying, but as much as they hated to admit it, she was one hell of an actress.

It was being a human being that threw her.

Onstage, Skye was grinning and bowing, basking in Mr. Tracy's praise. She'd waited all summer for this moment. Only the top ten percent of sophomore actors placed in Mr. Tracy's class, and, as the very first actress to read, she'd set the standard for the entire year. All she had to do was keep up the momentum, eat her tofu apples, and *no doubt* she'd land Sophomore Spotlight on Fall Fling's drama night. But all that would come. For now, she just wanted to soak up the moment.

Something thrilling happened to her when she was onstage, with the scorching lights beaming down on her and an entire audience hanging on her every word. In her very limited experience, sex didn't hold a candle to the tingles she felt from the top of her very discreet weave to the tips of her polished Chanel toes when she performed.

And adding to the thrill was her faux-hubbie, Nick. Where had he come from? Damn, he was a fine-ass white boy.

With floppy, curly, jet black hair falling in huge curls around his ears, full red lips and, oh, those turquoise eyes, he was devastatingly delicious. Cute style, too—he was rocking an old Parliament Funkadelic concert T, impeccably worn-in indigo jeans and those new, seersucker Air Force Ones. And you had to be blind, deaf, or dumb not to have noticed the instant chemistry they just had.

Batting her lashes and flipping her hair over a shoulder, she sauntered past Nick to the edge of the stage.

"Hold on, Skye," called out Mr. Tracy. "My actors never exit the set before hearing their feedback and doing a second reading."

"Oh, I'm sorry, Mr. Tracy," she said, backing up and standing next to Nick. She smiled humbly, anticipating a glowing review.

"My course is all about a free-flowing conversation, a fluid exchange of ideas. As the best of the best in the sophomore class, you're now ready for more intense criticism from your peers. However, I will not tolerate any mean-spirited remarks—the point of this class is to gain experience through constructive critiques. For this reason, each week I'll bring in a different senior drama major to offer a fresh perspective on your work." Mr. Tracy punctuated every other word with a dramatic flick of his hand as he swished up and down the center aisle. He was a big believer in what he called *utilizing one's entire body to communicate.*

"I want you to take advantage of this person, use him or her as a resource to help you grow as an artist. For four years, my seniors have honed their ability to tap into their own emotional reserve to create the most authentic performance. Use them, people. *Plunder* them."

From the audience, Kamillah looked at Skye and rolled her eyes. *Plunder this*, she mouthed, and Skye bit the inside of her cheek to keep from giggling.

"People, I'd like to introduce my senior aide for Week One," continued Mr. Tracy. "She's an actress you know quite well from both her work on television as a child star and her pitch-perfect performances in Armstrong productions. Whew! Try saying *that* three times, fast." He paused, giggling. "Anyhoo, Skye and Nick, she's been watching you from the upper balcony. Eden Carmichael, please come down and join our class."

The students all gasped and craned their necks to look up at the balcony. There was Eden descending the stairs, looking like an angel with her shimmering golden skin and floaty Prada sundress. Flashing her little sister an evil smirk that was undetectable to anyone but Skye, she drifted down the aisle and met Mr. Tracy at the front of the auditorium.

Skye was positive she would vomit right there in front of God, Nick the New Guy, and everybody. Why did Eden have to steal every moment? She had just given a kick-ass performance—on the first day of school, no less, after a three-month break from hardcore training—and now her perfect sister was going to ruin it for her. And Eden was loving it, that much was so obvious. Oh, that thunder-stealing wench.

This must be how Solange Knowles feels, Skye thought.

"So, Eden, we just heard from Nick Vardolas, a brand-new transfer student from Washington, D.C.'s Duke Ellington School of the Performing Arts—and I'm sure you're familiar with our very first Maggie the Cat of the year," said Mr. Tracy, gesturing dramatically towards the stage. "I'm curious to hear your thoughts on their performance before I give my critique."

"The truth? I thought Nick was fabulous," started Eden in her breathy, slightly unfocused voice. "I thought his Brick had the perfect mix of strength, fury, and vulnerability."

Nick's chest puffed out and he shifted from one foot to the other. Those Carmichael sisters were supercute.

"And good job, Skye. I thought you were a . . . *capable* Maggie.

But there was a certain fire missing. See, Maggie is a desperate character. She's a woman scorned, she's basically been abandoned by the
love of her life. I didn't feel that burning, that desperation."

Skye's fists clenched by her sides and her cheeks burned hot. She
looked at Kamillah and Regina, and they shook their heads in sym-
pathy.

"Mmm, I have to agree, Eden. Skye, you certainly nailed her rage.
But she should be simmering underneath that fury." Mr. Tracy continued pacing the stage. "Also, be careful not to flail your arms and
hands too much."

"Yeah, Skye," agreed Eden, "you're not flagging down a cab."

Mr. Tracy tittered at her joke. "That's exactly right! Class, you
should never use your arms and hands to help get your point across.
As the famous Method Acting pioneer Stella Adler always said,
'Reach out with your ideas, not your hands!'"

An almost-visible halo hovering atop her head, Eden continued.
"Mr. Tracy, do you want me to show her what you mean?"

"Oh, would you? I think the class would absolutely love to see
you in action," said Mr. Tracy, making little fluttery motions in the
air. If he were wearing pearls, he would've been clutching them.

"I cannot believe this sneaky bitch!" whispered Regina to
Kamillah, in shock at Eden's obvious scene-stealing. No one messed
with her Skye.

Mortified, Skye huffed and puffed and stormed off the stage,
leaving Nick the New Guy standing alone and slightly flustered.
Once onstage, Eden strode confidently up to Nick and whispered in
his ear, "Good job, doll." Then she took her place behind the
wooden chair, and delivered the first line. She was brilliant.

Where Skye was all manic energy, Eden was subtly magnetic.
And where Skye was clearly working hard, Eden made the character
look effortless. Seemingly out of nowhere, she'd transformed herself
into a sad, aching, desperately-in-love, thirty-five-year-old Southern
wife. The class was in a trance. And Nick was so captivated by the

senior's skills that he forgot he was acting. He'd never been so good.

In the audience, taking refuge next to her friends, Skye was fuming. Humilated wasn't strong enough to describe it. Throughout her life, her big sister had stolen her thunder. She was prettier, skinnier, more popular—just plain better. Watching her up there with Nick, Skye decided one thing was for sure: She was not about to let Eden win the entire war. She'd spent her whole life coming in second place, but not this time. The prize was Nick, and *she* was going to have him.

"I'm so sorry, Skye," whispered an incensed Regina.

"Yo, this is the worst," said Kamillah. "Why does she have to get *all* the shine, like, always? Doesn't it get old?"

"Oh, please, I'm fine. I knew she was gonna be here, she told me last night," lied Skye, giving her second great performance of the day. "Poor thing, it's so obvious she's totally destroyed about Trey— I mean, look at how she's overacting. I feel sorry for her, actually."

Regina and Kamillah looked at each other, instantly understanding that they were supposed to pretend everything was cool.

"You and the New Guy, though," said Kamillah, changing the subject. "What was that all about? That white boy looks good, mama."

"I don't think he's, like, *regular* white. His last name is Vardolos . . . he's probably Greek or Italian. He's really working a 'Teddy from *8th & Ocean*' moment, with his teal eyes and black hair. But in a darker way, like Vince from *Entourage*."

"Adrian Grenier," replied Regina.

"Huh?"

"That's his name. Vince from *Entourage*." Regina always knew all that stuff. A future filmmaker had to be up on the hottest new actors.

"Anyway, yeah, he's hot." Skye blocked out her sister, staring at Nick. Chewing on her bottom lip, her wheels were turning a mile a minute. "Regina, I need you to do some research. Find out for me where he's from, what his story is."

With an officious nod, Regina pulled her trusty steno pad out of her backpack and began taking notes. She never really understood why filmmaking majors were required to take two drama classes a semester. She was a terrible actress. Well, the benefit was getting to hang with Skye. Chewing on her pencil, she looked up at Nick, her new project. It was funny, she thought she recognized him from somewhere.

"As long as you know what you're doing, mama," said Kamillah, obviously skeptical. "You know teachers are always discouraging interdepartmental relationships."

"Of course she knows what she's doing—Skye *always* knows what she's doing," snapped Regina. Sometimes her intensity about Skye was downright creepy. Kamillah raised her eyebrow at her friend. *This girl really needs to go get her some.*

"Flawless!" Eden and Nick just finished their scene, and Mr. Tracy squealed with pleasure, throwing his hands in the air like he just don't care. "Skye, were you watching that? Next time, I want you to try it just like your sister."

9.
BLOSSOM AND PONY AND CUPCAKE, OH, MY!

TANGIE TAPPED MS. CARMEN'S slightly open office door, hoping this meeting wasn't about her first-day-of-school tardiness. When she didn't hear a response, she peered through the opening. Ms. Carmen was sitting at her desk, holding an envelope and reading what appeared to be a handwritten letter. As she read, her lips moved slightly and her brow was furrowed. Ms. Carmen looked so intense, Tangie was hesitant to interrupt, but her teacher *had* asked her to meet her. So, she took a deep breath and knocked again. This time, Ms. Carmen jumped in her seat, quickly folding up the paper and stuffing it in her desk drawer.

"I appreciate you meeting me after class, Cupcake," she said in the rapid-fire, no-bullshit tone that made her students tremble in their leg warmers.

"That's okay, I have my free period now," said Tangie. Looking around Ms. Carmen's office, Tangie saw snapshots of her on music video sets with superstars like Janet Jackson, Whitney Houston, and Madonna—and more recently, shots from tours with Britney Spears and Usher. Tangie was most impressed, though with a photo from the 1999 MTV Video Music Awards that showed Aaliyah at the podium with Ms. Carmen, accepting the year's Best Video award.

"I remember that moment!" Tangie was in awe. "I watch the VMA's, like, every year. And I remember, back in fourth grade, when Aaliyah won her award and invited you on stage to accept it with her." She shook her head, at a loss for words. "What was that like?"

"Fine. Interesting. Um, Aaliyah was always a hard worker." Ms. Carmen wasn't interested in going over her past. She wanted to talk about Tangie's future.

"Omigod, were you in *West Side Story* with Debbie Allen?" Tangie pointed to a framed clipping of a *New York Times* review of the hit Broadway show, featuring a shot of Debbie Allen as Anita.

"No, I was her understudy. I understudied a lot." Her eyes darkened a bit, and her scarlet lipsticked mouth shrank. "I didn't enjoy stage so much; I liked video work a lot better. I came along right when videos were becoming popular, so I feel like I grew up with them. Broadway is the pits. The rejection, the endless chorus lines, the bloody toe shoes—it's murder. You have to be tough to make it. Hard."

Tangie didn't really know what to say to that. She'd have killed even to understudy for Anita, and as bizarre as it sounded, she actually liked it when her feet bled. It made her feel as though she'd been working hard.

"I'll be frank," continued Ms. Carmen, "you impressed me today, Chicken. You were very late, which I don't tolerate—in fact, if it happens again, just don't bother coming. But you have . . . something. Where have you studied?"

Tangie groaned inwardly. This again. "Every summer since I was ten, I've attended Debbie Allen's Dance Camp. I'm actually a junior counselor there. And, um, let's see, over the years, I've taken all kinds of classes at DADA—ballet, flamenco, Martha Graham, tap, African, hip-hop, lyrical, contemporary. But I've never really had serious training in one area, you know?" Tangie knew she sounded like a hypercaffeinated freak, but she was out-of-control nervous.

"Why not?"

"My mom was a dancer, but her whole thing was that during the year I should focus on schoolwork." Tangie exhaled, her shoulder slumping slightly. She had known it was just a matter of time before she'd have to mention her mother. "So I really only trained in the summertime. That's why I'm probably behind most of your students."

Ms. Carmen's mouth tightened a bit. "It's not your mother's fault you're behind."

"No, that's not what I . . ." She trailed off, horrified.

"Listen, you're a little rough around the edges," Ms. Carmen interrupted, getting straight to the point, "but you have serious potential. Most of my dancers half-ass the choreography for thirty minutes, and then go balls to the wall at the end of class. They know that's when I evaluate your progress, during each day's final run-through." Ms. Carmen paused, folding her arms across her chest.

Tangie nodded, not sure whether she was expected to respond. *Balls to the wall?*

"But a real dancer, the kind whose name was destined to be in lights, *always* dances like the world was watching. And that's how you performed today—fast, furious, and full-out, each and every time."

"Really?" Tangie was floored. She'd felt out of her league around all those skinny bitches with years of formal training—not to mention a year of Armstrong over her. "I don't know what to say, I . . ."

"Don't say anything, Chicken, just listen. Tryouts for Fall Fling's Dance Night are coming up in a couple weeks. As you know, only a select number of kids are chosen to audition for Student Spotlight. There are only three Spotlight positions per class." Ms. Carmen stared Tangie down, her black eyes blazing. "As the head dance department judge, I must say—you stand an excellent chance of being picked to audition."

"What?" Tangie shook her head, disbelieving. *"What?"*

"Of course, you'll need tons of work. The list of potential Student

Spotlights are posted this Saturday. Today's Tuesday. You have three more days to impress the hell out of your dance teachers."

"Are you . . . you can't be serious!" Tangie thought she'd heard her wrong. After all, it was only the first day of school. For all Ms. Carmen knew, her performance in today's class could've been a total fluke.

"Of course I'm serious. I'm always serious. Are *you* serious?"

Tangie nodded, taking it all in.

"Good. Then talk to your counselor about a student tutor. You need some fine-tuning, Pumpkin, but I see amazing potential."

Tangie was breathless. "You really see all that in me?"

Ms. Carmen kept talking, as if she didn't hear the question. "You need help in some other . . . areas. And I only bring it up because I know how bright your future could be. Sweetie, you've got to work on . . ."

Oh, please, prayed Tangie, her stomach sinking, *don't say it don't say it don't say it . . .*

". . . Your body."

No-o-o-o!

"I don't enjoy saying it any more than you enjoy hearing it. But there's no room for hurt feelings in this profession." Ms. Carmen looked stern. If she felt any remorse at all, Tangie couldn't see it. "Why be the best dancer in the class if you don't have the physique to compete, professionally? In the real world of auditions and call-backs, you'd lose out to the willowy-thin girls."

"But, but that's just not my body. I don't think I can . . ."

"Yes, you can, and you will," she said, cutting Tangie off. "Chicken, I'm in no way suggesting that you starve yourself, or take diet pills, or do anything unhealthy. I'd rather you give up dance altogether than kill yourself. I'd just like you to become aware of your diet, talk to the nurse about nutrition, take Pilates." Ms. Carmen looked hard at Tangie. "Do you understand what I'm saying?"

She couldn't respond. If she opened her mouth, she'd have burst into embarrassing, blubbering tears. She couldn't help her big butt and big boobs—that was the way she'd always been built. Hadn't J. Lo been a dancer before she became famous for . . . well, being famous?

Ms. Carmen cocked her head and squinted at Tangie, furrowing her brow. "This is the reality of a dancer's life. Our bodies are our instruments. I can tell you the exact number of calories I've consumed, every day of my life."

Tangie nodded, her eyes welling up with tears "I understand. Th—thank you for your help. Can I go now?" Before her teacher could respond, she burst through the door and took off down the hallway. Sobbing hysterically, she ran and ran until she hit the end of the dance floor, and then she stopped, collapsing against the wall. All the positive stuff Ms. Carmen had said about her dancing meant nothing—all she heard was that she was a hippo in a tutu. Too fat to live.

For a good fifteen minutes after Tangie left her office, Ms. Carmen stared at the chair where the young girl had been sitting. She pulled the crumpled, handwritten letter back out of her desk.

Rereading the familiar handwriting, fighting back tears, she thought, *Please, God, let me be strong enough to get through the year.*

The dance wing was bustling with sophomore dance majors celebrating their first free period of the year. Tangie, on the other hand, wanted to throw herself in the Hudson River. Moving like a zombie through the packed hallway, not even caring where she was going, she replayed Ms. Carmen's speech a million times in her head.

In midthought, she realized she'd left her rehearsal bag in Ms. Carmen's studio, after the street funk class. Freaking out all of a sudden—Tangie wanted to get in and out of that classroom as quickly as possible—she spun around, knocked over a trio of tap-dancing boys, and rushed back up the hallway in the other direction. When she got to the studio, it was open and empty, except for one person.

Busta Rhimes's "Touch It" was pumping, and Trey was in the middle of the floor, expertly dancing the complicated, seriously sexy choreography of the video. He nailed every single step and hit each count so perfectly it was as if he had choreographed the damned thing himself. He could've easily crushed Usher, Omarion *and* Justin Timberlake! Watching him, Tangie was mesmerized by how smoothly he moved: really cool, as if he were barely working. *He really is as amazing as everyone says.* She stood frozen in the doorway. *He had a right to be cocky—he could quit school tomorrow and land a gig dancing backup on tour with Missy or anybody.*

Tangie was so caught up in the moment that unconsciously she began bobbing her head and marking Trey's moves. The song was so loud, and he looked so good, that she was just moved. When the song stopped, Trey walked over to the stereo and shut it off. Sweat glistening off his muscles, he lifted up his wifebeater to wipe the sweat off his face, and Tangie caught a glimpse of his six-pack; her mouth went totally dry. Was that even real (she remembered reading somewhere that some male models used makeup on their abs to make them look more sculptural)? His sweaty muscles bulging, he stretched out his hamstrings and rolled his head to the left and right, cooling himself down. When he looked to the right, he saw Tangie in the doorway and grinned.

She immediately got flustered and began stammering. "Oh, sorry, I wasn't watching you, I was just coming in to get my bag over there. I had a meeting with Ms. Carmen. I didn't mean to spy on you or anything, it's just that . . ."

"Be easy, ma. I ain't trippin'," said Trey, chuckling. He turned toward her, stretching his muscular arms behind his back and smirking sexily. *God, he looked so damn hard in his track pants, wifebeater, and do-rag holding back his thick, lush dreads.* "I know you, don't I?"

"I mean, I think we met once or twice. I'm best friends with Skye, you know, Eden Carmichael's sister? I've seen you a lot at their house when you two were, um, together. But you probably never noticed me or anything."

"I noticed you today in class," he said, slowly looking her up and down. Tangie felt her palms get all sweaty. "What's your name again?"

"Oh, I'm Tangie. Tangie Adams."

"Tangie. That's cute." He nodded, not bothering to introduce himself. Clearly she knew his name.

She had no idea what to say next. "So, I was surprised seeing you in my class."

"Yeah, that nonsense. I was in a Missy video this summer, I don't know if you saw it . . . ?" He knew she'd seen it. Everybody had seen it. "Anyway, I got caught, and they're making me retake this class as punishment. Whatever, man, it's all good. I already have casting agents getting at me, so I'll be breezy after graduation. I could take a freshman class and still be me, nahmean?"

"That's so exciting—agents," she said, feeling like an idiot. She'd barely spoken two words to Trey in her life, and now he was talking to her. *Really* talking. As a kid spying on Eden and him making out, she had never really imagined having a conversation with him.

"Yeah, they been hollerin' at me for a minute now, so it's no new thing. It's whatever." He shrugged it all off, too jaded to care. "Yo, are you all right? You look, like, upset or something."

Tangie giggled, trying to play it off. It came out sounding like a horse's whinny. "Oh, I'm fine, I just got out of a meeting with Ms. Carmen."

"Oh, God. What did Carm say to you?"

Tangie could feel herself turning red. She had no idea how to respond, so the truth came flying out. "She, um, told me I needed to work on my technique, and that I . . . I should lose some weight." The second she said it, her mouth went dry, and she lost the feeling in her limbs.

"Wait, ma, don't bug out! You can't take what she says

personally. Listen, she picks a kid every year to take under her wing. You know, to mold into the perfect dancing robot. The second I saw you I knew she'd say that to you."

"Why?" Tangie croaked, feeling tears stinging the back of her eyes. *So, everyone on earth thinks I belong on* Celebrity Fit Club, she thought, her stomach sinking. *Too bad anorexia isn't contagious, or I would've successfully caught it from Gigi twenty minutes ago.*

"Because your body's crazy and I couldn't stop staring at you," he said, looking directly into her eyes. "To Carm, dancers ain't supposed to be, like, sensual women. There supposed to be sexless little girls. And you—man, you most *definitely* ain't sexless, and you sure as *hell* ain't no little girl."

"Oh," she said in a very small voice, finally getting it. Trey Stevens wasn't saying she was fat; he was complimenting her. Flirting with her. "Well, thanks. But you aren't deciding who tries out for Spotlight."

"Look, I'm telling you—don't change a damn thing." He winked at her, and Tangie felt faint.

All of a sudden, everything Ms. Carmen said seemed really far away. And then the room started spinning, because Trey began walking toward her. With his muscular chest and arms and gangsta-cute do-rag, he couldn't have been more sexy. Instinctively, she backed against the door, the way the women always did in the movies or on TV when a guy was about to corner them for the big, dramatic kiss.

"So, what else did she say?" He stopped, inches away from her.

"I don't know, that I need to practice my technique," she breathed, her heart racing. Trey smelled like a mix of manly sweat and Issey Miyake Pour Homme, her favorite scent. Wait, he wore cologne to modern dance class? Mmm. Something about that seemed wildly . . . *adult*. ". . . And that I have natural talent but that I need a student tutor."

"Good thing you know one," he said, real low and sexy.

"You?"

He raised an eyebrow and looked smug.

"But I'm sure you have so many students. . . ." She stopped, real-izing she was sweating him way too hard.

"Listen, meet me at this studio tomorrow after seventh period. It's always empty after school. And look, don't worry about Carm, okay? I got you." He flashed that amazing grin again, and then slowly, shockingly, he leaned forward. He kept going, until their lips were so close together it was obvious he was going to kiss her.

Tangie held her breath and closed her eyes, feeling as though she'd just stepped into a movie (some cheesy teen movie about a cute but socially awkward girl who improbably lands the unattainable popular guy, starring a couple of WB regulars).

When nothing had happened almost five seconds later—no kiss, not even a peck on the cheek—Tangie's eyes flew open.

"What are you doing, girl?" he asked.

To her horror, Trey was laughing and pointing above her. Whipping around, she saw that the Fall Fling tryout schedule was posted directly behind her. He wasn't leaning in for a kiss, he just wanted to look at the schedule! She was humiliated.

"Don't be embarrassed," he said, in a low, unbearably sexy voice. "I'll kiss you when I know you can handle it." With that, he grabbed his bag, threw it over his shoulder and swaggered out of the room.

For a long time after he left, Tangie stood frozen in the middle of the studio, wondering if fifteen was too young to suffer a heart attack.

10.
THE RANDOM GET-DOWN

THE FIRST DAY AT ARMSTRONG HAD BARELY ENDED, and all anyone could talk about was Fall Fling week—already. At a normal school, no one would've cared about a recital happening two and a half months away, but Armstrong wasn't a normal school. It was full of hundreds of ridiculously talented ministars with supersized egos, kids that dreamed their whole lives of being the Next Big Thing.

Where most high-schoolers were reading *Seventeen* and getting their braces off, Armstrong kids were compulsively sucking on honey-flavored Ricolas to soothe their vocal chords, practicing jetés until their pinkie toes swelled to the size of Connecticut, and scanning trade papers like *Backstage* and *Variety* for the hottest new auditions (on the q.t., of course—if anyone got caught performing professionally, it was a wrap. Just ask Trey). It was a school full of intense showbiz-heads who thought *American Idol* was for losers but loved *So You Think You Can Dance,* and got seriously offended when J. Lo was labeled a triple threat; a true triple threat was someone who was equally brilliant as an actor, dancer, or singer, but when Jenny from the Bliz-ock sang, she sounded positively canine.

These kids *craved* fame. They'd craved it ever since they were able to walk, talk, and make jazz hands.

It was the in-between time: school was over, but everyone had about an hour before their extracurricular classes began (all Armstrong students were required to take outside art, music, theater, dance, or creative writing lessons—whatever their major—to sharpen their technique). While the social white kids gathered at the Starbucks at Seventeenth Street and Union Square West, the popular black-slash-Latino crowd hung out around the benches in Union Square Park—but it wasn't a segregation thing—it was more like a comfortable parting of the ways. Of course, there were a few exceptions: in the park there were always your token CAS (cool-as-shit) white or Asian kids who rocked throwback jerseys and believed that any Outkast track off *Aquemini* could easily murder "Hey Ya," while Starbucks was definitely dotted with "bipsters," aka black hipsters who got down with bands like Death Cab for Cutie and tried like hell to look dirty on purpose (that messy-haired, ancient-jeans look, while so cute on white kids, always looked a tad homeless-chic on black kids).

The Union Square North side of the park, facing Barnes & Noble, was where the impromptu jam sessions went down—everyone called them Random Get-Downs, because the kids participating always varied from day to day. The Random Get-Downs always started with one brave singer—usually a senior and usually a boy. After he started singing a capella, somebody would jump in with a guitar or drums, and if it was an R&B singer, some kid would start beat-boxing. And then other singers would join in, harmonizing, and inevitably, a couple of dancers would start grooving to the beat. The moment grew bigger and bigger, until dozens of kids joined in, freestyling and jamming.

The Union Square crowd loved it, especially in good weather, and would even throw money at the students (of course, it was against school policy to accept it, though many of them did). Since you never knew who could be watching—a talent agent, a music executive—everyone was always their sparkliest (in fact, Lacey Henderson, a vibrant blond triple threat who'd graduated five years before, was discovered during a Random Get-Down by Edie Falco, the actress who played Carmela on *The Sopranos*. Lacey ended up being cast as one of A.J.'s ditzy blond girlfriends on a *Sopranos* episode, and apparently, now, she was having a torrid affair with one of the actors in Tony Soprano's crew). The Random Get-Down moment separated the after-school bunch into two groups: the joiners and the watchers (aka, the spotlight-hungry and the self-conscious). But no matter who you were, Fall Fling was the topic du jour.

"S—so, do you think you'll be up for Freshman Spotlight tryouts? It's crazy how the teachers decide who's best during the first week of school." Regina was perched on a bench, trying desperately to think of things to talk about with her Little Sister, Izzy. There was something effortlessly cool about this girl; she had an exotic, uber-experienced aura about her; and it made Regina feel sort of lame.

Also, she'd just introduced Izzy to Skye for the first time, and it was so nerve-racking. She adored Skye, but she sometimes had a way of making her feel and look dumb—and she didn't want to look like a jackass in front of her Little Sister. And, on the lowest of the low, Regina was desperately hoping Skye would like Izzy, because then her stock would rise for introducing a cool girl into the It chicks clique.

"I don't know, my Beginners' Black-and-White Photography teacher looked at my portfolio today, and she thinks I might have a chance," said Izzy with a nonchalant shrug, her faux-emerald nose stud shimmering in the sun. "But these kids at this school, man, they take this ish so serious. It's really just a glorified talent show to impress the parents, it ain't like *Entertainment* fuckin' *Tonight*'s gonna be reporting on the damned thing." She rolled her eyes. "Doesn't every student automatically get a spot in Fall Fling, anyway?"

Skye looked at Izzy with a mix of curiosity and awe, as if she were a specimen under glass. After everything Kamillah had said earlier—and considering the fact that Izzy had already gotten way too close to her best friend, Tangie—Skye had wanted to hate her. But she *was* kind of fascinating.

"Well, yeah," started Skye, "but only a couple of the hottest kids from each class get Spotlight. If your teacher recommended you, that's like—I mean, I wouldn't sleep on it. That's serious."

Izzy shrugged, sliding down in her seat so she could lean her head against the back of the bench. Closing her eyes, she tilted her high-cheekboned, Iman-like face up towards the sun and sighed. *What the hell did Tangie and this beast have in common?*

Meanwhile, Skye was practically speechless. She'd never met a girl so spectacularly unimpressed by Armstrong. By everything, really. Didn't Izzy understand where she was? If she played her cards right, she could parlay her talent into something fierce—the list of Armstrong alumni read like the Hollywood Walk of Fame. Either she was on crack or she was very, very smart—and Skye suspected the latter. As she caught a glimpse of the slightly psychedelic tattoo snaking around Izzy's exposed belly button that read, "Please Do Not Touch the Animals," she decided—against her better judgment—that she approved. Izzy was exactly what their clique was missing.

In terms of casting, they already had the Princess (Skye), the Innocent Ingenue (Tangie), the sassy Around-the-Way Girl (Kamillah), and the Follower with Potential (Regina). By adding the Enigmatic Exotic, their group would have more social power than ever.

"So, um, you're new to New York, right? Do you stay in the student housing, or did your family, um, move here?" Regina was running out of topics. Izzy was just not the kind of chick who needed a Big Sister. And what idiot had paired them together, anyway? It was like forcing Hillary Duff to make conversation with Courtney Love.

"No, I stay with a friend," said Izzy, averting her eyes. "I was in L.A."

"Ooh, did you love L.A.?"

Izzy shrugged, pretending to pick some lint off her shirt.

Clearly, Izzy was uncomfortable, but Regina was desperate not to let the conversation fall flat. "So, um, is that where you're from?"

"Not really, I was just living there."

"So, then, your parents are still in California? Are they in the business?" "The business," naturally, meant "show business."

Izzy opened her eyes, squinting in the sun. She grinned playfully at Regina. "Are you filling out a survey or something?"

"Oh, um, no, I was just . . ."

"Jesus Christ, Regina, give the girl a break." Skye shot Izzy an apologetic glance. "This isn't *The View*."

"No, she's cool," said Izzy, comfortably flinging an arm around her Big Sister's shoulders. "I'm just playing. Seriously, ask me whatever you want."

Regina smiled thankfully at Izzy, but said nothing. She hated when Skye dissed her like that, but what could she do? Even though the girl could be awful sometimes (and after all, Skye was having a shitty day—the whole Eden thing had really sucked). When Skye actually was nice, it literally felt as if the sun were opening up and shining down directly on Regina.

"Well, speaking of Fall Fling, I already know who's a definite shoo-in, besides me, for Sophomore Spotlight on Drama Night." Skye flipped her waist-length extensions over her shoulder. "Today, I acted a piece from *Cat on a Hot Tin Roof* with this guy Nick, in Southern Playwrights? He's white, but not *white* white, you know? This boy can act his ass off. Regina, tell Izzy how sexy he was."

"He was very sexy."

"And so what if he's white, you know? Kerry Washington's engaged to a white guy. And he's mad cute! It's very chic."

"Omigod, girl, you're buggin'," said Izzy, rolling her eyes.

Regina's stomach lurched—her Little Sister, a *freshman*, was getting all saucy with Skye. Not good.

"Wait, what do you mean?" Surprisingly enough, Skye didn't look mad: she looked captivated.

"What's chic about messing with a white cat? It's just like talking to a black boy. They're all the same—Indian, Spanish, Asian, whatever. Ultimately, they're all tryin' to figure out how much game they have to put down before you let 'em hit it."

Izzy was right—why was Skye romanticizing hollering at a white guy? All of a sudden, Skye felt like some provincial bumpkin with no culture or life experience. Izzy was a year younger than her, yet she seemed to have boundless knowledge. "Wow. I totally hear you," said Skye.

"Have you ever messed with a white guy?" Regina finally found her voice again.

"I've messed with *lots* of guys, ma," Izzy answered cryptically, her eyes twinkling. She lazily raised her arms over her head and stretched, clearly finished with the topic. Besides, she and C.J. had smoked a blunt before seventh period and she wasn't in a talking mood—she just wanted to *chill*.

"Well," began Skye, too curious to pretend not to be interested, "what are white boys like? I mean, are they any different?"

Izzy sighed. "The only difference is that, sexually, white cats are more free. You know, they get down with sex toys, freaky shit like that. Black and Spanish boys don't go there—they got too much ego to mess with all the extras. It's like, 'If I'm not enough to get you off, then, peace.'"

Regina was speechless. Sex toys? Had Izzy used sex toys? Holy shit. Meanwhile, Skye was beginning to feel an uncute power shift. This was *her* school, dammit, and she wasn't going to let some freshman make her feel like an inexperienced dork.

"No, she's right, Regina. Black guys hate sex toys. I tried to get Julian to use the Bunny on me once? He was so offended he threw it out of the bed. It was hilarious."

"What's the Bunny?" Regina was both horrified and confused. This conversation was disgusting.

"Don't you mean the Rabbit?" Izzy opened one eye, peering at Skye. "It's that vibrator that Charlotte got addicted to on *Sex and the*

City. It's bonkers, yo—it's a regular vibrator, but it has this extra piece that massages your, um . . ."

"I *know* what the Rabbit is," said Skye, embarrassed and suddenly way over Izzy. Izzy shrugged and leaned back against the bench, folding her tiny hands over her stomach.

Just as Skye was racking her brains for more sex tips, to prove she was just as experienced as Regina's know-it-all Little Sister (despite having had sex exactly zero times in her life), Tangie came sprinting down Union Square West. Her cheeks were flushed, and her eyes were shining, and she had a huge smile on her face.

"What's up, y'all?" She plopped down on the ground, Indian-style, in front of the bench. "Izzy! What are you . . . oh, that's right, Regina's your Big Sister. Did she introduce you to everybody? You met Kamillah, right?"

"Yeah, she's a cutie. That's her over there with her man, right? What's his name, Negritude?"

They all giggled hysterically. "*Blackadocious*," said Skye, throwing up a black-power fist. Huddled in a cypher further in the park, Black saluted her back, in midrhyme. Even from a block away, the girls could see Kamillah by his side, rolling her almond-shaped eyes.

"So, Miss Tangie, I'm glad you're here. What do you think about sex toys? Have you ever used one?"

Skye knew Tangie had never used a sex toy; she just wanted someone else to feel stupid. Tangie was probably the least experienced girl she knew, besides Regina.

Tangie flinched. "Ew, Skye. What are you talking about?"

"Absolutely nothing," said Izzy, dying for a change of subject. Skye was so insecure and desperate for attention, it was sad. "So, why do you look so giddy?"

"Oh, no reason," Tangie singsonged, barely able to conceal her grin. She'd never felt this . . . odd in her life. Today had been a terrible day and a fabulous day. C.J. was obviously still pissed at her. And Ms. Carmen had basically said she was morbidly obese. But on the bright side, the very same teacher had also said she could see her getting Spotlight, and Trey Stevens had offered to be her tutor with him. *The* Trey Stevens! Tangie didn't know whether to be devastated or delighted.

She picked delighted. It was better for her complexion.

"Stop BS-ing," said Skye, already forgetting about the humiliating sex conversation in favor of potential gossip. "You're thrilled about something. And I thought you'd be so bummed about your witch of a dance teacher." Tangie had texted her earlier about her meeting with Ms. Carmen.

"What happened?" Regina looked concerned.

"Long story," she said dismissively. "Basically, my hip-hop teacher—the class I'm trying to *major* in—told me I had talent but that, I, um, need to lose weight."

"Goddamned bitch," mumbled Izzy, her eyes narrowing into slits.

All three girls looked at Izzy. This girl really meant business, didn't she?

Skye was the first to recover. "I know, it's totally rude, and you're not even close to being fat. It's like, if you're fat, then Beyoncé is fat."

"I know, right? And she dances her ass off. I mean, she's not, like, a trained dancer, but still." Tangie shook her head, indignant.

". . . But at the same time, that's the nature of the business, sweetie," her best friend continued. She shot Tangie a sorry-girl-it's-just-tough-love shrug. "When we were young, things like our bodies didn't matter so much. But you're an Armstrong dancer now, Tangie-Pants—shit is crucial here. Your teacher was just being real with you about the future, you know? You gotta get thicker skin."

Thanks for being so understanding, thought Tangie. Honestly, had Skye always been so bitchy? "I'm not stupid, Skye, I know what a professional dancer's body is supposed to look like. It was just a messed-up way to start my first day at Armstrong, that's all."

"Skye didn't mean to come off like that. She had a teacher that was mad critical today, too. Our Southern Playwrights teacher made Skye stand there while Eden . . ." Regina was just too much.

"Ignore me, sweetie, I'm PMS-ing," interrupted Skye quickly, planting a big, fake kiss on Tangie's cheek. Over her shoulder, she glared hotly at Regina. "So, look, why are you glowing? Clearly something fabulous happened."

"I don't know what you're talking about," sighed Tangie. The talk with Trey had almost made her feel better, but now her boobs felt as if they were growing with every breath she took. She folded her arms across her chest, put on a brave face and went for a change of subject. "I'm not glowing, I just have some good gossip. Guess who's in my Advanced Beginners Street Funk class?"

"Who?" Skye perked up at the mention of gossip.

"Trey!"

"*No!*" exclaimed Regina and Skye simultaneously.

"Who's that?" mumbled Izzy, not really caring. She was half asleep—the sun felt so-o-o good. She was so happy. Happy and hungry. Yeah, if she had had a brownie and some Doritos she'd have been even happier.

"He's my sister's ex-boyfriend," said Skye, her eyes widening with excitement.

"And?" Izzy didn't get it.

"He's a *senior*," added Regina, watching Izzy for a reaction. But there was none.

Exasperated, Skye continued. "This summer, he got caught dancing in a Missy video, which is *so* against the rules, so he has to take a sophomore class this semester. Trifling! How was he acting, Tangie—humilated? Serves the cheating mofo right."

"He didn't seem humiliated, actually. He told me that he wasn't tripping off having to take a sophomore class—he already has agents hollering at him and everything." Tangie smiled, faintly. "He was actually really nice."

"Wait, he *talked* to you?" In all his years with her sister, Trey probably had spoken no more than three words to Skye. And he'd definitely never bothered with Tangie. In fact, he had only bothered with girls he wanted something from.

"Yeah, we had a whole conversation. He complimented my lines," she said, shaking her head. "And he offered to tutor me."

"For real?" Skye was inexplicably furious. Trey was a god at that school—and the fact that he'd worshipped her sister had always given Skye a certain power by association. Why was Trey paying all this attention to Tangie? He was going to be her *tutor*? She certainly hoped she didn't think he had a crush on her or anything. "Well, that's cute of him, being sweet to my friend. You know, he's so devastated about Eden that he just wants company, I guess. He's still so desperately in love with her."

Tangie looked at Skye, noticing that the tips of her ears were bright red. She couldn't believe it—Skye was jealous! Everything always had to be about her. But on second thought, maybe she was right. It was ridiculous to think that Trey Stevens was flirting with her. Tangie decided not to bring up the fact that he had almost kissed her. "Yeah, he was obviously still in love with her."

"Of course he is," said Skye, her eyes darting in different directions. Just then, she began waving hysterically at Kamillah across the park with Blackadocious and his cypher. "I'll be right back, I think Kammie's trying to tell me something. Talk amongst yourselves, bitches."

She jogged away prettily, bouncing high and slow—it was just enough movement to cause her tiny breasts to jiggle and her flawlessly real-looking extensions to fly out behind her, as if she were in a Pantene commercial. It was all very choreographed, but every guy in the park was staring at her, so it evidently worked. Fortunately for Skye, most guys were too dumb to pick up on a look-at-me-I'm-sexy cliché when it smacked them in the face.

Tangie seriously doubted that Kamillah had called Skye over, but whatever.

"Yo, your girl's gonna have a f'ing stroke before she's eighteen," said Izzy, her eyes fluttering open.

Tangie giggled, rolling her eyes.

"You shouldn't talk about her like that," snapped Regina. "You don't really know her."

"Don't need to, homey," Izzy answered, lazily swatting away a fly. "I'm curious, why you let her go so hard on you? You're a person, Regina. She's no better than you."

Regina looked at Tangie, frowning. She had a point. She'd just been Big Sister-ed by her Little Sister.

"She really is right, Regina," Tangie said. For the second time that day, she realized how happy she was to have met her own friend, outside of Skye—especially with her turning into such a diva. "Skye acts obnoxious because you make it easy for her."

Regina thought about this. She had always let Skye off the hook because she knew she was a good person on the inside. It wasn't easy being Skye. Her mother starved her, her sister was Eden, and she was expected to be perfect. Regina just wanted to protect her, no matter how much it hurt. And Skye *needed* her. The girl trusted her to ghostwrite her life story, for Christ's sake!

"Oh, look, she forgot her Sidekick," said Regina, grabbing the pale pink, bejeweled handheld and standing up. "I'm-a go bring it to her. Be back in a sec." She turned on her heel and flounced off, her Pocahantas braids whipping around her head like the blades of a ceiling fan.

And then it was just Izzy and Tangie.

"Yeah, your friends aren't dramatic or anything, huh?"

Tangie giggled, liking Izzy more and more by the second. It seemed as if she were the only normal person at this school—which was funny, because all anyone could talk about was how exotic and different she was.

"Yeah, I kinda feel like everyone here takes themselves so seriously," Tangie said. "I mean, me included. Ms. Carmen told me I had a fat ass, and it, like, ruined my day. I don't know, there's just a lot of pressure here. More than I thought there'd be."

"I feel you. But you can't let this showbiz stuff get to you. It's supposed to be fun, right? If it ain't fun, why the hell would anyone put themselves through all this competition-ego-sick-body-image nonsense?"

"True."

Izzy was right. Dancing was the only time Tangie ever felt truly, truly happy, through and through. If she couldn't have it, she supposed she'd die. She wouldn't let anyone take that from her. Including herself. If she had to be stick thin to dance, then she would be.

"Can I ask you something?" Izzy asked.

"Go ahead, of course."

"What do you see in Skye?"

"I knew you were going to say that." Tangie sighed, sad that it was so obvious that Skye had turned into a real bitch. "She wasn't always like that. I think Armstrong really got to her."

"Well, all I have to say is I'm glad I met my TMI twin. Everyone else here is so damned fake, I can't take it." Izzy smiled at her and then turned her face back up to the sun.

Tangie grinned happily and leaned back on the bench, absent-mindedly watching the Random Get Down. She felt at peace for the first time in hours. Her first day at Armstrong had been super-stressful; she was thrilled to have met such a cool girl—and so soon.

Lost in her thoughts, she didn't even notice anyone coming up behind them. It wasn't until she saw Izzy drop her head back off the top of the bench and jokily say, "What's really good, Cedric James?" that she realized C.J. was even in the vicinity.

Tangie quickly sat up and turned around to face him. He looked back at her, and for one brief, terrible moment she thought he was going to walk away again. Instead, he kind of looked back and forth between Izzy and her, then turned a funny, greenish, I-could-possibly-throw-up-right-now color. If he was sick, it was catching, because Tangie immediately felt as if she had the flu.

Her muscles started throbbing, and she felt feverish and cold and shaky and weak. *It wasn't supposed to happen like this.* After the horrible almost-encounter at lunch, C.J. had sent her a text message, asking if they could talk after school—she wasn't ready to see him yet.

And how the hell did Izzy know him?

"I'm being rude, sorry," started Izzy, shaking her head. "C.J., this is my girl, Tangie. Tangie, meet C.J. Yo, did you smoke too much? You look *finished*, homey."

"No, I'm good, I'm good," he said, clearing his throat. "Um, wassup, Tange?"

"Nothing. I'm good, too. Great, actually." Tangie shrugged. Never in a thousand years had she thought she and C.J. would ever feel this uncomfortable, this . . . *wrong* around each other. She wanted to cry, but instead pulled herself together enough to address Izzy. "Actually, we already know each other."

"Oh, word? Wait, I thought this was your first day here."

"It is. But, uh, we went to middle school together, me and C.J. and Skye . . ."

"We're cousins." C.J. seemed to be heavily preoccupied with a hangnail.

"Y'all two?"

"What? Me and Tangela? No, uh, cousins we're *definitely* not. I meant Skye and me. Our moms are sisters."

"Okay, such a coincidence! This is nuts, right? It's like we were all destined to meet each other." Delighted, Izzy hopped off the bench and flung her arm around C.J.'s shoulders. Not in a possessive, flirtatious way—in a chill, cool-girl way. Tangie was instantly jealous of Izzy's comfortable affection for C.J. In public, she'd always been way too self-conscious about showing how much she liked him to go there.

"I met him over the summer, and just by coincidence I found out he went to Armstrong." Izzy winked at C.J. "How crazy is that?"

"Yeah, crazy," said Tangie, suddenly feeling like she'd been kicked in the stomach. It was all becoming clear. C.J. was the guy Izzy had told her about in Orientation that morning. He was the "older" sophomore boy she'd met during the summer! *This isn't happening,* Tangie told herself. *This isn't happening, no, this isn't happening. . . .*

"So, how were the rest of your art classes, Ceej?" Izzy continued. "Did you get Mr. Tannenbaum for oil painting?" She looked at Tangie, way too high to get the subtext of what was going on between C.J. and her new friend. "We had this sketch class before lunch; it was so bizarre."

While he answered Izzy, Tangie caught his gaze and narrowed her eyes slightly. He knew what it meant. She knew he and Izzy were together.

Not wanting to be too obvious, Tangie hung out a little while longer before leaving to change for her Monday after-school class, flamenco. She couldn't be around them. Tangie knew she'd never have a chance against Izzy. Izzy was different. She was cool, she was funny, she was fly . . . she was Izzy. And now C.J. was gone for good.

Name: Tangela Marcia Adams
Class: Sophomore
Major: Dance
Self-Awareness Session #: TA 1

You mean, like, is he my true love? Um . . .

Tangela? Are you okay?

Sorry, I was just . . . I don't know, I try not to think about all that love stuff. It's like, my mom was supposed to love my dad, but she left. My dad was supposed to love my mom, but he let her leave . . . and then married a twelve-year-old! Not really, but you know what I'm saying. It just feels like a lie. That's why it's actually better that me and C.J. are just, like, best friends. You know where you stand, everybody's happy, and nobody's hurt.

You wanna know something bizarre? There's this homeless lady I pass on the way to my subway stop, and she makes me think of my mom. It's just . . . she could be somewhere on the street right now, just like that lady. I wish she'd call.

I also wish my new friend wasn't messing with C.J.

11.
BEAUTIFUL BUTTERFLY

"SO, WHERE ARE YOU SEXY LADIES GOING TONIGHT?" Alexa
Carmichael (Lexie to her friends, Allie to her fans, Crazy Bitch to
her husband) was posed in the doorway of her daughter Eden's
outrageous-looking, *Teen Vogue*–decorated bedroom (for a feature
article the previous year, *Teen Vogue* had arranged for Isaac Mizrahi to
make over Eden's previously personalityless room. With its leopard-
print breadspread and fuschia polka-dotted wallpaper, the room was
so self-consciously funky-kooky it didn't look as though a real girl
even lived there. It looked like a set from *Mean Girls*).

Alexa was watching her daughter and Marisol get ready. Surrounded by an arsenal of lip glosses, eyeshadow compacts, and mascara,
the two girls were sitting cross-legged on Eden's fluffy, lipstick-shaped
area rug examining their reflections in the wall-to-wall mirror.

"Jesus, Alexa, how long have you been standing there?" Eden was
annoyed. Her mom loved nothing more than eavesdropping on her
daughters' conversations. She'd even been known to listen in on
phone lines (hence, Eden and Skye never even bothered with their
land lines anymore).

"Oh, only for a sec," Alexa replied, slinking into the room and
flinging herself dramatically across Eden's canopied four-poster bed.

"You know how I enjoy staring at your pretty face. I swear to God, Eden, four inches taller and you could've had that chubby Tyra beat." She gazed off into the distance. "I should've screwed Michael Jordan when I had the chance, the night of the *Coming to America* premiere party. Just imagine how long and lanky you'd have been. Oh, I'm just sick about it."

"I bet you are," Skye said, rolling her eyes at her friend. Marisol grinned and continued blending shimmery charcoal shadow into the crease of her lid—she was a pro at creating smoky, bad-girl eyes.

Ordinarily, Eden was blasé about almost everything, but Alexa had the unique ability to push her over the edge after about two minutes. "What the hell are you *wearing?*"

Alexa was dressed in an old Azzedine Alaïa floor-length evening gown from 1988. "It's vintage," she replied, as if that explained everything.

"Huh?"

"Eden, you *know* every Monday my ghostwriter comes over to help me pen my autobiography. Getting dressed in my fabulous old clothes helps me get into the mind-set of *who Alexa was*. Oh, what an exciting, dramatic life I've led!"

Only her mother would have used the word "pen" as a verb and referred to herself in the third person. It was a wonder Eden was as normal as she was. "Fascinating," Eden said. "Can you leave now?"

"So," Marisol said, as if Eden hadn't spoken, "what juicy stuff have you written about so far, Alexa?" Despite Eden's protestations, Marisol was fascinated. Like Marisol, Eden's mom had been born a total nobody. But she had had the guts and moxie to turn herself into a rich and famous star. A pill-popping, overacting, overdressed train wreck of a star, but still, a star. If Marisol attained half of her fame, she felt, she'd be satisfied.

"Oh, you know, stuff. Things. My career, my loves, my life," mused Alexa, who'd been an Emmy Award–winning TV actress (not to mention the first Jamaican Bond girl). From 1981 to 1988, she'd starred as one of the three glamorous, bitchy, fashion industry executives in the hit Aaron Spelling–produced nighttime drama *Shoulder Pads*—she had played Darla, the Spicy Black One. While filming the show, she had had an affair with Junior Carmichael, the very married, Tony Award–winning Broadway producer, and become pregnant with Eden. Eventually he had left his wife and married Alexa, but their marriage had since disintegrated into an extravaganza of name-calling, finger-pointing, infidelity, and public drunkenness. "Don't worry, I'm not going to say anything ugly about your father."

"Honestly, Alexa, don't do me any favors."

"I mean, I could if I wanted to. That hateful man made me stop working to raise you girls, effectively ruining my career. I've been totally unable to find my joy for so long, and it's all Junior's fault."

"You know, Alexa, it's so unhealthy to let a man steal your joy," said Marisol, getting all self-helpey, as usual. "You've got to find your safe place."

Alexa nodded vigorously, clutching her heart and biting her bottom lip. "I know, I know. You're so right," she whispered, her voice trembling with emotion.

"Repeat after me: *I am at peace with myself,*" began Marisol.

"I am at peace with . . ."

Eden slammed her M·A·C Chestnut Lip Pencil down on her thigh and shot Marisol a look. "Please! Two more seconds of this Lifetime for Women drama and I'm vomiting all over the rug."

"Whatever," muttered Marisol. "Just 'cause you're spiritually bankrupt doesn't mean you should hate on those of us seeking enlightenment."

Alexa was smiling sweetly, staring off into space. As quickly as her mood darkened, it brightened up again. *Is she not taking her Paxil?* Eden wondered. "So," began Alexa, "how was the first day of senior year, you hot little puddin'-cakes? Please don't tell me you spoke to the trifling Negro."

Eden and Marisol looked at each other and made a face. "Do

I look stupid? Trey's permanently deleted from my Sidekick."

"I am so glad to hear it. He was just another example of an aimless black man trying to tear the wings off a beautiful butterfly." Alexa finished off her cocktail, the ice clinking in the glass. "I don't know why you associate with that trash."

"Trey's dad is the district attorney."

"Oh. Is he single?"

"Gross, Alexa."

"So, how is school?"

"Oh, God . . ." Skye knew where this was going.

"You know, every day I kick myself for letting you kids convince me to send you to Armstrong instead of the Professional Children's School. You're just wasting time, wasting time, wasting time. We donate a ton of money to that school for those teachers to pay attention to you, but it's not like it goes to anything useful." Alexa turned away from the mirror and began pacing again, totally on a roll.

The Professional Children's School was where working teenage performers went (Alicia Keys and Mischa Barton were alumnae)—while students at Armstrong were strictly amateurs during their four years. No agents, no managers, no professional work period. Alexa thought it was pointless. "Speaking of wasting time, did you eat the tofu apple I packed for you?"

"Yeah, I ate it," lied Eden. She never ate lunch.

"Did Skye eat hers? I asked you to check up on what she ate for lunch—Edie, you know I'm depending on you to help out with her weight. She never listens to me, but she worships you. . . ."

"Alexa. Listen to yourself. Will you please shut the hell up?" Now furious, Eden stood up and stormed over to her mom. Marisol stayed on the floor perfecting her smoky eyes. She'd seen this a thousand times and was adept at tuning the two out.

"Well, what? I just want the very best for . . ."

"Shut up, shut up, shut up!" Eden stamped her feet like a three-year-old. It took a long time for Eden to actually show real emotion, but when she did, she exploded. "You're so clueless. You were in the industry, like, sixty-five years ago! You wore Fashion Fair makeup and bad Diahann Carroll wigs; what do you know? I'm gonna be famous as shit, Skye's gonna be famous as shit, and we're gonna do it without your help. Get it through your head, Alexa—we don't *need* you."

"Ohhh, yes, you do. Without me, you wouldn't have this room and these clothes and your beautiful face—you look *exactly* like me—and all the other things you take for granted. Without my name, do you think you would've been on that TV show? Ha! Well, at least you actually landed a show. I poured so much money and energy into your sister, and for nothing! *God*, all those directors whining, 'She's too eager, Lexie, you're pushing her too hard.' Well, what was I *supposed* to do? I only wanted the best for you girls!" Alexa took a breath, and then her face collapsed in a frenzy of sloppy tears. "You stupid, stupid, selfish little brat. I gave up *everything* for you girls. I could've been a real star, an opens-at-number-one-at-the-box-office star! And I never got my weight back after Skye was born—never." Now she was hyperventilating. "What about me?" she wailed. "What did I get out of all this? What about *meeee?*"

Eden just looked at her pitiful mess of a mom and shook her head. "I wish you could hear yourself," she finally said, slowly. "You're wrong about, like, everything. And about Skye worshipping me? Please. If you knew anything, you'd know she *hates* me."

Still weeping, Alexa threw back her shoulders like the star she had once been and swept out of the room. Eden felt weak. With a huge sigh, she fell backward on her bed.

"That woman wears me out," she moaned, flinging her arm over her eyes.

"Whoa, you're smudging your eyeliner!" Marisol rushed to her side, gingerly removing Eden's arm up from her face. She licked a finger and carefully erased Eden's bleary eyeliner. Once she was satisfied, she climbed on the bed next to her friend. "Drama, drama, drama."

"One of Alexa's finest performances," she said, exhaling.

"Better even than the famous *Shoulder Pads* scene when she snatched off Cybill Shepherd's wig."

"It was Kirstie Alley's," corrected Eden. "But whatever. I've decided Alexa's the cross I gotta bear for being so cute and talented," she said, only half joking. "You can't have it all, right?"

"That's where you're wrong, sweetie," said Marisol, pulling her friend to her feet. She reached in her bag and extracted two tabs of Ecstasy and two baby bottles of Skyy vodka. "You can have it all, and I fully intend to. Tonight, at the Freaky Flow album release party, I'm committed to making two things happen. I'm gonna get an F.F. exec to notice me, even if I have to grab the mike from Funkmaster Flex and belt out 'Real Love.'" The Mary J. Blige classic was Marisol's favorite karaoke song. She had a little dance routine and everything. "And number two," she continued, "we're getting you a powerful, rich, sexy, industry playa to make you forget all this Trey nonsense. Ya heard?"

Eden grinned and nodded. She and Marisol stuck pills on their tongues, clinked the vodka bottles together and knocked them back. Feeling all fizzy and tingly, Eden went back to the mirror to finish her face. What was she so upset about? She was *Eden Carmichael*, after all—and there wasn't anyone she knew who wouldn't want to walk in her shoes. She had a feeling it was going to be a good night.

It wasn't going to be a good night, however, for Skye, who'd listened to the entire conversation through the air vents in her room. Her tears were softening the inch-thick armor of her Clarins Extra-Firming Facial Mask, which she had applied twice a week ever since Alexa had told her she had a double chin in photographs. She felt like an ugly, talentless, miserable joke. Knowing that she'd ruined her mom's career, and that she would always be second best to her perfect princess of a sister?

Not one of the great looks.

* * *

Later that evening, Tangie was positioned in front of the full-length mirror on her closet door, marking the combination she'd learned in Ms. Carmen's class. Her face was slick with sweat, her leotard was sticking to her body, and her poufy curls were erupting out of her high ponytail like a tornado. She looked crazy and couldn't have cared less—she *had* to perfect Ms. Carmen's routine. She *would* be selected to try out for Spotlight. Over and over she practiced, hitting the marks so hard her muscles began to twitch.

She refused to take a break, because the second she stopped moving, all she could see was *Izzy and C.J.* And she wasn't ready to face the horrible truth—whatever that might have been.

Tangie was so lost in the choreography that at first she almost didn't hear her cell phone go off (so many people had her ring tone— "One, Two Step"—that she'd begun to tune it out). On the fourth ring, she finally snapped out of her dance trance and grabbed the phone off her dresser.

"Hello?" she panted, out of breath.

"Wassup, babe, it's Skye."

"*Girl*," Tangie breathed, relieved. She'd been trying to get in touch with her all night for a first-day-of-school review. "We have *so* much to discuss!"

"Yeah," Skye said, with a sniff. Her voice sounded shaky.

"You okay?"

"Yeah," said Skye, who was definitely not okay. "Allergies. Can I just tell you, T.? I'm so freakin' glad we're at the same school again. We're totally back together; I love it."

"Me, too, me, too!" Tangie was relieved to hear this. Skye had acted so snotty earlier, she was worried that Armstrong had totally changed her.

"Did you holler at C.J.?"

"Speaking of, I have gossip. Are you ready?" Tangie sank to the floor in front of the mirror. Balancing the phone between her ear and the crook of her shoulder, she swung her legs out in front of her and reached for her toes, stretching her hamstrings. She needed to be doing *something* while she delivered this news or she'd go crazy. "Guess who C.J.'s messing with?"

"Izzy."

Tangie sucked in her breath. "How'd you know?"

"Kamillah told me."

Tangie flinched. Skye said it matter-of-factly, as if she were discussing the weather. As if she didn't know her best friend had been in love with him since they were ten. "Well . . . how'd she know?"

"Please, Kamillah knows everything. She saw them kissing in front of Blue Water Grill after school."

"Oh." Tangie felt hot tears welling up in her eyes, but she refused to let them fall. "So it's positive, then."

"Look, we all know C.J. has no attention span. He'll be done with her in five minutes." Skye sounded weird, like she was really far away.

"It's just weird, 'cause me and Izzy kinda bonded today." Tangie sighed, hurt by Skye's couldn't-care-less attitude. "I can see us being really cool."

Skye inhaled sharply. She hadn't anticipated Tangie's bonding with someone else so fast. After all, she'd waited patiently a whole year to have Tangie at her school. Freshman year at Armstrong had been fun (she had definitely hyped it up to Tangie), but being without her best friend had definitely sucked.

What with living in Eden the Fabulous's shadow, coping with Alexa the Psycho Stage Mom, and dealing with Armstrong's hyper-competitive showbiz kids, she'd felt really lonely. She had missed her supportive, sweet, normal friend Tangie, who always calmed her down in the midst of crazy drama.

And now that they were finally together again, she'd already replaced Skye with some crazy alterna-ho?

"Listen," started Skye, "I know it's only your first day at Armstrong. As your best friend, I have to tell you, these girls are ruthless. Cutthroat. They'll stab you in the back. Trust no one."

"What do you mean? Izzy didn't even know I *knew* C.J.!"

"Tangie, Tangie, Tangie. *Calm down.*"

"Calm down? Excuse me?"

"All I'm saying is, keep your eyes open. And speaking of eyes, what are you doing letting Izzy put makeup on you? You don't know her from shit. Her mascara could've been infected with pinkeye!" *If you wanted to try smoky eyes, why didn't you just ask me?* she wanted to scream.

"Omigod, you're buggin'." Clearly, Skye was agitated about something. And frankly, she was too upset about the C.J. situation to deal.

Skye continued on her Izzy diatribe. "All the guys were so damned *pressed* for her today. I don't know, is she even pretty all like that?"

"Yeah, I think so. She's exotic." Tangie rolled her head to the left, stretching out her neck. Her feelings were hurt, she was upset, and now she wanted nothing more than to get off the phone.

"But is she a dime? I really don't see it." She paused for a while, thinking. "T.? I think I'm starting to get a double chin. At least, in pictures."

"You're insane. Everyone knows how pretty you are."

"But am I *pretty*-pretty? Like, 'America's Next Top Model if I were taller' pretty?"

"You're beautiful, Skye!" Tangie threw her hands up, exasperated.

"I think I peaked in eighth grade."

"Are you okay? Is something wrong?"

"Yeah, I'm chillin'. I just want to make sure *you're* okay." Skye wiped away the tears that were now streaming down her face and cleared her throat. "Don't let C.J. get to you. I love my cousin, but the boy's a selfish player. Get over him."

With that, Tangie said her good-byes and threw her cell on the bed. For years, she'd fantasized about her and Skye's going to

Armstrong together, and so far, it really wasn't that fabulous. Skye was so absorbed in her own world it seemed as if she couldn't care less about Tangie. And what was up with her tonight? Tangie hadn't heard her best friend sound so sad and cranky in ages.

Knowing Skye, her mother had probably done or said something to hurt her. And, knowing Skye, she'd never tell.

Name: Regina Marie Evangeline Leon Guerrero
Class: Sophomore
Major: Film
Self-Awareness Session #: RG 1

Right now, I guess I'm just confused. Actually, I'm always confused.

And what are you confused about, Ms. Guerrero? I mean, Ms. Leon Guerr—

It's just Guerrero.

Oh, I see. Is that ethnic?

My dad's Filipino.

Ah! Anyway, back to why you feel confused.

I have no idea what I'm doing here or what I want. Last year, I changed my major three times, from drama to screenwriting to film-making. It was like I wanted to drop each one before I failed. And on top of my school issues, I feel like I'm living two totally different lives.

12.
YOU'RE SAFE HERE

REGINA GOT OFF THE N TRAIN at the Eighth Street stop down in Greenwich Village's eclectic shopping district. It was seven thirty, almost dark out, and the block was hot. NYU was in the neighborhood, so there were tons of supercreative college students running around. With their vintage Pumas, ironic message T's, iPod nanos, and Echo Unltd. track jackets, they just looked like older versions of Armstrong kids.

Interspersed among the students were fresh-off-the-boat models rushing to go-sees, tourists holding up traffic trying to barter with the knockoff bag peddlers, and loud-talking Jersey kids with overgelled, bridge-and-tunnel hair. Everyone seemed to be fighting to get into the same boutique. Along with all the fun stores in the area—like Urban Outfitters, Jimmy Jazz, Zara, and H&M—there were dozens of street vendors pushing everything from bootlegged mix tapes, fake Balenciaga bags, and racks and racks of cheap-but-cute dangly earrings.

Smack in the middle of all this frenetic energy, on a busy corner of Astor Place, was the Harvey Milk High School. It was located directly above the Astor Place Hairstylist, where every major rapper at one time or another got the bomb edge-up. Not a lot of people knew the school even existed, and that was sort of the point.

The Harvey Milk school had been founded especially for gay, lesbian, bisexual, and transgendered teens that might've experienced violence or bullying at other schools. Basically, it was a safe place for the kids to go, where they wouldn't feel weird or crazy or ostracized. And every Monday night, in the basement, the school held a support group and social hour for gay and lesbian teens across the city— whether you were a student or not.

Regina had stumbled upon the support group online during her ultrasecret, Web-surfing sessions. Her cell phone alarm would ring at 3:30 a.m. and she'd wake up and surf gay and lesbian teen Web sites. After about an hour, she'd log off and jump back into bed. Yeah, it seemed kind of shady, but the only time she felt safe doing her research was when everyone in the world was dead asleep. She was just trying to figure things out.

And Regina had *a lot* to figure out.

Exhibit A: Regina had never had a boyfriend or even a crush. Her girls assumed it was because she was so shy, but that wasn't it at all. When Regina thought about guys, she felt nothing. It was like trying to feel passionate about a thumb. But the idea of kissing a boy, let alone having sex, made her want to throw up. It just seemed so entirely wrong, so unsexy and undesirable, that she wondered if she'd ever be able to fake it. The bigger question was, should she even *have* to fake it?

Regina didn't know. What she did know was that Kamillah and Skye could never, ever know that she felt this way. Ever. Let Kamillah think it was just a harmless girl-crush.

It wasn't that she didn't think they'd understand; after all, they went to a performing arts school. It was an extravaganza of drag queen talent shows, musical theater boys kissing in the hallways, dyke artists painting odes to the vagina—and then there was that infamous crew of drama kids that called themselves trisexual (meaning they'd "try" anything once, get it?) and made a huge deal about taking turns hooking up, girl-girl, boy-girl, boy-boy, and on and on. But Regina didn't fall into any of those categories.

She was in the most popular clique, Skye Carmichael's inner circle, for Christ's sake. Certain things were expected. Last year, some anonymous guys in their grade had passed around a list of the ten so-called "baddest broads" in the class, and she was number three (after Skye and Kamillah, of course). It was dumb, but *everyone* paid attention to the list. On the one hand, the attention was flattering—but on the other, it was so much pressure.

She was supposed to be one of the It chicks—a hot, sexy girl who went with an equally hot boy, someone on her popularity and hotness level. That was just the way high school worked.

So, every day Regina had to pretend. When anyone questioned why she never went out with any of the several boys that liked her, she maintained that she was just being selective. It was exhausting. It was scary, too—she lived in constant fear that her true feelings would somehow show on her face and everyone would know she was a fraud, just a fake-ass Skye-wannabe. Or, worse, she'd be labeled a Birkenstock-wearing bull dyke.

Finally, Regina had a place to go where she could be herself (whatever that was). Five minutes into her very first session, back in June, she had known she *belonged* there.

It was the first day of the summer-break session, and the group leader, a tiny, vaguely punk-rock Asian woman named Patrice, had just explained the Loyalty Oath. "In here, you're safe. You can spill your innermost thoughts and secrets, and we won't judge. Most importantly, we won't tell. Everything shared in these two hours is purely confidential, okay, people?" Patrice smiled at the group, her bleached-blond buzz cut shining white in the harsh artificial light.

"For those of you who don't know," she started, holding up a pink, triangular tambourine, "the pink triangle is the symbol of gay pride. When you're handed the tambourine, it's your turn to speak—

and everyone else listens. Now, who wants to go first?"

About eight kids eagerly raised their hands. Most of them didn't go to Harvey Milk, so they went through their school day getting bullied and made fun of, relentlessly. Group was the only place where they could say what was really on their minds, so they went for it.

"Did you want to share, um . . ." Patrice knitted her sparse eyebrows, struggling to read the 'Hello, My Name Is' sticker above Regina's left boob. ". . . Regina?"

Here I go, thought Regina. Her cheeks burned, and her stomach flipped over, but this was the moment she didn't even know she'd been waiting for.

"Um, okay," she managed in a voice so low it was almost a whisper. Patrice handed her the pink triangle. "Hi, everybody, I'm Regina."

"Class?"

"You're safe here, Regina," the class chanted in unison. *"We're here to listen with an open mind and heart."*

"It's true," continued Patrice, noticing Regina's slightly pale, clearly terrified expression."

"Uh, okay." Clearing her throat, Regina looked around the room. Surveying the circle of drag queens, homo-thugs and -thugettes, Lipstick Lesbians, and hormone-popping, pre-op transsexuals, she wondered what her Armstrong friends would think. *Freaks,* she thought. *Skye and Kamillah and everybody would think they were freaks.* "I don't really know why I'm here or anything. You guys seem to know exactly what . . . I mean, who you are. But I don't really know. I just know I'm, well, different than my friends."

Patrice looked her in the eye, nodding encouragingly. "In what way, Regina?"

"Well. This is weird. I mean, I . . ." She paused and stared down at her hands. Her thoughts were getting all jumbled up. Dimly, Regina realized this was the hardest thing she'd ever done. "I never really liked . . . guys. Or anyone, really. But I know I don't like *boys.*

I think they're . . . well, not hot. And that's fine, I guess. I just pretend I'm picky or shy, that's why I never mess with any guys. But the real problem is . . ."

Omigod, am I going to say it? Am I really going to just say it?

"I like my best friend. I mean, I think I *love* my best friend. And it's a girl."

"Mmm-hmm," muttered a couple of kids in the circle. Others nodded, totally getting it. They'd all been there.

"She's, she's amazing. And this isn't a unique thought—I mean, everybody likes her. But I . . . uh, she has zero clue about me. No one does. I've never told anyone about it, and I can't." She paused, thinking. "And it's not like I even want to do anything about it. My God, never. But I just couldn't keep it a secret anymore—I had to let it out, tell *someone.*"

Patrice waited for a moment or two to make sure Regina was finished speaking, and then she began to clap. The whole group joined her, their enthusiastic applause echoing in the cavernous room. And, oh—it felt really, really good to Regina! She hadn't anticipated how *freeing* it'd be to finally say it out loud, that she loved Skye. Something lifted in her chest, and for the first time in forever, she really did feel safe. Smiling, she finally looked up from her hands.

"That's all, I guess."

"Thank you for sharing, Regina," chanted the group, robotically.

What a wonderful group this was! Everyone was so loving, so understanding and nonjudgmental—it was fabulous. It was like, for two hours every week, she could be a totally different person! She wasn't awkward, shy, Regina the Follower, who couldn't even compose a sentence without getting approval from Skye. At group, she felt free to be whoever she really was. And everyone loved her for being her, not for the crew she rolled with.

I've come such a long way since that first meeting, thought Regina with a smile. Her heart thumping wildly with anticipation, as it always did

right before a meeting, she slipped through the shady-looking basement door (its only mark was a peeling bumper sticker that read:
GOT PRIDE?) and entered the huge meeting room.

As usual, the uncomfortably bright, fluorescently lit rec room
looked as if it were decorated for a seventies prom. Tiny, sparkling,
aluminum-foil stars hung from the ceiling on multicolored strings;
streamers with painted-on rainbows (the national gay pride symbol)
snaked along the walls; and everywhere she looked, there were
posters of famously "out" celebrities like Rosie O'Donnell, RuPaul,
Queer Eye's Carson Kressley, Ellen Degeneres, and the cast of *The L
Word*, as well as gay icons like Madonna, Janet Jackson, and Ricky
Martin. In the back of the cavernous room was a pool table and a tiny
dance floor with a disco ball hovering perilously above it. In the front
was a group of about twenty-five chairs, arranged in a circle. Group
had already started.

"Reggie-Reg!" everyone cried out in unison, thrilled to see the
most popular kid in the group.

"Sorry I'm late, y'all!" Blowing kisses to the queens and giving
pounds to the homo-thugs, Regina quickly made her way around the
circle. "What's good, Matthew? Your new weave is tight. Wassup,
Brianna, I'm feeling your new LeBrons . . ."

"Glad you could join us, Regina." Patrice gestured for her to sit
down, her stacks of punky, studded, sterling silver bracelets clanking
against each other. "Today we're exploring different kinds of love
relationships, whether they be monogamous, open, or strictly sexual.
The most important thing is to not feel exploited or unsafe in your
relationship. Trust your inner voice. If an act or situation doesn't feel
right to you, *stop*. Remember, *you* are the prize! Don't give your prize
away to someone undeserving.

"And right now, Guillermo has the pink triangle," said Patrice.
"Continue with your story, sweetie."

"Cool," said Guillermo, a small Latino boy wearing turquoise hot
pants, a see-through mesh tank top, and gladiator sandals. "My

whole thing is, I just feel like he's using me. He's so old and ugly, and he has *me*—this hot young piece of ass, right? Every time we're together all he wants to do is smash, and I'm, like, I have a mind, okay? I thought I'd learn something from that old fucker but the only time he talks is to ask me to rub down his joints with IcyHot after he hits it. I mean, *tha fuck?*"

"I see, I see." Patrice nodded quietly for a couple of moments, taking it all in. Finally, she spoke. "Well, group, what do we say?"

"Thank you for sharing, Guillermo," everyone said in unison.

Guillermo stood up and curtsied.

"So, would it be safe to say," started Patrice, choosing her words ever so carefully, "that the only time you feel that this older gentleman appreciates you is during intercourse?"

"That would be very safe to say, Patrice. *Hello?* I mean, what have I been talking about for the past fifteen minutes?"

"Being in a relationship that feels one-sided can be extremely hurtful. Guillermo, you've expressed very strong feelings for this older gentleman, yet you feel that he views you mostly in a sexual sense. How many of us have been in a similar situation?"

A tough-looking black girl wearing a white wifebeater, hugely baggy Sean John jeans, and Timberlands raised her hand. Guillermo handed her the pink triangle. "My boo ain't been messin' wit' me lately. I ain't been feelin' too good, like, I had the chicken pops, and she ain't even hollered when I was laid up. It's like, if I ain't doing the damned thing downtown, she ain't tryin' to hear it. You feel me?"

Patrice nodded slowly and gestured toward the circle.

"Thanks for sharing, TaKeedra," everyone said.

"That must've really hurt you when Sharonne didn't visit you while you were under the weather," Patrice began. "Do you think . . ."

"Maybe she ain't wanted to holla, 'cause she wasn't tryin' to catch it," interrupted a very tall, light-skinned boy with freckles. He was wearing a long blond wig and a fuschia minidress. "I mean, chicken *pox* ain't cute. Once, when my cousin Kina had them joints? I didn't see her in like two months? To this day, she has mad scars, like, *all over*. I kid you *not*, yo. Craters. So I told her . . ."

"Thank you for sharing, Paris. But next time, remember to wait for the pink triangle before you comment, okay, sweetie?"

Paris shrugged, muttering something about Revlon ColorStay foundation being brilliant for covering scars.

"I see we have another latecomer," said Patrice, looking up toward the door as a slightly sheepish, extremely straight-looking white boy walked in. As he sat down, she began catching him up with the discussion.

Meanwhile, Regina couldn't take her eyes off the boy. With his shiny black curls, tanned skin, and lush, red lips, he was drop-dead beautiful, and she felt sure she recognized him from somewhere. He looked up, catching her gaze. At first he shot her a quizzical, who-is-this-person-staring-at-me look, but then he broke into a devastatingly cute smile. And then Regina knew. Skye's crush from Southern Playwrights class, Nick Vardolos.

"Do you want to introduce yourself to the class?"

"Sure," he started. TaKeedra handed him the pink triangle. "I'm Nick. I came to one meeting during the summer, but I didn't say anything."

"You're safe here, Nick. We're here to listen with an open mind and heart," chanted the group. Paris was having visible difficulty pretending he didn't want to eat Nick with a spoon.

"Why don't you tell us a little about yourself?"

"Well, like I said, I came to one meeting over the summer, but I wasn't really ready to speak. What else? I just moved here from D.C. And I go to school here in the city."

"You got a man?"

"Paris, please. You don't have the pink triangle, sweetie." Patrice smiled at Nick, encouragingly. "Keep going!"

"Yeah, well, that's about it. I had a boyfriend back home, but that's done. Long-distance relationships suck."

In unison, the group muttered "Word," and "True, true." Regina stared, mouth agape. She couldn't *wait* for group to be over.

When the social hour started, the lights dimmed, the disco ball spun, and Destiny's Child's "Lose My Breath" blasted over the speakers. A huge group of boys crowded on to the dance floor, booty-popping and wriggling their hips. The kids who weren't writhing around on the dance floor huddled around the pool table, hung out on the couches, or ducked outside for a smoke.

Even though she didn't play pool and had a mild allergy to Michelle Williams (Beyoncé on the solo tip was hot, but Regina couldn't take DC3 seriously after Michelle fell out during that *106 & Park* performance), Regina usually relished the social hour. She was basically the unofficial social chairperson of the group, flitting from clique to clique, always leaving everyone wanting more (she'd learned from the master—Skye). But today she wanted no part of it.

Regina made a beeline for Nick. It was imperative that she (a) got his full story, and (b) made sure he never told a *living soul* that he had seen her at Harvey Milk.

"No way," she said, sliding into the chair next to him.

"What?"

"You're *Cat on a Hot Tin Roof*. You performed with Skye today."

"Oh. Yeah. Yeah, I did." Nervous, he ran his hand through his floppy curls. "You're an actor, too?"

She nodded, her throat feeling dry and parched. "Yeah. Well, no, I'm not an actor, I'm a filmmaker. But I have to take certain acting classes to fulfill my major." Regina barely knew what she was saying, she was so thrown off. Nick's presence in her support group was both juicy and *not good*. "Look, no one knows about this. About me. No one knows I come here."

"Sure. Yeah, it's all good." He shrugged. "Me, either."

Regina felt little beads of sweat trickle down her back. "Promise me you'll never tell a soul you saw me here, okay?"

"Listen, it's all good," said Nick, putting his hand on her shoulder.

"No, it's not," she said, starting to panic. "No one knows about me."

"I get it. I'm not exactly trying to let the whole world know I'm a fag, either. Plus, who am I gonna tell? I'm the new guy."

"So . . . are you out to anyone?"

"No." Nick paused and chewed on the inside of his mouth, lost in thought. After a couple of seconds, he threw his hands up. "Whatever. We're letting our freakin' hair down, right?"

"Totally."

"Okay," he said, with a grand sigh. "I *used* to be out . . . in D.C. Well, I was out to everyone but my parents."

"I don't get it. If you're gonna be out, why not go all the way?"

"My parents are Greek; I thought they'd fucking kill themselves." He shrugged. "Turns out, they're more into killing me."

"What do you mean?"

"Your turn to swear never to tell." He lowered his voice to a whisper. "Seriously."

"I swear. Seriously." Regina crossed her heart. She knew it was juvenile, but it just seemed appropriate.

"Me and my boyfriend, Jesse, used to go to the movies a half hour from my house—all the way in Potomac, Maryland—because it was out of the way. I thought no one would ever catch us." He shook his head, remembering. "See, my dad owns this Greek bakery. And the Greek community is really nosy down there, totally close-knit. Turns out, the concession-stand boy's dad was one of my father's business partners. And I guess the guy told his father, who told my dad. And, well, want the abridged version?"

"Yeah," Regina whispered, terrified of what was coming next.

"My dad beat my ass. See this?" He lifted up his sleeve and showed her a thick raised scar zigzagging across his shoulder. "He dislocated my shoulder. I had stitches, right there."

"Omigod, Nick!" Regina's hand flew up to her mouth. "That's terrible. I'm so sorry."

"Whatever. It's cool. I'm over it." He shrugged. "So, long story short, my parents were devastated. Mortified. They got this idea in their heads that having a gay son would be terrible for business."

"What? Dick Cheney's daughter is gay, and he's *vice president*!"

"Okay?" Nick rolled his eyes. "So, they sent me to live with my very macho Uncle Dmitri, who lives on the Upper West Side. And I'm allowed to go to Armstrong on one condition . . . that I be straight. That's what Uncle Dmitri's for. He rocks a handlebar mustache and he's a carpenter, so they think he'll teach me how to be a real man."

"This is crazy. This is a TV movie."

"Right? So, basically, if anyone finds out I'm gay, my parents are taking me out of Armstrong. And they're sending me to Greece to live with my grandma." He shook his head, chuckling. "The irony is that I'm being forced to act straight in a school full of gays. It's not like they sent me to a damned military academy."

"Oh, Nick. I'm so sorry."

"Whatever. I can do a mean straight impersonation. I mean, shit, I'm an actor." He shrugged and grinned. "I keep telling myself, hey, if Tom Cruise can pretend to be happy, so can I."

"What about your boyfriend back home?"

"It was kinda sexy for a moment, the whole star-crossed, tragic lovers thing. But in the end, he couldn't deal with my crazy family. So we broke up."

Regina squinted at him, thinking about his story. Nick was *amazing*. Everything she was terrified of, he'd been through already—he'd been outed, discriminated against by his family, forced to change schools. Regina knew, deep down, that she could trust him. She wanted to be his friend. "Please, please never tell anyone about me."

"I'd never," he said, and she believed him. "You don't know a lot about gay folks, do you? Illegal outing is, like, a federal offense. I'd *never*."

"Thank you."

"It's cool. Can I tell you something, though?" He reached out, fingering one of her two Pocahontas-style braids. "You have the shiniest, glossiest blue-black hair I've ever *seen*. Is that all you, or L'Oreal Feria?"

Name: Cedric James "C.J." Parker
Class: Sophomore
Major: Fine Art
Self-Awareness Session #: CP 1

I don't know, I just ain't been inspired lately. My art's sufferin'.

That's a shame, Mr. Parker. Do you know why you're having trouble?

Most definitely. It's Tangie. My boys would say it's corny to admit a girl got me shook, but I got no problems saying it. I guess I'm sensitive. I'm an artist, homie, I can't help it. Look, Tangie was my muse. Last year when my grandma had her stroke—the doctors, they thought it was a wrap for her—I was up all night long, every night, for a week. You know how I got through? Sketching Tangie's face, over and over—all different ways. I know all her expressions by heart. Anyway, yeah, I filled up a whole notebook. One day I'll show her.

Wait—Should I show her? Or is that wack?

13.

IT WAS THE LEOTARD

"TANGELA, HAND ME A NAPKIN, PLEASE," muttered Tangie's dad, Nipsey, without looking up from his plate. He, Tangie, and Mariska, his bride, were sitting on the living room sofa eating dinner on TV trays (in the five years since Tangie's mom had left, the dining room table had not once been used). Mariska's one and only specialty, barbecue, was spread out on the mahogany coffee table.

"Oh, here," Tangie answered, passing him a napkin. It was practically the first thing Nipsey had said to her since she had gotten home. She wasn't offended—her dad was a man of few words, to say the least. Tortured writers were notoriously silent brooders, weren't they? It wasn't always like this, though.

Tangie had actually had a really happy childhood. Nipsey had been a successful writer of a black erotica book series (gross), and he had formerly traveled around to book readings and speaking engagements. And he and Tangie's mom, Marcia, had seemed so in love. But when the books stopped selling and Marcia left to dance in Germany, Nipsey had sunk into a dark depression he hadn't yet recovered from. Tangie had thought he'd perk up the year before, when he married his Mariska, but things had gotten worse.

Now that her dad had someone to clean and cook and make sure the bills were paid (shockingly, Mariska made *six figures a year* from foot-modeling!), he had virtually turned into a ghost. All he ever did was yell at his agent over the phone, stare blankly into his laptop, and sleep. Tangie tried not to take Nipsey's depression personally. What did she need him for, anyway? She'd been virtually parentless since fifth grade—she knew how to take care of herself.

"Why no food, Tangela?" Mariska, who couldn't have been more than five years older than her stepdaughter, looked concerned.

"I don't really feel like eating. I already ate dinner—but thanks," Tangie lied. How was she ever supposed to lose fifteen pounds eating that fattening barbecue? If she'd learned anything, it was that Armstrong dancers were on a *totally* different level—and not just bodywise. Her courses were brutal, and the ethnic dance lesson after school had easily been the hardest technique class she'd ever taken. Playtime was officially over.

From now on, it was all about tofu, lettuce, and nonstop practice. Not only was Tangie determined to get Freshman Spotlight in Fall Fling, she didn't ever want to give Miss Carmen a reason to call her fat again.

"What?" Mariska's expression was blank.

"I'll wrap it up and bring it for lunch, don't worry," explained Tangie.

Her stepmother squinted at her, not understanding.

"*I'M. NOT. HUNGRY.*"

Mariska burst into inexplicable giggles and nodded vigorously. "Eat," she ordered, pushing the plate closer to her.

Rolling her eyes, Tangie plunged her fork into a sliver of barbecued pork and stuffed it into her mouth. Watching Mariska from the corner of her eye, she subtly moved the meat under her tongue and then quickly excused herself. "Dad, I hear my cell ringing upstairs; I gotta go."

He grunted something inaudible. Tangie hopped up from the sofa and ran down the hall to her room. Yanking a tissue out of the Kleenex box on her nightstand, she quickly spat out the offensive pork. *Wait, can you digest calories without swallowing?* she wondered, panicking. With an anguished sigh, she pushed the stuffed animals off her sari-printed pillows by Delia and flopped down on her bed. From the other room, she could hear Mariska muttering to her dad angrily.

Tangie felt bad about dinner. She didn't mean to be rude to her stepmother, but she was sore, exhausted, and too stressed about her body even to *pretend* to have an appetite. Her stomach grumbled. *I'm not hungry, I'm not hungry, I'm not hungry.* She repeated the words in her head like a prayer.

Trey had said he thought she was cute the way she was. *Voluptuous*—that was the word he'd used. Tangie grinned. She'd replayed the scene so many times in her head that it was starting to seem surreal. Trey was far outside her league; it was almost funny. Had he really been flirting with her? Maybe she had been so sad about C.J. that she was seeing what she wanted to see, to make herself feel better. And how the hell could C.J. be dating the one person she thought she could really be friends with at Armstrong? What were the chances?

Tangie rolled over on her stomach and reached into the bottom drawer of her nightstand, pulling out an oversize, pink scrapbook. It was her baby book. She remembered her mom telling her once that it was a baby shower present from her best friend . . . or was it from her mom, who had died shortly after Tangie was born? She didn't remember. Cracking it open, she flipped to the front, where there was a little plaque:

> *We welcomed our blessed baby girl,*
> *Tangela Marie Adams,*
> *to the world on July 17, 1990.*

Taped next to the plaque was a photo of her mom lying on her side in a hospital bed, holding a teeny-tiny, bald Tangie in the crook of her arm. Her mom looked beautiful, even with a messy French braid and no makeup. Tangie didn't like to look at the picture too long, so she flipped forward, past the pages marked THREE MONTHS, SIXTH MONTHS, NINE MONTHS, A YEAR, TWO YEARS—and so on.

On each page were entries to fill in milestones, like Baby's First Word, Baby's First Solid Food, Baby's First Step. Her mom had stopped filling in the entries after five years. It was an uncomfortable thing to look at; a stranger would've thought baby Tangela Marie had died at five. Tangie always wondered why her mom hadn't filled in the rest of the book.

Did her mom have a short attention span? Maybe she had had attention deficit disorder—back then, Tangie supposed, doctors didn't know about Ritalin. Or maybe she had gotten too busy with her dancing to remember. *I guess I'll never know now*, Tangie thought.

The old, familiar knot formed in Tangie's stomach, the way it always did when she sat down and really thought about her mom. She'd never met anyone else whose mother one day up and decided she was over being a mom. If she ever came back, that was the first thing Tangie would ask. *Why? Why were me and Daddy so disappointing, so terrible that you didn't ever call, or write, or visit?*

Sometimes Tangie thought she'd crumble to pieces under the weight of it, and other times she pushed her questions so far away, as if she'd never even had a mom. Almost.

But hope always lingered, like a loose tooth she couldn't help pushing with her tongue. Tangie hoped that when her mom came back, she'd be proud of the dancer she'd become. She hoped that she'd be excited that Tangie had gotten into Armstrong. And deep in some embarrassing, shallow place, she hoped her mom would think she was pretty. Tangie sighed, knowing that endlessly fantasizing about her mom's return was a waste of time. She knew that, but she couldn't help it.

Tangie flipped through the book till she got to the back. There, in an old envelope, she kept all her most precious photos. She sorted through them, eventually coming across her favorite snapshot of all time. Curling up against her oversize pillows, she carefully slid it out. The photo was worn and creased and stamped with a thousand fingerprints—but it was her and C.J., so it was perfect.

They were at the Common/M.I.A. concert in Central Park the previous May, right before things got bad. Skye had taken it when they weren't looking. They were standing facing each other, Tangie laughing with her head thrown back and C.J. with that crooked smile. He was just so cute.

It's like that line from Sex and the City, *Tangie thought. Carrie said that after a breakup, you should destroy all pictures where he looks sexy and you look happy.*

Her stomach started grumbling again. She slammed the picture down on the bed, furious at her hunger. Where was her willpower? Groaning, Tangie yanked her pink iPod mini out of her nightstand drawer, plugged in her earphones, and clicked on her "Ciara" playlist (all her favorite singers were also amazing dancers, like Usher, Aaliyah, Omarion, Chris Brown, and Justin Timberlake—for Tangie, great dancing was a prerequisite). She scooted down so she was lying flat on her back. Folding her arms over her ample chest, she frantically began doing sets of crunches. *One, two, three, four, and breathe. One, two, three, four, and breathe.* She turned up "Goodies" as loud as she could stand it, drowning out her hunger and her heartbreak.

She also succeeded in drowning out the sound of the knocking on her bedroom door. It wasn't until Mariska cracked it open and stuck her head in the room that Tangie realized someone was there. Startled, she jerked the earphones out of her ears.

"What is it? You scared me."

"Sorry, Tan-ge-la. You have friend?" She cocked her thumb over her shoulder, indicating that someone was standing behind her.

"Oh, who is it? Hold on," said Tangie, assuming it was Skye. She looked down to adjust her outfit—her denim mini, which she'd layered over her leotard and tights, had ridden up during her crunches. When she glanced back up, she saw that Mariska had opened the door wider. And that C.J. was standing behind her.

As Mariska left the room, C.J. shifted from foot to foot, looking unbearably adorable in his pastel-striped Polo and his usual baseball cap cocked to one side. He seemed seriously uncomfortable. Tangie was no better. She was paralyzed on the bed, fully caught off guard. As if the pressure of a let's-make-up conversation weren't awkward enough, she hadn't anticipated enduring this moment wearing her practice clothes—ugh, so unsexy.

"Wh—what are you doing here, C.J.? I still have on my leotard," she said, idiotically. *Perfect, when I finally say something, I sound like an idiot.*

"I thought we were talking tonight. We did text that, right?"

"But I was thinking we'd talk on the . . . on the phone."

C.J. shrugged, his beautiful, half-open honey-brown eyes looking drowsy-sexy. Clearly he'd been smoking. "That's a punk-ass move. I'm tired of this, like, awkward, back-and-forth nonsense. I wanna talk face to face."

"But . . . I still have on my leotard," she said, again.

"You want me to step out while you put on makeup and a homecoming dress?" The corner of his mouth turned upward, in a slight, mocking smile.

"Don't flatter yourself." Tangie's cheeks got hot and she had to fight to keep from grinning. He was adorable. "I just meant I wasn't expecting you to show up here, that's all."

"Like I ain't seen you in a leotard before. Come on, man—it's me. I've seen you at your worst. Remember Mud Butt?"

"Okay, *why* are you bringing that up?"

"Because it's some funny shit."

"It was your fault! Wasn't that your bottle of tequila?" She covered her face with her hands, remembering her mortification. "Ugh, why did I take the first shot of my life ten minutes after I'd eaten Mexican? Gross."

"I gave that bottle to Skye. If I'd-a known you wanted to hit it, I never would've let you." He looked at her, his eyelids drooping. "That ain't even you."

"Oh, really? How do you know what's me?" She was flirting.

"Come on, now," he said quietly, shooting her a look that said, *you know I know you better than anyone else.* "You're the kinda girl that shits in her pants after one shot."

Without thinking, Tangie grabbed one of her sari pillows and threw it at him. He ducked, grinning naughtily. "Don't lash out at me, Mud Butt."

"Oh, shut up," Tangie said, pretending to be annoyed. It was funny. They hadn't talked in three months, yet look at how easily they fell back into their old routine. Maybe he would forgive her, finally. But even if he did, that didn't change the fact that he was dating Izzy. She paused, considering this. "I bet you wouldn't care if Izzy did shots of tequila."

"Y'all two are completely different," he said with a shrug. It was that simple. Chewing on his lip, he realized things were about to get deep. "So, we gonna get into this?"

Tangie nodded, solemnly. "It was . . . it was just a surprise seeing you together, that's all."

"Why? I mean, do you even know her? Or are you goin' off on all the bullshit Kamillah and them are spreading?"

"I only just met her today. I mean, I met her at tryouts, but . . . well, I really like her. She's mad cool."

"Yeah, she is," he said quietly, pausing for a moment. "It ain't anything, T."

"Please, C.J. I heard you two were kissing."

"It ain't even like that, though. Seriously, we're just chillin'. She keeps talking about having a quote-unquote open relationship, or some mess? I think she got a man, anyway." He paused. "But whatever, it don't matter what we did. I ain't here to talk about her."

"Are you two in love, or something?" She lowered her voice, as if the possibility of this were too traumatic to say out loud.

"*Love?*" C.J. flinched as if he'd been slapped in the face. The word "love" was a serious affront to his player status. "Izzy and I are strictly just kickin' it—no more, no less. The situation ain't any different than it was with other girls I've messed with."

"It is different. They were all hos."

"There you go with that 'ho' shit. Devon wasn't a ho. Neither was Lauren—she was a sweet girl. She was a candy-striper."

"Ha! Candy *stripper*, maybe."

"You're really reaching right now. What's your point?"

"The point is, I *like* Izzy. I can really see myself being friends with her, you know? She's the first person I met at Armstrong."

"You're acting like you don't already have girls at that school. Your best friend goes there."

"Yeah, but . . ." *Skye's acting weird, and I kind of wanted to step out from her shadow and get my own thing started*, Tangie wanted to say. But she was talking to a boy, and a boy couldn't possibly understand female social angst.

"And you have me."

"Are you kidding? You haven't talked to me since June." She looked down.

"You ain't talked to me either." C.J. shrugged. "I mean, look, you were really ill that night. You were. But it's whatever, I mean, I'm over it. I don't want to fight with you—I hate it."

"You do?" All that time, she had been scared that he didn't even care. "I hate it, too. You're my . . . my best friend. Even when we weren't talking, I still felt like you were my best friend."

"Me, too," he said, nodding slowly. "I miss, you know, just hangin' out."

"What do you talk to Izzy about?" Tangie hated sounding so jealous, but what could she do? She *was* jealous. Had he written Izzy letters? Had he sketched her portrait?

"Why do you care so much? You're acting like she's the first girl I ever got with," he repeated, utterly clueless. "You never grilled me about Kelli, or Shana, or Keisha, or none of them. Why do you care, T.? *Why?*" He stepped closer to her, his eyes intense.

Realizing she'd gone too far, she suddenly wanted to delete everything she'd said over the past five minutes. "I don't care. I don't. Just forget I said anything," she blurted out, feeling exposed. She hated seeming jealous.

"Seriously, what's this jealous-girlfriend shit?" He was truly angry now, and his eyes were blazing. "I mean, you act like you ain't had a man for the past two years."

Tangie looked down. Not the whole Pete thing again! She'd started her whole summer-love lie three years ago, and it just kept snowballing, and now she couldn't tell the truth without looking, well, psycho.

C.J. continued. "And besides, it ain't like I ain't tried to . . . I mean, I'm sayin' . . . you're the one who didn't want . . ."

"I know, I know, you're right. Seriously, just forget I said anything," she interrupted, feeling an enormous knot in her throat. *Please, please, please don't say it*, she thought, hot tears burning in her eyes. *I already know it's my fault we didn't make this thing official—even though the whole world knows we belong together.* The Mariah Carey song ran through her mind.

"You know what? Maybe I should just bounce," he muttered.

"No, no, no!" She jumped up, stood there with her mouth opening and shutting like a *verklempt* barracuda, and then plopped back down on the bed. "Don't go. I need to . . . let me explain, okay?"

C.J. shrugged, his thumbs hooked in his jeans pockets.

"Listen, you're my best friend; I never imagined we'd be like this. Avoiding each other and not speaking for months? It's the worst." Her voice got lower, and she blinked back tears. She saw him start to move toward her and then stop himself. "I'm so sorry for what I said, C.J. I embarrassed you and hurt you, and I hate myself for that. Please, please forgive me."

His face softened a bit, but he said nothing.

"I mean, the 'hood outreach' thing . . . there's just no excuse. I can understand if you never want to speak to me again." She swallowed. "And I didn't mean it, *at all*. I was just drunk. You know I don't think that about you."

"Why'd you say it, then?" His voice was quiet.

"I guess . . . I was upset."

"*You* were upset?" His eyebrows shot up, stunned. "What were you upset for? I stepped to you and you shut me down—*I* shoulda been upset."

"It was because . . ." she stopped and sighed. Was she really going to go there, finally? "Because I'd been waiting a long time for you to tell me you liked me, and then when you did, it sounded like I was your last choice. Like, 'Oh, I've already messed with every other girl in our grade, so I guess I'll kick it to Tangie.' It just hurt."

"Hold up, *what*? That's what you thought?"

"I mean, that's what you said, C.J."

"That's definitely not what I said." C.J. pulled his baseball cap down low over his face, shoved his fists deep in his jeans pockets and began pacing around Tangie's room, as if completely flabbergasted. "I was tryin' to say that I was over dealing with girls I don't care jack about—that I was ready to do this with you, for real. How could you even *think* I'd put you on the same level with some random floozies? I thought you knew . . . I mean, you're the only girl I ever . . . you know how I . . ."

As she watched him struggling, Tangie finally began to understand what C.J. had tried to say that night. He really wanted to be with her. Finally . . . and for real.

Her heart pounding, Tangie hopped off the bed and hurled herself at him, practically knocking him over. When he recovered from the surprise, C.J. squeezed her so hard her feet almost left the ground. Closing his eyes, he buried his face in the hollow of her shoulder and inhaled. They stayed like that for a long time, locked in that clinging, airtight embrace.

If I dropped dead this very moment, I wouldn't be mad, thought Tangie. He was just so delicious, so tall and strong . . . and his muscular chest felt so good pressed up against her. It was almost unbearable.

She pulled away, overwhelmed and nervous. And what she saw in his face made her knees buckle. He looked as if he wanted to devour her.

"Hi," he said.

"Hi," she whispered back, shakily. And then, because he really had no choice, C.J. grabbed her shoulders, backed her against the wall and kissed her. Really kissed her. It was the kind of kiss that was so delicious, so *thigh-melting* that Tangie couldn't imagine actual sex feeling any better. And it went on and on, until all she could do was hang on to the back of his T-shirt for dear life and pray that he'd never stop. And he didn't. He slid his hands down her back and over her bottom, and then he pulled her up against him, hard. She gasped into his mouth.

"What?" he murmured.

"Nothing," she breathed. And then she grabbed his ass right back. Their kiss burned deeper and hotter, if that were even possible. Tangie was up on her tiptoes, her arms tight around his neck, shamelessly pressing every inch of her body into his. She couldn't get close enough. Neither could he—so, in one quick motion, C.J. grabbed the backs of her thighs and hiked her legs off the ground, wrapping them around his waist. He ground his hips against hers, sending a thousand electric tingles up and down her body. She was melting; her head fell back, and he planted a hot, openmouthed kiss on her throat—and when she felt his tongue dart lightly over her skin, she had to dig her fingers into his back to keep from moaning.

And then the room started spinning. All she knew was

C.J.—he was everywhere, his delicious scent, his body, his mouth. And that's when she decided that virginity was overrated. In fact, she would've happily handed it to him on a platter, right then and there. Wasn't the whole point to do it with someone you loved? You adored? You had waited *five years* for?

Yes, yes, *yes*!

C.J.'s hands were holding her face and he was kissing her again, slowly this time. Softly, he bit her bottom lip, and she began to tremble. If she hadn't been smushed up between C.J. and the wall, she would've fainted dead away. *Please, don't stop*, she wanted to say. *I did not imagine wearing my leotard during this moment, but who cares?— just never stop kissing me.* But then, he did.

C.J. wanted to look at her. He pulled back so that her face was just inches from his, their lips almost touching. Her lips were puffy, and her hair was crazy—and he'd never seen Tangie look more beautiful.

She knew what she was going to say before she said it.

"C.J. . . ." she breathed.

"Tangie."

"I love you."

He flinched.

Tangie held her breath, thinking, *Oh, no, was it a mistake? Did I ruin everything?* But then, he flashed one of his most devastating C.J. smiles, playfully kissed the tip of her nose, and whispered, "No, I love *you*."

Before she could answer—or scream, or cry, or perform a celebratory interpretive dance—they heard a hard pounding on Tangie's door. "Tan-gel-a? Tan-gel-a, no friend so late!"

C.J. abruptly jumped away from Tangie as if he'd just gotten an electric shock. With a yelp, she tumbled to the floor. He tried to help her up, but she pushed him away, getting up on her own and backing him into the swivel chair at her desk. She didn't want Mariska to see him anywhere near her. Quickly, she combed her fingers through her disheveled ponytail, yanked down her miniskirt and opened the door a crack, squealing, "Hi Mariska! What's up?"

"Time for friend to leave!" Her stepmother bounded through the door and pushed Tangie aside, wagging her finger at C.J.

Tangie's heart was pounding. "C.J. *was* just leaving, Mariska!"

"I was just leaving," he repeated, hopping out of the chair. Mariska stood in the middle of the room with her arms folded across her chest, glaring at C.J. as he walked past. But just before he shut the door behind him, he stuck his head back in the room.

With his mischievous grin, he said, "Sorry for molesting your stepdaughter, Mariska. Couldn't help it—it was the leotard."

Then he was gone and Mariska was yelling, but Tangie was too thrilled and excited and lip-bruised and happy to care.

14.
THE PARTY PENIS

BY THE TIME THEIR CAB TURNED on Tenth Avenue and pulled up to Marquee, Manhattan's sexiest, most chock-full-of-A-listers nightclub, Eden and Marisol were good and twisted. On the way uptown from the Carmichael's West Village penthouse, they'd downed two more vodka shots each—and this was on top of the X. Giggling hysterically, they were trying to convince their driver to give them a discount.

"Come on, Ahmed," purred Marisol, looking fabulous in a one-shouldered, fuschia Roberto Cavalli minidress. It was one of rail-thin Eden's castoffs, and on the voluptuous Latina it looked positively X-rated. "You know you don't wanna charge us no fifteen bucks!"

"We're too cute for fifteen bucks," said Eden, and it was true. In her leopard-print L.A.M.B. camisole, superskinny Kate Moss jeans, and cork-platformed, red-patent-leather Christian Louboutin stilettos, she looked like a supermodel. "Mari, sing to him!"

That was all the encouragement the Mariah-wannabe needed. "You want me to sing, Ahmed? I love to sing for hot guys like you. If I sing, we only pay ten, okay?"

"I make decision after you sing," the old Persian man grumbled, leering at the girls in the rearview mirror.

Leaning forward and squeezing her arms together so her breasts looked superluscious, Marisol launched into her favorite Mariah song of all time, "We Belong Together," as cars all around them honked, trying to go around their illegally parked cab. Overdressed Paris Hilton-ettes waiting in line were starting to stare.

"Okay, let's wrap it up, doll," said Eden. "The bridge-and-tunnel crowd is staring."

"Did you like it, playa?" Marisol batted her insanely long lashes at Ahmed in the rearview mirror (Eden's mom had had her personal makeup artist give the girls "first day of school" lash extensions the night before—the false lashes would last up to two weeks!).

"Okay, *yes*," he said, grabbing the ten dollar bill from Eden. He turned around in the seat and wagged his finger at them. "You are wicked, naughty girls. I am believing your father kicks himself for permitting you to leave without chaperone."

"Baby, my dad's kicking himself for holding up that bodega—he's been in prison since I was eleven!" The girls collapsed into peals of laughter, hysterical at the thought of Marisol's jailbird dad caring where she went at night. Tears streaming down her face, Marisol kissed a scandalized Ahmed on the cheek, leaving behind a smear of her signature brick-red lipstick. The giddy girls tumbled out of the cab, leaving Ahmed in a queasy mix of excitement and disgust. Actually, when Eden and Marisol went out at night, they saw that look a lot.

The line outside Marquee's front doors was epic, snaking all the way down the block and around the corner. The club was always packed, but tonight was even crazier, since Freaky Flow Records was having its fifteenth anniversary party. Eden and Marisol had no time for the line, though. Flipping their perfectly highlighted, Chanel Chance-scented hair, the girls sauntered past all the overdressed Lindsay-and-Mischa-wannabes and the fake hip-hop boys who loved them, knowing that every last one of them was staring (how could they not? Between Marisol's curves and Eden's perfect face, they were the definition of "starter divas").

Once they got up to the front, Manny, the muscle-bound bouncer, lifted the red velvet rope and swept them through—much to the chagrin of an Oompa Loompa–orange spray-tan victim in the back of the line, who yelled out, "Fugly beeyatches!" The girls were too giddy with hotness to even notice. Since Manny, a man more powerful in Manhattan than Mayor Bloomberg, was Marisol's first cousin, they were way too VIP to care about the little people. And, oh, how they loved exploiting their inside connection, squealing "Edie-and-Mari sandwich!" and dramatically throwing their arms around the six-feet-eight-inch former Seton Hall linebacker.

After sufficiently making everyone in line ill, Eden and Marisol finally stumbled into Marquee. The glittering, glamorous, two-story club was blazing! Big Boi's "Kryptonite" was blasting from the speakers so loud the girls felt the bass thumping in their chests. Taking up most of the bottom level was a steamy dance floor teaming with It-girls-in-training, faux-hawked fashion boys, glossy magazine editors, and slumming socialites (the white powder still clinging to their pert, plastic noses).

Upstairs was an extravaganza of VIP fierceness, complete with plush white banquettes, cocktail tables barely holding up under the weight of thousand-dollar Moët bottles, and bling, bling, bling. It was thick with supermodels, hip hop industry bigwigs, anxious looking publicists rocking Baby Phat, and a weeded-out mix of chart-topping rappers, apple-bottomed video vixens, and their fawning entourages—all pretending to ignore legendary party photographer Patrick McMullan, as he made the rounds. It was a major, major moment.

Eden and Marisol were hardly starstruck, though, since they'd been on the scene for years—everyone knew them; they were like perky little mascots. Plus, tonight wasn't about fun; it was about business. Marisol was dedicated to networking with a Freaky Flow baller, and Eden was all about finding a rich, hot man to make her forget Trey.

Mouthing the words to "Kryptonite," they squeezed their way to

the front of the dangerously crowded bar area, mowing down *America's Next Top Model* finalist YaYa in the process (she barely noticed, as she was deeply preoccupied with convincing some Italian gigolo that she was too intellectually advanced to perform the sexual act he was suggesting—she went to *Yale*, after all).

"What's going on, Bailey?" Eden leaned over the slick-with-cocktails bar and double-kissed the goateed Eurotrash bartender.

"I've spent half the night trying to convince Lindsay Lohan to sip water in between her cocktails," said Bailey, a filthy-haired aspiring drummer allegedly from Amsterdam (his accent went in and out). He'd been hooking up the girls since they first started hanging out at Marquee, when they were only fifteen. " 'Babysitter' is not in my job description, okay?"

"You know, Bailey, it's really *so* unhealthy to internalize other people's issues," lectured Marisol, launching into one of her self-help rants. "All you end up doing is co-opting their negative energy. I'm reading this fantastic book called *Parasite Friends: How to Stop Them from Sucking Out Your Life Force*, and it's really . . ."

"Interesting! I gotta read it." Bailey, who'd grown accustomed to her long-winded speeches, knew exactly when to cut Marisol off. "So, what'll it be, girls—the usual vodka and Red Bull?"

"You know how we like it, babe," replied a clueless Marisol, twirling one of her thick, jet black waves around a finger. While Bailey handled their drinks, she leaned toward Eden to talk business.

"Okay, we gotta get up to the second floor, and fast. I think I see Kai James up there." Kai James was the highly influential vice president of artist development at Freaky Flow Records—and he'd been responsible for the careers of most everyone on *106 & Park*'s countdown. Marisol had been stalking him with her demo for a year and a half. "See him? Up there talking to T.I. and Jermaine Dupri?"

Eden squinted swiveled around on her bar stool and squinted up at the second floor. "T.I. is so fucking fine. OMIGOD, Mari, speaking of fine . . . is that Smoove Killah up there?"

"Uh-huh," Marisol said, very blasé. "You've met him, remember? The night last summer when we ended up at Nas's rooftop joint?"

"Hold up—I was at a rooftop party at Nas's? I must've blacked out."

"You lush," Marisol giggled, grabbing her drink from Bailey and spilling it a little. "Remember, Kelis let you borrow that shimmery teal eye shadow? Well, whatever. You were so up Trey's ass last summer, you probably wouldn't have noticed if Donald freakin' Trump tried to kick it to you."

How the hell could Eden have forgotten meeting the sexiest rapper alive? What, was she on crack?

Famous both for his lyrical beefs with The Game and his highly publicized relationship with R & B songstress Pearl, Smoove was ridiculously sexy in that dangerous, bad-boy way. He was covered in tattoos, boasted a criminal record that would make 50 Cent blush, and had the hardest, most rock-solid abs.

And he was *here*. Eden couldn't take her eyes off him. Yummy.

". . . And anyway, I think the new songs on my MySpace page are finally dope enough for Kai James to hear. So much better than the tape I slipped him last year at Def Jam's *Vibe* Awards preparty." Marisol had paid C.J. forty bucks to design a business card depicting herself straddling a huge, phallic microphone (her idea). The business card listed her MySpace address, where one could listen to the three songs—her favorite was a soaring ballad titled "Y'all Can't Be Me"—she produced with her cousin Manny's good friend Lupe Fiasco. Marisol gulped down her vodka and Red Bull and pulled one of the cards out of the Fendi spy bag she'd borrowed from Eden. "Do you think he'll even remember . . ."

She abruptly cut herself off, realizing that her audience was so not paying attention. Eden was staring googly-eyed at Smoove, upstairs. "Hello? You're, like, *salivating* right now," she said, waving her hand in front of her friend's face. Giggling, she burst into song. *"You have a crush on Smoo-oove, you have a crush on Smoo-oove. . . ."*

"Omigod, shut up, Mari," Eden said, whipping her head around to see if anyone were listening. It made her dizzy, so she grabbed on to the bar for balance. Maybe this was her last cocktail. "What are we, twelve? Of course I think he's a hot bitch, but he's so off the market. Are you forgetting that Pearl is his wifey? You saw them on the cover of *XXL*."

"I prefer not to look at that incense-waving, peace-and-blessings, fake-Badu bee-yatch," said Marisol, rolling her neck. She made a practice of hating all R & B divas except for Mariah Carey and Mary J. Blige, whom she considered beyond criticism. "How's she gonna be all about peace when her man can't cross a state line without getting arrested for gun possession?"

Eden said nothing, just sipped her cocktail and gazed at Smoove across the room, her eyes glazed over.

Looking at her lovesick friend, Marisol had the kind of all-of-a-sudden, earth-shattering epiphany you can only have while drunk. "Ohhh, Edie, I'm getting a feeling, here. Smoove is going to be your next man, I can just *feel* it."

Eden burst out laughing, sloshing her drink a little. She thought Marisol was nuts, not necessarily because he was out of her league (ever since notoriously Negress-obsessed Robert De Niro had sent his assistant to get her number at the Tribeca Film Festival, she'd decided no one was too high-post for her), but because he was so publicly taken. "Are you nuts? Mari, I cannot compete with Pearl, okay? I just can't. I mean, the woman has a M·A·C contract."

Outraged, Marisol hopped off her bar stool and put her hands on her shapely hips. "Let me find out Trey cheating on you has you thinking you're wack. *What are you smoking?* Look in a mirror! And whatever, Pearl ain't even here. You snooze, you motherfuckin' lose."

Eden sighed with her whole body, suddenly feeling very drunk and very sorry for herself. "I guess Trey's cheating hit me harder than I thought," she said, her nose turning red and her eyes getting watery.

"Oh, *hell*, no!" Marisol grabbed Eden by the arm, dragging her off the bar stool and into the crowd. She blew a good-bye kiss to Bailey, and he winked. "It's time to make power moves. You watch— I'm not leaving until Smoove is feeling you and Kai James is begging me to sign with Freaky Flow Records."

Five minutes later, the girls had used their Manny connection to successfully hustle their way past the bouncer guarding the roped-off second-floor VIP section. As soon as they set foot there, their old friend Laurie Anne Gibson, the choreographer from MTV's *Making the Band*, called them over to her table, where she was sitting with her publicist, the singer Mya, and Freaky Flow exec Kai James's assistant, Tyrone. (Laurie Anne had fallen in love with Marisol's hustle at Bungalow 8 the previous summer, when Marisol had stood up on a banquette and sung along to Keyshia Cole's "Love" in front of the entire VIP section. Gibson had ended up becoming a sort of a "party mentor" to the girls—watching over her "Li'l Muffins" and making sure no one messed with them).

Within roughly five seconds, Eden got trapped in a conversation with some *Making the Band* finalist about how she had dressed up as Eden's mom's character from *Shoulder Pads* for five Halloweens in a row. Luckily, she was too busy gazing lustily at Smoove to pay attention to the fawning fan. Was it Smoove making her heart pound in her chest like a Lil Jon track, or was it the Red Bull?

Meanwhile, Marisol and Tyrone were a frenzied blur of tongues and hands and intertwined legs. Tyrone, a goofy, hip-hop-crazed recent Howard grad, was Marisol's "Party Penis." Party Penis was Marisol's term for a boy she hooked up with when she was out, but had no relationship with outside the club. Of course, everyone knew she was using him to get to Kai James—everyone except Tyrone.

"Kryptonite" turned into Lil Jon's "Throw Ya Hands Up," and the VIP section went crazy. Everyone at the table jumped up and threw their hands in the air, dancing and bobbing their heads. Tyrone grabbed Marisol's hand to dance, but she gave him a big, wet kiss and told him she'd just be one second.

"Tyrone is really feeling me," whispered Marisol in Eden's ear, watching him bop over to the bar. "It's so good for business, babe. I gave him one of my cards, and he's peeping my MySpace page on his BlackBerry right now, see?" They both looked over at Tyrone, and indeed, he was holding the BlackBerry up to his ear so he could hear her song. "So look, I'm probably gonna make out with him for awhile and then make the demo transaction. You cool? You look seriously twisted, girl."

"No, I'm chillin'. Woo-hoo!" Eden threw her hands in the air, and wiggled around in her chair. "Go do your thing!"

Marisol squinted at Eden, not buying it. "You've been staring at your boy all night. If you don't go kick it to him right this second, I'm-a smack you."

"What the hell am I gonna say to him?" Eden's brow was furrowed. He just looked so cool—so untouchable—leaning up against the ledge, a blunt hanging from the corner of his mouth.

"Eden Carmichael, never in my life have I seen you so unaware of your own hotness! You're a Leo tigress, so act like it! Listen, just go up to him with your special you-know-you-want-it walk, and ask him if you can take a puff. Just *do it*." Marisol grabbed her arm and dragged her up off the seat. "I'm gonna go chill with Tyrone, you go put it on Smoove. I'll be watching." She ran over to her Party Penis, wrapping her leg around his waist and grinding against him. *I love that girl, but she's a straight-up slut*, thought Eden, watching her. *She does have a point, though. What man is too high-post for Eden Carmichael? And besides, I don't care how many Soul Train Lady of Soul Awards she has, I'm so much badder than Pearl. That Erykah Badu ish is so 1997.*

Plus, she figured that even if he rejected her, she could always draw upon the experience in her Characterization class. Before she could talk herself out of it, she gulped down the rest of her drink, licked her lips, tossed her hair, and headed over to him.

Nonchalantly, Eden leaned up against the second-floor ledge, right next to Smoove. She flipped her party-frizzy, honey-and auburn-streaked hair over her shoulders, the Red Bull suddenly giving her a burst of insane self-confidence. She *knew* she looked irresistible—could he feel the electricity that was practically shooting from her fingertips? Looking him straight in the eyes, she went for it. "Wassup, playa? You tryin' to share?"

He studied her intently with half-open eyes for a minute or so, as if he were trying to figure out where he knew her from. Finally a slow grin traveled across his pouty lips. "Lemme find out Kendra from *Family Chatter*'s tryin' to get twisted," he said, in the gravelly, smoked-out voice that had made him a millionaire a zillion times over.

He recognized her!

"Yeah, well, Kendra's all grown up." Eden licked her lips and fixed her huge, amber-colored eyes on the rap star. "So how about that puff?"

He nodded reaaally slo-o-o-wly and took a deep drag off the blunt. "Open up," he croaked, and she did. Inexplicably, he made an *O* with his hand and put it over her mouth. Leaning forward until his hot-to-death face was inches from hers, Smoove blew smoke through his hand and into her mouth. It was the single sexiest moment of her life. Well, up to that point, at least.

Shortly after that, Eden and Smoove found themselves entangled in the 400-thread-count, champagne-soaked sheets at his Hotel Gansevoort suite, doing things she'd only dreamed of.

And every time her nails clawed his back, she hoped Trey could feel it.

15.

YOU CAN TAKE THE BOY OUTTA MARCY

"YOU GOT NINETY-NINE PROBLEMS, and they're *all* about a bitch," said Blackadocious, shaking his head at C.J.'s complicated love life.

They were chilling outside the bodega next to Armstrong, waiting for the first bell to ring and discussing C.J.'s predicament.

He'd told Black that he and Tangie had hooked up the night before, but kept the "I love you" part to himself. That was nobody's business.

"I know, son," C.J. said, sighing. He took a long drag from his cigarette. "I know. I think I played myself, no question."

"I'm saying, though, why'd you have to go so hard with her? Knowing you got Izzy on the side? That's just *reckless*."

"Go hard? There was no going hard. I just kissed her. I mean, basically."

"I know you, playa. You ain't just kissed her."

He shrugged. "Me and Tangie just got this thing. I can't explain it. It was like I couldn't help it, you feel me?"

"No, playa, I definitely do not feel you. Don't get me wrong, Tangie's fucking bad as shit—the badonk is crazy, cute face, real hair—but Izzy? Man, Izzy's *hard*. And you *know* she's out there with hers. You can just tell." Black looked dreamy-eyed, fantasizing about wild, dirty sex with Izzy. "I bet she deals with handcuffs and chains and shit."

"Man, I really don't need to know if she deals with handcuffs."

"You never been tied up?"

C.J. squinted at Blackadocious, utterly disgusted. "Hell, no, nigga, I never been tied up. That's some crazy white shit."

Black was silent, deep in thought. "Okay, me, either. But from what I saw on lusciouslydelicious.com, the shit is crazy."

C.J. rubbed his eyes. He was miserable with indecision. "The thing is? I'm feelin' Izzy. She's the first girl I met that ain't *pressed*, you feel me? She's into me and shit, but then again, not really. I mean, she keeps talking about an 'open relationship.'"

"What the hell is an 'open relationship'? Shorty's mad different, yo."

"Right? She told me she's, like, a feminist. I seriously think she's even dealin' with other dudes."

"You're cool with that?"

C.J. shrugged. Was he? "I don't know, I think her swagger's kinda sexy—she's like a dude. Plus, she's mad artistic, and she's fully down with my hustle, ya heard? With her, I don't have to hide my side gig and make excuses. She gets it, 'cause she's been through her own shit."

"That's obvious."

"Man, don't believe all them rumors. She ain't Common's baby mama, them G-Unit niggas never smashed her, and she wasn't no starving Ethiopian infomercial baby with flies on her face and a big stomach. That's just jealous bullshit."

Black looked disappointed. "Well, damn, what's her story, then? Everybody says . . ."

"No, *Kamillah* said." Disgusted, C.J. flicked his cigarette butt on the ground, stamping it out with his Tims. He'd never really liked Black's girl—she needed to get a life and stop starting trouble. "Izzy just went through a wilin' out phase, that's all. We never really get into details, but I think she got into some, like, extracurriculars

when she was a kid, but she rehabbed it out and now it's all good."
C.J. paused for a second, thinking hard about Izzy's situation. "See,
this is how shit pops off when you have an absentee father."

"That's original," muttered Black, sarcastically. "Who *ain't* got a
absentee father?"

"No, but her pops straight-up kicked her out."

"Word?"

"Word, yo."

"Damn, y'all *are* mad alike. Where she live at?"

C.J. opened his mouth to speak, and then closed it. Could he
trust Black? After quickly weighing the pros and cons, he decided,
what the hell. "Look, if I tell you this, you gotta promise you won't
tell anybody. Especially not Shorty."

"Who, Kamillah? Naw, yo, I . . ."

"Don't even start, mothafucka, you tell her everything. Promise."

Exasperated, Black threw his hands in the air. "Fine, my word is
bond. God-*damn*."

C.J. took a deep breath, hoping it wouldn't come back to bite
him in the ass later. "She lives with this, like, thirty-five-year-old
named Damon. Anyway, he's some high-post social worker who
wrote a book on runaways, and I guess he . . . well, she said he . . .
he *found* her."

"Found her?" Black's eyes were as wide as saucers. Some music
major passed him on the way down the stairs and almost knocked
him over with his tuba. "Found her *where*, son?"

"On the street." C.J. looked at the ground, knowing as soon as it
came out of his mouth that it was a mistake. "It ain't no big . . . I
mean, look, her pops is a straight-up bastard, yo. He kicked her out
and she ain't had nowhere to go. I don't know, I don't got the whole
story."

Black had no words, for once. It was too much to process. Izzy
had lived on the streets? She really *was* hard. "But she ain't, like,
smashing this cat, right?"

"He's in his *thirties*, Black. No, she ain't smashin' him," snapped C.J., more mad at himself for telling Izzy's secret than he really was at Black. "You really running amok right now, just wilin' outta control. And you wonder why nobody tells you anything."

"Damn," Black answered, breathlessly. On the DL, he surveyed the crowd, looking for Kamillah—he couldn't wait to tell her. "Shorty's mad different."

"Yeah, but she ain't no crazy groupie ho. She just got up with the wrong crowd. That's all, money. She doesn't even know Common."

"Okay, man, chill." Clearly, Black didn't believe him for a second. "Why're you so defensive? You're really feeling her, aren't you? Just admit it."

C.J. shrugged, sliding the brim of his baseball cap to the side.

"So, what about Tangie?"

"Man, the two ain't even in the same breath. Tangie and me, we grew up together. She *knows me* knows me. And even though we're mad different and we're always beefin' and shit, there's just something with us that's, like, undeniable. You feel me?"

"Yeah, I feel you." Black nodded, smiling a little. That was how he felt about Kamillah.

"And don't compare our shit to you and Kamillah," said C.J., reading his mind. "You got jump-offs left and right."

"Whoa, whoa, whoa! That don't mean I don't love her! I'm dedicating my first mix tape to that girl."

"Yeah, but, if me and Tangie were for-real kicking it, I'd never go out on her like that."

"Whatever, man. If y'all are so in love or whatever, why you with Shorty, then? How's that any different than how I be rollin'?"

"First of all, I ain't *with* Izzy like that. We chilled over the summer, and now it's a wrap. And secondly, me and Tangie weren't together." He sighed. "We ain't never been together. And honestly? It's on her. She was never 'bout it, so a nigga had to do his thing. But if she came to me on some 'let's do this for real' shit, I'd cut 'em all back. No question. Izzy, included."

"All I'm sayin' is, Tangie would never tie you up."

"Nigga, what is *wrong* with you? You got Tourrette's?"

The two were silent for a few moments, reflecting on C.J.'s dilemma. All around them, scores of Armstrong kids were restlessly waiting for the first bell, doing what Armstrong kids do—the singers were practicing their chords, the dancers were marking their routines, and the musicians were loudly blowing on French horns and other unwieldy instruments. And yet the owner of the bodega stormed out onto the sidewalk to yell at C.J. and Black, because they were allegedly affecting business with their "reefer cigarettes" and "baggy jeans." Silently, they picked up their backpacks and moved on to Armstrong's front steps. They weren't about to get belliger-ent—they'd both had enough shady experiences with racist cops and shop owners to know it wasn't worth it.

They sat down on the front steps outside the school, and without addressing the idiot bodega owner, C.J. and Black picked up where they left off.

"So, what're you gonna do?"

C.J. shrugged. "I'll see what Tangie's tryin' to do, and then I'll know how to deal with Izzy."

"I like it, man, I like it." And that was the end of that. "Yo, let me get one of those Newports?"

When C.J. stood up to reach into his jeans pocket for his ciga-rettes, he saw Skye pushing her way up the crowded stairs. She was heading in his direction and wearing the stormy expression that, when they were little, always preceded a violent, shrieking temper tantrum.

"Aww, shit," he said with a groan, "here comes my cousin."

"And?"

"She has that look, son."

"Uh-oh. She throwin' blows?"

C.J. nodded, looking very tired.

"Well, I'm out." Black stood up, gave C.J. a pound, and bounced. He was not planning to stick around for the beat-down.

Skye came to a screeching halt right in front of her cousin, all swiveling neck and attitude. Because of the sudden, lethal combination of his atrocious allergies and the overwhelming scent of Skye's Dior Addict perfume, C.J. promptly had a coughing fit.

When he recovered, Skye looked him directly in the eye. "So, how *are* you?"

"Better than a chick that says yes too soon."

"Ha-ha, Kanye." Skye tossed her hair and got down to business. "Okay, C.J., why am I pissed at you?"

"What, is that a rhetorical question? You're always pissed at me."

"So, you're telling me I have no reason to be pissed, is that it?"

"Spit it out, cuz. I ain't got time for your neurotic shenanigans."

"How *could* you?" She threw her hands in the air, totally exasperated. "How could you tell her you loved her, C.J.? Do you know what that did to her? What the hell were you thinking?"

C.J.'s stomach hit the floor. "Hold up, *what*? Were you there?"

"I didn't need to be there. She texted me two seconds after you left. Honestly, could you *be* more irresponsible? What are you gonna do now, break up with Izzy? Be Tangie's boyfriend? You know you have no attention span and can't even *spell* commitment, so why put it in her head?"

"First of all, whatchu know about me and Tangie? No one knows her better than me."

"Please, C.J. If you really knew her, you'd know that she's loved you since we were eleven fucking years old. She's never liked anybody else, and . . ."

"Whatever, man. What about wusshisname, Pete?"

"Have you ever met him? Yeah, neither have I. He's a total excuse, you idiot, a reason to keep you at arm's length. Because as long as Tangie has a man in her back pocket, then she has no right to flip out over your hos. Get it? God, guys are *so* ignorant."

C.J. was speechless. Was this true? "But if she supposedly feelin' me, then why would she make up some guy to throw me off? And how come she shut me down when I tried to holler?"

"Because she's *terrified*, C.J. Basically, she feels safer loving you from afar than going there and having it blow up in her face."

"What's she so scared of, though? I don't . . ."

"She's scared that you'd cheat on her, or leave her, or something. Come on, you're, like, the biggest playa anybody knows. And she doesn't want to be one of C.J.'s many hos."

"But she knows . . ."

"And the Izzy thing makes her feel worse, because she can't tell herself she's just a dumb slut. She really likes her. I mean, I don't get it, I heard she's like a teenage Karrine Steffans, but whatever." Skye took a deep breath. She'd been ranting at her cousin for a full five minutes. "Listen, Tangie's not a girl you can mess around with unless you really, really mean it. You can't lead Tangie on like that, she's not as . . . well, experienced as we are."

"How you know I didn't mean it?"

"Hello? *Izzy!*"

"And what? If Tangela had heard me, I'da never gone there with Izzy. But she didn't. Listen, I don't believe any of this nonsense. Did Tangie tell you this?"

"Well, no, but she didn't have to. I just know. I'm very . . . um, what's the word? Oh: *perceptive*." Skye stuck her nose in the air and flipped her carefully curled Jessica Alba wings over a shoulder. "My point is, stay away from Tangie. Unless you're willing to become a goddamn monk—no hos, no *nothing*—I don't want to see you anywhere near her. She's too good for you. Do we understand each other?"

He snorted, pretending to ignore her.

She looked him up and down. C.J. was wearing Pharrell Williams's expensive, fly-as-hell Ice Cream sneakers. "Okay that's the third pair of Ice Creams I've seen you rock in the past week. How the hell did you afford all those kicks?"

"How you think?"

"And that's another thing. I don't want Tangie around all your drugs and hustlin' and whatever. It's not her."

C.J. glared at Skye for a moment and then sighed, reaching for a cigarette. "You know what? How 'bout you take all this energy and worry about the fact that your last man dumped you for an Internet freak? And you know I sell to take care of Grandma and her bills. It ain't like ya'll are chipping in." He stuck the Newport in his mouth and lit it. "Do we understand each other?"

"Who told you that?" hissed Skye, her cheeks burning an angry maroon. *No one* knew that Justin, the NYU sophomore she'd hooked up with over the summer, had traded her in for a *King* model he had met on MySpace. Humiliated, she yanked the Olsen-size Gucci shades off the top of her head and slid them down over her eyes. Her public couldn't see her that shaken.

"It ain't important," said C.J. with a smirk. Kamillah was the one who had told him (he supposed she was good for something). "Listen, I'm busy. I gotta go make Tangie my girlfriend and then cheat on her with a bunch of cheap sluts. Good talk, Cuz."

C.J. moved to walk away, but then abruptly stopped in his tracks. "Mother-*fuck*!"

"What?" snapped Skye, whipping around to see what he was looking at. And then her jaw hit the ground. Pulling up in front of the school was the hugest Phantom Rolls anyone had ever seen. The car was steadily vibrating with the bass from Smoove's new joint, "Who Said Your Mom Could Ride?" A mesmerized hush settled over the crowd. Who was this cat? C.J. squinted, trying in vain to peer through the windows, but they were opaque.

After a couple of moments the back door finally opened. Those in the crowd held their breath.

Surrounded by a thick cloud of weed smoke, Eden Carmichael

emerged from the car, clearly dressed in her walk-of-shame party ensemble from the night before. But that wasn't all.

None other than a blinged-out, smoked-out Smoove Killah himself poked his head out of the car. And when Eden bent down to give him a kiss in plain view of the entire Armstrong population, it would go down as one of the juiciest gossip moments in the school's history. Eden Carmichael and Smoove Killah were as A-list as you could get.

Of course, not everyone was delighted by the new power couple. Watching them from Union Square Park on the other side of the street, Trey Stevens was shaking with fury. He pulled his hoodie down low over his face and stormed away from his usual harem of dance groupies, too mortified to look anyone in the eye. How could Eden punk him like that? Everyone knew Eden Carmichael belonged to Trey Stevens—whether they were together or not. And now she was making a joke out of them both by pimping herself out to a hood-rich thug (albeit a platinum-selling hood-rich thug) like Smoove Killah? Well, whatever. If she'd moved on that quickly, then so would he.

And he already knew how, and when, and with whom.

Name: Cedric James "C.J." Parker
Class: Sophomore
Major: Fine Art
Self-Awareness Session #: CP 2

Ever since I was a shorty, I was into taggin', you know? Graffiti. Three of the buildings in my grandma's project got me all over it. That's what I'm known for. I mean, I'm known for other shit, too, but this is what I'm proud of. When I was growin' up, dudes on the block called me Donatello. I used to think they were naming me after a Teenage Mutant Ninja Turtle. I just wanna leave my mark, you feel me? I been watching that old eighties flick, Style Wars, *over and over, just really studying those graffiti pioneers, like Lee and Mico, even Jean-Michel Basquiat. I want my shit hanging in MOMA one day, like them cats. I think I'm that good. Folks think graffiti's some ghetto shit, but really it's legit art.*

Of course it is. So, Mr. Parker, have you talked to Financial Aid yet this year?

Don't need to. I handle mine. Listen, I got mad expenses. My grandma's insurance ain't enough to cover her medical bills and prescriptions, let alone the rent. That's why I do what I do.

And what is that?

I work. I hustle. Everybody's got a hustle, don't they?

16.
UNSIGNED HYPE

FALL FLING, OCTOBER 23RD-29TH
ATTENTION STUDENTS:

....

1) General Fall Fling tryouts are scheduled for two weeks from this Friday, starting at 12PM. There's no truth to the rumor that all students are automatically guaranteed a spot—you must try out!!

2) Spotlight tryouts are at 7AM the same day. This is a closed audition! Based on your performances this week, your department teachers will select a handful of students to audition for Spotlight (each grade has only three Spotlights per dept. major). The list will be posted this Saturday in the courtyard.

3) Break a leg, folks—remember you're all stars and there's no such thing as too much practice!!!

The hell there isn't, thought Tangie, massaging her sore calf muscle. She was standing in the middle of Armstrong's bustling front lobby, studying the flyer tacked to the wall. The night before, after C.J. had left, she'd been so distracted and delirious that she'd ended up marking Ms. Carmen's routine until three thirty in the morning (at which point Mariska had screamed at her to "make radio *off!*"). But how could she possibly have slept after having been completely ravaged by the love of her life? Oh, had anyone ever had a sexier kiss? Maybe Kristin and Steven on *Laguna Beach* (on the first season, when they were superpassionate; not after she bitched him, her senior year), but that was it.

C.J. said he loved me, she thought giddily, smiling to herself. *He loves me, he loves me!* All morning long, she'd been replaying every last detail of the night in her head. Everything had come out—how they felt about each other, why they were fighting, everything. There was nothing to hide anymore! For the first time in their relationship, Tangie and C.J. each knew exactly what the other was thinking.

She knew why. It was that kiss. *That kiss!* Every time she remembered it, a zillion little tingles burned through her body and she got all dizzy. The way he looked at her, the way he touched her—God, he kissed so good. If they hadn't been so rudely interrupted by Mariska, Tangie seriously doubted she could've maintained her virginity status. *Omigod, I'm sweating out my roots,* she thought, sheepishly fingering her frizzy-as-hell curls, feeling as though everyone in the crowded lobby could tell she was all hot and bothered.

She just wished she knew what was up. Like, officially.

Did last night mean that they were a couple now? That he wanted to be with her, instead of Izzy? *Girl, stop tripping,* she thought, trying to pull herself together. *What C.J. and I have is so special—it's not like it's just some random hookup.*

"Tangie! Omigod, *Tangie!*"

She whipped her head around and saw Kamillah rushing toward her, clutching a tattered magazine. With her black-and-white striped leggings, she looked like a very fly zebra in a mad rush.

Panting, Kamillah grabbed her chest to catch her breath. "What it do, baby? I've been looking all over for everybody. Where's Skye and Regina?"

"I don't know where Regina is, but Skye was supposed to meet me here, under the Fall Fling flyer, and . . ."

"Cool, cool. Listen, mama's got some serious news. I wanted to wait till we were all together, but *I just can't!*" Kamillah started jumping up and down, her gorgeous, waist-length cornrows bouncing around like a handful of miniature jump ropes. "It's so good, it's so good, it's so good!"

"What is it? Who's it about?"

"Wait, let me pull it together. Come on, Kami, work it out, bitch, work it out." She took a deep breath and fanned her hand in front of her face. "First of all, let me say that you're really working the Armstrong bunhead look to the *fullest*. You finally got it! Love the torn sweatshirt over the leotard and . . ."

"Kamillah, what happened?" Tangie was starting to get nervous. Was this about her?

Slamming the magazine in Tangie hands, Kamillah said, "Okay, are you ready? This is an old issue of *The Source* that Black found in his archives—read the Unsigned Hype column. This ish is bangin-in-your-head mad crazy, yo!"

Whatever that meant.

Letting her oversize practice tote slip to the floor, Tangie scanned the page until she got to the Unsigned Hype column (the cult-favorite section where *The Source*'s editors profiled a talented group or artist that had yet to sign a deal). She couldn't imagine what Kamillah was so amped about.

After making a buzz in underground hip-hop clubs in the tristate area for a minute (and becoming a favorite among decidedly non-underground fans like 50 Cent and Roc-A-Fella on-the-comeup,

Beanie Siegal), the eclectic New Jersey rap outfit Backpackz & Beatz has recently gained a larger level of notoriety with the addition of a funky-as-hell songstress. Miss Aziza, an eighteen-year-old Ethiopian American, solidifies B&B's stage presence with her street-savvy hooks and a whirling dervish energy far more sophisticated than her years. With moves like Ciara, pipes like Mary J., and a boho street-punk style à la early Madonna, this exotic alto is most definitely poised to take the Fugees and Roots-influenced group to a level of national importance. Word is, Miss Aziza wrote a hefty chunk of their latest demo—and not just the hooks, either. And if the public's reaction at the recent Rap Olympics to hilarious, brilliantly produced tracks like "Get Off My Couch," and "Why'd You Ask My Mom for a Twenty?" is any indication, then Backpackz & Beatz has got hip-hop's next superstar on their hands (five gets you twenty that she'll be solo before she can legally drink).

Tangie let out an uncontrollably high-pitched yelp, deeply offending the two voice majors practicing their chords next to her ("Let's hear this bitch try to hit a perfect high C before her morning Red Bull shot," one of them muttered, nastily).

"What the hell?" Tangie couldn't believe it! Izzy was in a band that had gotten written up in *The Source*? And wait—just how old was she?

"I know, right?!" squealed Kamillah, shamelessly thrilled with the drama of the situation. She lived for this kind of stuff. "It's, like, crazy-insane ill! Your girl's had a *whole. Other. Life.*"

"But, but—how old is she?" Tangie stammered, not even sure what she was trying to say. "I don't get it, I just don't get it."

"Okay, the issue is from last year. She's a freshman now, so she would've been in eighth grade—which would've made her thirteen when the article came out." Kamillah bit her bottom lip, lost in concentration. "How could she pass for an eighteen-year-old at *thirteen*, yo? Did she tell 'em that mess? Or is she lying to us?"

"I just . . . I don't know what to think." Tangie shook her head, completely shell-shocked. Even though she had just met Izzy, she couldn't help feeling a little duped. But that was stupid, wasn't it? No one immediately spilled *all* her secrets to a total stranger.

"Oh, I know what to think," said Kamillah, her eyes flashing with excitement. "I'm saying, now you gotta wonder if all those G-Unit rumors are true, right? The article says Fiddy's a fan—d'you see that?"

Tangie nodded. She saw that.

"She had to have lied about her age in the band. Because that girl don't look like nobody's eighteen. Which makes me wonder what else she's lying about. She lied to them; has she lied to us?" Kamillah planted her hands on her hips and shook her head. "I don't know, T-Nizzle, I kinda feel like she's not to be trusted."

Tangie looked at Kamillah, slightly irritated. Why did she feel the need to defend Izzy, a girl she hardly knew?

A girl who was currently getting down with her soul mate.

"There's gotta be an explanation, right? I mean, we all have our secrets and Izzy maybe doesn't feel like going there, yet. Maybe she's scared folks'll be jealous because she's already been successful in the industry. I mean, she's done what everyone here's *trying* to do."

"What, you think she's the only Armstrong-ette that's had some shine?" Kamillah did not like the suggestion that Izzy was any hotter than she and her friends were. "Look at Skye and Eden!"

"Well, I don't know, maybe she just doesn't want to big herself up," Tangie interrupted, tired of talking about this with Kamillah. She wanted to get the story from Izzy, herself, rather than stand there and gossip about her. "It's really none of our business."

"You *really* think it's none of our business?" Kamillah asked in a sickeningly sneaky tone, her eyes narrowing. "Come on, now."

Tangie's breath caught in her throat. "What's that supposed to mean?"

"Oh nothing, it's just that, well—Skye told us about you and C.J.'s history."

"Our history?"

"Yeah, you know, your whole 'we-pretend-we're-just-friends-but-everybody-knows-we're-fronting' thing." Kamillah leaned in toward Tangie. "I mean, I can only imagine how you must feel, knowing he and Izzy are, like, messing or whatever."

"*Excuse* me? Wait, I . . ."

"And especially after what happened between you two last night."

Tangie wanted to die.

"I mean, you ain't gotta fake it in front of me," Kamillah said, lowering her voice to a just-between-friends whisper. "I know we don't know each other all like that, but you and Skye are BFF, which to me means you're automatically down. So you can tell me, like, *anything.*"

"Good to know," said Tangie through clenched teeth, her cheeks burning. She handed Kamillah back her magazine and grabbed her bag off the floor. "Um, I gotta go."

"Omigod, I upset you with all that Izzy shit," she blurted out, dramatically throwing up her arms. "Look, if it's any consolation, I think she and C.J. look crazy together, 'cause he's so damn tall and she's, like, a dwarf? I mean, she looks like something he plucked off his foot with some tweezers."

"Kamillah . . ."

"I have such a big damned mouth!"

"It's okay, you can't help it," muttered Tangie, walking away from her as fast as she could without actually sprinting. She didn't even know what direction she was going in; she just had to go. Kamillah was shady. She was dying for Tangie to say she was jealous of C.J. and Izzy so she could tell everyone! And what the hell had Skye told her friends about her? Were they looking at her thinking, *Poor clueless Tangie, she's pressed for a boy who couldn't care less?* How infuriating—before she'd gotten a chance really to get to know Skye's friends, they'd already decided who she was.

Maybe Kamillah was right. Maybe Izzy wasn't to be trusted. And maybe Tangie was just being naive, pretending she wasn't jealous because Izzy and C.J. had hooked up (*were* hooking up?). It *did* bother her. Before, Tangie had told herself that she didn't have a right to be angry with Izzy, because she had no real claim to C.J. But after the previous night, things were different.

Tangie was so deep in thought she barely heard her name being called until she ran smack into the source, almost knocking her over.

"Whoa! Slow down, babe!" Laughing, Izzy bent down to help Tangie pick up her books. Meanwhile, everyone in the hallway craned their necks to get a look at the outrageously cool-looking black girl with the faux-hawk and the T-shirt reading WHAT HAD HAPPENED WAS . . .

"So, what's good with you, Tangie Adams?" Izzy saw Tangie's expression and frowned. "You look like something's wrong."

"Me? No, I'm fine." Tangie's voice was cold. "Just sore—I practiced for five hours last night after I did my homework."

"Wait, we had homework?" Academics weren't a priority for her. "Yo, what's your girl's name? The one with the cornrows and the dashiki?"

"Kamillah." Tangie tried to sound bored.

"Earlier, she came up to me and randomly asked what year I was born. What the hell was that all about?"

"No clue." Tangie shrugged, rolling her eyes.

"That girl has mad issues. She's the one with the boyfriend, Negritude, right? Wait, no, Blackadocious." Izzy giggled. "I'm sorry, that'll *always* be funny, yo."

"I know, right?" Tangie said, slightly annoyed that she wanted to giggle, too.

"So, um, not to change the subject or anything," started Izzy, while doing precisely that, "but, yesterday in the park . . . was there mad tension between you and C.J., or was I just high as shit?"

"Tension? No, we're cool," Tangie answered quickly. "Why? What did it seem like?"

"I don't know, but I sensed beef between y'all two. What, is he some shady motherfucker and I just ain't figured it out yet? You can tell me, I won't be pissed."

"Um, yeah. I mean, no!" Beads of sweat popped out on Tangie's upturned nose. She paused, wanting to choose her words very carefully. "He isn't shady. We've, um, been friends since we were kids, and we had this whole, stupid falling out. But we're cool now. Why, did he . . ." she began, her stomach flip-flopping. "Did he say something about me?"

"No, I was just wondering," Izzy said, chewing on her bottom lip. Then she paused and took a deep breath. "Just so you know? I know what folks are saying about me, but it's nonsense. Lies."

"People are talking about you?" Tangie raised her eyebrows, trying to look surprised by the suggestion. "I haven't heard anything."

"Come on, T. I've moved around, like, a lot—eight times since kindergarten. I know how bitches are with the New Girl, especially when she's somebody like me."

What did she mean, someone *like her*? Just then, Tangie desperately wanted to grill Izzy, force her to come clean about everything— The *Source* article, the starving-Ethiopian infomercials, C.J.

"And I don't care what most people say about me," Izzy continued, "but I *do* care what you think."

"Really?" Despite wanting so badly to be mad at her, Tangie couldn't help feeling flattered.

"You're my TMI twin, girl!" Izzy smiled. "Not to be corny, but I'm just glad I met somebody cool. You're so different from the rest of these shallow, vain Armstrong bitches who're too caught up in their image to have a real conversation."

"Yeah, I know what you mean." Tangie looked at her for a long time, her irritation slowly subsiding. She just liked the girl.

"Listen, I'm not a ho," continued Izzy. "I'm really not. And just so you know, I don't, like, just get up with random . . . especially not after . . ." She took a breath, and looked Tangie directly in the eye. "Okay, yes, I do have a past. When I was younger, I made some mistakes, messed with the wrong mothafuckas . . ."

Who, Common?

". . . And now, I'm really not trying to waste my time with foolish boys." Izzy ran her fingers through her gelled faux hawk, looking effortlessly charismatic and sexy.

Okay, Tangie, just be cool, don't ask her about him, she told herself. And then she opened her mouth. "So, um, what about with C.J.?"

"What about with C.J.?"

"Are y'all, like, boyfriend and girlfriend?" So much for being cool.

"No, no, no, not even. We're just chilling." Izzy cocked her head, thinking. "I mean, this summer we were kickin' it, but now it's just a friend thing. It's against my personal philosophy to get too serious, anyway."

"Oh, okay! I thought you guys were together," Tangie giggled, feeling absolutely giddy with relief. She'd gotten herself all worked up over nothing! They hooked up over the summer, when Tangie and C.J. weren't even speaking. That, she could handle. And as for Kamillah's having seen them kissing? Whatever. Tangie would be a fool to believe anything that girl said. She was such a gossip.

Feeling confident that their friendship could be salvaged, Tangie finally relaxed. "So, are you talking to anybody?"

"Mmm. There's this one guy, but I don't know." Izzy sighed, looking past Tangie at nothing. "We got a lot of history—some good, but most of it's bad. He got me in some situations back in the day, but . . . well, whatever. I guess some folks just stick to you, whether you like it or not. Nahmean?"

Tangie nodded. Did she ever.

"But in general, I'm just trying to chill, have fun." Izzy linked her arm inside Tangie's, and the two girls headed off in the direction of their first class. "C.J.'s funny, though, isn't he? Ever since school started he's been mad distracted."

"Please, girl. He's been moody since the fifth grade." Tangie grinned, finally feeling comfortable discussing him with Izzy.

"I think I know how to cheer him up," Izzy said with a giggle. "Listen, if I tell you something, do you promise to keep it a secret?"

"Come on. Do you really need to ask?"

"We have to do a nude portrait for charcoal sketching class, and guess what? I'm posing for him tonight. Crazy, right? I mean, I've posed for artists before, so it ain't a thing . . . but it's hilarious how nervous *he* is!"

Tangie tried to smile, but she had a feeling it came out more like a shaky grimace. She worried that she was going to vomit all over Izzy's scrunchy ankle boots. *No, no, no, no-o-o-o-o!* she screamed inside her head, suddenly feeling as if she were standing in the middle of a tornado, struggling to keep her feet on the ground and not get sucked up, wailing and flailing, into the sky.

Izzy was posing nude for C.J.? That was not a "just friends"–type thing to do. She wanted to be mad at Izzy again, to punch her in the face and ruin her perfectly sexy pierced nose. But, honestly, it wasn't Izzy's fault. It was C.J.'s fault. All Tangie knew was, it was totally shady that he had kissed her the previous night—and so passionately, so convincingly—knowing that he was about to see Izzy naked for hours on end. He had held her in his arms and told her he loved her.

Tangie was a fool for thinking he'd pick her over Izzy.

"What's wrong, ma?" Izzy asked.

Her eyes burning with just-about-to-fall tears, Tangie managed to squawk, "Have you ever been in love?"

"Hell, yeah, something fierce," Izzy nodded, completely oblivious to the fact that right near her, Tangie was struggling not to have a nervous breakdown. "And you know what?"

"No, what?"

"It ain't worth it, girl," Izzy said, with a haunted look. "It hurts. It hurts like shit."

I know, thought Tangie, following her into their classroom. She felt numb. *Believe me, I know.*

Name: Aziza Abdelrashid
Class: Freshman
Major: Fine Art
Self-Awareness Session #: AA 1

So, how are you adjusting to your new environment, Miss Abdelrashid?

It's cool.

Have you shared anything about your past?

Like I really want these pampered showbiz shits to know what happened to me.

Miss Abdelrashid, you'll have to open up if this process is going to work. You have to trust people.

After what happened to me, would you trust people? Look, all I wanted to do was get outta my house. My father, man, he just never understood me. I guess in Ethiopia, girls do what their daddies say, even if they're sadistic dictators who don't know how to keep their mothafuckin' hands to themselves. I guess Ethiopian girls don't watch Ultimate Hustler *on BET, they don't pierce random orifices, and they sure as hell don't run off with their boyfriend's hip-hop band. But I can't help it, I'm a free spirit. And I've always been a sexual person. I own it. Got to, because ever since I developed, practically every male in my life has tried to use me, in some way or another. But I don't let the past mess with me. I love sex, I love my power, and I love the way it feels when I got somebody sprung. But no, I don't trust most people . . . except I have connected with two kids here, C.J. and Tangie. That girl doesn't know how cute she is, for real. I kinda just want to protect her. And C.J.'s a brilliant artist . . . he's also hot to* death. *They have really good, pure hearts and remind me a lot of each other. I actually wonder why they never kicked it.*

17.

GAYER THAN A PINK FEATHER BOA

". . . AND THE THING IS, THESE DAYS, the Hollywood game is all about who you know," Nick whispered to Regina and Skye. They were ten minutes into Stretch Technique class—aka, the most torturous course in the drama department. In Stretch Technique class, drama students learned how to "stretch" their personalities to the limit, temporarily becoming different people. This time, everyone was supposed to pick from a choice of three characters (either an elderly person, a lisping five-year-old, or a stutterer), separate into groups of three, and attempt to have a natural-sounding conversation, in character, while the notoriously sadistic Mr. Johnston made his rounds, publicly tearing everyone's performance to shreds. Basically, it was a nightmare.

So, everyone just pretended to rehearse until it was his or her group's turn to be observed by Mr. Johnston. Nick was feeling especially chatty, excited to have found a kindred spirit at his new school. After bonding at the Harvey Milk support group the night before, he and Regina had ended up hanging out at the Astor Place Starbucks for hours, and then texting all night long (well, after the season premiere of *Lost* ended, anyway). They had a ridiculous amount in common—everything from the immigrant parents thing

(Nick's parents were Greek, while Regina's dad was straight-off-the-boat Filipino), to an obsession with the cult novel *Homo Thug*. It was thrilling, like discovering you had a long-lost twin. The only time Nick and Regina could take a break from the draining task of pretending to be straight was when they were together.

They promised each other, over grande banana coconut frappaccinos, that they'd keep the support group and their true identities a secret forever.

Nick liked Regina so much that he was determined to be nice to her gorgeous but deeply obnoxious friend with the outrageous weave (even though, if truth be told, he did kind of love Skye's bitchy diva 'tude—she was like Nicole Ritchie without the weird-looking ex-fattie DJ boyfriend).

"It's your basic, standard *nepotism*, okay? It's not like back in the eighties, when a starving actor could move to New York, get his SAG card doing a couple Mentos commercials, understudy for an off-off-off-off-Broadway play, and get discovered one day while bussing Robert De Niro's table at Da Silvano."

"Damn," said a mesmerized Skye, her eyes widening. God, Nick got sexier by the second—those aqua-blue eyes, that floppy mop of shiny black curls, that grungy-hipster stilo! And could he *be* any savvier about the industry? "Who did that happen to?"

"Nobody, it's just an example."

"Oh."

"What I'm saying is, it's almost not even about talent anymore."

"I know, just ask Regina," Skye said with a giggle, tossing her hair for Nick's benefit. He didn't laugh—neither did Regina. "Omigod, Geena-Geen, I'm kidding! You know I think you're brilliant."

"Yeah, you really nailed your Southern Playwrights scene last period," said Nick, sticking up for his new friend.

"Thanks," she said, quietly. Regina'd hardly uttered two words since class started. Nick was confused—where was the sassy, chatty, confident girl he gossiped with all night, the most popular girl in

Harvey Milk's support group? *That* Regina would never have let Skye get away with a dis like this—no matter how "just joking" she pretended to be.

"But on the serious tip, I *so* hear what you're saying, Nick." Skye licked her lips and squinted thoughtfully, trying desperately to look intense. "But you'll have an easier time getting castings than us. There are zero roles for black women in TV and film. Like, none."

"But I'd think you wouldn't have a problem, though," he answered, wondering why she kept squinting. Did she need contacts? "Wasn't your sister Kendra on *Family Chatter*?"

Skye looked pale. "Yeah, well, I was up for a role, too, but my mom didn't want two kids in showbiz. Something about our household needing some normalcy, I don't know."

"And you know who her parents are, right?" Seeing Skye's face, Regina wanted to get the subject off her sister. "Her mom played Darla on *Shoulder Pads*, and her dad is Junior Carmichael, the Broadway producer."

"Holy shit, are you serious? Are you *serious*? Dude, that's so fierce!"

Fierce? Thought Skye. *Did he say "fierce"?* Maybe it was a D.C. thing.

". . . So what are you talking about, no roles for black women? You have connections out the ass!"

"Oh, stop, I'm no more connected than anyone else," Skye answered mock humbly, waving him away. She took a deep breath and thrust her chest in Nick's direction. "And no one I know could help the black-chicks-in-Hollywood situation. Leaving out Halle and Angela, look at our black actresses: Nia Long, Kerry Washington, Joy Bryant, Zoe Saldana . . . oh, wait, she's Dominican, isn't she? Well, that's black enough. Anyway, if they're lucky enough to get a big-budget mainstream movie like *Mr. & Mrs. Smith* or *Alfie* or that Kate Hudson horror movie . . ."

"*Skeleton Key.*"

"Right, thanks, Reggie. They always play the supportive best friend, you know? The only other options for us are those embarrassing blaxploitation comedies like *Soul Plane*. I *hate* those!"

Nick flinched, taken aback by the venom in Skye's voice. "A lot of good actors got their start in those low-budget comedies. Jamie Foxx had *Bootie Call*, Halle Berry had *BAPs* . . ."

"Okay, well, what about all those Thug with a Heart of Gold, rapper-turned-actor vanity projects, like *ATL* or *Get Rich or Die Tryin'* or *Waist Deep* or anything starring Snoop or Ice Cube or The Game. Omigod, and let's not forget Tyrese—and Ludacris." Skye rolled her eyes. "Poor, pretty Meghan Good, she's, like, the *queen* of those."

"You're buggin'!'" Nick shook his head, passionately disagreeing. "Between *Crash* and *Hustle & Flow*, Luda's having such an A-list moment, it's, like, not even funny!"

"Well, he's an exception," started Skye, unsure about her argument now.

"And hold up, you can't hate on Cube! *Friday*? *Barbershop*? I mean, they're not gonna sweep Sundance, but these movies are solid entertainment. And some of those hood flicks are true classics."

"I know, I *love* those old-school nineties gangsta films," said Regina, finally exerting some semblance of personality. "Like *Boys 'n the Hood* and *Juice*, and . . ."

"And *Menace II Society*!" Nick perked up, turning his back on Skye to focus on Regina. "That's another actor, Larenz Tate—he's been in some good joints. I mean, *Love Jones* is the best romance ever. Am I right?"

Trying desperately to get his attention back, Skye leaned forward so far in her chair she almost fell over. "I guess *Love Jones* is kinda cute, but . . ."

"Omigod, I live for *Love Jones*!" Regina gave his shoulder an enthusiastic squeeze to punctuate her point, and Nick grabbed his heart in ecstasy. Skye's mouth dropped open in horror—what the hell was *happening*? "And what about *Dead Presidents*? Larenz acted the shit out of that."

"Dude."

"God, whatever happened to N'Bushe Wright?" Regina wondered.

"I don't know, man," Nick began, looking at Regina as if she were the only girl in the room. "Was she in *A Bronx Tale?*"

"No," said Regina. "That was Taral Hicks."

"Speaking of *A Bronx Tale*, did you hear the main kid just got arrested for murder? I think he did guest spots on *The Sopranos* a couple times, right?" Regina and Nick were on a roll—that was how their conversation had been the previous night at Starbucks. It had been all over the place, the words spilling out uncontrollably, as if they had had a lifetime to catch up on.

"Regina, where'd you come from all of a sudden? I never even knew you watched those ghetto movies." Skye was fuming. What was Regina's problem? Why was she trying to soak up all the shine in the room? She *knew* Skye was trying to kick it to Nick, and now she was cock-blocking—which was so unlike her!

Shrugging, Regina answered, "Some of those movies really have a lot of artistic merit. They're not ghetto. You should watch sometime."

"She's right, Skye." Nick gave Regina a private, playful look. "You know what? I think your friend's definitely a film snob."

"Omigod, I am not! Nick, you're so bad," Skye said, laughing a little too hard, smacking him on his arm. *I'm losing control over this situation fast*, she thought, panicking a little. Didn't he think she was hot? Why was he all over Regina? It didn't make any sense—fine, Regina was sorta cute, in that brown-skinned-with-Asian-eyes way that always made a fantastic video ho, but Skye was *beautiful*. And sexy, and talented, and easily the best-dressed sophomore girl (okay, Kamillah was a tad funkier . . . but Skye had better shoes).

I'll just have to try harder, she thought. Licking her lips, she tilted her chin down and looked up at Nick through her lashes (a tip she had learned from years of watching Eden deal with their dad). "You know, I loved your stutter during Stretch exercises. No one would know it was your first year at Armstrong."

"Thanks," he said, used to receiving compliments on his acting. At Duke Ellington, he'd played the emcee in *Cabaret* and brought the house down. "So, I'm curious—why does someone who's been on a top-ten prime-time show, had a publicist and an agent and all that, even need to go to a performing arts school?"

"Oh, I don't know," sighed Skye, gazing off into the distance and trying to look pensive. "I guess one can never stop developing one's craft."

Nick looked at her for a moment, then glanced at Regina and burst out laughing. And then Regina collapsed into giggles. She knew it would definitely piss Skye off, but she couldn't help it.

"What's funny?" Skye's cheeks turned bright red, and her hands formed tiny fists at her sides.

"Nothing, nothing," said Nick, trying to keep a straight face. "We just think it's hilarious when actors say stuff like, 'my craft.' It's so James Lipton on *Inside the Actors Studio*."

"Oh. *Ohhh*." Skye threw her head back and erupted in a laugh faker than TomKat's relationship. "You didn't think I was *serious*, did you? Omigod, I was totally joking. 'My craft.' *Please*! Listen, I really don't take this acting shit that seriously. I mean, I *do* have a life outside drama."

Just then, Mr. Johnston sashayed over to their group, his curly, wet, gray ponytail trailing behind him. Without missing a beat, they transformed themselves into their assigned characters.

"Oooh, my po', achin' back!" exclaimed Skye, doubled over in her chair, leaning on an invisible cane.

"S—s—s—sorry, m—ma'am. I w—wasn't p—paying att—tt—ttention," said Nick, squeezing his eyes together in concentration as he attempted to sound out every consonant.

"Thutup, thtupid, *thtupid*!" Regina punctuated each "thtupid" by slamming her fists down on her thigh.

"My God, stop, please! Stop the madness," hollered Mr. Johnston, clutching his head. Everyone in class looked up from their groups to see who he was torturing now. "You people are giving me a massive migraine. Listen, Stretch class is all about *stretching* your personality, becoming someone eons away from who you are. Right now, you three sound exactly like Nick, Skye, and Regina—after a couple of Quaaludes."

The three looked at each other, stumped. What was a Quaalude?

"Honestly, Skye, I expected more out of you," said Mr. Johnston, continuing his tirade. "You did win the freshman Stretch competition last year, didn't you? And your sister, Eden—didn't she play Lady Macbeth in *Macbeth* in the last spring festival? Now, that was some stretch."

Skye sighed and nodded, almost visibly shrinking before everyone's eyes. *Poor Skye*, thought Regina, wanting to give her a hug.

"Well, then, why do all your elderly ladies sound like *Driving Miss Daisy*? And Regina, you have *way* too much spit in your mouth."

Regina quickly swallowed, her cheeks turning red.

"Just so everyone knows, drama auditions for Fall Fling's sophomore night *will* consist of a Stretch scene," he announced, addressing the class. "So, make sure you get this right, actors, because your future depends on it. Now, Skye, I want you to close your eyes. *Feel* the age in your bones. *Feel* the arthritis, the nonexistent sex drive, the smell of Icy Hot. Do you smell it?"

Skye closed her eyes. "I smell it."

"Do you taste the *sourness* of your dentures?"

Skye felt nauseous. "Check."

"Good, now step to the front and give me a monologue in character. Let's show the class why you won the competition last year."

Looking him squarely in the eye, she stood up, threw her

shoulders back and glided to the front of the room. So it was true, what all the upperclassmen had said about Mr. Johnston. He was famous for putting his students on the spot, making them perform at the most random, unpredictable times. His big thing was that actors should always, always, always be prepared to "turn it on." And it only made sense that the first student he picked was Skye, the girl who everyone knew—whether they liked it or not—had more talent in her little finger than all the actors in their grade put together.

Once in front of the class, Skye took a deep breath and exhaled, trying to find her center. It was important to be fully relaxed before taking on a character, but for some reason, Skye felt blocked today. She was usually so good at channeling! *Come on, girl*, she told herself. *Concentrate! Just remember the "As If" exercise you learned in Characterization class, freshman year. Mr. Johnston wants to test me? Fine, I'll act the hell out of this character.*

Skye took a breath and started whispering, "as if" she were an old woman lying on her hospital bed, floating in and out of a morphine-induced haze; reassuring her vigil-sitting daughter that yes, yes, indeed, she was a good daughter. The best kind an old woman could ever, ever hope for.

Meanwhile, Nick was very disturbed. "Why do you let Skye talk to you like that?" he whispered to Regina. "Dude, she's such a shallow bitch."

"Don't say that," Regina said under her breath, her eyes fixed on Skye. When she performed, it was as though no one else were in the room. "You just don't know her. She has a lot of pressures—her mother's an alcoholic lunatic, her sister's addicted to pills. I mean, her life sucks. Honestly, when it's just me and her, she's amazing." She sighed, realizing she barely even believed herself anymore. "She's different when we're alone. No one understands."

Nick looked at her, his expression softening. Regina was in love with this girl, and there was nothing anyone could say to change that. "Wow, it's like that, huh? You're, like, gone for her."

She nodded, sadly. "Please don't tell . . ."

"Come on, girl, I think we're a little beyond that. You're the only one in school that knows I'm a big old fairy. It's safe to say I'm keeping your secret."

Regina smiled.

"But if you want my opinion, you could do a hell of a lot better. She shits on you, Regina. She really does. And you're better than that."

It was the second time since school had started that someone had pointed out how badly Skye treated her. Sighing, she thought about this. Did he have a point? Skye *was* shitty to her, a lot of the time.

A perfect example: during freshman year, Skye wore a ridiculous pair of super-high stilettos to school, during a snowstorm. And in front of the crowd waiting outside for the first bell to ring, she slipped and fell face first into a slushy snow puddle. When she pulled herself together, humiliated and soaking wet, she turned to Regina and yelled, "Look, I know you have a crush on Vineet, but every time you see him, you don't have to jump all over me and knock me on my ass! Control yourself, *please*." It was such a ridiculous attempt to take the attention off herself—not only was Regina humiliated, but Vineet's girlfriend tried to kick her ass during lunch (and of course, Skye was nowhere to be found).

And then there was the time, during the summer, when she overheard Skye patiently breaking down their clique to a soon-to-be Armstrong freshman they had met in the Hamptons. She said that every Popular Girl like her needed a sidekick who was pretty, but slightly *less* pretty than herself—like Regina—to truly complement her sexiness. To make matters worse, Skye had then pointed to Kristen Cavalleri and her big-nosed friend Alex H., as their *Laguna Beach* counterparts. Regina was furious. How could Skye compare Regina to mousy Alex H.? That girl had *never* had a man, and she always seemed awkwardly tomboyish next to the other girls. (*Oh, no,*

Regina had thought at the time, *maybe I* am *Alex H.*!)

Frankly, Regina was tired of always being the understanding friend, taking Skye's abuse and making excuses for her. So what if her home life sucked? Whose didn't? Nick was right, she *was* better than that.

Lost in thought, Regina barely noticed the end-of-class bell sounding. She snapped back to attention when Nick gave her a good-bye kiss on the cheek, promising to text her later. Seconds later, Skye dragged her out into the hallway.

"Regina Marie Evangeline Leon Guerrero, what the hell's gotten into you? You *know* I like Nick; how could you throw yourself at him like that? You were all over him! It was so embarrassing I can't *even*! And hold up, how do you even *know* him so well? I asked you to research him, not *rape* him! I mean, I thought we were *girls*, Regina! Since when do you like white guys, anyway? You said you thought hipster boys looked *homeless*, and . . ."

As Skye stood there, yelling at her, Regina's eyes began to glaze over. She could barely even hear her anymore. And then she had an epiphany.

This was bullshit. Yeah, she loved Skye—she couldn't help that—but Regina didn't have to take this. That's when it hit her.

"Actually, Skye," she started, interrupting her tirade. "Nick was just telling me how much he liked you."

Finally, *finally*, Skye stopped talking. "Get out."

"I'm serious. He told me he wanted to step to you, but he didn't think you'd take him seriously." She shrugged. "And I told him about your party on Friday, and he's all over it."

"Shut up!"

"It's true, he's really feeling you. Go get your man, girl."

Skye jumped up and down, hugging Regina so tight her gum popped out of her mouth. "I love you so much; you're the best friend ever, ever, ever."

If Regina felt even the tiniest bit of regret for purposefully encouraging Skye to throw herself at a guy gayer than a pink feather boa, it faded away when she realized Skye hadn't even bothered to apologize for yelling at her.

Serves her right.

Name: Nikolas Vardolas
Class: Sophomore
Major: Drama
Self-Awareness Session #: NV 1

You don't have to come prepared, Mr. Vardolas. Think of this as a stream-of-consciousness conversation.

This is kinda weird. I still don't really get why we have to do these little sessions, but, hey, I'm open to new things. Let's see. I miss my ex-man, Raheim, in D.C. I'm wearing my hair longer than usual; it's a little too floppy-hipster-soccer-boy for my taste, but I've been getting positive feedback. Generally, I try to be a happy person. I really like it here, actually. I met some supercute girls in my Southern Playwrights class. You know, tons of style, great hair, just fly as shit. Skye reminds me of Tyra before she began retaining water. . . . You know, those fabulous green-hazel eyes and the honey-amber weave? But she should slow down a little with the Pussycat Dolls ensembles. And I adore Regina. She looks like a cross between Amerie and Kimora, but less glam, you know, more earthy. Total dyke, but she has yet to embrace it.

SHIT! I wasn't supposed to say anything. You swear to God this is confidential?

18.

TUTOR WITH BENEFITS

TANGIE WAS READY FOR HER TUTORING SESSION; all warmed up and stretched out, and dressed in her regulation dance rehearsal outfit of black footless tights, a black tank leotard, and pink ballet slippers. To look less bootylicious, she'd slipped on some supershort warm-up shorts, rolling down the elastic waistband twice for a more hip-hugging fit (that way, they accentuated what she thought was her best feature—her flat tummy). She was ready, but where the hell was Trey?

They were supposed to meet in Ms. Carmen's studio right after school, but seventh period had ended twenty minutes ago. *Dear God, please don't let him stand me up,* Tangie thought, nervously fiddling with the huge, curly bun on top of her head and pacing back and forth. She stopped to check her watch, deciding that Trey had five more minutes before he was officially an asshole.

Sighing, she resumed her nervous pacing in front of the huge, wall-to-ceiling mirror before accidentally catching a glimpse of herself in the mirror. She stopped again and twisted from side to side, examining the circumference of her butt. *Okay, I've been dieting for a day now,* she mused, furrowing her brow. *When will I notice a difference?* If truth be told, she didn't look too hideous in a leotard, but naked? Naked was a different story.

And then she froze, remembering. *Naked.* Izzy was posing naked for C.J. tonight. It was the first time Tangie had thought about it in fifteen minutes. All day long, C.J. had been texting her, but she'd ignored him. He didn't know she knew about the nude portrait, and she didn't feel like hearing what he had to say. Finally, during seventh period, she'd forced herself to dance hard—so hard that everything else was shut out of her mind. Until now.

How could C.J. play her like that? How could he declare his love for her and her alone—when he knew all along he was going to have sex with Izzy that night? (oh, sorry, he was going to sit there, like a good boy, while she got naked "in the name of art." *Please.*) Everything she'd hoped was true was a lie. She *wasn't* different from his other girls. If she were, he would've deaded the Izzy thing the second he left her house the night before! Tangie didn't want C.J. under those terms. She wasn't trying to share. And she was not going to be made a fool of.

Nothing like a tutoring session with a virtual god to let C.J. know what's up, thought Tangie. She tried to smile at her reflection in the mirror, but came up short. Who was she fooling? She was devastated.

"Girl, whatchu smilin' at?"

Jerked out of a trance, Tangie spun around to find Trey leaning in the doorway, a duffle bag thrown over his shoulder.

"Omigod, you scared me!" She grabbed her chest, exhaling and giggling a little. "How long have you been standing there?"

"Long enough," he said, flinging his bag on the floor. Taking his time, he walked over to her and, without hesitation, pulled her into a full-body hug. "What it do, girl? You lookin' good."

His chest and arms were muscular and hard, but he was just a couple of inches taller than Tangie, which felt a little odd (she was used to C.J.'s hugs—he was so tall that she felt like a teeny-tiny, ultra-protected thing with him, which she loved). Tangie was mildly shocked that her presence warranted such a big bear hug, as if she had been a long-lost friend he hadn't seen in, like, five years. But, not knowing how else to react, she went with it. After they had swayed back and forth a couple of times—awkwardly, she thought—Trey finally released her. And Tangie released a very tiny sigh of relief. She just wasn't ready for the object of her wildest pubescent fantasies to become so, well, *real*.

"I'm good. I was just, well, I was wondering if maybe I had the wrong day? Or time?" Tangie instantly regretted saying this. Could she have been more uncool? She sounded way too eager, as if she'd been counting down the minutes until Trey showed up.

"Why?"

"Oh, no reason. Really, no reason."

"Hold up, we ain't said we'd meet after school?" Trey looked sincerely confused, as if it honestly hadn't hit him that school had ended half an hour earlier.

"Yeah, yeah, yeah! No, it's fine. Anyway . . ."

"Oh, you mean 'cause I was late?" Trey waved his hand in front of his face, as if to say, *Aww girl, I'm too high-post to be worried about insignificant nonsense like time.* "Look, I gotta get outta here. You tryin'-a bounce?"

Was it Tangie, or was this conversation getting more and more awkward by the second? "But . . . I thought we were gonna practice. If not, that's okay, I mean, you're a senior, and I'm sure you're, like, mad busy. . . ."

"You're cute. No, you really are." He grinned, tweaking her nose between his index finger and his thumb. Again, Tangie was taken aback—by how casually comfortable his gestures were. He acted as if they'd been hanging out forever. "Of course we're gonna practice. I ain't the nigga to go back on my word. I said I'm your tutor, and I'm your tutor. No, I meant let's go somewhere else to practice."

"Oh! Like where?"

"My house." He grinned. "My moms used to run a dance

company, back in the day. And she had the living room built into a little studio so she could teach private lessons."

"Really? I've never seen a New York apartment big enough to fit a studio." Tangie's heart was beating too fast; she was nervous about going to his house. He did understand that they were just training, right? She hoped she hadn't given him the wrong impression.

"Yeah, well, it ain't an apartment. It's a four-story brownstone. In Brooklyn Heights."

Tangie had never known anyone to live in all four floors of a brownstone—they went for at least a million dollars! In New York, those old Victorian brownstones were usually separated into single-family apartments on each floor, like where Tangie lived. Even Skye's family lived in an apartment, and her parents were famous.

"Wow, that's impressive," she said, wondering why everything she said sounded naive and immature.

"Whatever, man. My pop's the district attorney, nahmean? So he's working with crazy-insane change."

She nodded, fresh out of things to say. Trey was unbelievably sexy, but his ridiculously forced gangsta-speak was starting to make him less godlike to Tangie (she cut him some slack, though, figuring it must be hell on your ego to be a straight male dancer in a gay male world). Which was a good thing, because she was finally able to relax a bit.

"So, you tryin'a do this thing, girl?"

"Yeah, let's go. I just have to be home by eight o'clock for dinner."

He grinned, comfortably throwing his arm around her shoulders and walking her over to the door. "Not a problem, ma. I got you. Trust me."

C.J. was shook up. He was way too cool to show it, but the fact that Tangie hadn't responded to any of his text messages that day was really messing with him. And he hadn't seen her all day—she wasn't chilling in Union Square Park with her girls at lunch; she wasn't hanging by her locker during break. Was it Skye? *If she said something to Tangie about my alleged "playa status," I'll force-feed her a Krispy Kreme*, he thought, hurrying up the now almost-empty stairs leading to the dance wing. He had to get to Tangie before she left for the day; she had to know how he felt.

It didn't make any sense—as soon as they started talking again, they stopped talking again. For the first time, C.J. felt as if he and Tangie were in the same place at the same time. He hadn't planned that moment in her room; it had happened because it was *supposed* to happen. His mind going all over the place, he made his way down the dance wing's never-ending hall, stopping every five seconds to peer into each studio window.

Just when he was going to give up, he spotted her walking out of a studio up ahead. But she wasn't alone.

Some guy had his arm wrapped around her shoulders and was whispering in her ear. And then, in the worst wannabe-gangsta display C.J.'d ever seen, the guy looked back at the studio door, gave his chest a pound, kissed his fist and threw up a peace sign. And Tangie giggled.

Trey Stevens.

But the worst part? Even from all the way down the hall, C.J. saw her smiling. He clenched his hands in fists, and he gritted his teeth in disgust. Tangie was hollering at Trey Stevens? *Trey Stevens?*

Tangie must've felt C.J.'s eyes boring holes in her head, because all of a sudden, she glanced behind her. For a millisecond they both froze, and then Tangie looked ahead again, turning the corner with Trey.

C.J. left the building stunned, in a daze. He wondered if last night—hell, the past five years—had even meant anything. What was the point of Tangie's even saying she loved him, if she was hollering at Trey? For the first time in his life he felt played.

And that shit was not cool.

* * *

The hallways were almost completely empty as Trey walked Tangie through the dance wing and down the stairs with his arm around her. But the second they went through the double doors leading outside to the front stairs—which was still crowded with kids—Trey dropped his arm and started walking about a foot in front of her. He stayed that way until they were about three blocks away from Union Square. And then he grabbed her hand and pulled her over to the curb, hailing a cab with his free hand.

"Wait, you live in Brooklyn Heights, right? We're not taking the train?"

"The train?" He burst out laughing. "For real, yo, you're hilarious. There's no subway when you're ridin' with me, ma. Okay, cool, here's a cab. Come on."

If Tangie had been worried about making conversation with him, she shouldn't have been, because Trey talked throughout the cab ride home. He never even paused to make sure she was listening (she was). She was so relieved to have the pressure off her that she never stopped to wonder if he would ever ask her anything about herself (he didn't).

On and on he talked, about the importance of the "danger face" when pop-and-locking, about how Armstrong was trying to "shut down his gangsta," about how he believed Ms. Carmen would relax if she "got some." Trey was still talking as the cab pulled in front of his gorgeous, gingerbread house–looking brownstone, and was still talking as he led Tangie inside.

Trey's house was very rich-looking and very creepy, in a dollhouse kind of way. It appeared to have last been decorated a hundred years before. It was full of antique gold-framed mirrors, twinkly crystal chandeliers, ceiling-high potted plants, and the kinds of stiff-backed velvet chaise lounges and chairs that no one was supposed to sit on. Everything was covered by a fine layer of dust. Before Tangie had a chance to say the house was beautiful, Trey led her up a steep, winding flight of mahogany stairs and down a Persian rug–lined hall to a pair of tall French doors.

"Here's the studio," he said, pushing open the doors. Tangie gasped. It was stunning.

Intense sunlight poured through the enormous picture-frame windows, giving the polished-to-death wood floors an otherworldly, amber glow. In the far right corner was a massive, shiny, baby grand piano, covered with a beaded and fringed, multicolored Spanish throw. Built into the opposite wall was a complicated sound system, its high-tech modernness the only thing out of place in the studio. Except, maybe, for Tangie.

"Omigod, Trey, this studio . . . it's beautiful."

"Yeah, it's *ai-iight*," he said, finally letting go of her hand to pick up a remote siting on top of the piano. He pressed a button, and the stereo started playing Missy Elliot's "Lose Control." That was the song from the video that he had starred in over the summer.

"I love this song," said Tangie, instantly beginning to feel wiggly. No matter how she was feeling, the song always made her want to dance. "I know people must tell you this all the time, but you were amazing in that video. That choreography was off the hook." She looked at him shyly.

"You want me to teach it to you?" He offered so quickly it had to be the reason he had turned the song on in the first place.

Her mouth dropped open. Tangie couldn't believe what was happening. She was going to learn one of the hottest video routines of the summer from Trey Stevens, who'd oh so controversially experienced dancing it firsthand (with the likes of Ciara and a dozen insanely talented Krumpers, no less!)? "You can't be serious. Are you serious?"

"I'm always serious. Are *you* serious?"

Tangie cocked her head. Hadn't she heard someone else say that today? Who was it?

Whatever, it didn't matter, because right now Trey Stevens was standing in front of her, teaching her the first eight counts of the routine. He spent the next twenty minutes going over the routine with her, over and over, until finally she learned it. After that, they plowed through the routine so many times they lost count. They danced and laughed and messed up and kept dancing, until it was almost an hour later and they had collapsed on the floor, sweaty, exhausted, exhilarated.

"That was . . . so much . . . fun," panted Tangie, her leotard soaking wet, her mascara smudged around her eyes. There was a halo of curls around her hairline that had escaped from her bun while she was dancing, a telltale sign that she'd just grooved her ass off.

"Listen, I gotta tell you, you're *fire*, okay? I can't believe you ain't dancing professionally right now."

"What?" Coming from him, this was the best compliment Tangie had probably ever received. "No, *you're* fire—*please*. I was just trying to keep up."

"Don't be modest, ma, you just rocked it so deadly. I'm seriously scared of you right now." He sat up with his legs out in front of him, and then he stretched over and touched his toes. Realizing that she should stretch out, too, Tangie imitated him.

"Well, thank you. It's 'cause I have such a good tutor."

He looked over at her, grinning, and Tangie's stomach flip-flopped.

"So, Miss Tangela Adams, who I've known since she was in middle school . . ."

She giggled, spreading her legs far apart and reaching her right arm over her head to touch her left toe. After dancing with Trey, she felt much more comfortable with him. "Yeah?"

"Tell me your life story."

"Please, there's nothing to tell."

"There's always something. What, you tellin' me you ain't got any secrets?" One of Trey's dreadlocks slipped out of the big knot at the nape of his neck, and it fell in his face. *This is Trey Stevens*, she silently reminded herself. *I'm sitting six inches away from Trey Stevens in Trey Stevens's house.*

She shrugged. "Let's see. Well, my mom went into labor with me while she was lying in bed watching MTV. And the second she went into labor, the "Baby Got Back" video came on. She used to tell me she knew I'd be a dancer, because I came out of the womb doing the running man, like the girls in the video. But I think it's the reason I came out so bootylicious."

Trey burst out laughing. Which was good, because Tangie was immediately mortified that she'd called attention to her body. She hated the fact that it was always her first instinct to make fun of herself when she was nervous. *So not sexy!*

"Okay, *and* . . . ?"

"Okay. Um, for my kindergarten jazz-dance recital, we dressed up as Disney characters, and I was Tinker Bell. I became obsessed with flying after that, and I dressed up in my costume and jumped off a car that was parked in front of our apartment. I popped my kneecap out of joint. See?" Tangie rolled up her footless tights and pointed to a shiny, raised scar the size of a quarter beside her knee. "Not one of the great looks," she said, surprising herself with an out-of-nowhere Skye-ism.

"Aww," said Trey, as if the hideous scar had been cute. Out of nowhere, he rested his hand on her thigh, then leaned over and kissed her knee. Jolts of electricity ran from the exact place his lips were to the tips of her toes. Tangie sucked in her breath. What was going on? And *eww*, her leg was so sweaty and gross—how embarrassing!

"Keep going," he said. "You're more interesting than you think, Miss Tangie."

"Um . . ." she began, really struggling now, because Trey had left his hand on her leg, which was now all tingly and electric-feeling, and she was feeling dizzy and unable to concentrate. "I . . . I don't know what else. Why don't you tell me something about you?"

"Come on, ma. You gonna tell me you don't know about me already?" He ran his hand a little further up her thigh, and Tangie broke out in goose bumps. Trey acted very nonchalant, as if he weren't halfway up to her goodies—which made her feel as if she were going crazy.

"You know, I got caught out there for doing the Missy video this summer. You know they're making me take a sophomore class. And you know I used to deal with your homegirl's big sister."

Perfect chance to change the subject, thought Tangie. She flipped her legs out from under her, knocking his hand off her thigh in the process, and lay flat on her back, stretching her arms out above her head. For the first time in minutes, she could breathe. "So, what happened there? It's so sad about the two of you. I mean, you were the couple everybody wanted to be."

"Don't believe the hype, Miss Tangie." She was starting to like his calling her that. "We was bad for a lot longer than we was good. Look, she's crazy. Bananas. Eden has this perfect princess rep, but she's a straight-up junkie, yo."

"Hmm. The pills," said Tangie, nodding. Dimly, she felt she was betraying both Skye and Eden by agreeing with him.

"She hit me once."

"She hit you?"

"With her dad's car. I'm tryin' to tell you, Eden Carmichael is totally unhinged." He raised an eyebrow. "People ain't always what they seem," he said sagely.

"Were you hurt? When she hit you, I mean."

"Hell, yeah. But it hurt my feelings more than anything else." Trey stretched out on the floor next to her and turned on his side, propping himself up on his elbow. He was looking down at her as she lay flat on her back. Suddenly, she realized that that position could be very vulnerable.

"Listen, folks project shit on to me, like I'm this hardcore thug-life motherfucka. But I'm really a humble cat, very gentle and sweet. When I'm hurt, I'm hurt." He cast his eyes down, looking pitiful and adorable. Tangie did everything in her power not to grab him and press his head to her chest, soothing him and running her hands through his thick, masculine dreads.

"You seem sweet to me, Trey."

He looked up again and into her eyes. "It's 'cause we got a connection, girl. I can tell. See, I can *sense* things about people. And I sense that we was *supposed* to meet each other yesterday."

Tangie was too jittery to look at his face. They were so close she could smell his obscenely sexy sweat, mixed with Issey Miyake scent. "Really?"

"Most definitely." He swiped a lock of hair out of his face, sticking it behind an ear. "But I'm tryin'-a get to know you better, ma."

"There's really nothing much to know."

"Okay, then, tell me this," he said, slowly sliding his hand further up her leg, over her knee, and up, up, until he rested his hand high on her thigh—under the hem of her short shorts. She held her breath again. "You got a man?"

"I . . . no. No, there's no man." *Please, God, please, make him take his hand off my thigh. . . .*

"Why you ain't got a man? You unhinged, too?" Taking care not to touch anything too controversial, he ran his hand up under her shorts, not stopping until he reached the elastic waistband rolled down around her lower stomach. And then, lazily, he drummed his fingers on her taut stomach. At which point Tangie stopped breathing altogether.

"Is that supposed to be funny?" She was going for Sassy, Confident Girl, but instead sounded like Bratty Little Sister.

"Actually, no," he said, slowly leaning his head down toward hers. "I've been hurt before, Miss Tangie. I ain't about to let anybody hurt me again. You feel me?"

"Uh-huh," she thought she said; but she couldn't be sure, because then his mouth was over hers, and he was kissing her. Her first instinct was to tense up, worrying that he could tell she'd been kissed only twice before in her life—and both times by the same guy! But the thought floated away as she began to relax under his soft, sensual kisses, parting her lips and running her hands over Trey's broad shoulders. (Besides, even if last night was all a lie, at least she could now say she was officially experienced!)

The kiss got deeper and hotter, and then he slid the strap of her tank leotard down over her shoulder and laid his open mouth hotly against her neck, and she surprised herself by moaning. As he pulled the strap down further, he kissed down her throat, across her chest, giving her soft love bites and running his tongue along her sweaty skin. Helplessly, she moaned, trailing her fingers down his back. And then he reached behind him and grabbed her hand, slowly guiding it across his rock-hard stomach and down, down, down into his shorts and then she wrapped her hand around his surprisingly big . . .

"*Holy shhhh. . . !!!*" Trey hollered, leaping off her and grabbing his crotch in agony. "Omigod, omigod, omigod . . ."

"What? What is it, what'd I do?" Tangie wailed. Quickly, she sat up and snatched her hand out of his shorts, as if she'd just burned it on a scalding-hot curling iron.

"Omigod, Tangie, you killed my . . . !" Trey was doubled over, clutching his crotch and grimacing. He seemed barely able to speak.

For a second she sat frozen in horror. What had she done wrong? She could have sworn you were supposed to squeeze it really hard! Oh, no, had she squeezed it *too* hard? *That's what I get for getting all overconfident after my one-and-only night of passion,* thought Tangie, her mind racing with panic. She had to get out of there, immediately.

Overcome with mortification, Tangie yanked the strap of her leotard back over her shoulder, scrambled to her feet and ran for the door. Groaning, Trey got up and awkwardly limped after her, managing to grab her by the waist before she made it out of the studio.

"Wait, Tangie. Wait," he said, the pain seeming to subside

somewhat. "Listen, ma, it's okay. I'm fine. I doubt I'll be able to reproduce, but . . ."

"Oh, no-o-o," Tangie wailed, hot tears shooting from her eyes. She covered her face with her hands, wanting to die.

"Hey. Yo, stop crying. It's all good." He wrapped his arms around her limp body. She didn't hug him back.

Whispering, Tangie said, "I'm sorry. I've never touched a . . . I didn't know . . . I just—I didn't know how."

Grinning, he pulled away from her and put his hand under her chin. "It's my fault. I forgot how young you are. But can I tell you somethin'? You might not know how to do all that extra shit yet, but I ain't *never* been kissed that good before. Ever."

Tangie looked at him, her eyes sad and damp. Was he messing with her? "You're just saying that to make me feel better."

"No offense, girl, but you just Lorena Bobbitted me. Why would I try to make you feel better?"

She smiled a little and finally looked back into his eyes. "Well, thanks, then. If you mean it."

"Not only are you a sick kisser, you're the best dancer at Armstrong. Well, the best *girl* dancer. You ain't beat me yet."

And that was enough to make her forget her huge, embarrassing fumble—temporarily. Trey Stevens thought she was a good kisser and a better dancer. He must really like her. That could really lead to something. They might grow closer and closer, soon becoming inseparable. Would he introduce her to his parents, and take her to dinner dates at Nobu and then to the senior prom? Would she become the envy of every girl at school? Would they one day—while basking in the afterglow of a passionate, post-tutoring lovemaking session on the studio floor—feel guilty for flaunting their love in front of a school full of people who, sadly, just weren't as dynamic as they? Would they feel compelled to tell their classmates and peers, "Really, don't put us on a pedestal—we're normal, everyday people, just like you!"

With visions of her and Trey's glittering future dancing through her head, Tangie wiped the tears off her cheeks, smoothed her out-of-control curls back into her bun, and looked him dead in the eye. "Go put on 'Lose Control' one more time, and we'll see if I don't beat your ass," she said, her eyes twinkling. And then they danced for two more hours, and Trey told her he'd call later to say good night (*aww—so cute!*), and all was right with the world.

On her way home in the cab Trey had gotten for her, Tangie flashed back on being with Trey, and C.J. kissing her and saying "I love you." Then she saw him painting Izzy's naked body. She was glad he had seen her with Trey. It was C.J.'s turn to be jealous.

19.
TANGIE WHO?

AT EIGHT O'CLOCK THAT NIGHT, C.J. sought refuge in Izzy's bedroom. Even though they'd hung out all summer, it was only the second time he'd ever been to her apartment. Every other girl he'd ever dealt with had been unable to wait to bring him home, introduce him to the parents, show him her fuschia photo albums, talk a lot of nonsense about when she was a kid—they had all tried to get too close, too quick. But Izzy was different. She showed C.J. only what she wanted him to see, when she wanted him to see it—and that shit was sexy.

And so was her room. It was the coolest-looking girl's room C.J. had ever seen. She'd painted each wall purple, blue, green, or red, covering them with vintage rap concert flyers featuring old school MC's like Run DMC, Eric B. and Rakim, and Kurtis Blow (it was one of her many addictions, scrounging eBay for classic hip-hop memorabilia). She had even made her own rug, by sewing together scraps of concert T-shirts from the flea market. And hanging above her bed was a funky sculpture of the letters in her name, which she'd constructed from broken-up pieces of old vinyl records. Basically, the whole thing looked like the movie set of a bedroom belonging to the Funky-Fresh Tough Girl character.

C.J. was exactly where he wanted to be, sparking up a bowl of his most premium weed with Izzy. He couldn't believe that hours earlier he had been about to end it with her. Was he nuts? She was the only girl he'd ever been able to count on—she was straight-up, no games. He'd been so stupid, obsessing over Tangie all that time, when he had a sexy, mature woman right in front of him. It was all good, though, he'd woo Izzy back into his arms tonight. Ladies loved cool C.J., right? Now, if he could only erase the vision of Tangie, making googly-eyed faces at Trey. *Forget her,* he repeated to himself, over and over. *Forget her, son. If she's goin' for hers, then I'm 'bout to go for mine.*

"So, you sure your, uh, guardian or whatever . . ."

"Damon," interrupted Izzy, taking a long, deep drag off the bowl. "Just Damon."

C.J. frowned, still not getting who he was to her. Izzy lived in a Hell's Kitchen apartment with a thirty-five-year-old man that wasn't related to her, and no matter how you looked at it, that was seriously ill.

"Okay, Damon," he said. "You sure he don't care that we're smoking at his crib?"

"He's at work," she shrugged, not really answering the question. She took another drag and passed the bowl to C.J., who was hunched over her desk, distractedly drawing in his sketchbook. For someone who was always the epitome of cool, he looked anxious. "Don't worry about Damon. He's never here. After work, he either volunteers at the community center or works on his goddamned book."

"He writes books?"

Izzy sighed, gazing up at the ceiling. "He already wrote one about teen runaways. This new one's called *The Lolita Syndrome,* whatever that shit means. I'm so over hearing about it."

"So, he just lets you smoke?"

"I mean, he wouldn't buy it for me. But he's real chill about stuff like that, as long as I'm honest and do it in the house." She lazily stretched and settled back into the pillows. "Look, Damon's a *social worker*. He's real big on letting me express myself and shit."

"That's kinda serious," he said, rubbing his thumb along the paper to blend the charcoal. "My grandma don't believe in expression. It's against her religion."

She giggled. "Once, he told me my 'wings' were too beautiful to be clipped. That's a quote."

"Well, you said he's a writer." C.J. could barely concentrate on what she was saying. He couldn't think straight—despite trying to focus his attention on Izzy, all he could see was Tangie losing her virginity to Trey Stevens. It wasn't supposed to happen like that! It was supposed to be him! He pounded his fist on the table, trying to drive that vision out of his head, and realized that, to his horror, all this time he'd been drawing a sketch of Trey in tights getting run over by a bus.

"You okay, Ceej?"

"Yeah, yeah, I'm cool. I just, uh, killed a mosquito. You tryin' to hit this?" He offered Izzy the bowl and she shook her head. Instead, she pulled a silver flask out from under her mattress and took a hearty gulp.

Fixing him with her gold-lined black eyes, she murmured, "How about we do what we came here for?"

"Cool," said C.J., exhaling. Finally, the perfect chance to step to her again—when she was naked and vulnerable. "Let's do it."

Without hesitation, she grabbed the hem of her camouflage T-shirt minidress and yanked it up over her head. She wasn't wearing a bra, only an impressive stack of gold bangles and a pair of see-through lace boy shorts. C.J.'s mouth went dry—her body was even crazier than he remembered.

Her breasts were small but perfectly perky (he'd later tell Blackadocious they were "apple-size handfuls of lusciousness"), and her taut, bronzed skin would've made Christina Milian weep with jealousy. Even with the sprawling angel tattoo rising out of her boy shorts, Izzy was flawless. Of course, he'd seen her naked before—they'd had sex all summer, but it was always quick, in the bathroom at someone's house party or in the back of a cab. He'd never had time actually to study her body.

Izzy was as matter-of-fact as C.J. was awestruck. She rolled over on her side and propped herself up on an elbow, hitting a perfect swimsuit-calendar pose. But without the swimsuit. "So, are you gonna act like you've never seen my "girls," or are you gonna get to sketching?"

C.J. swallowed drily. "Damn, girl, you gotta give some warning before you throw down like that."

Izzy grinned. "Sorry. I told you, I've done this before. Being naked ain't no big thing to me. The human body is beautiful, don't you think?"

"Who'd you pose for?'

"Oh, I did it to make quick cash when my dad first kicked me out. I posed for an art class at the local community college, no biggie." She caught his slightly disturbed, slack-jawed expression and giggled.

"Wait . . . but weren't you underage? How'd you work that?"

"Fake ID, silly. They had no clue I was thirteen!" Izzy's eyes twinkled. "Besides, the professor was a guy. I could convince a man I was twenty-five if I wanted to. Y'all believe what you want to believe."

"Huh," nodded C.J., completely mesmerized. Staring at her naked body, he began to feel like a bumbling, prepubescent virgin with no coordination. He reached for his charcoal pencil, fumbled, and dropped it on the floor. Embarrassed, he snatched up the pencil and threw himself into his sketching. Knitting his brows in intense concentration, he traced the outline of her form, using feather-light strokes. As he sketched, his eyes moved back and forth from her body to his paper. And then he did a double take.

"Hold up! When'd you get your nipples pierced?"

"They've always been pierced, I just take them out sometimes.

They start to itch in the summer." Giggling, she flicked one of the tiny hoops. "You like?"

"I like it all. Did it hurt?"

"Yeah," she said, her eyes twinkling, "but it's the good kind of pain. You know, like a tattoo. It hurts like shit, but you know if you just hang in a second longer it'll be so worth it."

C.J. paused, thinking about that. "But you can't *know* it'll be worth it, right? I mean, while you're in the pain," he said, thinking of Tangie and Trey. What a shame. A buck-naked goddess was sprawled out in front of him, and he still couldn't shake thoughts of Tangie.

"Nothing worth having comes without a little bit of pain, baby," she said, wisely. "Anyway, I did it when I was young, like, in seventh grade. I just wanted to be a rebel, you know, pierce everything, tattoo everything, dye my hair every color. Just to be different."

"You are different, Izzy."

"But in a good way, right?" she said softly. For a split second, she looked very young.

"Absolutely."

"I mean, not like I care what people think of me." She ran her hand through her messy faux hawk and bit her bottom lip, fixing him with her wildly exotic, seductress eyes. She looked irresistible, and she knew it. Like a model in one of those black-and-white Calvin Klein ads. With a sigh of sexual frustration, C.J. slammed his charcoal pencil on the desk. He couldn't concentrate anymore. She looked too good. It was amazing: even with all the tough-girl trimmings—the blue-tipped hair, the tattoo, and the nipple piercings—Izzy was amazingly feminine. He knocked his sketchbook over getting up from the desk and stormed over to the bed. To his surprise, Izzy put her hand out, stopping him.

"Slow down, baby. I thought this was about the art."

C.J. was speechless, standing in the middle of the room like an idiot. Hadn't she clearly been putting out a "C.J.-I-want-you-now" vibe? "Wh—what do you mean? I . . . *yeah*, it's about the art. But . . ."

"But what?" Izzy looked up at him innocently, still in the swimsuit-calendar pose. Her eyes were serious, but her mouth was curled in a devilish grin. She was torturing him, and she knew it. It was what she did best, manipulating guys. C.J. was cute, she liked his gangsta, but she'd decided long ago that no guy would ever have the upper hand with her again.

"Weren't you the one so worried I wouldn't understand it wasn't anything deeper than an artist sketching a nude model? Or am I tripping?"

"No, I . . . I did say that. I did say that. It's just that I really feel like we got something going here."

"Oh, baby. You're just higher than a motherfucker, that's all." She chuckled, lazily tracing a finger around her breasts. C.J.'s eyes almost crossed. "We clearly said we'd be better as friends, didn't we? I'm just doing you a favor, here. I believe in your talent, baby, and I wanted to help you get Spotlight at Fall Fling."

He nodded, his mouth dry. *Stay focused*, he told himself. *Remember why you're here.* "But . . . listen, Izzy, I think we should talk. I've been thinking, and I feel like we could really do this."

"Do what?" she said, slowly trailing her finger down her perfectly flat stomach and down toward her shorts.

"Um . . . what I'm trying to say is, like, I think we're good together. For real."

"Is that really the point, Ceej?" Izzy slowly ran her hand around her hips, over her thighs, teasing him. "Or did you just come here to hit it? I mean, I was under the impression that it was . . ."

". . . About the art," he said, barely breathing. *Why did I ever say that?* "Yeah, I know."

Abruptly, she pulled her hand from inside her shorts and sat up, her whole demeanor changing. "C.J., sit down," she calmly ordered, and he did. "You're here to sketch my portrait, and that's it. I don't know what you thought, but I'm not going there with you."

"Aw, girl, it ain't even about that. It's just that, I mean, you can't deny that we got a good thing going."

"All I know is, you got a job to do." Izzy looked dead serious, but she really wanted to giggle. *God, guys really were all alike, weren't they? Dangle the goods in front of them, slap 'em around a little, and next thing you know they were professing their undying love. So predictable. And so fun.*

C.J. looked at her for a moment, dumbstruck, and then shook it off. "Cool, cool. No, it's all good," he said, deepening his voice in a feeble attempt to recover some of his swagger. What had just happened? She'd managed to flip the balance of their relationship in a matter of minutes. The fact was, C.J. was whipped. And he didn't even know what had hit him.

Tangie? *Tangie who?*

Name: Tangela Marie Adams
Class: Sophomore
Major: Dance
Self-Awareness Session #: TA 2

. . . And I'm still in shock about hooking up with Trey! This is the most, like, sexually explicit week of my life! I don't know what's going on with that. I went from just kissing one boy in my whole life, to . . . well, aaaagh!

If you're feeling uncomfortable, we can . . .

No, no, no, it's fine. I just don't know what's up with me and Trey now. I mean, was that a one-time thing? How am I supposed to act around him? What if I see him in the hall, what am I supposed to say? I just don't know how to do these things, how to be this, like, vixen who hooks up with boys and keeps it moving like it isn't a thing. It is. It is a thing. Isn't it?

Ms. Adams, I sense that you worry quite a bit.

Worry? Uh, yeah, I worry. I worry that my butt is too big, that I'm going to say the wrong thing, that everyone will find out I'm not good enough to be here, that I'm eating too much, that during the year I went to a different school my friends moved on. Most of all, I worry that I'm too ordinary. But I think that's an Armstrong thing. . . . Everyone's terrified of being ordinary. It's like it's a disease. Everyone's trying to prove they've got some uniquely special thing that's gonna make them a star. Except for Izzy. She's got the opposite issue. She's so unique it's like she's pretending to be normal.

I can see why C.J. likes her. That's what scares me; I totally get it.

20.

FIDDY DON'T WANT IT WITH SMOOVE

EDEN WAS IN HEAVEN. Tipsy enough to dull her anxiety and twisted on the kind of seriously potent homegrown weed available only to superstars, she was desperately, clingingly, unequivocally in love. Smoove was half man, half amazing.

Fine, so they'd only known each other for two days, but it seemed like for-ever. He was so generous, so caring. In those two days, she hadn't had to lift a finger. His driver—actually, it was just his third cousin, Puddin'—had chauffeured them anywhere they wanted to go, in Smoove's Rolls Royce Phantom with the plush, cream-on-cream, perforated leather interior. And in two days they had gone everywhere.

Settling into the pillowy backseat of the Phantom while Smoove did a phone interview with *XXL* magazine, Eden thought about how sick this school year was turning out to be (and she'd had the nerve to worry that her senior year would be wack without Trey—*please!*). In just two days, Smoove had shown her off at all the hottest spots—dinner at Spice Market, lingerie shopping at Le Perla, industry talk with Dame Dash at 40/40 Club. Paparazzi followed them everywhere, shouting things like, "Who's the mystery girl, Smoove?" and "Come on, one shot'll put my kid through college!"

and "Where's Pearl at, Smoovie-K?" To tell the truth, Eden was wondering the same thing.

If he and Pearl were truly hip-hop's supercouple, then where was
she? Why was he taking chances being seen all over the city with
Eden? She couldn't help assuming she was about to take Pearl's place
as hip-hop's first lady (okay, second). Especially after their conversation at Smoove's Hotel Gansevoort penthouse earlier that night.

Eden had been perched on the bed surrounded by all the sexy
designer dresses he had just bought her at Barneys. Pretending to
decide what to wear, she was really just stalling, trying to work up
the balls to ask the question "Baby, can I ask you something?"

"Come on, ma. You tryin' to kill the magic with questions?" He
was in the palace-size bathroom, getting an edge-up from his barber,
Flawless. Flawless was Smoove's half sister's baby daddy.

"Oh, no, it's nothing bad. I'm so-o-o happy, you know that," she
said, hopping off the bed and running into the bathroom. She leaned
in, watching Flawless work his magic. "I just . . . I just have to ask,
what's up with you and Pearl? Everyone says you're engaged, but, I
mean, I don't know."

"Yo, you can't take all that tabloid nonsense seriously," he said,
nudging Flawless for backup. Flawless nodded in agreement. "That's
a bunch of folks with too much time on their hands. Smoove *definitely* ain't engaged to Pearl."

"Okay, but are y'all together? Everyone says you two are, like,
supertight." She took a deep breath, not wanting to sound like
Needy Relationship Girl, but also trying not to get caught up with
another cheater. "I know we just met and all, but I just want you to
be straight with me."

"You wanna know the truth, ma?"

Eden nodded.

"Pearl is crazy, ya heard? *Bananas.* I'm talking about drinking all
day and night, being physically and emotionally abusive. And look,
Smoove's from the *block*, you understand? My whole life I've been

around all kinds of knuckleheaded lunacy. But I ain't never seen a woman so mentally unbalanced. Flawless, cosign my shit."

"*Unbalanced*, yo," cosigned Flawless.

"I ain't even gonna lie, at one point we was tight. But a nigga like Smoove is used to having some freedom, yaknowwhatI'msayin? I had a mother, may she rest in peace until I get there, and I don't need another one. Like, I'd go to her crib after chilling with my boys, and she'd straight-up answer the door with a gun pointed in my face. I'm saying, *my own* piece! Tell me that ain't some animalistic, bugged-out shit."

Silence.

"Flawless?"

"My nigga?"

"Cosign my shit."

"Oh!" The barber snapped to attention. "Yeah, that was some bugged-out shit."

"And then at Mariah's VMA after-party, she was wild'n out when she saw me kicking it with Ashanti. Ridiculous. I mean, who don't know she's Nelly's wifey?" He shook his head in exasperation. Flawless quickly jerked the razor away from his hairline, preventing a serious mishap. "Anyway, she smashed a Moët bottle on the floor, then sliced me with the jagged bottle. I'm saying, she marked Smoove for life—look!" He held out his right arm for Eden to inspect, and she saw the shiny, raised scar zigzagging across his forearm. "What can I tell you, ma? Pearl's a dysfunctional bitch. And Smoove ain't about the drama, so I deaded it. It's over. You believe me? Huh, boo?"

I believe him, she told herself now, sinking into the Phantom's buttery leather backseat. *Who wouldn't? Pearl was a nightmare.* Well, Eden wouldn't be. She knew how lucky she was, and she wasn't going to ruin it. Forget about the fact that Smoove was the sexiest, most generous man she'd ever met. How many seventeen-year-olds got the chance to be wined and dined by one of the most powerful players in hip-hop? There was nothing sexier than a guy with power, real power—somebody with an entourage that basically tap-danced on command, somebody who could make things happen. She felt so special, like the Chosen One.

Of course, Marisol had been telling her all along that she could pull a truly A-list guy like Smoove, but for years Eden was so up Trey's ass she couldn't see her own dating potential. Who knew where a relationship with Smoove could lead, what it could do for her career?

His interview finally over, he clicked his blinged-out Razr phone shut and faced Eden. "You chillin', ma?"

She nodded, smiling prettily. "How'd your interview go?"

"You know. Same ish, different day. All the media wanna talk about is (a), my beef with Game, and (b), my ties to the streets." He conveniently left out (c), his relationship with Pearl.

"Ties to the streets?"

"Yeah. Don't get me wrong, I'm strictly official these days. Smoove got too much paper to be dealing with knuckleheads. But when I was a shorty, you know, I got into some scraps. Some gang shit, some drug shit. I'm just so sick of all these reporters focusing in on my former violent tendencies. It's about the music, ya heard? I'm an artist."

"I know what you mean," said Eden. "My parents are kinda well known in the theater world, and at my school, teachers always wanna focus on . . ."

"I mean, I *have* been shot eight times," Smoove continued, deeply uninterested in Eden's attempt to relate. "I just ain't tryin' to talk about it twenty-four-seven. I guess it made a boy a man, though. Did I ever show you this scar from where my pops stabbed me?" Talking so fast his words were jumbled together, he lifted up his arm and showed her the scar on his arm. Eden caught her breath. *Wait, didn't he just show me that, like, two hours ago? And he said it was from Pearl, right?*

The consummate actress, she gasped in a perfect combination of awe and horror and ran her finger across the scar. "Damn, Smoove, did that hurt?"

"Naah," he said, running his hand up her thigh and leaning in to nuzzle her neck. "No more than your fingernails on my back."

"Smoove, stop!" she giggled, slapping his hand away. "You're so bad."

"Yeah, that's me. A bad, bad, motherfucker. Right, A-OK?" A-OK, his personal assistant and the foster child of his mom's best friend, was sitting in the front seat.

"No doubt, Smoovie-K," A-OK called back, his voice barely audible over the bass of Young Jeezy's "Thug Motivation 101." "You a bad, bad motherfucker."

"A-OK *wilin'*!" Smoove leaned forward into the front seat, giving A-OK pounds. A-OK and Puddin' began enthusiastically hyping up the platinum rapper, hollering, "Who's harder than Smoove? Fiddy don't want it with Smoove! T.I. don't want it with Smoove!" Eden eyed this display of hopped-up testosterone with a mixture of surprise and amusement. It was kind of . . . weird. When she met Smoove at the club the other night, he had seemed like a smoked-out, laid-back man of few words, almost too cool to open his mouth. But tonight, he was more hyper than Brittany Murphy at a slumber party. Why wasn't he paying more attention to her?

"Um, Smoove? Where are we going tonight?" Eden grabbed his hand, pulling him back toward her. She placed his hand on her thigh and nuzzled his neck. Just then, her Sidekick started buzzing, and she clicked it open. It was Marisol, of course.

"Did you tell Smoove I can sing in both English *and* Spanish? Spanish is very hot right now, with the whole reggaeton thing popping off. . . ."

"Not now, babe," Eden whispered. She hung up. It was the third time her best friend had called or texted since Smoove had picked her up earlier that night. "Sorry, baby—where did you say we were going?"

"La Esquina," said Smoove, nuzzling her neck. "It's the blazin'-est restaurant in the city right now."

Puddin' nodded, keeping his eyes on the road. "Yeah, nobody can get in, ya heard? You gotta show, like, ten forms of identification and shit."

"True, true. A-OK, did you bring my ID?"

"You cool, Smoove," said his trusty assistant. "You know I got you."

"That nigga, A-OK! You always got me; you my motherfucker!" And then it started all over again, the three of them giving each other pounds and hyping each other. Eden slumped back in her seat, annoyed. She was not used to being ignored. Then again, she was in a whole other league now. Smoove Killah wasn't a high school boy, he was an adult—a very famous, very rich, and *powerful* adult. She should have felt lucky that she was even riding with him.

Except that there was one thing that she just couldn't deal with.

"Smoove? Can I ask you something?" She put on her girliest, most I'm-so-cute-how-could-you-deny-me voice.

"Yeah, sexy?"

"You gotta stop saying the N-word. It's just so . . . déclassé."

Smoove looked shocked for a couple of seconds and then burst out laughing, reaching up in the front seat and slapping A-OK and Puddin' on the backs. "Yo, d'you hear my shorty? She's on some righteous shit, yo! She's on some ole 'We Are the World,' It Takes a Village shit!" He turned back to Eden and threw his arm around her. "You're so cute, girl. No, really you are. Yeah, man, I can cool it with the 'nigga' this and 'nigga' that. Though I suggest you listen to the classic Tribe Called Quest joint, 'Sucka Nigga,' and then report back to me. You might switch up your position, ya heard?"

"I doubt it," she said, wrinkling her nose with distaste. She kissed his cheek, hopefully distracting him from the fact that she was fussing. "But thanks for respecting me. I'm really proud of you."

Just then, her Sidekick started buzzing again. She looked at the display screen and thrust it against her ear, hissing, *"What?!"*

"Yo, you hollered at your boy yet about a Smoove-Mari collabo? Tell him I'd *murder* the hook on his next joint. . . ." Marisol begged.

"Go away," Eden hissed, slamming the phone shut. She briefly toyed with the idea of tossing the Sidekick out the window.

"Yo, Puddin'," started Smoove, "pull over here on Delancey. You got this, P.?"

"You *know* I got this," said his driver, making a right. He pulled up to the curb in front of an abandoned warehouse on a seedy street filled with discount stores, bodegas, and fake designer-bag stands. Leaving the music pumping at full blast, Puddin' hopped out of the Phantom. He lit a cigarette and pimp-walked up to the warehouse, where he knocked on the door. An Asian guy dressed like Big Daddy Kane—full-on gold chains, Adidas tracksuit, clean white shell-toe Adidas sneakers—appeared. Eden saw that he was clutching an extremely large machine gun (an Uzi?) under his arm. He and Puddin' had a quick conversation with lots of gesturing, and then they both disappeared into the warehouse.

"What was that all about?" Eden didn't know why she was whispering, but the situation seemed to call for it.

"Puddin' is going on a weed run. This Chinese playa down here on the Lower East Side? He's got the best herb in the city. Strictly underground. He grows it in some field in Long Island."

"Yeah, he's on some word-of-mouf shit, like Ludacris," A-OK called out over the music, Kelis's "I'm Bossy." "You gotta be in the know to get his herb."

"Yeah, so don't go tellin' all your high school girls," said Smoove with a grin. He leaned in and gave Eden a kiss (finally!), which was immediately interrupted by the loud, reverberating crash of something ramming the back of the car and knocking them to the floor. In a single impressive, almost gymnastic move, A-OK grabbed a tiny silver from the dashboard and hopped out of the car to assess the situation. Eden struggled to get back on the seat, but Smoove held her down on the floor next to him. "Don't move," he whispered. "A-OK's got this. He's an ex–Navy SEAL."

"Wait, I thought he was your personal assistant."

"Yeah, but he's also a trained killer. Don't be scared."

Then they felt another huge jolt, and Eden screamed. She twisted out of Smoove's grasp and hoisted herself up over the backseat, where she peered out the shattered rear windshield. Smashed up against the back of the Phantom was a pale pink convertible, with vanity plates reading FIGHTING BITCH. A-OK rushed over to her side and knocked on her window, hollering at her to roll it down. Not only did the girl ignore him, but she slammed open her door with such force that it knocked him to the ground and his head hit the concrete. Hard. A-OK was out cold.

And then all hell broke loose.

"MOTHERFUCKAAAAH!!!" screamed the girl in a voice Eden thought similar to a cracked-out Minnie Mouse. She kicked A-OK's unconscious body out of the way and stormed up to the Phantom, pounding on the back window. Eden and Smoove looked up from the floor, terrified. The girl sported gold fronts and an early Mary J. Blige blond wig that was dangerously askew. And she looked ready to tear somebody's head off.

"Open this door, motherfuckaaaaah!" the girl repeated, her heavily glossed, black-lip-lined mouth curling into a sneer. She pounded on the window until Smoove, his Navy SEAL down, had no choice but to deal with her. "Stay here," he said to Eden, and he crawled out of the car. The girl proceeded to take off her clear plastic stripper platforms and beat him over the head.

"Who's that bitch? Who's that bitch? I been waitin' outside Hotel Gansevoort all day, and I followed you, money, I followed you for twenty minutes! Who's that anorexic, mariny bitch? That ain't her hair, Smoove, I promise you that!"

"Cinammon! Cinammon, get a holda yourself, why you trippin', ma? Listen, I told you it wasn't gonna work between us."

"Lyin' jackass! What about *our baby*? You don't gotta do right by me, but you better take care o' your own seed or I'm suin' your skinny ass like Misa did Diddy! I ain't playin' witchu, Smoove. You know I'll go to Pearl. . . ."

He grabbed her by the neck and shoved her against the car. "You better not go to Pearl, you understand me?"

"Leggo o' me, you fake-ass Fiddy!" She kneed him in the balls, and he doubled over, letting her go. "Why you even care if I go to Pearl? Huh? You supposed to be her ex, remember?"

"You better not go to Pearl, Cinammon," he repeated, his voice hoarse with pain.

"He's still with her," she hysterically squealed at Eden, pressing her face against the now-open back window. "Don't believe the hype, baby, he's still with her! They *engaged*, okay? Don't trust him, girl! Oh, and I hope you ain't gave up the goodies yet, cuz this nigga got *syphilis*!!"

Sneaking up behind Cinammon, a newly conscious A-OK grabbed her from behind and dragged her, kicking and screaming, back to her car. Crying hysterically, she sped away, leaving smoking black skid marks on the street.

Once Eden was sure she was gone, she crawled off the floor and scooted out of the car. Smoove was sitting on the curb, doubled over in pain, while A-OK was pacing back and forth, yelling on his cell phone at Puddin' to grab the shit and get in the car. Finally, Puddin' came running out, and A-OK began berating him for not having his back when Cinammon hit the fan.

"Okay, what the *hell*?" Eden looked down at Smoove, her hands on her hips. She was angry, hurt, embarrassed, and scared—not to mention *so* not used to ghetto drama. "Who the hell was that trashy ho? You didn't tell me you have a baby mama! And she's right, why do you care so much about what Pearl thinks? I thought it was over!"

"Baby, baby, baby, *calm down*," started Smoove, trying to buy time so he could figure out an excuse. With much difficulty, he stood up and pulled Eden into a tight hug. At first she tried to pull away, but then she gave in, willing to hear him out. "Shhh," he said. "Were you scared? That scared you, didn't it?"

"Hell, yeah, it scared me! I thought she was gonna kill us! Who was that?" Just then, her Sidekick buzzed again. She peeked at the screen, and it was a text from Marisol: *Tell him I can sing two verses and the chorus of "Vision of Love" without breathing.*

"Honestly, I don't even know that girl. She's just a fan that came by my hotel room when I played the Hammerstein Ballroom. Listen, we just met, and I ain't had time yet to cut back all my bitches. But since the moment we met I been spending all my time with you. You know that! When would I have time to even holla at another shorty?"

"What was she so mad for if y'all aren't talking? And what about the baby?"

"When you got a well-known name, it happens all the time; you know, you get these hos tryin' to trap you for life with fake paternity suits and shit. Look at what happened to Kobe, yo."

Eden shook her head, confused. "I just . . . maybe we should slow down some."

"Listen, that baby ain't mine! Come on, look at me. Do you seriously think I'd hit that? Did you *see* that girl?"

Eden thought about this. It was true, Cinammon was kind of gross. "Well, I . . ."

"Seriously. I meant it when I said I wanted you in my movie. I'm really feelin' you, ma. I know we only known each other for a minute, but I feel like we can take this to the next level. And it scares me, kind of. But at the same time, I kinda wanna see where this thing goes."

Eden looked at him for a long time, then nodded. It was true, whether she liked it or not. They did have a connection that was hard to deny. And she was no idiot. She knew how these high-profile guys rolled. There were groupies everywhere.

"Listen, there's always gonna be some ho trying to blow up my spot. When you're high profile like me, they're *all over*. You just have to trust me. You trust me, don't you?"

Eden looked at him for a long time. She wasn't a little girl; she knew how guys like Smoove rolled. But could she handle it? Everyone had always told her she was a star, since she was a baby. She belonged with somebody as high-post as Smoove. She had the face, the body, the hair, the style.

And the trade-off was priceless. All she had to do was look hot on his arm and he'd give her more publicity than she'd know what to do with. She silently mused over this until they pulled up to La Esquina, on Kenmare Street on the Lower East Side. Eden was surprised to see that the supposedly fancy restaurant looked like a run-down California taco stand.

But when they walked in, Puddin' whispered something in the manager's ear, and the slick-haired Latin man ushered Eden, Smoove, and Smoove's entourage through a secret door in the back. Smoove and company followed the manager down a steep flight of stairs, through a steamy, busy kitchen, and then into the restaurant—a dark, cavernous underground VIP palace teeming with celebs, socialites, and glittering New York personalities. The restaurant was *beyond* happening. Feeling a surge of power, Eden flung her arms around Smoove's neck and almost knocked him over with a lusty, openmouthed kiss—in plain view of Lindsay Lohan, Sienna Miller, the thrilled paparazzi, God, and everybody.

Hell, yeah, this was going to be so-o-o worth it.

21

GOOD COMEBACK

TANGIE WAS HOT, SORE, and exhausted after stamping her way through an after-school flamenco lesson and then training with Trey. Well, *sort of* training; they spent half of the hour hooking up—again—though this time, because Trey's package was still sensitive, they didn't go much further than kissing. She stopped in the Starbucks across the street from Armstrong to nestle into an over-stuffed love seat with a low-fat frappaccino and the latest issue of *Seventeen*.

All she wanted to do was relax, catch her breath, and not think about anything annoying—like the fact that she was starving on her dumb diet or that this was the second evening she'd made out with Trey Stevens. And yet she felt as if she weren't supposed to tell any-one. Most of all, she didn't want to think about C.J. doing Izzy's nude portrait.

It was only the first week of school; she wasn't supposed to be this stressed yet, was she?

With a sigh, Tangie settled back into the crushed-velvet love seat, sipped her frappaccino, and flipped to the Chris Brown article. Awww, he was so cute. Too wiped out actually to read the damned thing, she stared at his photos in the back-to-school fashion spread.

Okay, I guess I kinda see what folks are saying. Chris Brown does look a little like an innocent version of C.J. With an exasperated sigh, she slammed the magazine shut and dropped it to the floor. It wasn't fair—what did she have to do to break free of that boy? Not even a secret (*very* secret) affair with Dance Fever was making her forget their issues.

She wished she could drop her stupid diet and eat an Entenmann's powdered donut or something equally sweet and calorie-ridden.

And then, all of a sudden, Tangie was inexplicably, uncontrollably furious. She was furious at her diet, furious at her hair (it was humid outside, so her curls were living *quite* large), furious at self-obsessed, big-mouthed Skye, and most of all, furious at C.J. Over the past few days, she'd tried to push the reality of the situation out of her mind, but the truth was clear. She had spilled her soul to him, he had said she was the only girl he'd ever loved—and he'd lied. He lied! Her soul mate!

She wanted to kill him. And it was time to let C.J. have it.

Cheeks flushing an angry crimson, Tangie stormed out of Starbucks, leaving her half-finished frappaccino on the table. Masses of messy, frizzy curls were popping loose from her bun, she was sweaty and stinky and makeup free, but she didn't care—C.J. was long overdue for a verbal beatdown.

And Tangie knew exactly where to find him.

It was 7:50 p.m., and C.J. was already on his second hustle of the day, at Virgin Mega (he'd already worked the after-school shift at Foot Locker). Not only was he exhausted, he had just gotten a call from his grandma, who'd accidentally spilled her blood pressure pills down the toilet (and she could end up in the emergency room if she didn't take her nighttime dose). Now he'd have to come up with the seventy-five bucks needed to buy her a new bottle before he went home. So far today, he had had one strike from his boss, Bob, for being late. Two more, and he'd be sent home early, his pay docked for the day.

But the real icing on the cake? Seeing Tangie with Trey Stevens. Every time C.J. pictured that corny poser with his arm around her, he felt nauseous. He wished he could just focus on Izzy in her sexy boy shorts. It was much less stressful.

Drama. Always. *Why?*

Rita, the aspiring Puerto Rican model-actress working the register next to him, started giggling.

"Why you so happy?" C.J. snapped.

"I'm all excited cuz we've got special guests coming in tonight."

"For real? Who's coming in?"

"You didn't know?" Rita smacked him on the arm. "Omigod, C.J., where's your head at today? Big Boi and Andre 3000 are coming in to meet with Virgin Mega's publicist. Something about setting up an in-store promotion for this movie they're working on called *Idlewild*."

"That's wassup," said C.J., without looking up from his book, too stressed out just then to care. All he wanted to do was wrap up his shift, hit the nearest 24-hour Duane Reade for his grandma's meds, and take his ass home. He didn't want to talk or think about girls, or answer any questions from any of the few customers who were in there.

"Damn, babe, why you so distracted tonight?" Rita looked over at C.J., smiling to herself. She thought it was so cute and sexy, the way he was always so deep into his sketching that he ended up blocking out the entire world. It was all very "tortured artist." (Rita realized, though, that having a crush on C.J. was not an original thing. Every girl working at Virgin Mega—and two of the boys—wanted him.) But tonight, he was extra preoccupied.

"I ain't distracted," he said.

Not yet.

Tangie burst through the front door, still wearing her Armstrong dance-regulation uniform. She was headed straight for the checkout counter.

And she did not look happy.

"Okay, *now* I'm distracted," he said.

Tangie stormed right over to C.J.'s register and flung her gym bag on the floor. "C.J., we need to talk. Right now."

"Hey, Tangie."

"Hey, girl," she said, giving Rita a forced smile. "My bad, I didn't even see you."

"No, it's cool." Rita turned toward C.J., resting her hand on his upper arm. "I'm, uh, gonna go stock in show tunes. You can handle things out here, right, C.J.? Cool, see ya, babe."

As Rita walked away, Tangie breathed a very small sigh of relief. She had never really loved the idea of C.J. working with a six-foot-tall, two-pound model who, to her knowledge, looked as though she had never experienced a zit or period bloat.

He sighed, setting down his charcoal. "Let's do it. Why you ain't answered any of my texts? What's your problem?"

"My problem? What's *my* problem? C.J., why'd you say you loved me if you didn't mean it?"

"Why'd you say you loved *me* if you didn't mean it?"

"Oh . . . just . . . shut up." She was flustered and angry that her words were pouring out on top of each other.

"Well, clearly I was buggin'."

She swallowed hard. "Wh—what?"

"You gonna pretend like you don't know what I'm talkin' about?" Trey and Tangie, Tangie and Trey—he couldn't get them out of his mind.

"I *don't* know what you're talking about, and stop trying to change the subject!" Tangie slammed her hand down on the register counter. "C.J., why did you do it? Why'd you even come over? Why'd you kiss me like that? Why, why, why when you knew *the very next night* you and Izzy were gonna do a fucking *porn* shoot!" She whispered the word *fucking*. After all, they were in semipublic—she might have been furious, but she still had manners.

"Tangela, you're really gonna go hard like this in public?"

"C.J., you really gonna go hard like that in private?"

He paused, swiveling his baseball cap to the back of his head. "You know, you getting very heated for somebody hollerin' at a twinkle-toed wanksta. Congratulations, T., that's real smart."

Tangie just looked at him, opening and closing her mouth and trying to figure out what to say. "Excuse me? First of all, what I do or who you see me with is none of your business. And we're not even together. He's my tutor, though I don't know why I'm explaining this to you in the first place."

"Motha*f*—." C.J. tore off his hat and threw it on the floor, now furious. "I never thought I'd hear you sound so stupid, T. Listen to yourself. Your boy's a known playa. What are you *doing*? You really wanna play yourself out like this?"

Tangie felt herself about to get hysterical, but she fought back the tears. "Just shut up. Shut up."

"You're a good girl, Tangela. I just can't understand why . . . I mean, I can't . . ."

"Oh, I see what this is about. I sit around for years and watch you hit off every slutty trick in our grade, but, I get friends with Trey Stevens and you flip out." She folded her arms over her chest. "Maybe you're jealous."

"How I'm gonna be jealous of what's already mine?" He looked at her so hard she felt his gaze burn through her body.

She cleared her throat. "Oh, no you didn't!"

C.J. waited for her to say something more. "Good comeback, T."

She sputtered in frustration, wanting to punch him. That was the problem with arguing with somebody that knew you inside and out. "Why do you even care about who I'm with or not with? You got your girlfriend. You're good."

"She ain't my girlfriend, and I ain't gonna say it again. And whatchu care for? You're good."

Tangie didn't say anything.

"Yeah, I thought so," C.J. said.

"You know what? Whatever, I'll just say it, I don't care. You're crazy to think that I'd ever like Trey more than you. Crazy. Okay? Are you happy? I said it." She looked at him, waiting for him to say the same about Izzy. Panicking, she swallowed hard and decided to ask him the question she'd been avoiding for days. It was pathetic and needy, but she didn't care. Tangie was way past shame—she just needed to know the truth.

"C.J., do you . . . do love her more than me? Are you picking her over me?"

C.J. wouldn't look at her. First of all, he thought the question was stupid; Tangie should have known better than that. And secondly, he was sick of Tangie's making him look like a damned idiot—first at Skye's party, when she had shut down his offer to really get together; then when she had made that dumb "hood outreach" comment (which he pretended to be over); and now, when she had the nerve to run off with Trey Stevens after revealing her undying love to C.J. Apparently, she didn't know what—or who—the hell she wanted. And obviously, C.J. couldn't trust her. That hurt more than anything.

So in answer to Tangie's question, all he did was shrug.

In a blind rage, Tangie made a fist and punched him in the arm, hard. Then she slapped him across shis face. *Hard*. He recoiled, grabbing his bicep.

"God-*damn*! Be easy, yo! What the . . ."

"The other night was just a lie, wasn't it? Be a man and tell me the truth. It meant nothing. And *I* meant nothing." She was hysterical. A group of thirteen-year-old girls looking for the *Bring It On 2* DVD were staring at her, wide-eyed. "Just tell me it meant nothing, and I'll never bother you again!"

He couldn't believe she was going there. "If that's what you think, then I ain't got shit to say."

"Fuck you, C.J." She snatched her bag up off the floor, so pissed and hurt she was shaking from head to toe. "Just stay outta my life, okay?"

"Will do." His hand covered his cheek.

Just as she was about to turn around and head for the door, she caught a glimpse of what C.J. was working on in his sketchbook. It was Izzy. Naked. Tangie's mouth dropped open. She looked from the book to C.J., and then back again at the book. Quickly, he slammed it closed and looked at her.

"And what?" His voice sounded like it was laced with venom.

Shaking her head in disgust, she got the hell out of there.

Name: Nikolas Vardolas
Class: Sophomore
Major: Drama
Self-Awareness Session #: NV 2

You must be under a dreadful amount of pressure, Nick. You know, pretending to be someone you're not.

Yeah, but what choice do I have? I wanna stay at Armstrong; and if anyone finds out about me, my dad's shipping me off to my grandma in Greece. And believe me, Grandma Vardolas is not someone you'd wanna run into in a dark alley. The woman has a mustache and a goatee. Besides, I can handle it. I'm an actor, remember? I play straight so well, no one would ever guess the truth. I just need to hold on until college, anyway. Then I'll be far away and I can do whatever the hell I want. Wanna hear something funny, though? I think, well, I heard that Skye might like me. Insane, right? I've been thinking, maybe I should just suck it up and take her out.

It would please your father if you dated a girl, wouldn't it?

Are you kidding me? He'd love it! And dating Skye would really, like, drive home my whole "straight boy" act at school, too. I mean, the girl's such a Black Barbie—every guy in school will think I'm the Man. Let's just hope no one finds out that the Man gets his eyebrows waxed every Thursday.

22.

YOU DON'T HAVE TO BEG

SKYE WAS CONFUSED. She and Nick had had all the makings of a totally romantic first date, but now it seemed like the sexy, floppy-haired actor thought her walk-in closet was sexier than she was. Gazing into his eyes and speaking in a baby-soft, Paris Hilton whisper, she was declaring that she'd never met a guy so talented, funny, and superbly dressed.

Meanwhile, Nick's gorgeous teal eyes kept darting from her to her open walk-in closet. Fresh out of ideas, she stared down at her Goth-black nails (she had noticed in *Star* magazine that Lindsay, Mischa, and Nicole always rocked supershort nails and black polish—so chic!) and pouted, wondering where it had all gone wrong.

The evening had started off really well. Skye and Nick met up after school at Union Square Park, and she had paraded him around to all her girls for approval. Everyone agreed that he was the cutest white boy on earth, besides Justin. Of course, the unanimous approval made Skye like him even more.

They had decided to meet up at seven at the Angelika, Soho's famed indie film theater, to see *Hustle & Flow*. Skye was not into "hood" movies, but since Nick was an avid follower of black independent cinema and seemed to be obsessed with Terrence Howard, she decided to suck it up. *It's all about sacrifice when you're really feeling someone*, she told herself.

So she met him at the Angelika at 7:07, careful not to be exactly on time or to look as excited as she felt. As she walked along Houston Street and saw him standing in front of the theater, hot in his vintage Pumas, newsboy cap, and fitted message T reading I'M KIND OF A BIG DEAL, she wanted to die. His downtown-chic ensemble was the perfect contrast to her boho-sexy Catherine Malandrino paisley halter dress—together, they were the biracial equivalent of Justin and Cameron—though Skye's skin was much, much better than Cameron's! While they grabbed low-carb muffins and soy lattes at the Angelika's first-floor café and Nick went on and on about Terrence Howard's illustrious career, she was in another world.

Visions of their glittering future kept flitting through her mind—the two of them falling in love and becoming their grade's Trey and Eden! And right before graduation, they'd end up landing the same high-profile agent after their stellar performances in the senior festival. They'd move to Los Angeles together, and within months he'd land a Steven Soderbergh film with lots of smoking and talking and male full-frontal nudity that would go on to sweep the Cannes Film Festival. Meanwhile, she'd get tons of buzz playing a juicy supporting role in a Reese Witherspoon film about a couple of spoiled, trashy socialites who suffer a public falling-out after succumbing to anorexia and sex-tape scandals. Annie Leibowitz would then photograph Nick and Skye for a *Vanity Fair* cover story on Young Hollywood, and soon after, paparazzi shots of the photogenic lovers shopping at Fred Segal's and making out at the Coffee Bean and Tea Leaf would sell for thousands. They'd go on to win their first Golden Globes before turning twenty—Nick for playing a porn star with a heart of gold in *Porn to Be Wild*, a movie about Jenna Jameson's life; Skye for her role as a tough-talkin' supermodel in peril on *24*. And all their Armstong friends would read about their glamorous lives every week in *Us Weekly* and *In Touch Weekly* and want to slit their wrists with jealousy.

Sskye wondered if, after the movie, they should slip into the theater's vintage photo booth—a first-date souvenir would be so cute on her *E! True Hollywood Story*. Oh, she was in heaven. It was obvious that they were destined to become a supercouple. And she thought Nick was on the same page, until a few things suggested otherwise.

First of all, whenever she reached for his hand during the movie, he'd all of a sudden have an urge to fidget with his hair. And when she slipped her foot out of her Sigerson Morrison wedge to run it up under his jeans, he jerked away, whispering something about her toenail scratching him. What? She'd just had a chocolate-mint pedicure at Bliss!

And as they walked up Broadway to her favorite Mexican restaurant, Gonzalez y Gonzalez, Skye stopped Nick in the middle of the sidewalk to kiss him (an idea she had stolen from *Cosmo*'s "Why Don't You . . ." section), and he quickly spun around and blurted out, "Omigod, look at those flat-front khaki Bermuda shorts in the H&M window! They'd look *insane* on your superlong legs."

Clearly Nick thought she was hot, since all night long he'd showered her with compliments on everything from her "sparkly caramel highlights" to her "radiantly dewy skin." So why didn't he want to touch her? Maybe he was a virgin. Or worse, maybe he had some contagious disease, like that awful bird flu. Or maybe, horror of horrors, he was trying desperately to stay faithful to some chick back in D.C. Was that it?

So, while Nick went to the bathroom to wash his hands, Skye whipped out her pink, Swarovski crystal-studded Sidekick. She had to call Regina. As weird as that girl was, she was *always* there for her.

"Reggie-Reg?"

"Hey, Skye."

"Are you mad at me or something?"

"Huh?"

"Why'd you tell me this white boy was feeling me if he wasn't? Don't start shit if you don't have your information straight!"

"Wait, what are you talking about? Nick definitely likes you, Skye." Regina's heart began to race, and she hoped her voice didn't give it away. "What happened?"

"Well, I don't know," Skye wailed. "I kind of feel like he thinks I'm cute 'cause he keeps bigging me up. But he, like, refuses to come anywhere *near* my ass!"

"Well, *of course* he thinks you're cute," said Regina, trying to think of an excuse quickly. "Look, maybe he's just a romantic and doesn't want to rush into anything. Remember how Carrie was buggin', like, after a *week* because Aidan didn't want to sleep with her? And he told her that he wanted to go slow, because he'd slept with lots of girls too soon and it never went anywhere—and hello, whatever happened to romance?"

Skye's eyes widened, and she hopped up and down in her seat. "Oh, yeah, I remember that! So-o-o cute. And yeah, Nick's definitely the sensitive, romantic type. I need to pull back on the slutty thing so I don't terrify the poor boy."

"Yeah, just chill, I know he likes you," said Regina, her gut churning. It felt a lot like the time she had debuted her first amateur film at the Studio Museum of Harlem's Children's Theater Showcase, back in fifth grade.

"I *knew* he was feeling me!" Skye cried. "Okay, wish your girl luck." It all made perfect sense. Nick definitely thought she was sexy, but he was Sensitive Boy. He wanted to go slow, to savor her. And what was more flattering than the cutest white boy ever wanting to *savor* you? Suddenly reinvigorated, Skye decided to invite Nick up to her house—not for anything wild, just to get to know him on a more intimate, personal level. And since Eden had disappeared somewhere with Smoove Killah and her parents were doing business in London, the two would really be alone.

* * *

Back at her house, Skye and Nick were sitting on either side of her bed. The atmosphere was perfect for a romantic-but-taking-it-slow tête-à-tête—she'd lit her Regaud candles and dimmed the lights to give her room a sophisticated, French feel. She even plugged her iPod into the speakers and played her special "Sexy Time" playlist, which kicked off with Gwen Stefani's "Luxurious" (too slow jam–ish, maybe?). But either Nick was a total waste of pouty red lips and turquoise eyes, or Skye was not as cute as she thought.

All he wanted to talk about was his favorite screenplays, her opinion of Armstrong's drama department, and what it was like to grow up as showbiz royalty. It was kind of flattering that a guy would be so interested in her biography, but she wouldn't have wasted her überexpensive candles on a damned interview!

Was he ever going to pay attention to her? Apparently not, as he was now exploring her room, peering at picture frames and admiring her "Wall o' Glamour," i.e., her collection of pinup shots of classic, old-Hollywood divas.

Poor Nick. He was *dying* to rave about the perfection of Josephine Baker's finger waves, and to inform Skye that he could see in the picture that her prom date's suit jacket was too roomy in the shoulders, and most of all, he wanted to raid that closet of hers! Outside of the filthy-rich bitches on *My Super Sweet 16*, he'd never seen such an extensive wardrobe, never seen a bigger walk-in closet. Skye had racks and racks of sexy dresses, bags, and accessories. She had more than one hundred pairs of shoes, and a whole wall devoted to jeans. And her sweaters were *color-coordinated*.

But Nick was doing his damnedest to ignore it, because rifling through some girl's closet was the gayest thing ever. God, he wished he were there with Regina instead, so he could be open about the fact that he was dying to dress Skye up in her fabulous ensembles—the way he used to do with his friend Jenna's Barbies, back in the day.

Focus, Nick, he told himself. *Just remember, dating Skye will confirm your straightness, and then you can stay at Armstrong! Eyes on the prize, eyes on the prize* . . . Furrowing his brow, he tried to channel the straight-est guy he knew. Hmm . . . Billy Blanks, the tae bo guy? Vin Diesel?

"Hey, Nick? Come here a minute, I'm about to open a bottle of wine. Do you want red or white?" Skye had decided to move on to Plan B . . . get him wasted.

Nick was so lost in thought he jumped at the sound of her voice. With a frustrated sigh, he turned away from the Wall O' Glamour and sat back down on Skye's bed. And before his brain could censor his mouth, he blurted out the following: "You know, I couldn't help but notice that you have some *sick* ensembles, girl! You have to try something on for me."

Skye looked at him for a moment, baffled. "You're joking."

Always the actor, he quickly recovered with a line he knew she'd fall for. He lowered his voice, trying to sound all gravelly and butch, like—well, like Vin Diesel. "No, it's just that . . . well, it's a shame to let that kick-ass, supermodel figure go to waste in jeans. Don't get me wrong, you look hot as hell, but I want to see you in something straight-up sexy, like a hot dress."

Slowly, an excited grin spread over her face. Nick thought she had a supermodel body! So cute. And *that* was why he was so preoccupied with her closet—he just wanted to see her all dressed up, like in *Pretty Woman*, when Julia Roberts gave Richard Gere a lit-tle fashion show in that fancy boutique. Awww.

"Of course I'll try it on for you, silly boy. You don't have to *beg*."

Skye rushed into her closet and slid a turquoise Tocca halter dress off the rack. "No peeking," she called out teasingly, shutting the closet door behind her. After pulling it on, she studied herself in the full-length mirror and decided she looked irresistible. To cap it off, Skye pinned her thick, honey-streaked weave atop her head and pulled down some sexy, loose tendrils in the front. And then she slipped two cutlets—those jellylike falsies that give you an instant boob job—into her bra. *Give him Sexy Bitch*, she told herself, and she swept back out into the room. Giggling, she struck a sultry pose and blew him an over-the-shoulder kiss.

"Well? What do you think?"

Nick sat down on the edge of her bed, gaping at her in awe. "Skye, you're a goddess," he murmured, enthralled.

It was all Skye could do to keep from squealing—she had finally gotten to him! So *that* was what his hook was. Fashion! It made perfect sense—the artfully tousled curls, the gazillion-dollar Helmet Lang jeans—he was a total metrosexual. And, of course, he was an actor, and weren't they always looks-obsessed? If all she had to do to keep Nick's attention was dress like she had paparazzi chasing her, then that was what she'd do.

"So happy you think so," she purred, striding over to where Nick was sitting on the edge of the bed (she made sure to cross one foot in front of the other, à la Miss J. on *America's Next Top Model*). Standing over him, she tilted her chin down and peered at him through her lashes. It was one of Eden's signature sexy looks, which Skye was borrowing.

"I think you look incredible in that dress."

A thankful smile broke over Skye's face. "You really do?"

"Incredible," he repeated, looking her up and down.

That was all she needed to hear. There was no more denying how he felt. Suddenly, Skye bolted off the stool and flung herself on top of Nick, knocking them both backward onto the bed.

"Skye, w—wait," he cried out, but she shook her head vigorously and kissed him, hard. Nick was still for a second, but then he grabbed her shoulders and gently, but firmly, rolled her off him. He jumped off the bed, leaving her sitting there, humiliated and furious in her smeared M·A·C Lipglass.

Hysterical with embarrassment, Skye hollered, "Do you know how many guys would kill for me to kiss them like that? What's wrong with you? Or is it *me*?"

"Of course it's not you, you're fabulous!"

"You think I'm fat, don't you? Don't lie to me, jerk!"

"I'm serious! You know how hot you are, Skye."

She glared at him. "What is it, then? You have somebody back in D.C., don't you? That's why you're so quiet about your past."

Nick chewed on his bottom lip in silence, trying to buy time.

"Well, is that it?" Skye pulled herself together, folding her arms across her chest. "I just *mauled* you, Nick. The least you can do is be honest."

Finally he exhaled. "Yeah, I got somebody back home."

So it really *wasn't* her! She knew he liked her—all those compliments! "Well, long-distance relationships are notoriously wack," she said pointedly, raising an eyebrow.

Nick chuckled and nodded. "That's what they say."

"So that's the story, then! You're a faithful boyfriend."

"Yeah," he said with a sheepish shrug, looking everywhere but at her.

"You're a dying breed. Just so you know."

He smiled at her, his pouty red lips looking so kissable her knees went weak. "Listen, I had a great time with you tonight. But, I . . . I think I should probably go."

"Yeah, okay," she said, analyzing the situation as she watched his cute ass head for the door. It absolutely wasn't over. With fresh hope, she got up and met him at the doorway. Rising up on her tiptoes, she kissed him on the cheek and whispered, "She's a lucky bitch."

Nick hugged Skye, pressing every inch of his body against hers. Then, miracle of miracles, he leaned in and kissed her long and softly on her glossy lips. *That D.C. chick is so done,* Skye thought triumphantly.

23.

YOU SAY THAT TO ALL YOUR TUTEES

TANGIE HAD BEEN CRYING FOR HOURS, curled up on her bed, when her cell phone went off. *Trey!*

Quickly, Tangie tried to pull herself together. Wiping her damp eyes and nose with her sleeve, she grabbed a tube of lip gloss from the nightstand drawer and slicked it on. Which was clearly ridiculous, because Trey couldn't see her. But it made her feel better.

"Hello," she croaked, hoping she didn't have that telltale scratchy, crybaby voice.

"Wassup, girl, you been cryin'?"

"Um, no. I think I'm coming down with a cold," she responded, her stomach flip-flopping. She'd talked to Trey only once on the phone, and it had been to set up today's tutoring session. Her mind raced, trying to find something to talk to him about. The extent of their sorta-kinda relationship was two tutoring/hook-up sessions. There was a lot of dancing and kissing, but not much talking. She never really saw him in the hallways during school, either—and when she did, he was always busy dealing with his faithful followers.

"You better fight that shit, ma. They got Spotlight announcements coming out on Saturday! I don't want all my hard work to go to waste," he said jokingly.

"I know, I know."

"So, how you feelin', ma?"

"Um . . ." she didn't know what to say. She had just told him she had a cold. "How are you?"

"Chillin'."

"Yeah? Cool."

Silence followed.

"So, um, are you sore? From practicing?"

"Naahh. I'm Trey Stevens, girl! Trey Stevens don't get sore—my shit *stays* smooth, knowwhatI'msayin'? I'm always up for the challenge."

She didn't know what else to say, so she just giggled idiotically.

"So, you been thinkin' about me?"

"Um, I don't know." Tangie giggled again, her cheeks burning hot. "Have you been thinking about me?"

"Man, I can't *stop* thinkin' about you. I don't think about nothin' else." Silently, he cringed at the TV. His team, the New York Jets, had just fallen way behind in the game.

"Our session was fun today, right?"

"Huh?" The Jets were killing him. He felt like kicking the screen, but the Sony *Wega* 62" plasma TV had been a Christmas present from his dad.

"Practice was fun, right?"

"Yeah, yeah, yeah! You major, girl. Seriously, you got skills."

"I bet you say that to all your tutees." *There*, she thought. *I did it! I flirted!*

"*Tutee?* That shit sounds funny. *Tutee.* Listen to you, with the crazy lingo. You're cute, you know that?"

"Oh, stop it," she said, suddenly embarrassed at her corniness. Who said *tutee*?

"Hey, I want to talk to you about something."

"You do? What is it?"

"I really . . . well, I feel like I'm really starting to like you, nahmean?" He flinched as the Jets lost the ball again. "It's weird, it's like, things are happening really fast with us."

At first, Tangie was so shocked and flattered that she couldn't speak.

"You there?"

"Yeah, yeah, yeah, I'm here. I was just gonna say, I kinda feel the same way."

"Cool! But I want to be responsible here. I'm older than you, more experienced, and I've learned that relationships, know whatI'msayin', they're all about honesty. Trust. Openness."

"Oh, of course. I know." Tangie had no idea what he was talking about, but she'd heard the word "relationship" in there, and that was definitely a good thing.

"Tangie, I want to be open with you about something."

"Trey? Is something wrong?"

"No, I'm cool." He wasn't. He was so furious, he could barely concentrate. The Jets *sucked*.

"Okay. You can tell me anything."

"Can I, Tangie?" He lowered his voice to a whisper. "This is shit I never talk about wit' nobody, so I really need to know I can trust you."

"Of course you can, Trey." Tangie sat up, rod-straight, in the bed. She couldn't believe how fast things were moving! She felt as if she were living in a movie.

"You know about me and Eden, right? I mean, yeah, everybody does. What folks don't know is that she hurt me. She hurt me bad."

"I'm so sorry. What . . ."

"I loved Eden so much. I put my all into that relationship. I *lived* for that girl, and she broke my heart with all her shadiness." He paused for effect, sniffing a little. "That did something to me, yo. It hardened me a little."

"I can understand that." Tangie's hand went to her heart; she was moved by his honesty.

"And now, I gotta be *careful* with mine. You know, take baby steps."

"You're right. That's the best thing."

"It was crazy, being part of such a public couple, and then having a public breakup. Man, I *feel* what Brad and Jen went though, nahmean? On sort of a smaller level, but it's the same shit. Everybody was in ours. Spreading lies and extra nonsense just to say something."

Tangie shook her head. "I can't imagine."

"Yeah, so now, I really don't like folks in my business." He paused, letting his words sink in. "I need to keep our thing between us, ya heard? The more people we involve, the worse off we'll be. And, Tangie?"

"Yeah?"

"I want to *protect* what we got. Look, people like to spread lies about me, like I'm a playa. I'm not, but I wanna spare you all the drama. As soon as folks find out you're kicking it with me, they're gonna start whispering all kinds of nonsense in your ear. Who they seen me with, where I been . . . just lies." He lowered his voice to an oh-so-sincere whisper. "Let me protect you from that, ma."

Tangie couldn't help it—the smile started small, and then it spread all over her face until she was cheesing like a first-grader posing for her very first school photo. She had no idea Trey felt so strongly about her! She'd never felt so special. "Trey, I . . ."

"Oh, wait, hold on." The Jets made their first down. "Okay, go 'head."

"No, I only wanted to say that I totally understand." And she did. Going public sounded like more stress than she could handle. And since Trey had suffered through a nasty breakup in front of the whole school, he was more experienced with this stuff than she was. So, yeah, maybe it was better to keep things quiet for now. Except for the fact that, at some point, she'd have to tell Skye. This was too big to keep from her.

"So, you feel me, then?"

Tangie nodded, and then realized he couldn't see her. "Yeah, I do. Let's definitely keep things quiet. It's for the best."

"Cool, cool!" Trey sounded chipper. "So, then, we're on the same page, right?"

"Totally," said Tangie, grinning from ear to ear. "Everything'll strictly be between me and you. It's the mature thing to do."

Trey was surprised and relieved that she bought it. He couldn't remember it's ever having been that easy, convincing a girl to keep her mouth shut. Usually, the girls he messed with were way too experienced to believe his story about being "hurt before." But Tangie? It was like taking candy from a baby.

When Tangie hung up the phone, she felt exhilarated and closer to Trey than ever before. She decided, then and there, not to shed one more tear over C.J. What was the point, when such a mature, thoughtful—not to mention endlessly popular—boy wanted to be with her?

It felt, in fact, too good to be true.

24.

THE NAME'S EDEN CARMICHAEL

IT WAS THE THIRD DAY OF SCHOOL, and once again Eden was dropped off by Smoove Killah. A pattern was forming. The car would roll up in front of Armstrong's bustling-with-kids front steps, and Puddin' would open Skye's door, grab her bag, and help her out of the Phantom. Smoove would then step outside the car to kiss her good-bye, while half the kids in the crowd took "candid" shots of the couple on their camera phones (the other half pretended not to stare—after all, Smoove was no different than they; weren't they *all* artists?). Then, as Eden walked up the stairs to the front doors, the crowd would part as if she were a queen. Or Lindsay Lohan, at least.

This was the first day, though, that three giggling, screeching, ninth-grade drama majors ran up to her with a copy of the *New York Post*. Clearly, they had not gotten the "stars are just like us" memo, because they were as giddy and amped as a couple of *TRL* audience members.

"Omigod, you're Eden Carmichael, right?" The crew's spokesperson was a busty redhead with braces and a T-shirt reading SAVE THE DRAMA FOR YOUR MAMA.

"Mm-hmm." Eden yawned, too hungover and sleep-deprived to form complete sentences. She'd been out till 4 a.m. the night before at Damon Dash's birthday party, and had spent the last three hours having X-induced sex with Smoove. Of course, her daily breakfast of two Valium and a Twix had done nothing to curb her overall wooziness.

"My older sister Jodie's in your grade. Last year, she played a New Orleans townsperson when you were Stella in *A Streetcar Named Desire*. She always said you were the most generous, giving actor she'd ever worked with," the redhead babbled.

"Mmm, Jodie. What a performer." Eden had never met Jodie in her life.

"Anyway, I'm Candace, and this is Jen and Stacy, and we're crazy stoked to meet you! You know, I was actually on the fence about the whole drama thing, but when I saw you perform your tryout monologue at the Armstrong auditions last year, I was so moved! And your *dad*! He was in the very first Broadway play I saw, *Purlie* . . ."

Eden's eyes were crossing behind her oversize Dior shades. *Are there really three of these girls, or am I seeing triple?*

". . . And, anyway, I know it's the tackiest, but will you sign my Page Six?"

"Page Six? Why?" Eden jerked back to life, snatching the newspaper out of Candace's hands. Smack in the middle of Page Six, the *New York Post*'s wildly famous gossip page read by everyone in Manhattan, was a huge photo of her and Smoove walking into La Esquina. They were arm in arm, and he was whispering something in her ear. With her tiny D&G minidress, wild mane of auburn-streaked hair, and mile-high stilettos, she looked like a bona fide movie star. And the sexy, world-famous rap star? He looked positively smitten.

"Can if I borrow this for a second?" she blurted out, breathless.

"But I . . ."

"Thanks, you're fabulous," she said, bolting up the stairs and through the front doors, en route almost mowing down a group of kids practicing a mime routine. It was probably the fastest Eden had moved since she had been a toddler.

She headed straight for the senior lounge, where most of the twelfth-graders hung out before classes. Marisol was in her usual pre-first-bell spot, sprawled out in a purple beanbag chair with her iPod headphones in her ears. She was humming along to—who else—Mariah Carey, and flipping through the latest copy of *Backstage*, a trade magazine for people in the performing arts. Eden rushed over to her best friend and, without saying a word, tossed the newspaper in her lap.

"What the . . ."

"Just read," ordered Eden excitedly.

Marisol picked up the newspaper and started reading. Ever so slowly, her already enormous eyes widened to twice their size. With a delighted squeal, she grabbed Eden's miniskirt and yanked her down next to her on the beanbag. She read the caption aloud: *"All eyes were on Smoove Killah and his new mystery lady at the exclusive eatery La Esquina on Wednesday night. The name's Eden Carmichael, and the game's landing hip-hop's sexiest—and formerly most taken—bad boy. According to reports, Smoove and the frighteningly young former child star (who also happens to be the daughter of Tony-winning Broadway producer Junior Carmichael and TV actress Alexa Evans) are knocking down walls at Hotel Gansevoort. No word yet on how the rapper's on-again off-again lovah, neo-soul diva Pearl, is taking all of this."*

"No," said Marisol, in utter disbelief.

"Yes."

"*No.*"

"I swear to God."

"You're a fucking superstar, do you understand me?"

"I understand that I'm *fucking* a superstar."

Marisol yanked the headphones out of her ears. "This is crazy-insane ridiculous, okay? Do you realize that the whole world reads Page Six? Do you realize that you are now tabloid fodder? Do you realize what this will do for your *career*?"

"You mean *your* career," teased Eden, giggling. She knew that by lunchtime, everyone in school would've seen Page Six—oh, it felt good to be famous.

"Okay, yes, I clearly expect to get a hook on one of Smoove's joints out of this, but we're talking about you."

Eden raised her arms over her head and stretched. The Valium was really kicking in. "Can you believe the part about us knocking down the walls?"

"You're mom's gonna die."

"Please. Alexa'll be thrilled she got a mention."

Marisol scanned the item again. "Damn, girl, it says that you 'landed' him. It's in print, mama. You're his main girl! You're famous! You're like the black Brangelina! Smeden? Edoove?"

She wrinkled up her nose. "Ick, spare me. Remember when everyone used to call me and Trey 'Treyden'?"

"That was on such a smaller scale; are you kidding? Trey might think he's major, but he's just high school major. There's a difference, babe." Marisol kept rereading, shaking her head in awe. "Tell me you're not *hyped* Trey's gonna see this! Come on, admit you're loving how jealous he's about to be."

"Honestly, I don't care. I'm not really trippin' off Trey. He's so done in my mind." Eden yawned, feeling drowsy. "I don't know, the biggest thing is getting that buzz."

"Hell, yeah, it's all about the buzz. At the end of the day, there's really only so much the goddamned senior talent showcase can do for our careers. The best of us'll get agents out of it, but then what? The first year out is pure hell—unless you got buzz."

"Right, humiliating budget castings, cattle calls, off-off-off Broadway—I just can't. I mean, I'm beyond that." Eden looked around, making sure no one was overhearing this. She didn't need any diva rumors threatening her golden-girl image. "Look, getting an agent isn't gonna be hard for me. I mean, I already had a hit TV show. I want the best parts, the best castings, and to do that I need *attention*—something beyond starring in all my dumb high school plays."

Marisol raised her eyebrows in surprise. It was the most she'd heard her friend say in, like, three years. "If it's attention you wanted, attention you got, Edie. But answer me this: are you even feeling Smoove? Or is it just for the press?" She lowered her voice.

Eden shrugged, eternally blasé. "He's a sweetie. Like, really cute and generous. I mean, he pays for everything and doesn't want me to lift a damned finger. Look, he even gave me his Visa and told me I could get whatever I want." She pulled the platinum card out of her Marc Jacobs wallet, and Marisol almost suffered a seizure.

"Shut *up*!"

"I know, I know! Listen, meet me at our bench in Union Square after school and we'll go to Intermix, okay? It's so on."

"It's *so* on, bitch!" Marisol bounced up and down in the beanbag and kissed her best friend on the cheek. She couldn't believe her luck. "Wait, but hello? Is he, like, any good? In bed?"

"I mean, he's *aii-iight*. Honestly? He's a little . . . um, out there."

"Classify this. Is he out there like R. Kelly peeing on fourteen-year-olds?"

"No, but . . ." Eden stopped, not sure if she should continue. "He, well, he likes me to whip him with my bra while he lies in a fetal position and sucks on the heel of my stilettos. That's bugged, right?"

Marisol paused. "Sweetie, don't tell anybody that."

What Eden really didn't want to say was that everyone in Smoove's entourage was parking, and that a crazy jump-off had threatened her life, and that Smoove quite possibly had syphilis. Being around him was kind of scary, but kind of thrilling, too.

On Smoove's arm, Eden was a star. And the fact that their relationship was thrusting her back into the public eye after five years of being a virtual nobody—well, it made his shadiness so worth it. Eden really was beyond the first-year-out-of-high-school acting trenches. It would be humiliating for a former child TV star to be reduced to playing Girl Number Three in an infomercial, or understudying in some play no one had ever heard of. And honestly, there were worse ways to get media attention than dating a Grammy-winning rapper. Weren't there?

Name: Regina Marie Evangeline Leon Guerrero
Class: Sophomore
Major: Film
Self-Awareness Session #: RG 2

*I don't know if it's a strictly Armstrong thing or if it's like this at
other schools, but there are certain girls that have this, like, glow
about them. You see it in class, in the hallway, at lunch, everywhere.
Their hair's always tight, they've got the best clothes. And the teachers always adore them, you know, calling on them first and giving
them the starring roles in every production. I don't know how you get
that glow, but when you do, it's like you can do no wrong. You're perfection. Eden Carmichael glows. And so does Skye.*

You say all these wonderful things about Skye, but you're
deceiving her. Can you explain that?

*Here's the thing. I love Skye, but sometimes she can be . . . well, some-
times she's pretty nasty. A lot of people would say our friendship seems
one-sided. But guess what? Not anymore. Don't get me wrong, I do
feel so terrible about what I did—you know, the whole Nick thing—
but in a weird way, I feel like things are finally equal between us.*

Am I evil?

"IS IT JUST ME," ASKED KAMILLAH, "or are our boys mad distant this year?"

It was lunchtime, and she, Regina, Skye, and Tangie were sharing a tiny bench in the massively crowded courtyard. It was a surprisingly hot ninety degrees outside, somebody was blasting Nelly Furtado and Timbaland's "Promiscuous" out of iPod speakers, and the always-animated Armstrong students were even more hyper than usual.

On the opposite side of the courtyard from the girls were Kyle, C.J., Vincet, and two other guys huddled around Black in their usual cypher. Kamillah had a point; they couldn't have been farther away from the It chicks if they had tried.

Were they trying?

"What do you mean?" Tangie didn't get it.

"You're kinda right, Kamillah," said Regina, squinting across the courtyard at the little cypher. "Last year, we weren't, like, two different crews—we all rolled together. And now we barely talk."

"What's that all about, yo?" Kamillah crossed her arms and pouted. Was Black suddenly over her?

"I know what it's about," said Skye, happily sipping on vitamin water through a straw. She was in a positively giddy mood after the previous night's date. "It's C.J."

"C.J.?" Kamillah was both intrigued and relieved. Thank God it wasn't *her* man.

Tangie raised an eyebrow. Just hearing his name made her want to vomit. What, was Skye going to tell more of her secret exploits?

Tangie and Skye had been verbally circling each other, kinda-sorta not-talking. "What'd he do now?"

Skye rolled her greenish-hazel eyes. "You haven't noticed how weird he's been acting? All cagey and secretive. It's so obvious he's avoiding us. It's 'cause he's messing with Izzy and he knows we know what everyone's saying about her. He's not trying to hear a lecture."

Kamillah squinted over at the huddle and gasped. "Omigod, look! Exhibit A, thank you very much."

They all craned their necks to study the group and realized that Black wasn't alone in the center of the huddle. Izzy was so short they hadn't seen her at first, but there she was with Black, bobbing her head and freestyling. And the boys *loved it.*

When she finished rhyming, their little huddle exploded into laughter, and Black pounded her on the back, clapping and bigging her up. The girls looked over at her with a mixture of jealousy, disgust, and admiration. The girls spent all their time trying to look and act hot for these guys, and then a random chick dropped out of the sky and stole them out from under their noses.

"I can't *stand* that girl," sneered Kamillah. "She's trying so hard to be down it's embarrassing."

"She really isn't, though," said Tangie, watching them. No matter how much it hurt to see them together, she had to accept it, or she'd go crazy. She was trying to be mature; just like Trey said. And it wasn't very "girl power" to drop Izzy, her TMI twin, because of some guy.

Some guy that had broken her heart.

"How can you say Izzy isn't overdoing it, Tangie? Look at her; she's so fake!" Kamillah was furious that her man was fawning all over Izzy, in plain view of the entire school. *Oh, he's not getting any for weeks*, she thought.

"No, really, she's actually an aspiring rapper. Her lyrics are kinda tight. I've heard them."

"Oh, please," said Kamillah. "I've seen girls like that my whole life. Trying so hard to act down with the boys, you know, talking about mix tapes and Air Force Ones and, like, Kobe vs. A.I. But guys see through that 'look at me, I'm so cool' act."

"Yeah, once they hit it!" Skye giggled at her own joke. Nothing was going to bother her today. She had a new man!

Meanwhile, Regina was watching Skye closely, wondering why she looked so damned happy. What exactly had *happened* on that date?

"I'm just saying, I *know* Izzy better stay away from Black." Kamillah's neck swiveled recklessly. "I can't believe she and C.J. are talking. But then again, I can—they're peas in a fucking pod. Both got shady pasts."

Skye looked at Tangie from the corner of her eye, wondering if she was uncomfortable. "Is all this C.J. talk bothering you, sweetie?"

"Why would it bother me?" She narrowed her eyes at Skye. "I mean, me and C.J. are just friends. Really, it's all good. And it's really nobody's business but mine."

Kamillah's head swung back and forth between the two girls. *Damn. What the hell's up with them?*

Skye shrugged, happy to go back to daydreaming about Nick. "Whatever you say, babe. Just know that I think your boy lost major points messing with that trash."

"I thought you liked Izzy," said Regina.

"Uh, no. She's o-*kaay*. At first I thought she'd be a cute addition to our crew, but the grace period is just about up. Look at her, laughing way too hard. Really, what's that funny? I just don't trust her."

Kamillah decided it was time for a subject change. She was getting too heated up. "Oooh, Skye, how was your date last night? Do you love him?"

"Omigod, yes! Those eyes. And he's so into me, you know? But wait, the best part is—that white boy can kiss!"

Tangie wondered when she'd have the nerve to break *her* relationship news.

"I knew it would work out," said Kamillah, clapping excitedly. "Y'all had mad chemistry in Southern Playwrights."

"I know, right? I wouldn't be surprised if we *both* got picked for Spotlight on Saturday, just on the strength of our line reading the other day." Skye shivered with glee. "Can you imagine? Oh, we'd be such a power couple! Don't you think, Reggie-Reg?"

"Uh-huh," Regina said blankly. *Hold on, Nick had kissed Skye?* No, no, no—that wasn't in the plan!

He must've been thinking that the straighter he acts, the longer he gets to stay in New York, thought Regina. And what was straighter than dating Skye?

"Tangie, I can't wait for you to meet Nick," Skye was gushing. "You'd love him."

"He sounds cute," said Tangie, distracted. She was just as excited about Trey as Skye was about Nick—so why was she so nervous about telling Skye? *Because I know she'll be mad as all get out.*

Somehow, Skye would turn it around and make it seem as though she was being disloyal to Eden (yeah, the same Eden who could barely stand to breathe the same air as her little sister). Maybe it was better to not say anything at all.

And anyway, what would Tangie say? That she and Trey kissed and stuff, but only during their tutoring sessions? That they never spoke during school, but they really had an *amazing* connection when they were alone? That Trey wanted to keep their "thing" a secret? Tangie totally understood his reasons, but Skye might not. You kind of really had to be there to get it.

"So now that I've invited Nick to my party on Friday night, my ensemble has to change," said Skye. "I'll probably wear my blingy Giuseppe Zanotti stilettos instead of the Cynthia Rowley espadrille wedges."

"Cute," said Tangie, hardly listening.

"Girl, I can't wait for your party!" Kamillah hopped up and down in her seat. "Your joints are always off the hook! Did your dad get you Funkmaster Flex again?"

"No, Vineet's gonna DJ. But you know he's tight."

"Please, he's gonna rip that shit!" Kamilah grinned. "I love Vineet. That's a sexy Indian boy."

"You think everybody's sexy," said Regina, who had also been really excited about the party until about five minutes before, when she realized that the Nick and Skye thing could quite possibly go up in flames.

"What am I gonna wear?" Tangie wondered aloud. This was a big deal, her first Armstrong party. She had gone to Skye's school's out thing last year, obviously, but it was different—she was still an outsider.

"With those curls," said Kamillah, "you could come naked."

"Definitely liberate the curls from the whole dancer-bun thing," agreed Skye. "Go big. Think wild, you know, all over the place. Wanton."

Tangie nodded, taking mental notes.

"So, you gonna invite Izzy?" Kamillah's eyes twinkled.

Skye shrugged. "It's really up to C.J., I mean, she's *his* jump-off, you know? Personally, I think she's a bad influence."

"Oh, shit, here she comes, y'all," whispered Kamillah, smacking Skye on the leg. "Be nice."

Izzy sauntered lazily over to them from the opposite side of the park, clutching a newspaper.

"Hey, Tangie, what it do, girls?" Everyone gave her a warm welcome, like they hadn't just been ripping her to shreds. "Yo, your boys are crazy. Black's got some ill lyrics. You ever hear them?"

"Of course," said Kamillah, which was a lie. Black didn't like to practice in front of her; it made him nervous. Oh, she wanted to slap Izzy—how dare she know more about Kamillah's man than Kamillah did?

"Anyway, about me and Nick, I really think that the world's ready for the first interracial power couple, don't you? We'd be really cute."

"Speaking of power couple," started Izzy, "did y'all see the paper? About your sister? Crazy, right?"

"No, what?"

"Isn't your sister's name Eden?"

"Of course."

"Yeah, I got my *New York Post* right here. Madness, right? I used to love Smoove, before he started singing on his own hooks like god-damned Ja Rule. So wack. Why can't he get Mary J. or Mariah or, hello, *Pearl*?"

Kamillah snapped up the paper and, seeing Eden's picture, screamed. She quickly read it out loud. "Skye, you bitch! You knew about this and didn't tell me?"

Skye's skin looked green. "Of course I knew about it, I just wanted to surprise you!" She took the newspaper from her and scanned the page. She'd seen her big sister and Smoove get out of the car together just yesterday, but now the *Post*? And Eden hadn't said shit about it, either. "Yeah, Eden's so excited. She's really feeling Smoove, it's so cute."

Kamillah was bouncing off the walls. "Wait, has she introduced you to him?"

"Of course she has! *Hello!* I'm her sister. He's really cool, so unlike his public image, you know, shooting up Hot 97 and shit. He thinks of me like a baby sister," she said, totally lying. She folded up the paper and stuck in her purse. "You know what? I gotta go to class. Mr. Lopez wanted to see me before practice."

"Yeah, I'm-a go with you," said Kamillah, hopping off the bench. "I wanna hear more about Smoove."

"You coming?" Skye looked at Regina quizzically. She usually followed her everywhere.

Regina had actually planned on hanging back and looking for Nick, to get to the bottom of that kiss. But, as usual, she followed Skye's orders—it was just habit. "Oh, yeah, sorry. See y'all later."

Ignoring Izzy completely, Kamillah, Skye, and Regina said good-bye to Tangie and skittered away, whispering pointedly. Tangie and Izzy looked at each other and each rolled their eyes.

"Listen, I'm sorry that Skye acts so shady around you."

"Please, I feel bad for that girl," said Izzy, shaking her head. "Poor Skye."

That was a new one. "What do you mean, 'Poor Skye'?"

"Clearly, she was the last to hear about her own sister being in Page Six, and she was embarrassed and hurt." Izzy shrugged. "I mean, I've heard about her sister—she sounds like a satanic Miss America or something. It must suck to be Skye sometimes."

Tangie nodded, considering this. She was impressed that Izzy—a virtual stranger—could see through Skye like that. But it was a little disconcerting, too. *What can she tell about me?* Tangie wondered.

"Why couldn't she just be honest about Eden not telling her?" asked Tangie. "Everyone knows her sister can't stand her, but she's always pretending that they're, like, supertight. It's really sad."

"Ain't y'all supposed to be best friends?"

Tangie smiled sadly. "Yeah, something like that."

"Then what's up with all that secrecy and shadiness? How're y'all best friends if she can't come clean with you? And vice versa." Izzy shrugged. "Life's too short, ma."

She was right. Izzy was always right. It was weird, like she wasn't really a teenager at all, but a thirty-year-old woman sent back to high school to teach everyone a lesson. Tangie just wished Izzy would take some of her own advice and come clean about her past—

she couldn't stop thinking about that "Unsigned Hype" review from *The Source* (it was all anyone could talk about, ever since Kamillah had begun passing the article around during Voice Criticism class).

Shadiness aside, Tangie felt like she could trust Izzy. And with her and Skye growing farther apart, she really felt lucky that she had someone else to talk to.

She would've felt even luckier if Izzy hadn't been going with the boy she loved.

26.

I'M AN IT CHICK

"ACTORS, ACTORS, PLEASE SETTLE DOWN," begged Ms. Zola, her fingers massaging her aching temples. Ms. Zola's improv class was always loud, and she always had a migraine. "You heard me, I said *settle down!*"

The class quieted.

"Thank heaven for quiet." Ms. Zola gingerly sat down on the edge of the stage and dry-swallowed one of the migraine pills she always clutched in her hand.

"Okay, on your seats you'll find a list of random words. Memorize them. In five minutes, you'll each be expected to recite the words, using the emotion I assign you. For example, if the emotion is 'fury,' you will recite the words in anger. If the emotion is 'elation,' you will recite the words in a joyful way. Understand?"

The class responded, "Yes, Ms. Zola," as she'd instructed them to do on the first day.

"This is stupid," Nick whispered to Regina. They purposely sat in the fourth row from the stage, so they could gossip without Ms. Zola hearing them. "Purple, zebra, cake, notebook, station wagon? How are we supposed to convey emotion with this shit?"

"Hell if I know," Regina answered. She wondered how she'd

be able to convey any emotion other than anxiety.

Ever since she had found out that Nick and Skye had kissed, she had felt as though her insides were turning inside out. Her little scheme had gone way too far.

She'd imagined they would go on one date, and during that one on one, outside the school setting, Skye would *really* see that they had no chemistry and somehow figure out that Nick was gay. She'd be humiliated, and that would be that. All Regina wanted was the secret satisfaction of knowing that Skye, perfect Skye, who always liked to embarrass Regina, felt *dumb* for once. Who knew that she'd truly start to like him?

Regina didn't *really* want to hurt Skye, not forever, anyway. Just temporarily. And she certainly wasn't trying to offend Nick, with whom she'd shared more in three days than she had shared with anyone in her whole life. What if Skye told him that Regina was the one who had started the Nick-likes-Skye rumor? He'd never speak to her again! *Ugh*, she thought, *I so didn't think this through.*

While Nick tried to memorize the assigned words by mumbling to himself, Regina tried damage control.

"So, uh, what are you gonna do about Skye?"

He rolled his eyes. "Reggie, how did I get in this situation? Seriously, it's all my fault. I went out with her for the stupidest, shallowest reasons, you know?" He leaned into her ear and brought his voice down to a barely audible whisper. "She's just so cute, and I knew that if folks saw me with her, there'd be no question that I was straight."

He paused, shaking his head in frustration. "Look, my whole life, girls have always been attracted to me for some reason. . . ."

"It's the eyes."

"I know, I was just being modest," he said with a devastating smile. "Seriously, though, they're *always* attracted to me. But, like, back in D.C. when I was out, usually within seconds of conversation they'd figure out I'm the biggest Sally. And then we'd become best friends and discuss Marc Jacobs's new line."

"Oh, Nick."

"But obviously, that didn't happen with Skye." He sighed, laying his head on Regina's shoulder. "It was really hard, harder than I thought it would be, to act straight around her. I mean, Skye's closet is a gay fashionista's wet dream. I wanted to roll around naked in her *shoes*."

"I know. She does give good shoe."

"I freaked out at one point, 'cause I asked her to try on a dress." Sheepishly, he grimaced at Regina. "I know, I know, so-o-o *Project Runway*! But I couldn't help it. Anyway, I thought she might've caught on, so I . . . well, I kissed her."

"No, you didn't!" Regina pretended to be shocked. "I can't believe you actually went there! Is, like, physically hooking up part of the no-really-I'm-straight plan?"

"I hadn't planned on it, but I had to do *something*! And, ugh, it was so unsexy." He groaned, thinking that taking Skye on a date was the worst decision he'd ever made. "You know what's funny? I thought the dress thing would be a dead giveaway for a girl as savvy as Skye. But she, like, didn't get it at all. *At all*."

"You know you're gonna have to tell her," Regina whispered, realizing what was at stake.

"Are you fucking kidding? You're the only one who knows! I can't do that, Regina, you know I can't."

"Listen to me, Nick. You're a brilliant actor, but nobody's that good. At some point she will figure it out. And then it'll be so much worse for you, because you'll have led her on for much longer."

"But what if she tells?"

"She won't," Regina said quickly. "Listen, I know her. Being in on such a huge secret will make her feel so special and privileged— she'll eat it up!"

Nick covered his face with his hands and mumbled, "God, do I have to? Can't you tell her?"

"No!" she answered forcefully. *If I told her, then she'd know I tricked her.* "I mean, I—I think that it would be better coming from you. More mature."

"I guess you're right," he said, sighing.

"And I promise. You can trust Skye never to tell anyone."

"I'm not worried about that. She's friends with you, so she's gotta be cool." He smiled at her, and she smiled back. "God, I *hate* the I'm-gay conversation. The shocked expression followed by 'not that there's anything wrong with that.' It's so tired."

"I can't imagine. Really, I can't."

Nick nodded slowly, thinking. "So . . . are we gonna talk about the irony of this situation?"

"What do you mean?" she asked.

"The fact that you're asking me to out myself to your girl, but you can't do the same?" He looked at her with soft eyes.

"Omigod, I could never tell her. I just can't. She . . . everybody already knows me one way, you know? I'm an It chick." She sighed, as if it were a tremendous burden.

"Can I be an It chick?"

"Are you kidding? Nick, you were *born* an It chick." Regina giggled and then got serious again. "I just can't imagine what Skye would . . . I don't know."

"I know how you feel. And believe me, I'm not judging you. I'm just as closeted as you are. But it's because I have no choice. If I could be out, I would." He hooked his arm through hers. "The thing is, sweetie, you're not being yourself. Do you realize you act totally different at group than you do here? That's not healthy. It's like being constantly constipated."

"*Ew.*"

"But look, no pressure. I know how scary it is. When my parents found out, they told me they had a friend once with a similar condition, and he cured it with vitamins." Nick sighed, remembering that traumatic night, and then shook it off. "I love your wedges. Louboutin?"

"Nah, they're Steve Madden knockoffs."

"You have way too much flava to be a lesbian. Maybe you're bi."

"Shut up before somebody hears you!" They giggled quietly. "Listen, just break it to her gently. You should tell her before her party on Saturday. That's when she's planning on hitting you with the Skye stealth bomb, just so you know."

He wrinkled his nose. "I don't even want to know what that is."

"It's a whole production, featuring lingerie and these chocolate-covered strawberries her housekeeper makes. Man up!"

"Oh God."

"I'm curious. Have you ever been with a girl?"

"You kidding? Of *course*! All gay boys start off with girls, that's usually how they figure out they're fags."

"Really?"

He nodded. "I hate vaginas, though. They're so squishy and hidden. Penises are just so much . . . cleaner, 'cause they're all out in the open."

"I think we just figured out what you should say to Skye," said Regina with a naughty grin.

"Fine, fine, fine!" he said, smiling. "Look, you want me to tell her? For you, I'll tell her. You're a really good friend to that girl. I hope she knows what she's got."

"Yeah, me, too," Regina said, feeling like the world's biggest jerk.

The longer Nick kept up his charade, the more devastated Skye would be when she found out. And Regina had to keep Nick from finding out that it was *she* who had told Skye that he liked her in the first place. Nick would never trust or talk to Regina again.

27.

DANCE THERAPY

THE BOOM BOX ON TOP OF THE PIANO was blasting the Ying Yang Twins' "Shake." The studio was steamy with the sweat of twenty-five sophomore dancers—and one senior—all trying to outshine everyone else. It was Friday, crunch time.

This was the last day they could showcase their talents before the teachers decided which students would audition for Fall Fling Spotlight. Tangie, for one, was giving it her all. Every so often she'd catch herself in the wall mirror as she danced, and find herself shocked at how intense her face looked. She'd never, ever worked this hard in her life. For her, Ms. Carmen's Advanced Beginners Street Funk was more than a required class, it was therapy.

With each pop-and-lock, she imagined punching C.J. in the head for toying with her emotions. With every body roll, she convinced herself that being in such close proximity to Trey (he was dancing two people away from her) didn't make her stomach flip. With each kick, she smashed Skye's betrayal into pieces. And with every Russian leap, she aimed to prove that Ms. Carmen was right about her: she *was* special enough to audition for Spotlight—even though her technique and training might have been the Skinny Bitches. But most of all, when Tangie danced, she convinced herself she was *the best.* There, in class, dancing her heart out, things were good. And it showed.

Standing in her usual spot in front of the piano, Ms. Carmen slammed her cane to the ground with every beat, occasionally hollering out insults to certain students—for example, "Your extension sucks, Tutti-Frutti," and "Harder, Pony, hit it *harder*—floppy is for losers," and "Practice much, Sugar? Learn the damn *steps*!" But even though she prided herself on being able to analyze each of her students' movements simultaneously, Ms. Carmen found herself staring at Tangie longer than she stared at the others.

It was obvious that Tangie had taken her advice and gotten a student tutor, because in just the first week of school Ms. Carmen had already noticed a profound difference in her technique. Tangie was much sharper, much more focused, and—there was something else. What was it? She actually was beginning to *move* differently. She was dancing with a new confidence, a sureness that she hadn't had a week before.

Ms. Carmen had to let the thought go, because, just then, three girls nearly fell on their faces while performing a near-impossible partner stunt (here and there, she enjoyed spicing up her choreography with some unnecessarily advanced moves just to separate the truly spectacular dancers from those who should maybe have taken up knitting).

"What the . . . everybody, take five! *Take five!* Yao, turn off the music." Yao, a shockingly flexible, bowlegged Vietnamese boy scurried over to the piano to turn off the stereo.

"Gentlemen, what's wrong with you? The damned partner stunt is abysmal. Sadder than sad. Corpselike. Look alive, please! Unless you want your partner to break her neck—at which point your parents will sue my ass, and I'll make sure you'll never have an ounce of happiness in your sad little lives—*get the hell out of the way* when she backflips into the split!" She shook her head in disgust, pacing back and forth in front of the heaving, exhausted class. "Tangie and

Robert, come to the front. Everyone, Robert is the only man in the room that did his lifts correctly."

Tangie was too nervous to move.

"Tangie, are you having a seizure or something? Come up, *now!*"

Jumping a little, Tangie hustled to join Robert at the front of the studio. She was in a sort of blissed-out daze, incredulous that Ms. Carmen had singled her out for the second time in one week. She certainly *felt* as if she'd brought it today, but it was another thing entirely to have Ms. Carmen notice! She just hoped Trey was watching.

Frankly, her classmates couldn't believe Tangie's luck, either. No one was surpised about Robert—after all, the tiny (five foot two, eighty-eight pounds) transfer student from Holland was an amazingly limber dancer and famous for his break-dancing stunts. But the new chick with the Melyssa Ford body? She had way too much ass for anyone ever to take seriously as a real dancer. Please!

"Somebody push PLAY," Ms. Carmen yelled, to no one in particular. A caramel-skinned girl with Afro-puffs turned the song on, and Ms. Carmen began barking out orders. "Okay, Tangie and Robert, just mark through the beginning, but do the partner work full out. Here it comes—*five, six, seven, eight, and ONE!*"

For a stunt that lasted only a couple of seconds, it was extremely complicated. And even though they'd nailed it five minutes ago, it was different performing such an intricate move in front of a studio of jealous dancers who wanted you to mess up. Despite the pressure, Robert spotted Tangie like a pro, and she leaned into her backflip. Then everything went wrong.

When she landed in the split, he was supposed to dive over her in a flying somersault—but, sadly, that didn't happen. Instead, he hesitated and ended up falling right on top of Tangie.

The first thing the principal always told Armstrong students at Orientation was that laughing at another student's honest efforts to create art would earn a student a demerit—five demerits and one was banned from performing in the next showcase. No one laughed at

Tangie and Robert, but there *was* a smattering of sarcastic applause.

Out of nowhere, Trey emerged from the group and swaggered up to Tangie and Robert, edging the tiny break-dancer out of the way. Before Ms. Carmen could object, Trey looked at Tangie, winked and whispered, "On the *two*, okay?" Without thinking, she nodded, and they broke out into the routine. And they were *good*.

Their chemistry was so obvious it looked as though they'd been partners forever. Trey and Tangie were in sync; they anticipated each other's moves, responding in a way that made it look easy. There was no getting around it—their version of the routine was sexy, funky, and brilliant. All anyone could do was stare at the couple in jealousy, wondering why they didn't look that good. And when Trey and Tangie got to the partner work, Trey was a strong spotter, and he performed the flying somersault without a hitch. Finally, Trey bowed and smoothly walked back to his row, leaving Tangie breathless and exhilarated at the front of the class.

Everyone was totally quiet, in awe of what they'd just seen. The guys wanted a piece of whatever Trey was selling, and the girls wanted the story. Were Trey and Tangie messing? He didn't dance like that with just any girl. Who'd this new chick think she was?

Tangie didn't care. All she knew was that she'd just performed, in public, with Trey Stevens. She also knew that (a) it was official, dancing had to be better than sex, and (b) she hadn't imagined the thing between her and Trey. It was right there, plain as day, for the world to see. Not only did *the* Trey Stevens like her, he was cool with showing an entire class how he felt!

What happened to "Keep things on the D.L."? thought Tangie. It was as if he were so overcome with passion for her that he had to break his own rules! Oh, she'd never felt more special in her entire life.

Without commenting on their performance, Ms. Carmen ordered Tangie to return to her row, and then addressed Trey. "Don't you ever . . . *ever* come to the front of my class without my instruction. I don't care how good you *think* you are, Trey Stevens, this is not your studio, it's *mine*. You are a student. You are a teenager. You've never been anywhere, you've never done anything. You've done one stupid video that impressed your friends. Would you like me to applaud?" She turned to face the class. "Everyone, please clap for Trey, because he's so magnificent."

The students clapped grudgingly. Trey chuckled, looking down and nonchalantly scratching his chin. Clearly, he was not bothered by the humiliation.

"A-yo, for real? You're a trip, Carm," he said, winking at her.

"You think you're so bad? No real company and no real entertainer will hire a kid who thinks he knows more than the choreographer. I promise you that."

Trey rolled his eyes, folding his arms across his chest. "I ain't said I know more than every choreographer. Just the one standing in front of me."

The studio was dead quiet, except for a few gasps. Ms. Carmen turned bright red. When she finally spoke, her voice was very slow and eerily calm. "Until you understand that you should be humbled in my presence, and thankful that I didn't kick you out of this school for that music-video stunt you pulled this summer, I want you out of here. Out!"

"Cool, I'm gone." Trey gave his chest a pound, kissed his fist, and threw a peace sign at the class. His signature move. "I'll catch y'all. Stay breezy, Carm."

"Good luck graduating without this class," Ms. Carmen called out after him as he exited the studio, not bothering to close the door behind him. She turned back to her stunned students and said, "Class dismissed. Please rehearse the changes over the weekend, I'll be drilling you on Monday. Tangela, I'd like to see you in my office, please. Right now."

Tangie'd be damned if she'd let Ms. Carmen ruin her high. Standing in the doorway, too nervous—and excited—to sit down, she looked at her teacher expectantly.

"Did I do something wrong, Ms. Carmen? I thought you liked my performance."

"Oh, of course, Chicken. You were good." Ms. Carmen sat behind her desk, crossing her graceful, still-shapely dancers legs in front of her. She motioned for Tangie to sit down, and she did.

Tangie frowned. "Then I don't understand."

"I asked you to find a dance tutor. Did you choose Trey Stevens?"

Tangie frowned. Was that what this was about? "Yeah, he's my tutor. How did you know?"

"I've watched this boy for over three years, I know his style. I can see his influence in you. And frankly, I'm worried."

"Am I not doing well?"

"You're doing as well as you can do for your third day of school," she said. "It's not that Trey's a bad tutor—he's very good, in fact. But he's not right for you. I need you to promise you'll switch immediately. I can recommend a beautiful senior dancer named Kendra. She's an amazing contemporary and hip-hop dancer. Christina Aguilera has already contacted her to audition for her tour after graduation, and . . ."

"But why do I need to switch? Is this because of the way he acts in class? Because, when we're alone, it's different, and . . ."

"Oh, God, stop," moaned Ms. Carmen. It was worse than she thought. "Listen, Tangie, you're a smart girl, right?"

"Of course, but—"

"You ever had a boyfriend?"

"Um, no."

Ms. Carmen sighed. "I don't trust Trey with you. This might sound inappropriate coming from a teacher, but I spend more time with you people than your own parents do. Understand?"

"Yeah, I guess."

"I've seen him do this before: hone in on some young, cute dancer, and then ruin her life. He's a very selfish kid. And I don't want an involvement with him to throw you off your course."

"But we're not involved, I—"

"I saw you two dance," Ms. Carmen blurted out, interrupting Tangie. I know 'together' when I see it. Listen, you're at a school full of cute, talented boys. You're a beautiful girl. Leave this one alone. Your career's more important than some guy." Ms. Carmen's expression turned steely. "May I remind you that I'm watching you closely for Spotlight?"

Tangie inhaled sharply. Was Ms. Carmen giving her an ultimatum?

Anyway, it was none of Ms. Carmen's business. What was up with her? One minute she was complimenting Tangie, giving her special attention and insisting she had something special—and the next minute, she was being mean. It really wasn't fair. It also wasn't fair that Tangie was expected not to hang out with Trey. C.J. got to like somebody and date, but she couldn't?

Sorry, Carm. Not gonna happen.

After their meeting, Ms. Carmen spent a long time sitting at her desk, thinking about Tangela Adams. She was a great girl—talented, sweet. But she was also running after the wrong guy. Unfortunately, Tangie wasn't the first pretty but naive young student of Ms. Carmen's to fall for Trey Stevens.

Despite dating that little actress (what was her name, Edith?) all those years, he'd always had a thing for de-virginizing sweet young dancers with fabulous futures ahead of them. And many times Ms. Carmen had seen what had happened to the girls when he dropped them. Their dancing suffered, they lost concentration; and come Fall, Winter, and Spring Fling audition times, they ended up losing out on the real star-making parts. And the way a student performed in her underclassman showcases affected how she was cast in the most make-or-break showcase of all, the Senior Festival—when the industry's top casting agents and company directors were in the audience.

Ms. Carmen pulled a crumpled letter out of her desk drawer.

She'd reread the letter every day since the first day of school, when she'd met Tangie. By now, the writing was smeared and blurry from Ms. Carmen's tears.

"Oh, Marcia," she whispered, holding the letter to her chest. "Tangie might end up hating me, but I won't let your daughter ruin her career over some guy. Especially after what you went through."

And then she carefully folded the letter back up and placed it back in the drawer. She hoped to God she was taking care of Tangie the way Marcia Adams had asked her to.

Name: Aziza Abdelrashid
Class: Freshman
Major: Fine Art
Self-Awareness Session #: AA 2

Let's talk about your relationship with Damon, your care-
giver. How, um, close are you?

*Yeah, yeah, yeah, I live with a thirty-five-year-old man, so what?
You'd have to be pretty sick to think I'd mess with somebody that age.
Plus, the man's engaged, okay? I don't know why folks can't see it
as the positive thing it is. If he hadn't shown up at the shelter that
morning, doing research for his damned book, who knows where I'd
be right now. And I'm not staying there forever, either—just until I
figure out what to do next. I know I can't go home. That much is
clear.*

*Sometimes I wonder how my life would be if things were different. If
I'd grown up in a different house, if I'd used a condom that night,
and if I had wanted so-called normal things, like making the cheerleading squad.*

Armstrong doesn't have a cheerleading squad, Ms. Abdelrashid.

*Whatever, Homey, that's not the point. What I'm saying is . . . I
can't deny what I'm good at, which is music and dance and art—
expressing myself creatively. One day the name Izzy Duz It will
mean something. You wait.*

28.
DRAMA AND A HALF

IT WAS 9:45, AND SKYE'S BACK-TO-SCHOOL JUMP-OFF was just getting good. Her personality was on full blast. She was moving from group to group, passing around red cups, and laughing, always laughing. (She'd learned that social trick from Eden. Whenever her sister was in large groups, she constantly erupted into "Clearly I'm the life of the party" giggles. It made her the center of attention, because who wouldn't want to be in on a joke that made Eden Carmichael laugh so prettily?)

Skye had been waiting for this night ever since her deliriously memorable School's a Wrap party the previous year. Hopefully, her first get-together of the school year would be even crazier!

First of all, Skye wasn't a lowly freshman anymore, so she had more social pull than before, and tons more folks were coming through. Secondly, she had the apartment to herself! Eden was out God-knows-where with Smoove Killah, their mom was at Milan's Fashion Week, and their dad was in L.A., presenting a TV pilot to NBC. Not that her flighty, distracted parents would've cared about the party, had they been around. As far as Alexa and Junior Carmichael were concerned, Skye and Eden could spend their days snorting blow off the toilet seat, as long as they maintained their weight, popularity, and status in Armstrong's drama department.

The living room was getting hot and crowded. Earlier, Skye had enlisted Vineet, Black, and Kyle to move the furniture out and had Vineet set up his DJ stand on Marcia's antique Chippendale desk. Skye had their cleaning lady buy tons of liquor and mixers; and C.J. promised to bring over some premium weed (for business purposes only, as he was still pissed at his cousin for butting into his business about Tangie the other day). Of course, he wasn't there yet, because he'd insisted on coming with Izzy instead of with his boys, even though Skye'd begged him not to. She was nervous enough without having that attention slut soak up all the male energy in the room.

Skye knew from watching Eden's parties that the hostess was never supposed to act as if the party weren't hot yet. So she'd made her closest friends get there at eight to be in good-time mode when folks started trickling in. And now, everyone was twisted.

Vineet was spinning Cheri Denis's "I Love You," and Skye and twelve or so of her best girlfriends—plus Nick, who was an amazing dancer—were huddled in the middle of the floor, dancing up a storm and sloshing red plastic cups filled with Red Bull–vodka cocktails. While waiting for C.J. to bring the weed, the boys hung out by the makeshift DJ booth, patiently bobbing their heads as Black spat out a rhyme they'd heard roughly a dozen times in the past week. Tangie and Regina were the only two not wasted. Regina was too worried she might slip and say something dangerous to Skye, so she was only smoking tonight. And Tangie didn't want to drink. The last time was at last year's School's a Wrap party, and she wasn't going to suffer another night of hell.

There was nothing worse than trying to make conversation with dozens of drunk kids when you were stone-cold sober. So Tangie did what she always did when she was feeling awkward and weird—she danced her ass off.

She was in the middle of the circle on the dance floor, leanin' wit' it and Beyoncé-butt-popping and twirling and shimmying, and the girls were chanting "Go, Tangie, go, Tangie," and she felt better than she had in a long, long time.

Tangie was determined to have fun that night at all costs. She was in a fabulous mood, mostly because of her after-school tutoring session with Trey. This time, they'd actually talked more than they danced or kissed. And it was a good conversation—Trey had really opened up to her. He told her that it really hurt, the way Armstrong folks tended to treat him more like a statue in a museum that a real person, because they were so in awe of his talent. And they talked about how much he was bench-pressing these days (250 pounds), and he'd also shared intimate details about shooting Missy's video (the catering was *fire*!). Tangie had left the studio on a giddy high—it was as if they were getting closer by the second.

That afternoon had provided all the more reason to ignore Ms. Carmen's warnings. Trey had never treated her like some naive girl he could take advantage of—he was really sweet. Her teacher probably was just concerned that Tangie would lose focus if she got into a serious relationship. But Ms. Carmen didn't have to worry—Tangie'd never let a boy get in the way of her dreams. First and foremost, she was a *dancer*, damn it.

She was a dancer who quite possibly was about to be Trey Stevens's new girlfriend. Instead of continuing to feel so out of place at Armstrong, instead of obsessing about C.J. and worrying about her relationship with Skye, she'd be too preoccupied with her own boyfriend—yes, *boyfriend*—to worry about all that. It was crazy to think about. Her whole life was about to change, and no one knew it but her.

She still hadn't figured out how to tell Skye. Tangie knew Skye would take the news of her dating Trey as some sort of betrayal. But what was she supposed to do? She liked him, he liked her, and didn't she deserve to be happy? *Hell, yeah*, thought Tangie as the music changed to Sean Paul's "Temperature" and she and Nick began winding down to the ground. *I'm having fun tonight, no matter what.*

It was a good thing Tangie made herself that promise, because at that precise moment, Izzy and C.J. burst through the front door together. *Together* together. When she saw them, Tangie almost froze solid on the dance floor, but she pulled herself together in time.

As they walked in, C.J.'s arm around her shoulder in a vaguely possessive way, Izzy had an unimpressed "Well *of course* he adores me" look on her face that fascinated Tangie. *If C.J. was all boo'd up with me like that, Stevie Wonder would be able to see my happiness,* she thought.

The boys immediately went over to them, giving C.J. and Izzy pounds, and talking and laughing just as if she were one of the guys. Tangie was instantly grateful she was sandwiched in between Kamillah and Nick so she could observe C.J. and Izzy without any-one's noticing. And what she saw almost knocked her out.

C.J. was all over Izzy, in ways that were perceptible only to Tangie. He rubbed her shoulders, smiled at her a tad too long, even kissed her on the cheek. He looked totally, completely, and utterly smitten.

But Izzy? Not so much. When she saw Tangie, she shrugged out of C.J.'s embrace and headed for the dance floor, but C.J. grabbed her arm, stopping her. Tangie could see her giggle and whisper some-thing to him, and then he shrugged, letting her go. From the dance floor, Tangie watched them like a hawk. *Something has changed,* she thought. *He looks thoroughly whipped.*

Izzy ran over to Tangie, jumping in between her and Nick and giving her a hug. Tangie hugged her back, determined not to be a jealous wench—she was above that. They danced around in the group a little bit until Skye made a huge point of grabbing Kamillah and pulling her away from Izzy.

Rolling her eyes at Skye's idiotic behavior, Tangie leaned over to Izzy's ear, yelling over the music, "Wanna go to the kitchen?" Holding hands, they half walked, half danced into the kitchen, where the counter space was cluttered with used red plastic cups, tons of liquor bottles, and three half-eaten Domino's pizzas. The Mexican-tiled floor, which Alexa had spent $30,000 installing the previous spring, was filthy, caramel-colored with sticky, congealed beer. A couple Tangie had never seen before—a lanky black guy in a T-shirt reading WILL F&*^K FOR FOOD and a black girl with reddish-burgundy hair—were heavily making out against the wall. The guy was standing with one foot in an ice bucket, but didn't seem fazed.

Tangie was relieved to be alone with Izzy, free from worrying about what her friends would think, or how C.J. would react. "Izzy, you look so cute, girl!" Izzy was wearing an oversize turquoise tunic T-shirt with a slouchy, funky belt over ripped jean shorts and gray leggings. "My butt is way too big to wear leggings outside of rehearsal," Tangie added.

"*Please*, if I had your ass I'd be naked constantly," said Izzy, pulling a Corona out of the fridge. "And I see you curled your lashes, and you're rocking the Maybelline Great Lash mascara, like I told you! Girl, you're the baddest bitch *in* here!"

Tangie twirled one of her curls and made a kissy face, and they both burst out laughing.

Izzy opened her Corona and took a huge, unladylike gulp—of course, she still looked sexy as hell. "Omigod, girl," she continued, "I'm so tryin' to get a piece of that pizza. I've been smoking all night, and I'm starving." Pushing past the precoital couple, she grabbed a slice and lustily bit into it. Even with cheese hanging from her mouth, she looked good.

"Who were you smoking with?" Tangie knew the answer; she was just being nosy.

"C.J. You know he has that good ish. Actually, I think he brought some with him, I'm not sure." She leaned against the counter, tearing into her pizza.

Tangie felt the need to keep herself busy, so she poured an already open Red Bull into a plastic cup. "Yeah, he probably did."

"You smoke?"

"Not so much." *Not at all, actually, and I wish C.J. would stop sell-ing it before he ends up on Rikers and ruins his life. But whatever. Not my problem to worry about anymore.* "So, uh, what's going on with you guys?"

"Who, me and C.J.?"

"It looks like you're getting serious." She couldn't resist.

"Serious? Ha! Not even." Izzy shook her head violently, her gelled-up faux hawk slicing the air. "I'm only fourteen, I'm trying to have a good time, meet people, chill. Ceej knows what's up."

"I wish I could be like you. I think I take things way too seriously—especially boys."

"You can't give them too much power, girl," Izzy said, chewing on her pizza. "It's all in how you play the game. Never let them think you care too much, or they'll have the edge over you. It's very impor-tant for a woman to have control over the situation, always."

"But how do you get control? I never learned how to play that game," said Tangie, thinking of Trey.

"You gotta get your man whipped," Izzy said with a matter-of-fact shrug. She took a swig of beer and wiped her mouth with the back of her hand. The deep purple polish on her nails was chipping. "It's easy. You give a little somethin', then cut him back. Give a little more, then cut him back. In a week you'll have him begging for it."

So *that* was how you whipped a boy. Tangie folded her arms across her chest, deciding that Izzy was quite possibly the wisest person she'd ever met. How'd she know this stuff? Maybe her mom had passed on those secrets when she gave her The Talk. Maybe that was why Tangie was so inept around boys; her mom had disappeared before it was time to teach her how to be a woman.

"How'd you learn this stuff?"

Izzy shrugged. "Experience. Some good, most bad. It's simple. You see what boys do to get you so hooked, and then you flip it and do the shit right back to them."

Before she could answer, Tangie felt her cell phone vibrate in her pocket. She peered at the tiny screen and then gasped, breaking into a huge, silly grin. It was Trey! The text simply said: *miss u, dimples. hlla back soon.* He was thinking about her! She looked up and saw that Izzy's expression had brightened when she saw Tangie get so excited. She was genuinely happy for her, without even knowing what it was about. That was when Tangie realized that Izzy was a damn good friend.

Tangie knew then that they'd be cool forever, no matter what drama they were going through. She felt a sudden urge to tell Izzy all about Trey. She had to get it out or she'd *explode*—and she knew telling Skye would be a disaster.

"Izzy, if I tell you something, will you promise not to tell anyone?"

"You're so on the stealth tip, I love it." Izzy grinned. "What's the secret?"

As Tangie told her about everything—from the first day of class with Trey to their tutoring sessions to the moment when he performed with her in front of the entire class—she felt a staggering sense of relief wash over her. Now that someone else knew, the situation finally felt real.

And deep down—*deep* down—Tangie wanted Izzy to know that she had a life. She wanted her to know she wasn't some lame, loveless loser standing in the shadow of her more sophisticated friends. That she was seeing someone, too. Even deeper down, she hoped that maybe Izzy would mention it to C.J.

Wouldn't *that* be fabulous?!

Kamillah had waited all night for this moment. She'd timed it perfectly. Obviously, she didn't want to unleash the drama too soon and risk having the rest of the night be anticlimactic. But she also didn't want to hold out much longer, because she was about to be too twisted even to tell the damn story.

First, Kamillah waited until Izzy and Tangie were safely out of reach (it was not that she didn't want to include Tangie, it was just that she was so oddly attached to Izzy). Then she dragged Regina away from Nick on the dance floor, found Skye redoing her makeup in the bathroom, and forced them both into the stuffy, closet-size laundry room for the unveiling.

"Y'all ready?" Kamillah held something behind her back, her pouty, bronze-glossed lips curving in a naughty grin.

"Yes, yes, yes," squealed Skye with childlike, totally uncool glee.

"Okay. Unveiling on the *one*," said Kamillah, and then all three of them began the countdown, "Five, six, seven, eight . . . and ONE!"

Kamillah sang, *"Ta-daaah!"* at the top of her voice, a beautiful, lilting high C, and pulled a book from behind her back.

Regina frowned, disappointed. "I don't get it. What's that?"

"Omigod, is that Wendy Williams's autobiography?" Skye was thrilled, but way off. "I've been dying to read that! She gets all up in everybody's business, like Whitney and . . ."

"It's called *Do You Know Where Your Children Are? A Portrait of the Modern Teen Runaway*," said Kamillah, holding up the book so the cover faced her friends; it featured a grainy black-and-white shot of four dirty-looking teens sitting on a church step, linking arms, their back to the photographer. One of the teens was holding up her middle finger at some enemy off camera.

"So?" Visibly disappointed, Skye snatched the book out of her hand. It looked like the kind of book they'd have been assigned to read in health class as some sort of scare tactic. "Why is this so earth-shattering?"

"Because guess who wrote it? This social worker named Damon Jeffries, who specializes in oversexed, lying, too-fast-for-their-own-good teenage girls. Aka Izzy's quote-unquote *guardian*!"

"Wait . . . *what*?" Regina was confused.

"Omigod, omigod, omigod, it's so good I can't even get it out!"

Kamillah hopped up and down, barely able to avoid hyperventilating from excitement.

Skye stamped her foot, getting impatient. "Kammie, if you don't tell me this story right now . . ."

"Okay, listen! So, Izzy, right? She lives with this old guy, Damon Jeffries, okay? C.J. told Black, who obviously told me. You would not believe how many Damons I had to google to find him! But I knew he wrote a book on runaways, so that narrowed it down. Anyway, he's not related to her *at all*—he's just some whatever old-ass man."

"That's so ill," whispered a wide-eyed Skye.

"I know, right? I thought so, too, so I looked up his book on Amazon. The description said that this guy, Damon Jeffries, lived with a group of homeless teens in New Jersey for, like, six months, and wrote about their lives."

"*Ewww.*" Skye wrinkled up her nose. "Unsanitary."

"When I started reading the sample chapter online, I had it FedExed for *next-day* delivery!" Kamillah grabbed the book back from Skye and flipped to a Post-it-marked page. "Listen to this, okay?" And then she started reading the chapter introduction:

From the start, A. was different. A massive personality struggling to break free from a tiny, five-foot-one, ninety-pound body. A born saleswoman, or the best entertainer you ever saw—it was hard to tell. What was clear was that they all looked up to her; she was like a celebrity to these kids because she could do everything—sing, dance, sing, draw, tell a story, anything you wanted. She was remarkably feminine, yet was quick to fight if a friend was in trouble (and, according to F., "She could rap better than the guys."). A. had that rare seductive ability to shift her personality slightly, depending on whom she was talking to, making everyone think she was their best friend. Somehow, she made you believe she wasn't homeless, that she was just hanging out with her friends and at the end of the night would go back home someplace, to a warm bed and MTV, not a filthy sleeping bag on the freezing concrete floor of the Newark bus depot.

I met A. when she was thirteen, and by then she'd already lived a thousand lives. For two years, she'd been posing as an eighteen-year-old. She'd been kicked out of six schools, sung with an underground hip-hop band, posed nude for a men's magazine, and was running from something. Was it the ex-boyfriend she'd told me about, the one who dangled her off the side of a project building when she tried to leave him? Was it her parents, who apparently were "foreign" and "didn't understand her"? I don't know about the ex-boyfriend, but I tended to believe the foreign part, because she looked so exotic—she had the golden-caramel skin, high forehead, arched nose, and large, deep-set black eyes of Northern Africa. With A., it was hard to tell when she was putting me on, but honestly, the true story was unimportant. What mattered was where she was going, not where she'd been. And that made her more powerful than most adults I've known. No past horror was going to cripple this girl—she was going to be Someone. Actually, she already was Someone. Which was why I had to know her, to find out what made her vibrate on a different frequency from the rest. Like them all, I'd become an A. disciple. And this is how.

Everyone was silent for a second, staring off into space and struggling to piece it all together. Finally, Skye spoke up. "Okay, I don't get it."

"It's Izzy," said Regina, her voice low, her eyes huge. "He's talking about Izzy."

"But how can it be Izzy?" Skye glared at Regina. "I mean, yeah, it does sound like her, but he said her frst initial was *A*!"

"It's 'cause her real name's Aziza, fool!" Kamillah exclaimed, thrilled at her deductive powers. "Can you believe this shit? Izzy used to be *homeless. Homeless!* Seriously, y'all, that's *so* her—did you hear the whole part about her looking exotic and all that?"

Regina and Skye were stunned speechless, both staring at Kamillah as if she'd just announced she was getting a sex-change operation.

"So look," started Kamillah, "here's what I think happened. I think this guy, Damon, followed her around for his book, and then he fell in love with her and asked her to move in with him."

"You honestly think Izzy's dealing with a man in his thirties?" Regina was disbelieving.

"What, you don't see that? I most definitely see that."

Skye clapped her hand over her mouth, loving the drama. "Wait. What if he was, like, married or something and then she broke it up? I knew there was something shady about that girl, I knew it."

"I'm still in shock."

"Oh, Regina, you're so naive," sniffed Skye. "Not everyone is exactly the way they represent themselves, you know. You have to learn that if you plan on being in the film business, because Hollywood types are a trip. I mean, I'm used to them because I grew up around that element."

Regina looked as if she'd just been slapped.

"Okay, so, look, y'all," started Kamillah. "We have to figure out what we're gonna do!"

Regina rolled her eyes. "What we're gonna do about what?"

"Hello? Izzy's totally seduced two members of our crew."

"Which two members?" Regina asked, messing with Skye.

Skye stamped her foot, frustrated. "Tangie and C.J., *hello!*"

"We can't let them get caught up with this bitch, y'all," insisted Kamillah. "She's danger."

"Yeah, did you see C.J. with her tonight?" Skye's eyes were bulging out of her head with excitement. "He was practically drooling. I don't know what she did, but never in my life have I seen him like that over some chick, you know?" She sighed. "Tangie must be *dying.*"

"Actually, I don't know if Tangie's tripping," snapped Regina. "She's been hanging with Izzy all night. She doesn't seem that fazed."

"Whatever," said Kamillah. She wasn't trying to hear anything positive about Izzy tonight. "Bottom line, y'all—you think it's time for an inflation." She paused, trying to remember the correct word. She was definitely drunk by this point. "Um, invention?"

"*Intervention,*" said Skye, rolling her eyes.

"Yeah, that."

Skye exhaled grandly, lost in thought. "Yeah. I'm cosigning this intervention. Above all else, we *must* preserve our sexy."

Kamillah nodded. "Let's shut down this shady liar, y'all!"

Regina looked at the door and sighed, feeling as if she'd been taken hostage. She didn't really care about Izzy and her sketchy past—after all, she had bigger problems. All she wanted to do was escape and find Nick. Until his situation with Skye was resolved, Regina would never feel right around her best friend. *Forget Izzy,* she thought. *I'm the shady liar.*

Skye's apartment had gotten so packed that moving was almost out of the question. She was too smoked-out and drunk to care. Vineet was still spinning the hottest songs, and drinks were flowing, and the boys were sexy—who cared if things got a little out of hand? It was all love, right?

Speaking of love, Nick couldn't have been more adorable. Every single person Skye introduced him to had fallen madly in love with him. He was a fantastic dancer, and he watched all the right reality shows, and his one-liners were hysterical. And he wasn't all caught up in trying to act hard and antisocial, like most guys. Even though Nick was brand-new, she could tell he was going to be *major* at Armstrong. Oh, what a sexy, photogenic, charismatic couple they'd make!

If only he hadn't spent every waking moment with Regina. All night long—except for Skye, Regina, and Kamillah's brief moment in the closet—he'd been practically Velcroed to her side. He couldn't possibly like her over Skye, so what was it? Their little friendship was obnoxious and ridiculous, and Skye was over it. She wanted answers, and she wanted them now.

She slammed her red plastic cup on her mother's shabby-chic console table and began searching the apartment for Regina and Nick. She was determined to catch them in the act, but instead she caught another couple cuddled up on a wrought-iron love seat in the foyer. Gin. Slurred words. Louis Vuitton luggage.

"Alexa!"

"Skye!"

"What are you doing back home? And what are you doing with . . ."

"Johnny," warbled Alexa.

"Actually, my name's Etienne," mumbled the chubby boy in Alexa's arms. Skye remembered he played the banjo and had spent most of freshman year out with the measles.

Alexa threw her head back and emitted the loudest, screechiest cackle. "Well, that explains things!" And then she lost her balance and toppled off the love seat onto the floor. Her skirt was up to her waist, and her lacy thong was in full view.

"Alexa, come on, you have to go to bed." Skye bent down to grab her mom, almost losing her balance. With great effort, she hooked her arm around Alexa's waist and hoisted her up.

"Can I get you to sign an autograph before you go?" Etienne was thrusting a damp cocktail napkin and a pen in their direction.

"*Back off, bee-yatch!*" screeched Skye, dragging her mom through the crowd on the way to the master bedroom.

"Skye, what the hell are you wearing?" Alexa sneered.

Skye was wearing a leopard-print Roberto Cavalli minidress she'd "borrowed" from Eden without asking her. She knew she looked hot, and everyone had been complimenting her all night.

"Is that Edie's dress? Take it off right now! Your hips are bigger than hers, you're gonna stretch it out!" Alexa started crying. "Oh, Skye, why would you do this to Edie?"

An embarrassed hush fell over the room—the only noise was Young Joc's "It's Goin' Down" banging from the speakers—

and everything was spinning. Skye was humiliated. She just wanted to get her mom out of there and disappear forever. "Alexa, shut up," she hissed through clenched teeth. "Come with me *now*."

Leaning heavily on her daughter, Alexa staggered out of the room sobbing. "Why do you always have to be so mean to Edie?" She was half screaming, half slurring. "You're so jealous of her, and you shouldn't be. There's no comp—comp—competition. You know? Nothing to be jealous of if you're not even in the running, right?"

As Skye dragged her mom down the hallways, trying desperately to ignore her ravings, she ran into Nick. The second she saw her crush, she tried to turn around and go in the opposite direction. The last thing she wanted was for him to hear Alexa's drunken ramblings.

"Skye! Skye, wait up. What's going on?"

She turned around, panicking. He *couldn't* see her like this! "Um, I . . . this is my mom, and I . . ."

Alexa raised her head for a moment and waved. Then she passed out.

"Holy shit, let me help you." Nick jumped over to her other side, hooking Alexa's arm around his shoulders. "Just tell me where we're going."

"Down the hall. Keep going, all the way down to the back room." Skye was so ashamed of her mom she could barely look at him.

But how cute was he, helping her out like this! Such a gentleman. "Thanks, Nick. You're the sweetest."

"It's cool. I was just in the living room talking to Regina, and we were wondering where you were."

Why are you bringing up Regina at a time like this? she wanted to scream.

"Yeah, it's right through there," she said, pushing open the master bedroom door. The three of them toppled into the room, startling a partially clothed couple intertwined on the bed. Yanking on their clothes, the couple jumped up and scurried out, giggling.

"So," started Nick, "you want me to carry her to bed?"

Skye opened her mouth to respond, and then, to her shock and horror, she burst into tears. "Wh—wh—whatever," she blubbered. "Let's just put her d—d—down right here! On th—th—the floor!"

"Are you sure? I don't think . . ."

"D—d—don't worry about it," she said, hiding her face behind her hair. Nick put his arm around her, attempting to soothe her, but she shrugged him off. She didn't want him to see her like that.

After a couple of deep breaths, she managed to pull herself together. But just barely. She flipped her hair back and flashed Nick a big, fake smile.

"Seriously, she likes sleeping on the floor. Something about her back, I think?" That was a lie, but Skye was so furious with Alexa, she thought if she touched her one more time she'd vomit all over the room. So, slowly, Nick and Skye lowered Alexa down to the floor, where she landed with a thud.

He looked down at Alexa, shaking his head in pity. "So that's your mom, huh?"

"Yeah. She's not supposed to be here." Sighing, she stepped over Alexa's limp body and staggered over to the bed, sitting down and resting her head in her hands. The room was spinning. Skye closed her eyes and groaned, feeling extra tipsy. Nick, concerned, sat down next to her.

"Are you sure you're okay, Skye? What's wrong?"

"Nothing's wrong," she said, flipping her head back up. *Flirt, damn it, flirt!!* "So, you chilling? I'm happy you came."

"Yeah, me, too. Me and Regina were saying . . ."

"I like your outfit," she interrupted. Nick was wearing a turquoise polo with a skinny tie, ratty jeans, and vintage Chuck Taylors. He looked styled by Kanye West.

"Yeah?"

"You look, like, mad sexy." She was using her baby-soft Paris

Hilton voice. She leaned over to him, pushing her tiny breasts together with her arms.

"Thanks. I almost wore a fedora with it, but I thought that was a little extra."

"Nothing on you is extra."

"Actually, Regina said . . ."

If Skye heard Regina's name one more time, she was going to scream! "Regina, Regina, Regina! Seriously, spare me!"

"Uh, sorry." Nick was taken aback.

Skye exhaled sharply. "Whatever, it's fine. Now, where were we?" She pouted, trying hard not to look as wrecked as she felt. "I was hoping we could get to know each other better."

"You know, I have to . . ."

"What, find Regina?"

He chuckled. "You're hilarious, you know that?"

"But in a cute way, right?" She leaned in to him, her lips one millimeter away from his. Nick held his breath.

"Nick," she began, trying to keep her voice steady, "I found my mother trying to sexually harass the boy who plays the piano when we do our relaxation exercises in my theater movement class. I'm vulnerable, here! I'm a sure thing!"

He burst into nervous laughter and then kind of sat there, thinking. She smelled really good, and her mouth was right there, inches from his. *It was just so easy.* He kissed her for the second time. The second Nick realized what he'd done, he jerked away from her, horrified. And then he abruptly stood up, causing her to fall over.

"Sorry, I didn't mean . . . I shouldn't have . . ." he muttered awkwardly, and then he raced out of the room, leaving her alone on the bed.

This time, Skye didn't think Nick's nervousness had anything to do with his girl in D.C. In fact, she had a hunch that it was a cover-up. No, this was about Regina.

Shakily, Skye walked out. She wasn't two feet from the bedroom when she ran smack into, who else, Regina. *Of course*, she thought. *Were Nick and Regina ever apart for more than seven seconds?*

"Skye, where have you been? I was looking for you. Have you seen—"

"Who, Nick?" Skye snapped. "Yeah, I've seen him. But all he sees is you."

"What are you talking about?"

"You know what I'm talking about, you slut. You *know* I like him, and yet you continue to throw yourself at him! I thought you were my girl!"

"Skye, I *am* your girl. If you just listen for a second, I have something to tell you."

"I don't wanna hear it," Skye said, sobbing. Her party was ruined. Her mom had humiliated her, and the one boy she liked at Armstrong was in love with her girl. "I don't care. I already know what you're gonna say. Just save it."

"You already know?"

Skye looked up at her, frantically wiping her mascara-streaked cheeks. "Never talk to me again, Regina. We're done, okay? *Done!*" She ran down the hallway into her bedroom, flinging herself onto the bed, where all her guests had thrown their jackets and bags. She cried and cried, wanting the party to end. Wanting everything to end. Why did Alexa have to be so awful? Why was she always comparing her to Eden? Why did Nick think she was a gross cow compared to *Regina*? Regina, whose photo should have run alongside the word "regular" in the dictionary.

Feeling sorry for herself, she hopped up and started rifling through the purses and jackets, looking for Nick's bag. (She remembered him coming in with a very grown-and-sexy Prada manbag. . . . All the boys had started mumbling that the bag wasn't real, those haters.) She wanted to find evidence, proof that he'd been hanging with Regina—a photo, a note, anything. Finally, she found it at the bottom of the pile. Skye began to frantically go through the bag, opening his wallet, flipping through a small notepad. Nothing. There was *nothing*. Skye opened the zippered compartment along the side and felt around inside. Her hand brushed against a smooth, flat, squarish thing at the bottom of the bag. She pulled it out and saw it was a DVD.

The DVD was called *Mandingo Madness*, and it featured a grainy shot of three very dark, very muscular men doing jumping jacks on a beach. Nude.

Mandingo Madness.

Mandingo Madness?

Just then, a group of people she'd never seen in her life burst through the door. Automatically, Skye stuffed the tape up her dress and scurried out. She knew exactly where she was going—to lock herself in Eden's room, throw this in the DVD player, and pray to God it wasn't what she thought it was.

Tangie and C.J. had ignored each other all night. Except for a couple of glances across the room—the kind where you just kept catching each other's eye and it seemed you'd been staring at the person, but really you hadn't. She wished he'd just leave. She'd barely even seen Skye, Kamillah, or Regina all night, but it didn't matter. Izzy was there. And together, they were having a ball—dancing like crazy and not caring who was looking. It was so nice to be friends with a girl who genuinely couldn't care less what other people thought about her. It made Tangie feel invincible, as if nothing could go wrong. And, really, what could go wrong when Trey Stevens was text-messaging her every twelve seconds?

Every time her cell went off, she'd grab Izzy, and together they'd hop up and down and squeal at the message. (So far, she'd been sent "still remember the way your lips feel," and "roses are red/flowers are blue/folks say I move like water/and you sort of do, too.") Of course, when Tangie and Trey's relationship was purely based on electronics, she conveniently forgot how stressed out and nervous she was in his actual presence. It was a lot more thrilling imagining what *could* be, instead of actually being faced with the torture of how to act in *front* of him. But Tangie wasn't thinking about all that. Right now, she felt like the luckiest girl in the world, like a girl that good things happened to.

Vineet spun Chamillionaire's "Ridin' Dirty" into Lil Jon's classic, "Get Low," a song Tangie despised (she hated dancing to crunk; it was way too slow), and she and Izzy walked off the dance floor to go chill on the couch. They were immediately intercepted by Nick, whom they'd hit it off with earlier that night during Beyoncé's "Crazy in Love." Tangie was dying to pee (all that Red Bull!), so she left Izzy and Nick, and headed in the direction of the guest bathroom in the hallway. The line outside was insane. Luckily, Tangie knew Eden had a bathroom in her room, so she hung a left at the end of the hallway and ran up to the bedroom door. Surprised and relieved to find that Eden had left the door unlocked, she sprinted through her room and into the bathroom.

Refreshed, Tangie came back out into Eden's room.

It was strangely quiet (even with all the rah-rah-rah party sounds outside) and untouched, like the room of a beloved dead girl that had been preserved exactly the way she had left it. It was squeaky clean, with not a thing out of place. Above her bed was a painting of Eden that was done on her sixteenth birthday by some famous downtown artist Alexa had been having an affair with. The shelves were lined with trophies from Eden's many summers at drama camp, and every surface was covered with framed photographs: Eden on the *Family Chatter* set, Eden with Spike Lee, a twelve-year-old Eden at a podium with Courteney Cox, presenting an award at the Golden Globes. Propped on her desk was a floppy "Kendra" doll, complete with the pigtails and denim overalls that her *Family Chatter* character always wore.

Wandering around the room, Tangie wondered what it must feel like to be so loved. Was it weird, or did it get normal after a while? It must have been something, knowing you could walk into any room, anywhere, and have people literally gasp at your beauty. Gazing at a group of pictures of Eden with her friends, all shiny, popular, perfect-looking girls, Tangie remembered when she and Skye used to hide in Eden's bathroom to spy on her and Trey making out. She remembered being mesmerized by the sheer number of pictures of Trey that Eden had plastered all over her walls, the desk, *everywhere*. And now, nothing.

Suddenly, Tangie was struck with the realization that she was *standing in the room of Trey's first love*. Tangie began to wonder—what had made him fall in love with Eden? What were their secret jokes, their private thoughts? Suddenly, an intense, almost ferocious need came over Tangie to investigate his and Eden's relationship. After peeking outside the door to make sure no one was around, she found the previous year's Armstrong yearbook on a shelf and slid it down.

Flipping through the Juniors section, she came across the superlatives—of course, Trey and Eden were "The Couple Most Likely to One Day Appear in *People*'s Most-Beautiful Issue." In the front of the book, Trey had written, *Dear Edie-Bird, You make me wanna say yeah, just like Usher. Love, Your Thug*. Then she flipped to the dance department photos and saw a huge, glossy shot of Trey doing a backflip on the hip-hop spread. She ran her finger along the picture, sighing. *His body*. Oh, he was so beautiful, it was sickening. Maybe in this year's yearbook he'd write something as sweet to her.

Tangie wanted more. Glancing guiltily at the door, she ran over to Eden's desk and ripped open the drawers, looking for any signs of Trey. Finally, she came across a small box filled with pictures. Grinning, her heart racing, she took them over to the bed and sat next to the yearbook. She spread them out, memorizing each. She was obsessed.

There were little-boy shots of Trey, photo-booth pics of him and Eden at the Angelika, Spring Festival tickets, programs from performances they'd been in. Closing her eyes, she tried to imagine what it must've felt like to sit in the audience, watching Trey dance his ass off, thinking, *That's my man.* . . .

"What the hell are you doing, Tangie?"

She whipped her head around, dropping the pictures to the floor. It was Skye. She looked as if she'd been crying—her face was puffy and tear-streaked.

"Skye! I . . ." She trailed off, not knowing what to say.

Skye stormed over to the bed and ripped the pictures from Tangie's hands. "What are you doing with these? Are you spying on Eden?"

Tangie shook her head, her cheeks blazing hot. "No. No! I'm not spying. I was just, well, I was coming out of the b—bathroom and—"

"Look, spare me the stuttering. Just tell me what's going on!"

"Okay, fine." Tangie swallowed. "I . . . I have something to tell you. You know Trey's been tutoring me after school, right?"

Skye slowly looked back and forth, from the pictures to Tangie. And then, in one heart-stopping moment, she understood. "Omigod, no. *No!*"

"Skye, let me "

"I can't believe it," she murmured, as if in a daze. "You like Trey."

Tangie was quiet a moment, her heart racing. And then she just went for it. "Skye, I wanted to tell you, I just didn't know how. I . . . we I've been hanging out with him. He's my dance tutor. Honestly, it wasn't about anything, but now it's gotten kinda, I don't know, official in the past couple of days. And—"

"Let me get this straight. *You* like *Trey.*"

"Yeah, Skye. And he likes me, too."

For a minute Skye didn't say anything. Then she rolled her eyes up to the ceiling, shook her head, and exhaled. "God, Tangie, at least try to have an original thought."

"Huh?"

"Everybody likes Trey. That's his whole thing. That's like saying,

'Wow, I sure am into H&M.'" She smirked. "He probably doesn't even take you seriously, Tangie. Not to be harsh, but . . ." she let herself trail off.

Tangie blinked, taken aback. "This is why I didn't want to tell you! Forget it. Just forget it."

"So, what, are you his *girlfriend?*"

"No, it's not like that yet. We're . . . we don't . . . he doesn't like other people in his business." She was stumbling over her words, doing a lot of gesturing. "We're taking it slow. He's . . . Trey's not really into labels."

"And why do you think that is, Tangie?" Skye threw her hands in the air in exasperation. "Come on, wake up, baby. He doesn't want you to tell anybody, because he doesn't want Eden to find out. Did you ever think about that? He's crazy about her. She's the love of his life. Jesus Christ, I thought I knew you better than this."

Tangie stared at her, her lower lip trembling. "After everything I went through with C.J., why can't you just be happy for me? How can you do this to me?"

"How can I do this to you? *To you?*" Skye was so outraged she could barely find the words. Her voice was a low rumble. "I take you under my wing, introduce you to everyone, give you a social presence at the damn school, and you go and steal my sister's boyfriend?" She paused to catch her breath, her chest heaving. "I even talked to C.J. for you. I bombed his ass out for you."

"Yeah, I know."

"I told him he was an asshole for leading you on the other night, and that he shouldn't stay away from you until he knows he can be a faithful boyfriend."

"Why did you do that, Skye? And why would you tell the biggest gossip in the school about it? You humiliated me. You made me look like I couldn't handle my own business."

"Well, you can't! I mean, you were so *open* after he left, and you know he's just gonna disappoint you."

"Why are you so sure, Skye? Why couldn't he be really ready to settle down?"

"Honey, you have this totally skewed perception of him, cuz you like him, but I know my cousin. The boy is so damn out-for-self it's not even funny."

I hate that she's right, thought Tangie. But she wasn't about to tell her.

"Listen, I learned so much last year at Armstrong. Your first year, it's a sink-or-swim situation, you know? You're dealing with cutthroat competition, and egos, and you really start to become savvy about people. No offense, but even though you're a sophomore, you're on a freshman level, maturitywise. There's a savviness about people, about the industry, about *life*, that you learn that first year—and you're not there yet."

Tangie's mouth dropped open, shocked. *Oh, no, she didn't!*

"Skye, don't talk to me like I'm Regina, or one of your little groupies. I've known you since you used to make out with that Lil' Bow Wow poster you taped to your pillow. Don't pull that manipulative, *Mean Girls* nonsense with me."

Skye flinched with her entire body, totally caught off guard. It wasn't really like Tangie to mouth off like that. Well, if Tangie wanted to go toe to toe, Skye would see to it.

"As for your little crush on Trey . . . Who do you think you are? You weren't here last year, you didn't see what Eden and Trey were. You can't just sweep in and be the new Eden. There is no 'new' Eden, okay? No one can be her."

"I'm not trying . . . Oh, whatever!" Now Tangie was screaming too, not caring who could hear. "You know what? I barely even know you anymore. I shouldn't have said anything."

"But I bet you told your *best friend* Izzy. God, it's so obvious to everyone why you hang around her. You just wanna be close to C.J., any way you can. It's so sad."

That was the lowest blow. So Tangie struck back as hard as she could. "You're two-faced and, you don't know anything about loyalty. Thanks for telling Kamillah all my C.J. business. Why do you even care if I'm messing with Eden's ex-boyfriend? It's so pathetic, how you try to act all close to her. Everyone knows Eden, your own sister, hates you, Skye. Open your eyes."

Skye flinched. "Get out of my house."

Quietly, Tangie put the pictures back in the book, stuffed it in Eden's drawer, and walked out. She wanted to go home and forget this night had ever happened.

Izzy and Nick had spent the last twenty minutes dancing up a storm, and now she was dying of thirst. So the two of them, now fast friends in that we-just-platonically-dry-humped-to-a-Lil-Jon-mix-for-twenty-minutes way, beat a path to the kitchen, dissing people's outfits and laughing hysterically the whole time. Just as Izzy was starting to revise her opinion of Armstrong kids (they weren't *all* stuck-up showbiz shits!), she and Nick opened the kitchen door. And there, through the crowd of loud, overacting friends o' Skye—all with their party personalities on full blast—Izzy spotted Kamillah leaning back against the counter with Skye and Regina. She was holding a book under her arm. Izzy couldn't see the title, but she'd have spotted that cover anywhere.

In a flash, Izzy unhooked her arm from Nick's and elbowed her way toward Kamillah When Kamillah saw Izzy emerge from the crowd, headed straight for her, she clutched the book to her chest for protection. And then she saw Izzy's face, and her stomach flipped.

"What the fuck," hollered Izzy, snatching the book from Kamillah. The entire kitchen went quiet. Skye's and Regina's eyes widened, and they took two steps back, suddenly wishing they didn't know Kamillah.

Nick finally caught up to Izzy and grabbed her arm, trying to comfort her. "Whoa, baby, slow down. What's up?" And then he saw her holding the book. He glanced at Regina and mouthed the words, *Holy shit!*

Ignoring Nick, Izzy stepped closer to Kamillah. "Again, I ask you, what the *fuck* are you doing with this book?"

"What, it ain't a free country?" Kamillah rolled her eyes, obviously nervous but pulling out her Harlem tough-girl act for show. Especially since half of their grade was watching. "Clearly you got issues, love, and I really ain't the one to help you work them out."

Izzy glared at her for a moment, her eyes eerily blank, and then she smiled. It wasn't a happy smile, it was a "Stand back, the shit's about to hit the fan" smile. "Oh, okay. That's cute. I get it, you're cute, right?"

"Come on, Izzy," said Nick, trying to pull her away.

"No, no, no, this bitch thinks she's cute." She shrugged her arm from his grasp and turned back toward Kamillah. "I'm just really tryin' to understand your choice in reading material, that's all. You about to run away from home?"

"Look, Izzy, why don't you find your own crew, okay? Because C.J. and Black and them? They're *our* boys, so just go find some other clique to run through. Like, maybe, the G-Unit?" There was a collective gasp from their audience, and somebody whispered, *"Let me find out she went there! Kamillah's goin' hard, yo!"* "And by the way," she continued, "if I ever see you put your hands on my man again, you slutty homeless liar, it will *not* be cool. Know this."

"Know this? Know *this*, ho." And before Kamillah knew what hit her, Izzy had snatched one of her Afro-puffs in her fist and dragged her, screaming, down to the floor. The book went flying, and Nick gracefully caught it in the air. The kitchen was in an uproar; the drunken tenth graders were cheering and climbing over each other trying to see the action. As Izzy and Kamillah slid around on the beer-sticky floor, clawing and scratching and screaming, Skye stood on the sidelines. After her blowup with Tangie, she'd downed two vodka shots and was too drunk to do more than stamp her feet and shout, "Girls! Stop! *Not sexy!*"

Finally, Nick and Regina managed to pull Izzy off Kamillah and onto her feet. They held her back as Kamillah struggled back up, her face and arms covered with scratches, her lip swollen and bleeding, and her once-cute Afro-puffs now resembling auburn-streaked tumbleweed. Her mascara was everywhere and she was missing an earring. Izzy, however, looked just about as stunning as she had when she walked into the room. Kamillah hadn't gotten in one punch. Yeah, Kamillah might be from Harlem, but Izzy was from the streets. The streets, *for real*. And now everyone knew.

"*You can't put your hands on me!*" screamed Kamillah. Izzy lunged toward her again, but Nick and Regina each grabbed one of her arms and held her tight. Quickly, Skye slipped her arm around her friend's waist and hurried her out of the kitchen. The crowd parted as Kamillah staggered out, ranting and sobbing like a crazy person. "You're gonna hear from my daddy's lawyer, Miss I'm-bonin'-a-thirty-five-year-old-man! Miss I-git-naked-all-up-in-*King*-magazine! You just wait, Izzy or Azeeda or Alibaba or whatever the fuck your name is! You just *waaaaaiiiiit. . . .*"

And then she was gone. Nick and Regina finally let go of Izzy. Breathing heavily, Izzy assured Nick and Regina, "I'm fine, it's cool, let me go. Really, it's cool." Watching her closely, they let go of her arms but stayed put on either side. Without saying another word, she turned around and pushed her way out of the room. Nick tried to follow her, but she held her arm out, saying, "Leave me alone, babe, I gotta think for a minute."

The second she got out of the kitchen, she started to run. Without even knowing where she was going, Izzy ran out Skye's front door, hopped on the elevator going down, and then tore through the downstairs lobby into the night air. Izzy had never wanted to be farther from a group of people in her life.

Once she was safely two blocks from Skye's apartment building, she collapsed on the stoop of a Victorian brownstone. Without thinking, she pulled out her cell phone and began dialing his number. She knew it was wrong, she knew he was the worst person for her, but right now Izzy wanted to talk to someone who *knew* her. Who really cared about her. She promised herself she'd forget his number, never speak to him again. After all, everything was his fault—her father kicking her out, those hellish months she had lived on the street, the terrible thing he had made her do. Despite all it had taken for Izzy to stay away from him, she still loved him.

"'Sup?" Izzy heard loud, thumping bass in the background. He was clearly at a gig with the band. Her heart raced. God, she missed her band. She wondered who sang their hooks now.

"Baby?" She could barely get the word out.

"Aziza? Is that you?"

Izzy burst into tears at the sound of his voice. She'd never cried in front of anyone but him. "Can you come and get me?"

Silence. "Where you at? I'm on my way."

It was late, and the street outside Skye's apartment building was dark and empty. Tangie was sitting on a bench in front of the building, tears streaming down her cheeks. She'd been there for a while now. Tangie couldn't believe that she and Skye had said such hateful things to each other. Skye was her best friend. They'd been looking forward to going to Armstrong together since the fourth grade, and now that they were, it was awful.

A group of Armstrong kids on their way up to Skye's party breezed past her, and Tangie covered her face with her hands. She'd have died if they had seen her swollen, damp eyes, red nose, and wet cheeks. Everything would be fine once they made it through the front door; then she could make a run for it and catch a cab home. *Just keep your head down, Tangie, just . . .*

"Tangela?"

She looked up, her face damp with tears. It was C.J., standing right in front of her clutching a brown paper bag filled with bottles. He must've just gone on a beer run. Luckily for him, he had a convincing fake ID.

"Not now, C.J., I gotta go."

She stood up and tried to push past him, but he grabbed her elbow with his free hand. He looked into her face, saw she'd been crying, and his eyebrows shot to the ceiling. "Yo, what's wrong? What is it? Is it *Trey*? What'd that motherfuckin' Sally do to you? I'll kill him. Where's he at . . ."

"What? No, listen . . ."

"Is he up there?" He pointed up toward Skye's penthouse apartment, his face screwed up into an almost comical expression of fury. He looked like a five-year-old who'd just been sent to time-out. "I'll stick a ballet shoe up his ass, T., you know I'll do it. He don't want it with me. He really don't."

"C.J., he's not even up there!" Tangie yelled.

Tangie plopped back down on the bench, and finally, C.J. sat next to her.

"Okay, so tell me what he did." He set down the brown paper bag and pulled a lighter from the pocket of his indigo Sean John jeans.

"This is so embarrassing," muttered Tangie. She covered her face with her hands, not wanting him to see her looking a puffy, miserable mess. "It isn't about Trey, okay? Please, just calm down."

"Oh." He relaxed a little, lighting a cigarette. "Good thing, though, because if that *Nutcracker*-ass bitch *ever*—"

"C.J., please! He's not even a ballet dancer. God."

"Okay, okay. What's wrong, then?"

"I don't wanna talk about it." As she sat there next to him, Tangie realized she'd been so caught up in her fight with Skye that she'd forgotten about her falling out with C.J. And the fact that she never wanted to speak to him again.

"Actually, it's none of your business," she snapped.

"Oh, yeah, I forgot I'm, like, totally mad at C.J.,'" he said, making fun of her in his faux-Tangie voice.

"Oh, shut up."

"You think I'm not equally as pissed at you?"

"You have no reason to be pissed at me."

"Whatever, man. I'll let you tell it." He took a long, slow drag of his cigarette and exhaled away from Tangie's face. "Maybe we should agree to disagree."

She looked at him. "Do you think we can?"

He shrugged. "After Skye's joint last year, we ain't talked for three months. You really tryin' to go through all that again?"

She shook her head.

"I mean, fine, you can hate me—I ain't that happy with you right now, either—but it's just stupid not to *talk*." He bumped his shoulder against hers. "You feel me?"

"I don't know," she said with a sigh. Why were all her relationships so damned difficult? "I still can't believe . . . I mean, you lied to me."

"I didn't lie to you."

"You were gonna do a nude picture with your girl the night after you said you loved me."

"I didn't lie, I withheld information. There's a difference."

"Oh, my God, same thing!"

"The portrait was for school, there was nothing sexual about it."

"Whatever."

"Tangie, we been friends a long time. I've never lied to you. Why would I start now?" He looked at her, but she wouldn't look back. "I meant everything I said to you that night. I meant everything I *did*."

She cleared her throat, starting to feel tingly. She wanted to smack him for reminding her exactly how good that night had been.

"If you . . . if you meant it, why didn't you break it off with Izzy afterward?"

"First of all, there was nothing to break off. We weren't together, T. We had a school project. And second of all, everything happened so fast. I ain't had time to process everything."

Tangie was silent. In the distance, she heard the blare of a police siren. "Well, you're together now, aren't you?"

He shrugged. "I don't know. You with Trey Stevens?"

"He's just my tutor, C.J."

"Then Izzy's just my art partner." He sat there, thinking. He took one more puff and flicked the cigarette butt out into the street. "We ain't gonna get anywhere with this, are we?"

Tangie shrugged, threw back her shoulders, and finally looked at him. "Maybe it's obvious that we should just stay friends."

"Oh, word?"

"Yeah. Word."

He smiled. She sounded hilarious saying "Word." "If we're just gonna be friends, let's just hug it out, then."

Tangie shrugged nonchalantly. "Okay, let's do it."

They leaned in and shared the most awkward, clumsy hug ever. Once they were safely back on either side of the bench, C.J. became deeply preoccupied with a hangnail, and Tangie concentrated on picking lint off her lacy Forever 21 camisole top. After what felt like ages, she finally got up the nerve actually to look over at him. And when he returned her gaze, he was so caught off guard—mesmerized, really—by her big, beautiful, sparkling eyes, that he started coughing. Really coughing. Alarmed, Tangie immediately began beating him on the back.

"You tryin' to kill me? God-*damn*," he croaked, when he could finally talk.

"I thought you were dying! Seriously, C.J., you gotta stop smoking."

"How come you're strong all of a sudden when it comes to beating my ass?"

"Ha-ha-ha! Who's your daddy?!" she giggled, dragging him off the bench and putting him into a headlock. They were acting ridiculously immature, like kids, but they couldn't have cared less.

"Yeah, right, mud butt. I'm a gentleman." C.J. slipped out of the headlock and pulled her leg out from under her so that she fell on her butt. Laughing hysterically, she tried to get back up off the sidewalk, but C.J. wasn't about to let her. After a frenzy of wrestling—during which Tangie bit his forearm and, in pain, he yelled *mud butt* loud enough to wake up the West Village—C.J. grabbed Tangie's wrists and pinned them on either side of her head. And then things didn't seem so silly anymore, because he was on top of her, and it was *C.J.*

She smelled him and felt the weight of him, and all of a sudden she didn't care about anything anymore. Trey seemed like a distant schoolgirl crush, like that embarrassing Sisqó phase she had gone through in fourth grade, circa "Thong, Th—thong, Thong, Thong."

"Let me up," she said, breathing hard and squirming around under him. She didn't want to look him in the eye.

"Nope." He grinned at her, and she wanted to die. *Kiss me, kiss me, kiss me,* she thought. And for a moment it seemed as if he would.

Slowly, he lowered his face to hers, his lips only an inch from hers, and she closed her eyes, breathless in anticipation, and then, with a loud grating squeal, his butt started playing the "What You Know About That?" ring tone. Startled, they both froze, and the moment was gone.

"Oh, shit," he groaned, awkwardly hopping to his feet. He reached in his back pocket and pulled out the blaring cell. Flipping it open, he saw that it was a text message from Rita, his coworker at Virgin Mega in the Village. *Wow, ma,* C.J. thought, *your timing really leaves something to be desired.* He looked at Tangie and smiled, but she wasn't looking at him.

The text message said: *You ain't gonna believe this shit. Remember how Big Boi and Andre 3000 was coming in today? I guess you left your sketchbook on the counter, and he saw your nude portrait of that chick? He wants to talk to you about using it on his solo album cover. Holla back ASAP . . . This is big things, son.*

He read it three times, and each time it sounded better and better. Could this really be happening? Dazed, he just kept repeating, "What the, what the, what the," over and over until Tangie grabbed his arm and shook him.

"What, C.J.? What is it, what happened?" She knew it was

something good. She looked so excited for him, eyes shining bright, her smile lighting up her face. He looked at her, realzing that, no matter what happened, he loved this girl. He'd always love her. And if he told her what he was so excited about, she'd never speak to him again.

"I can't tell you."

She flinched. "You can't tell me? You used to be able to tell me everything."

"I know. I just can't this time. Believe me." He reached out to touch her arm, her elbow, he didn't know what, but she jerked away. "Just trust me, okay?"

Tangie looked at him for a second, then shook her head. What was she thinking, letting him back in even for five minutes? All C.J. did was hurt her. And she had a fly, outrageously sexy, real man—a dancer, no less—who liked her and understood her. It would be the last time she let C.J. get to her. For real this time.

No Skye, no C.J. *It's gonna be one hell of a school year*, she thought, storming down Gansevoort Street in the hot September air.

29.
THE LOWEST BLOW

IT WAS 9:55 ON SATURDAY MORNING, the moment every Armstrong student had been anxiously awaiting since the first day of school. Practically the entire student body (or anyone who thought he or she had a chance) was crowded in the lobby, counting down the minutes till 10:00—which was when Mr. Jaworsky would finally reveal the Spotlight Eligible List. But until then, everyone was forced to listen to him deliver a mind-numbingly boring speech.

". . . And as you all know, Spotlight is an honor *so prestigious* that each grade awards *only three students per major*! But aside from the prestige factor, it's also an *invaluable* opportunity to showcase your own personal talent. Every year at Fall Fling, Spotlights get to perform a one-minute solo in their particular field . . . and in the case of the Fine Art and Creative Writing Students, their work will be displayed in a beautiful, special edition Spotlight program, which will be for sale in the lobby during Fall Fling week! So, ladies and gentlemen, are there any questions?"

Tangie looked around the sophomore section of the lobby. Nope, there were no questions, only the charged silence of overanxious students ready to rip off Mr. Jarworsky's wiry red toupee if he didn't unveil the damned list, already.

Tangie was alone in a crowd full of cliques, best friends, and couples. As far as she was concerned, she was no longer speaking to Skye or C.J. And she'd made plans to meet Izzy that morning, but she'd disappeared sometime during Skye's party—and now she wasn't answering her cell. So there Tangie stood, her stomach full of butterflies and her head aching from the previous night's drama, counting down the seconds till Mr. Jaworsky shut the hell up!

"Well, if there are no questions, then let's get right to it, shall we? Behold, everyone, the list of students eligible to audition to be a Fall Fling Student Spotlight!" After making a loud, cheesy drumroll sound effect with his mouth (which left the front row soaked with spit), Mr. Jaworsky lifted a curtain thumbtacked to the bulletin board. Underneath was an extensive list of names written in oversize black type (the bigger the font, the more visible from the crowd—and the less likely the students were to bulldoze each other to get to the front).

And then all hell broke loose.

As the students found their grade and then searched under their major for their names, they began to roar. There were bitter tears, thrilled giggles, excited high fives, and brain-rattling wails of grief. One blue-haired punk punched the wall and was immediately taken to Mount Sinai Hospital's emergency room. A lesbian couple happily embraced each other and fell to the floor, wildly making out. A tiny Persian girl stood in the middle of the crowd and screamed at the top of her lungs, as if she were being nailed to a cross (a senior volunteer quickly sent her home in a cab). It was utter chaos.

Tangie saw none of the action, though. The second that Mr. Jaworsky raised the curtain, she squeezed her eyes shut, too terrified actually to look at the board. What if Ms. Carmen really *had* given her an ultimatum and wouldn't give her a chance at Spotlight if she continued to see Trey? And, even worse—what if, in the end, Ms. Carmen didn't feel she was good enough?

Just as Tangie mustered up enough nerve to open her eyes,

someone reached around her from behind and gave her a huge, happy squeeze. She spun around and saw her new friend Nick, with Regina. "We made it, we made it," he was shouting, and Skye figured he meant him and Regina. But then Regina kissed her on the cheek and said, "No, no, I didn't make it. He's talking about you, silly!"

Her head was pounding—*Please be true, please be true, please be true* Tangie whipped around to face the board, and right there, at the top of the tenth-grade dance majors column (it was alphabetical) was her name. *Tangela Marie Adams.* She'd made the cut! She was officially one of Armstrong's best and brightest!

She wanted to scream, to dance, to shout the news from the rooftops. *It's proof—I really deserve to be here!* she told herself happily. She and Nick and Regina grabbed on to each other and jumped around in a circle, like giddy little kids, laughing and cheering.

After they calmed down a bit, Nick and Regina said they were going to brunch at the Coffee Shop (they were trying to avoid Skye, who was mad at them both, and wanted to leave before they ran into her) and asked Tangie to come. She declined.

There was somebody she had to see.

Across the room, C.J. was surrounded by hordes of people—his boys, his customers, a group of slutty freshman girls with a graffiti fetish—congratulating him on making the list. Everyone wanted to talk to him, but he was barely paying attention. He was staring at Tangie, watching her face light up as she discovered her name on the board. God, she was so pretty. And she looked happier than she'd been in ages. C.J. was proud of her. He wanted to grab her, kiss her—but that was stupid, wasn't it? She hated him. And she was making her way over toward the senior section.

Trey. Obviously, she was going to see Trey.

He quickly pulled out his cell and pressed Izzy's speed-dial number. But she still wasn't picking up. Where the hell was she? It seemed like every girl in his life was peacing out on him. C.J.

glanced back in Tangie's direction, but she'd long since disappeared into the crowd. So he turned his attention back to the freshman girl who was asking him if he was looking for a muse.

Maybe he was.

Tangie knew she was breaking all their rules about publicly acknowledging each other, but she couldn't help it. Skye and C.J. were out of the question, and Izzy was MIA—so she *had* to tell Trey the good news. Grinning with anticipation, she pushed her way through the crowd to get to the seniors. Once she was close, she stood on her tiptoes and looked for his telltale dreadlocks—and almost immediately, she spotted him. Tangie rushed over to where he was standing, with all the cool seniors, and when she was within shouting distance, she called his name, their don't-ask, don't-tell policy be damned.

Trey turned around, and Tangie *knew* he saw her. But he didn't smile or say hi or anything. Instead, he kind of glanced at her with a blank expression, as if he didn't recognize her, and turned back around.

Trying to hold back the tears, Tangie felt as if she'd just been punched in the stomach. She looked—and felt—like a fool. And she didn't even bother to wipe away the tears streaming down her face.

Skye stood outside the building fuming, waiting for her sister to come outside so she could drive them home in Smoove's Phantom. Of course, Eden had made it. *Of course.* Eden was the Miracle Sister, she was the Perfection Princess, who got Spotlight every damned year. *Well, what about me?* Skye wanted to scream. She'd made Spotlight last Winter Fling *and* Spring Fling, so why wouldn't she at least get to audition this go-round? Plus, she had been good that week; she had been damned good. Hadn't she?

Well, the old-lady thing had bombed in Stretch class, but all her other performances had kicked ass. What about Maggie the Cat? It seemed as if everyone with a pulse had been picked but her. Tangie and Nick and C.J., and *Izzy*, of all people! Even Marisol had been picked, that oversexed, fake-ass Mariah. Maybe Kamillah hadn't made it either, and they could console each other and bitch out the other girls.

It was the party. It had jinxed her somehow. The night before, everyone had turned against her—Tangie had stolen her sister's boyfriend, Regina had stolen her crush, Nick had toyed with her oh-so-delicate emotions, and Alexa had tried to have sex with a chubby crasher. And now this? This was the lowest blow.

Skye heard the front doors open and close, and she turned around, hoping it was Eden. It wasn't. It was Tangie.

They froze, staring at each other for a moment. Skye didn't know what to say—she looked at Tangie and no longer saw her best friend. She saw a girl who had stolen her life. Tangie, who hadn't even gotten into Armstrong her freshman year, was now possibly going to make Spotlight *and* was hooking up with the goddamned king of the school? The guy that belonged to Eden, and by association, *Skye*? It was just wrong.

Tangie opened her mouth, but before she could say a word, Skye mustered up her coldest, bitchiest voice and said, "Congratulations, Tangela. You really needed it more than me." With that, she spun on her heel and set off on the walk home. It was a good thing, because Eden was so busy with her admirers she had forgotten about Skye anyway.

Tangie stood there, watching Skye as she stormed down Union Square West. *Would anything ever be right again?* It was only the first week of school and so far Louis Armstrong Academy was all about the drama.

Visit Tia's blog "Shake Your Beauty," for *It Chicks* news, contests, and product giveaways!
www.tiawilliams.net/blog